The shining splendor ... cover of this book refl... story inside. Look for ... buy a historical roman... the very best in quality ...

UNDENIABLE DESIRE

"You feel it, too, don't you, Lark?" Brent's voice was as soft as a caress, and as electrifying as a bolt of lightning.

"I feel nothing," Meadowlark answered stiffly.

"You may be an expert at hiding your feelings, but I know you're as aware of . . . whatever . . . it is between us as I am."

Their eyes locked. She knew what a mouse must feel just as a giant hawk swooped it from the field.

Brent's head dipped forward. He kissed the tip of her pert little nose. And then his lips molded to hers.

Meadowlark's toes curled. She was hardly aware of her arms curling around his neck, or her fingers ravaging the hair against his collar. The strands were even softer than she'd imagined. A ribbon of fire twisted through her stomach as his kiss deepened. She was lost . . .

JUDITH STEEL

ZEBRA BOOKS
KENSINGTON PUBLISHING CORP.

In memory of Kay Blosser Garcia

Very special acknowledgments to two
important women in my career—
Joyce Flaherty, my agent; and
Carin Cohen Ritter, my editor.
Thank you, ladies.

ZEBRA BOOKS

are published by

Kensington Publishing Corp.
475 Park Avenue South
New York, NY 10016

First printing: November, 1991

Printed in the United States of Ameria

Prologue

Flies! Nasty, buzzing flies everywhere!

Meadowlark Russell shuddered and frantically beat her hands around her head. She winced as her fingers jerked through strands of long, blue-black hair. Tiny, winged bodies bumped and whined about her lithe form as, twisting and turning, she entered the office of the Indian agent representing the San Carlos Reservation.

"Father?" Frustrated, she batted at the pesky fly that followed her. "Father, where are you?"

The room was a disaster. Papers were strewn all over the floor. A chair was overturned.

A sinking sensation knotted her stomach. It scared her to look around and know that Maurice Russell was usually so neat and tidy that she took great delight in teasing that he could hardly wait for the wind to blow just so he would have an excuse to fuss with the room's only framed picture.

Something was wrong. Dreadfully wrong.

She bent to pick up one of the scattered papers. When she rose, a horrible odor assaulted her thin, almost patrician nose. Swaying, she reached out and caught herself against the wall to keep from falling.

Death! It had a smell all its own. Like a gnarled finger at the end of a stiff, skeletal arm, it seemed to beckon, motioning from behind the closed door leading into the room where her father kept his most important files. She hesitated, trying to block the possibility that *he* could be . . .

Anything could have gotten locked inside the building. A dog. Maybe a rabbit. Her body sagged against a splintered board. Without a shadow of a doubt, though, whatever it was, was dead.

She took a faltering step forward. Two days! She had only been away from the reservation for two days. Everything had been fine when she left. It had been months since the last threat. So why was she thinking the worst?

Because there had been so many warnings during the past year. So many, they had begun to laugh them off—at least for all outward appearances, she reasoned. On the inside, she knew her father had been as terrified as the rest of them. Yes, the Apaches residing at San Carlos were well aware of how lucky they were to have an honest, caring man looking out for their welfare. No one wanted to take the threats seriously.

Meadowlark swallowed hard. Sooner or later she would have to see what was behind that door.

Her legs trembled as she inched slowly forward. Her damp palms slipped on the knob and it took several tries before she secured a grip.

The door creaked open. Her eyes widened and her heart thundered in her breast as she lurched into the room. Her father lay sprawled with his face down across the otherwise spotless floor. A groan rumbled from deep inside her soul as she gradually sank to her knees.

His thin body looked grotesque in its normalcy. She could have imagined he was only sleeping if it weren't for the damned flies. They swarmed everywhere—on the floor, in the air, on his . . . body. Frenziedly, she flailed her arms, beating at the insects until the utter futility caused her to slump in defeat.

Then, tentatively, she reached out to stroke his graying head. The hair was so fine it sifted through her fingers like strands of silk. Her lips curved slightly upward. It was a distinct contrast to the bristles fluffing his blond beard. There were times, as a little girl, when she would giggle and squirm when he would teasingly rub his chin over her ticklish skin.

Suddenly, Meadowlark snatched her hand away. She could only stare in horror at the sticky, smothering blood.

Her lids drifted closed over shimmering amber eyes as she bowed her head. Nausea churned her stomach. Then she rocked back to sit on her heels and pulled a thin-bladed knife from a scabbard hidden inside her high-topped moccasins.

She ran her free hand through her hair. Tears scalded her tawny cheeks as she held out several coal-black strands. The keen edge sliced through them as if they were nothing more substantial than air. Soon the floor was littered with her long, shiny tresses.

She moaned and began to sway back and forth. The sound lifted in crescendo until her haunting Apache wails of mourning echoed over the flat, barren wasteland called San Carlos Reservation.

Chapter One

Brent McQuade swiped for the hundredth time at the soot and ashes steadily filtering onto his new blue uniform. He cursed as the train rocked back and forth on the uneven rails, literally throwing him into his seat. Hard metal grated down his tender spine as he slid into place with a bone-jarring thud and another muffled oath.

Over six months ago, he had ridden this same train headed east, going home to Philadelphia, thinking that when his enlistment with the United States Cavalry was up in September, he would retire from the army and take a nice, quiet job in Washington, maybe get married and think about starting a family.

Harrumph! He'd be caught dead before he'd consider such an asinine notion again. Women! Why did otherwise intelligent men seem to think they couldn't get along without the fairer gender? From this one man's opinion, life would be much happier *without* the encumbrance of females.

His lips compressed into a fine line. He had wanted as far away from Washington as he could get, and decided he might as well continue his career doing something challenging and exciting. Whether Miss Elizabeth Fitzpatrick cared to think so, or not, he was a damned good officer. Every bit as good as her father, the colonel.

One day, she would turn around and realize just what, and whom, she had rejected.

Brent wiped his palms down his cramped thighs. Now he was returning to Arizona Territory under the command of a man he truly admired, Brig. Gen. George Crook.

He remembered when Crook had led his first campaign against the Apache ten years ago. The general had dealt punishment swiftly and thoroughly, then extended his hand in friendship and fair treatment to those Indians who chose to live in peace. He had won their trust and respect, along with Brent's, because of his daring and unconventional ideas.

But now it was 1883 and the government was tired of dealing with renegade Apaches like the notorious Geronimo. So Crook had been ordered to return to Arizona to find and capture the fierce Apache leaders and their bands.

Brent's teeth ground together. Finally, his dream had been answered and he had been assigned to General Crook. But what did he get to do? Damn it all, he would be sitting on his ass in "Hell's forty acres"—the San Carlos Reservation itself—playing nursemaid, while the general and the rest of his command tracked Geronimo all the way to the Sierra Madres.

An agent. Capt. Brent McQuade, an Indian agent. Oh, the general had assured him it was a very important assignment, that only his most trusted officers were to be placed on *all* of the reservations, but that knowledge did little to appease Brent's pride and sense of decency.

Yes, it was important for the Apaches to know Crook's intentions were to treat them as fairly as possible and protect them from the agents in league with the crooked politicians operating out of Tucson. But Brent was worried about the one or two honest men who would be replaced for no good reason—like Maurice Russell. He hated like hell to walk in and tell the man he was out of a job when Russell had done so much for the Indians under his supervision.

And he certainly hoped the sudden change in authority wouldn't cause the Apaches to do something stupid—like running to Mexico and Geronimo.

Brent settled more comfortably in his seat. He supposed Crook's ideas were sound. But of all the damnable luck! What a miserable way to utilize his own talent and expertise. Brent hated to seem to serve his own interests, but while stationed at Fort Apache he had made quite a name for himself because of his ability to track and bring in renegades. Now his biggest challenge would be in deciding how much flour to order, or how many beeves to butcher.

Well, perhaps he deserved the assignment. He was probably lucky the general even deigned to bring him along. Very few people connected with the army had been as vocal as himself concerning the harsh and uncompromising attitudes directed toward the hapless Apaches.

But then very few officers of the United States Cavalry had a long-lost brother, recently returned from the dead, who had once been a feared Apache war chief.

The left side of Brent's mouth quirked upward. The White Fox. Who could have known the white-haired Apache was in reality Brandon McQuade, the boy abducted from a wagon train almost twenty-three years ago?

And who would have thought that Brand would now be married to Hillary, Brent's first real love, or so he had thought at the time?

Brent sighed, glad to think that he would be seeing Brand and Hillary soon, for they were somewhere in the area near Fort Apache doing what they could to help the Indians adjust to making their way in the white man's world. Yet, at the same time, he nursed a pang of melancholy. First Hillary, then Elizabeth. Was he destined to always love and lose?

He tipped his hat forward to block the sun from his face and tried to accommodate his six-foot body into a three-foot space. A vertebra in his neck popped and he began to relax. Flipping open the lid on his watch, he groaned and yawned. Ten more hours. Only ten more hours and the end of his life would begin.

Meadowlark Russell ran her fingers through the short, curly cap of hair framing her too-round face. She had never seen any of the other Apaches' hair curl when shorn, so why did hers?

She sniffed with derision. Though she tried to claim no part of her white blood, it was the only explanation. Ugh!

Suddenly, her breath clogged her throat. Thinking of her white heritage reminded her of her father. Two weeks ago she had discovered his body, and the memory still caused her anguish. Although the pain and grief had lessened somewhat, the anger and frustration taking their place was a living, gnawing ache consuming her every waking moment.

Whenever she closed her eyes, she envisioned that terrible afternoon, relived the terror of finding her father's body. She had spent hours then, walking in a dazed stupor, removing paperwork and files, transporting them to another empty building.

Meadowlark shuddered. She had purposely returned to the scene of death with every intention of burning the office to the ground, as the Apache always did with the possessions and dwellings of those who had died.

But as she had raised her arm, preparing to toss the flaming rags tightly secured to the end of a long stick, a brown hand had suddenly materialized and grasped her wrist. Swinging around, prepared to battle anyone who dared try to stop her, she had come face to face with her friend, Scorpion.

Scorpion, whom she had idolized and trailed like a puppy dog through all of her growing-up years. Her best friend. The man everyone took for granted that she would one day marry.

If it had been any other person, she probably would have shoved him aside and flung the torch into the pile of brush she'd stacked inside the office. But he had quickly wrapped her in his comforting embrace, soothing her with gentle words of wisdom.

And now that she thought about it, over and over, he had been very smart. Setting fire to the structure would have brought the army's wrath upon her, and she would never have been able to implement her plan.

Blinking rapidly, Meadowlark refocused on the stack of papers awaiting her attention. Her hand shook so badly when she started to sign a requisition for more yard goods to make clothing for the new arrivals on the reservation, that she dropped the quill.

Shaking her head, she admonished herself to get control of her emotions. It would not do to smear the initials on the order, for it was the one thing she had been able to think of that might flush out whoever was responsible for her father's death.

It had been so simple, once she had come up with the idea to take her father's place. He had allowed her to work with him the past several years, and had trained her well on what the Apache needed to survive on the reservation.

Who would know whether it was Maurice, or Meadowlark Russell who signed the papers? Only one person would think to question the requisition's signature. Only *one* knew Maurice Russell could not possibly lift the pen.

A sly grin curved her lips. She had practiced her father's initials and signed orders whenever he'd been away from San Carlos. Hers was an almost perfect duplication.

Then her amber eyes sparked with suppressed rage. Jagged nails dug into the palms of her hands. First her mother, and now her father. Both gone within the year.

She shrugged and willed the tension from her shoulders, mentally shaming herself for the thoughts racking her brain. It was as if she blamed her parents for her every misfortune, especially her poor father. But he had always been the one to see the good things in life, always told her everything would be all right. He had promised. He had lied!

Without thinking, she reached into a large, deep pocket in her skirt. Her fingers curled around a beaded pouch, one of the last things Meadowlark's Apache mother, Estrella Russell, had lovingly crafted and presented to her husband. And inside the pouch, she felt the round hardness of Maurice's pocket watch. It was the only material possession of her father's that held any value to her and her memories.

She took a deep breath, hating the sentimentality that had prompted her to forsake Apache tradition and keep the pouch and watch. It was that hated *white* emotion cropping out again and it angered her to acknowledge its existence, for any reason. But when she remembered how she used to bounce upon her father's knee, reaching for the shiny gold object as he dangled it in front of her, and how she giggled and nearly tumbled from his lap until he would stop and crush her in a warm hug. . . .

The door to the little hut she had commandeered for her office suddenly swung open. Meadowlark jerked her hand free of the pocket, straightened her back and swiped at the traces of moisture damping her cheeks. Her smile was tremulous, but her greeting warm.

"*Hola,* my friend. What brings Scorpion to the agency on such a cold day?" The reservation wasn't huge, but Scorpion's band, and hers, the Warm Springs Apache, were located near the northwest corner where few traveled.

The warrior grinned at Meadowlark's joke. It was mid-January and the temperature was warm enough that a man could go about comfortably in only his breechclout and leggings. "*Hola,* little pigeon. Why you all time work? Is *muy bonita* outside."

She cocked her head to one side and grimaced. He had always thought it wonderfully amusing to call her *pigeon* instead of Meadowlark. Although she was tempted to take him to task, as he no doubt intended, she let it pass because she was so proud of how well he was learning his English. What did it matter that he sometimes jumbled his English, Mexican and Apache together? At least he tried.

As the sadness began to finally fade from Meadowlark's golden eyes, Scorpion leaned on the edge of the stacked crates serving as her desk. "Come. Let us ride."

"No. I should—"

"How long since you ride?"

Meadowlark flushed. She hadn't exercised the mare since the day she found her father. Somehow, she suspected that Scorpion was well aware of the fact, just as she knew how he had always held her father's thoroughbred mare in high regard, unlike most of the Apache whose only use for a horse was that of necessity, not pleasure.

She looked from the stack of papers up through the small opening serving as her window. Only a few white clouds drifted across the endless expanse of blue, blue sky. Her decision was made as soon as a light breeze swayed the barren branches of a scraggly cottonwood. Work could wait. The weather was not always so obliging.

"Let's go." Within a heartbeat, she had stepped out of the voluminous skirt, beneath which she wore a pair of loose-fitting leather britches. Although the Apache women frowned upon her defiance of tradition, there were many times she could not do the work she needed to do in a skirt. But she did try to be inconspicuous about it.

Scorpion just winked and reached for her hand. "Is good."

The mare was stabled in a small corral next to the building, so it only took a minute for Meadowlark to bridle the animal and swing onto the horse's broad back. As she and Scorpion rode away from the agency, Meadowlark nodded at several black guardsmen. The Negro cavalry had been garrisoned with the Warm Springs Apache for many years and had long since ceased to be an oddity. In fact, the Apache greatly admired their daring and courage in battle.

Meadowlark frowned, though, recalling the day the soldiers herded her band from their beloved Black Mountains in New Mexico Territory to San Carlos. All of the separate Apache bands had been crowded onto the one reservation, with no distinction made between them, and no regard at all paid to the fact that most of the bands could not tolerate each other. There had been nothing but trouble since.

As she gazed over the dry, flat desert, it was readily apparent why that particular location had been chosen. The land was even more worthless to the whites than it was to the Apache.

Scorpion led the way as they crossed one of the two creeks that sided the plain comprising the San Carlos headquarters. Meadowlark looked over her shoulder and turned up her nose at the five or six shabby adobe buildings that blended so perfectly among the sand and sparse shrubs. How she longed for tall pines and sweet-smelling flowers and green grass. How she missed the beautiful mountains.

She sighed. There was no sense in wishing for what could not be, *yet*. Tossing her head, she reveled in the wind as it ruffled her fine, soft curls. Hatred, worries and grief faded into the distance, to be replaced by the first sense of freedom she had experienced for a long, long time.

Scorpion grinned and kicked his horse into a canter.

It didn't take Meadowlark's long-legged mare a minute to catch up with and overtake his compactly built mustang. She flashed the warrior a bright smile and marveled again at the marked difference between Scorpion and the majority of Apache men. Rather than being short and fairly squat, his body was long and lean.

He presented a handsome figure indeed with a red bandanna tied around his thick brown hair. Even his facial features were more refined than would normally be expected. Scorpion's thin nose and high cheekbones accentuated the long oval shape of his face. He was quite appealing, now that she thought about it.

Her musing was interrupted when Scorpion slowed his horse and reached out to take one of her hands. With his free arm, he gestured contemptuously about the barren, brown countryside. "We leave this place, yes? *Venga* Mexico."

Meadowlark's insides tumbled into a knotted mass. She suddenly found it difficult to swallow. "I . . . I don't know."

Scorpion's face contorted. "More soldiers come. Time for Apache over. We be free with Geronimo."

"For a while," she added under her breath. Yet she read the serious intent in Scorpion's expression. Why was it so important that she go with him *now?* It had been almost a year since the raid on San Carlos.

Perhaps it was the eminent threat of General Crook's return to Arizona Territory. Perhaps Scorpion felt time was running out. Even in her own mind, she realized that maybe not tomorrow, or next month, or even next year, but *soon,* the Apache nation would be restricted to reservations or . . . disappear from the face of the earth forever. It was inevitable.

However, Meadowlark hesitated to follow Scorpion. Her mother had been one of old Loco's band, forced to leave the reservation with Geronimo and Juh last April. They had made it all the way to Mexico with only a few minor skirmishes with the United States Cavalry.

But once they crossed the border, the Mexican army caught up with the fleeing Indians, most of whom had no weapons with which to defend themselves, and engaged in what could only be described as mass slaughter. Over eighty Apaches were massacred, and only eleven of those were men. The rest of the bodies were women and children. A few weeks later, Meadowlark learned that one of the victims had been her mother.

The Mexicans. Meadowlark shivered. Even worse than her contempt for the United States Army was her hatred of the Mexicans. It was *they* who initiated the bounty on Apache scalps. *They* who continued to trade in Apache slaves. *They* who committed the worst atrocities against her people.

Suddenly, her fingers tingled and she realized Scorpion was squeezing her hand to get her attention.

"Say you come, little pigeon. Nothing here for you now."

She blinked. Nothing? He was mistaken. Her father's killer was nearby, she was certain. And the Apache, with no other choice but to remain on the reservation, depended upon her—as her father before—for their very lives.

"I cannot."

"Why? Government take care of reservation Indians. You have no place here. Family in Mexico."

Meadowlark stared into his intense brown eyes. They reflected her own wavering features. Everything he said was true, but she had taken her father's responsibilities as her own. She was honor-bound to stay. "The Apache are my family, too. I cannot turn my back on them."

A muscle in Scorpion's jaw jerked, and for a moment it appeared he would argue. Finally, he only asked, "Soon?"

She sighed. "Maybe." Who knew what the future held? Perhaps someday they really would be able to leave the reservation and make a new life. Perhaps a gila monster would soar like the eagle.

Scorpion's long, slender fingers trailed up her palm and warmed the pulse throbbing in her wrist. "I would speak with . . . your mother's sister."

Meadowlark winced and ducked her head. For a moment, she had thought he would speak her mother's name. It was taboo to repeat the name of a dead person. And if that name happened to be the same as a word in their language, another word was made up. She smiled. For that reason, it was very difficult for the white soldiers, or any one else, to learn the Apache language. It changed as frequently as the seasons.

When Scorpion leaned over and tenderly kissed her

compressed lips, Meadowlark started. It had been a long time since he had touched her mouth with his, and the unfamiliar custom sometimes caught her by surprise.

Then his words registered and she shifted her legs on the mare's warm back. He had voiced his intention to speak to her aunt. So, it would finally happen. Strange, she had thought when the time came she would feel more emotion—excitement, anticipation, *something.*

She loved Scorpion. Had loved him for as long as she could remember. But it was the love of a sister for a brother, not what a woman should feel for the man who would one day become her husband—not the feeling her father had for her mother.

There was a pleasant sensation, however, in knowing that someone wanted her. She would not have to take on every responsibility alone. He could possibly even be of help in finding the murderer.

Scorpion's hand moved over Meadowlark's shoulder and cupped the back of her head. He kneed his mustang closer to the big mare and leaned forward in an attempt to take her in his arms.

She shied away. "W-we should return now."

His confident grin, and the manner with which his brows narrowed together, caused her stomach to turn a little queasy. It was almost as if he mocked her for stopping him, yet his next words belied his expression. "I am patient man. Is good, no?"

Relieved that he didn't seem angry after all, she nodded and reined her horse around. With a quick glance over her shoulder, she kicked the thoroughbred into a gallop. Scorpion threw back his head and let out a bloodcurdling Apache answer to her challenge.

Brent McQuade rode into the San Carlos agency in the wake of a small dust devil. Shiny motes swirled in the air, settling on his wrinkled uniform and between his teeth. When he blinked, it felt as if his lids grated against splinters.

Damn! It was an all-too-familiar feeling. He was home.

However, as he gazed around the drab, inhospitable grounds, he was thankful for the years he spent at Fort Apache in the foothills of a large mountain range. On his infrequent visits to San Carlos, he had always sympathized with the poor soldiers garrisoned here. They suffered during the summer months through heat that had been recorded upward of one hundred and thirty degrees. And at night the temperature dipped as low as fifty.

Removing his hat, he carefully dusted off the brim, then ran his fingers through his hair where the leather band had plastered it to his damp scalp. Yes, he could certainly understand why San Carlos had been dubbed "Hell's forty acres."

The agent's office was the largest building to his right. It was easy to find, since there were only five or six structures on the whole reservation.

As his gaze settled firmly on the cracked adobe and weathered wood beams, he wondered for the hundredth time how Maurice Russell would take the news that he was being replaced. The older man was small and thin with hair the color of granite cliffs and what Brent could only describe as a "meticulous" nature.

He wasn't at all the type of person Brent would imagine holding down such a tough, thankless job. Yet Russell had done a hell of a lot of good and bucked pressure from quite a few corrupt officials, if what General Crook had said was true.

Two iron tie rails and a water trough half filled with green water were located in front of the agency office. Brent stiffly dismounted, brushing away another coat of grime before hitching his horse.

After he loosened the tired gelding's cinch, he smoothed out and buttoned his jacket, used his handkerchief to polish his boots to a clear shine, and stepped over to knock on the rough-hewn door. No one answered. He rapped a second time. Nothing moved. He tried the knob. It turned easily beneath his fingers and the portal creaked open.

The complete disarray that greeted his eyes was unbelievable. He gingerly stepped over a pile of small branches and dead leaves curiously mounded just inside, then waded through crumpled papers and across smashed and empty boxes to peer inside the far room. It, too, was unoccupied except for more debris and a dark stain in the middle of the floor.

The hairs on the back of his neck quivered and he quickly left the building. The smell that accompanied him caused his nose to wrinkle with disgust as he fought his way through a horde of lethargic flies. How odd. The office appeared deserted, yet he carried several requisition orders with Russell's initials.

It was all very confusing.

He spied several soldiers lazing in the shade of a long, low building across the way, and started toward them. Maybe one of them would know where Russell was. Damn it, he wanted to get this unpleasantness over with and settle in as soon as possible.

Brent hid a smile when the young men jumped to attention at his approach. Several tried unsuccessfully to shrug into discarded coats, and one hurriedly stomped a swollen foot back into a scuffed boot.

"Afternoon, men. Any of you seen agent Russell?"

Brent pretended to pay no attention to their state of undress. It certainly wasn't unusual for a soldier to slouch around on a quiet day, although the army never let them forget for long that they were military men and were to appear as such when the time demanded.

A flustered private glanced toward the other two. Their faces were devoid of recognition. The tallest young man cleared his throat and answered, "Beg your pardon, Cap'n, but we only been here a couple o' days. Don't recollect the name."

Brent sighed. "Thanks anyway. What about your commanding officer? Is he on the post?"

A freckle-faced youngster who didn't appear to be a

day over fourteen saluted importantly. "No sir, Captain, sir. He's on patrol. Be back in two days, sir."

Another long sigh emptied Brent's lungs. "Who's in charge while he's away?"

Three blank stares greeted the question. "Don't suppose you know whoever *he* is yet, either?"

While the privates hem-hawed and scuffed their toes in the sand, Brent's eyes turned skyward. A sudden movement caught his attention and he turned to see two Indians entering the compound.

A long-legged, blooded thoroughbred mare was guided by a small Apache with a shock of short, curly, incredibly black hair. A typical stocky desert mustang was ridden by a tall, long-coupled man whose legs would drag the ground if he straightened them out.

He watched as the boy reined his horse in front of a roughly constructed lean-to that looked as if the next hard gust of wind would blow it away. The other Indian tied his mount in front of a small, shabby adobe, then leaned against the rail, observing the youngster as he rubbed down the mare.

Brent nodded, pleased to see that at least some of the Apaches appreciated their horseflesh.

Meadowlark washed her hands in the tepid trough water. She tried to appear nonchalant when Scorpion announced, somewhat imperiously, that he was leaving and would be back to see her in a week or so..

When Scorpion stepped forward, acting as if he would like to touch her, maybe even kiss her good-bye, she suddenly became very busy searching for a towel. It came as an extreme relief to hear him mutter under his breath and, at last, grunt as he mounted his horse.

As the hoofbeats faded into the distance, she let out a long breath. The missing towel was found on the ground beneath the trough. She shook it out and tossed it over her shoulder, then cupped her hands and splashed the warm water over her flushed cheeks.

After washing as thoroughly as possible, she dried her face and scrubbed her neck with the damp cloth. She had just reached down the front of her tunic to continue the cooling ablutions when gravel crunched directly behind her. Thinking Scorpion must have forgotten something, she turned her head, all the while dabbing at the water dripping down her chin.

The first thing that caught her eye was the bright reflection off a pair of polished black boots. A soldier. Ugh! That was all she needed now, another argument over *why* the cattle herd just delivered was twenty head short.

She wiped the moist towel across the back of her neck, intent on taking her time, as the army so often made *her* hurry up and wait, until the incongruous notion of shiny boots in the middle of a dry, dusty afternoon captured her curiosity.

Glancing back, her eyes followed the outline of slim calves snugly encased by black leather, up trimly muscled thighs accentuated by navy blue trousers with a yellow stripe running along the sides of his legs and up lean hips. So, he was a cavalry man, was he? Nothing so unusual about that out here on the reservation.

But she could see areas of brighter color here and there, as if the soldier had taken the time to try to brush the dust from his person. It amused her to think he had missed more of the annoyingly clingy granules than he'd wiped away.

Her gaze lingered briefly on the belt girding his waist and the gold buckle clasped across a flat, tight belly. She swiped the towel over her forehead and cheeks before bravely continuing her appraisal. Broad, broad shoulders filled out a double-breasted jacket as if it had been made for him. Another oddity. Few officers and no buffalo soldiers wore such .

Suddenly, her gaze darted to the soldier's face. There was only one feature there she noticed. The pale blue eyes held her attention, forever it seemed. They were almost transparent and it felt as if she could stare straight through them.

Of course, Meadowlark had been raised knowing it

was rude to stare—in fact, Apache women never looked a man in the eyes—but she could not help herself. She became mesmerized. Her skin even tingled, as if she had just been cleansed by a fresh spring rain.

Brent had been so intent on watching the movements of the towel that he was taken aback when the little person turned, only to regard him with an expression he couldn't even begin to read. The rich, amber eyes colliding with his were surrounded by the longest, thickest black lashes he had ever seen.

He swallowed, unable to figure out what to do with his hands, which seemed too anxious to reach out and touch the unruly mop of curls framing a sweet round face with the smoothest skin and most tempting lips imaginable.

The question kicked him in the deepest, most vulnerable, section of his gut. How could he have seen this beautiful creature and not recognized right away that she was a woman?

But even as his eyes took in her trim figure and gorgeous features, his heart went out to her for a completely different reason. His years spent around Indians had taught him that it was Apache custom for a woman to cut her hair when someone close died, and he recognized the emptiness in those huge, almond-shaped eyes for exactly what it was.

Finally, he blinked and shrugged off the drowning sensation crushing his chest.

"Pardon me, ah, ma'am, but do you know a fella named Russell?"

Chapter Two

When the raven-haired woman continued to stare, Brent McQuade blinked, breaking the strange, compelling lure of her eyes. Assuming a nonchalance he was far from feeling, he furtively glanced down the front of his jacket, then farther.

He cleared his throat. Perhaps she just hadn't heard him. From her expression, she appeared as startled by their encounter as he. "I'm looking for a man named—"

"Yes, I know. The . . . agent."

She spoke so suddenly, yet quietly, that her words drifted over him like a soft caress. He stiffened to ward off the pleasant sensation. He'd learned his lesson where women were concerned, and this little beauty was definitely every inch a woman.

"Well . . . good." He waited, but when it appeared that was all she was going to offer, prodded, "Can you tell me where he is, please?"

Meadowlark slowly laid the towel on the edge of the trough, then straightened her tunic. When she darted a nervous glance back to the officer, a small flame ignited in the pit of her stomach. Men had looked at her before, but none had *ever* had such a disconcerting effect.

She didn't like the way he made her feel. It had taken days to regain what poise and self-control she had left after the trauma of finding her father. Now, here *he* came along, and within a minute's time she went all weak and queasy again.

Straightening her shoulders, she drew her body up to all of its five-foot height. The soldier towered over her, but she refused to allow that to intimidate her. "The agent is not here."

Brent rolled his eyes. Was everyone on the reservation a little slow, or was he just used to the precision of the way things were run in Washington?

He ground out, "So I surmised. Do you know where I can find the man?"

"He . . . he . . . won't be back."

"What?"

"I said, he . . . won't be back." Meadowlark gulped. She was a terrible liar. Had never done it before in her life. At least most of her answers so far had been as close to the truth as possible.

"Damn!" Brent took off his hat and slapped it against his pant leg. Dust formed a small cloud around his knees.

Meadowlark shifted from one foot to the other. "W-why? What do you want with my . . . with him?"

"I . . ." He paused and eyed the woman closely. No, he'd better wait. He didn't want Russell to hear the news secondhand. This was something that needed to be handled face to face. "It can wait."

Her silence made him a little edgy as he glanced around the headquarters area. His eyes fell on the agent's office and he recalled the disarray he'd discovered there. "Perhaps you could tell me what happened to Rus—"

Meadowlark noted where his gaze had stopped. "You mean the office? It was . . . uhm, condemned."

"Condemned?" Brent couldn't believe his ears. Was this some kind of joke?

"Yes. I just recently moved everything over here." She indicated the tiny hovel where one beam sagged through several crumbled adobes.

Brent blinked, then looked with utter disbelief from the larger, seemingly better kempt building, back to one that appeared little more than a hut. But, she was the one who should know, so rather than argue, he concentrated on something else she had said. "*You* moved the files and all?"

She licked her lips and nodded.

For some unexplainable reason, the gesture caught him completely by surprise. His belly tautened at the sight of her delicate pink tongue darting from between full, perfectly shaped lips. Uncomfortable with his sudden reaction, he snapped, "Who gave you the authority to tamper with government property?"

His voice sounded gravelly and much more gruff than he'd intended and he winced. It wasn't the woman's fault he responded so strongly to her innocent movement. He was irritated with *himself.*

Meadowlark's hands fisted at the soldier's arrogance. "I've helped with the paperwork for years. I wa . . . am . . . the . . ."—she ground her teeth together—". . . agent's daughter." She stopped abruptly. If she weren't careful, he would demand more explanations than she was ready to give.

"I didn't know Russell had a . . . daughter."

Then he frowned. The woman just closed her eyes and grimaced. What had he said? He'd been tactful and caught himself before mentioning "Apache" daughter—for it was plain to see she had Indian blood.

His eyes devoured her high forehead and prominent cheekbones, sweet round face and gorgeous peach-tinted skin. But it was still her unusual whiskey eyes that taunted his good sense.

The same eyes Brent was so openly admiring, narrowed as Meadowlark glared. "Does it surprise you more, soldier, that a daughter exists, or that she is half Apache?"

A wide grin curved Brent's lips. She was a feisty little thing, too. "I just didn't know, is all."

Meadowlark's stomach turned upside down. Wouldn't you know it. The white man had a dimple. A cute little indentation on the left side of his sensuous mouth.

Brent welcomed the distraction of a fly determinedly attempting to alight on his nose. "Why don't you show me this new office. I would like to look through a few of those files." The job, he reminded himself. The reason he had come here in the first place.

Meadowlark seethed. There was that arrogance again. Those files weren't there for just *anyone* to "look through." "Sorry," she lied. "But I cannot give permission."

Brent saw the devilish glint in her eye. The woman was up to something, but what? And, permission? Just who did she think she was talking to? "Look, little lady, I don't need . . ." Wait. He couldn't up and tell her *he* was now the authority at San Carlos. He had vowed to talk to Russell first, and by his honor, that was exactly what he would do.

"Very well. Tell your father that Brent McQuade is here and needs to talk to him. It's important." He flopped his hat back on his head and stalked away.

Meadowlark stood with her hands on her hips, watching the straight set of the soldier's retreating back as he unhitched his horse and rode off in a cloud of dust. She felt a slight quiver as she realized the small victory was hers.

Then her eyes narrowed. The handsome soldier was gone for now, but if he came back and called her "little lady" again . . .

Early the next morning, Brent walked through the dusty compound on his way to Maurice Russell's "new" office. As he neared the old building, he couldn't help but wonder again why it had been condemned. As far as he could see, it was in much better condition than any of the other structures, even those being used by the troops.

He shivered and cupped his hands around his mouth, blowing warm breath on his stiff fingers. Damn! but it was cold.

Just as he passed the deserted building, he hesitated, then stopped. He could have sworn he detected a movement, or something, inside. Stepping over to the door, he peered through the grimy window. The room was empty. All appeared quiet.

Brent stuffed his hands in his pockets and continued on his way. Once, he looked over his shoulder. Then he laughed to himself. Must be seeing ghosts.

By the time he reached his destination, though, his thoughts centered on only one thing—or person. The woman. From when he had left her yesterday, until he'd gotten up that morning, she'd been uppermost on his mind. Never in his life had he encountered such an impertinent, aggravating female.

Who would have guessed that nice, quiet, unassuming Maurice could sire such a firebrand? Yep, she did have a temper.

Meadowlark Russell. Hhmm. *Cougar* Russell. *Grizzly* Russell. Now those fit her much better. Nevertheless, there *was* something intriguing about her name.

His teeth gritted when he remembered the calf-eyed lieutenant at mess last night. The man had talked about the woman called "Meadowlark" in such glowing, adoring terms that the cherry pie almost curdled in Brent's stomach. Poor young fool. The boy was setting himself up to learn about women all right—the hard way.

But the fellow had saved him the embarrassment of having to *ask* her name. After all their conversation, like a stupid idiot, he had forgotten to find out her name. Lord, who was acting the young fool?

Brent reached out to push open the door, which was barely held in place by two leather straps serving as hinges. His knuckles cracked when it didn't budge. Barred? The door was barred. Why? Maurice had never kept the office locked before.

He gingerly flexed the fingers on his right hand, then knocked as loudly as possible. Something strange was going on here. Real strange.

Wood grated against wood just as Brent raised his fist

again. The door creaked ajar. The slender form of a tousle-haired girl blocked as much of the opening as she could fill. She raised her head and gazed at him bleary-eyed.

Brent could hardly take a breath. Meadowlark Russell stood before him, with black curls nestled against her rosy cheeks and falling onto her forehead. Her white teeth gnawed at that pouting lower lip and his mind formed an immediate image of what she might look like, rising in the early morning, naked, from his bed.

He decided to act quickly, before he lost all train of thought having to do with business. "I've come to see your father. Would you tell him I'm here?"

Meadowlark blinked and started. Him! Her hands flew to her flushed cheeks. From the warmth of the sun, it had to be midmorning already. She'd overslept. For the first time in her life.

"You! Again!" Unreasonable anger swelled in her chest. It was the soldier's fault. Because of him, she had tossed and turned and finally lain awake most of the night trying to figure out how to keep him diverted or, better yet, how to get him to leave.

Brent frowned and shrugged.

Meadowlark rubbed her forehead. What excuse could she give? Oh, she couldn't think. "Uhm . . . I'm sorry, again, but you are . . . too late."

Brent's frown turned into a full-fledged scowl. He'd purposely come early. From the few times he had been around Maurice, the man had never gotten out this soon. "Can you tell me where he is? Perhaps I could meet him there."

He sucked in his breath when she pulled herself up and set her determined little features. She had to be the most beautiful woman he had ever seen, even sleep-tousled. Then he corrected himself. *Especially* sleep-tousled, and with that cute sprinkle of freckles across the tip of her nose.

Meadowlark couldn't seem to look him in the eye. "Uhm, I don't know where."

He sighed. "Now, why doesn't that surprise me?" Damn it, there wasn't any reason for him to believe she would be purposely evasive. Was there?

She cocked her head. Suspicion narrowed her eyes. "Pardon me?"

Brent took a deep, calming breath. It was those whiskey eyes that caused his chest to constrict. "Never mind. I'll come back by later."

Meadowlark muttered to herself, "Do you *have* to?"

He had turned away, but swung back. "What was that?"

She gritted her teeth, but managed to snap, "I'll be waiting." And beneath her breath she added, "Like a rabbit awaits the coyote."

A smile lit Brent's face as he tapped the brim of his hat with two fingers and jauntily sauntered off, whistling off-key.

Meadowlark slammed the door, then jumped to catch it and prop it in place again. In Apache, she repeated every foul word she had ever heard, and made up a few of her very own. What had she done to deserve being plagued by that *white* man.

Her stomach felt like it had turned permanently wrong side out.

He had given her a reprieve. But how long would it last?

A little over twenty-four hours later, Brent rode back into San Carlos. He counted the tally he'd taken of the beef herd and figured that there would need to be another purchase and drive made soon.

According to his calculations, there was enough meat for maybe three weeks, but a person never knew from one week to the next how many Indians would turn up for their allotments. It seemed on days when supplies were given out, their numbers swelled considerably.

He reined his mount over to the hitching post in front of the agent's office. In order to be sure Maurice'd had time to return, Brent had not gone back last evening. He ran a finger underneath his collar and tugged. All of a sudden, the damned thing was cutting off his air.

He hated to acknowledge, even to himself, that the real reason he'd waited was because new sensations he'd felt during the past few days had stirred old memories. Memories of Elizabeth and the pain he'd suffered since she jilted him. Hopefully, a long evening spent drowning his sorrows and the subsequent hangover, would be enough to get him past another meeting with little Miss Meadowlark Russell.

As Brent dismounted and tethered his horse, motioning for the young officer who'd accompanied him to do the same, he prayed that Maurice would be home. Yet when he knocked on the lopsided door, he experienced an undeniable yearning for *her* to open the portal.

His prayers weren't to be answered.

Meadowlark winced at the insistent rapping. This was the moment she had dreaded. Wait. Worry. Hurry up and wait some more. And the man hadn't even the decency to come back yesterday. She'd lain awake all last night, sweating, suffering, trying to think up a believable story.

Now as she pulled the door open, she was irritable and annoyed to find him looking so . . . haggard and blurry-eyed? His bandana was askew. One jacket pocket was unbuttoned and the flap stood up.

With a grim sense of satisfaction, she noted that he must have had as bad a night as she, if not worse. For the first time since meeting the handsome officer, she smiled.

When he just stood there, his hand still raised in midknock, she cocked her head and studied him for a brief minute. Oh, yes, he was still maddeningly good-looking, even with a dark stubble lining his square jaw. His shoulders appeared somewhat hunched, as if he pondered the problems of the world.

Well, it so happened she had a few troubles of her own. "Good morning, Captain . . . Uhm, sorry, but I seem to have forgotten your name," she lied. McQuade. Brent McQuade. The name was emblazoned in her mind, but it did her heart good to see the slight flush that darkened his already ruddy features.

Somehow, his name had sounded familiar, and after he left yesterday, she had gone through the files and stacks of papers until she found dates where he had visited San Carlos and her father. At that time, he had been garrisoned at Fort Apache. So, what was he doing now, at San Carlos?

Brent stifled a groan. Did the woman have to shout so early in the day? "McQuade, ma'am. Captain Brent McQuade, at your service."

"Miss. I'm still a 'Miss', thank you." Meadowlark scowled. She didn't know which was worse, being called a "little lady" or "ma'am." Then she realized what she had done and could have kicked herself. Why hadn't she just left him with the impression that she could have been married?

Glancing then into the smiling face of the young lieutenant who always seemed to be trailing after her at the most inconvenient times, she found the answer to her question. Too many people at San Carlos knew she was unmarried. She was also sick of thinking up lies. One day she would trip over her own tales.

The pounding in Brent's head seemed to ease a little when he heard no man had claimed her hand. It was a mystery why he had even wondered about her marital state, but he had, after seeing her with the other rider that first day. Suddenly, he cleared his throat. Not that it made any *real* difference to him, of course.

"Well, that's real fine, *Miss* Russell." He loved the way her eyes sparked fire and her little nose tilted upward when he prodded her some. Then he leaned forward and peered inside the room. "I'm still looking for Mau—"

"No! I mean, you are too early." She hadn't meant to be so abrupt, had only intended to stop him from saying the name she couldn't bear to hear.

"Too early?" Brent was incredulous. Yesterday he'd been too late to catch the agent, and now he was too early?

"Are you telling me he spent the night on the reservation?"

She looked nervously at the dried slab of board beneath his still shiny boots and shrugged.

Brent slowly pulled off his gloves, fisted the cuffs into his left hand, and slapped them against his right palm, over and over. Too much time was being wasted. Important matters needed his attention *now.*

He looked into her wide, too bright eyes, and down to her perfect little mouth with that inviting lower lip. A long sigh shuddered through his weary body. For *her* sake, for Maurice's, and for his own piece of mind, he would wait one more day. Just one. "No sense in my hanging around here then, is there?"

She shook her head and hoped she didn't look as relieved as she felt.

"Well, I'll be going." But his legs refused to obey his brain's command to move. His eyes devoured her from head to toe. Today, she wore a blouse that was gathered at the neck and fit low over her smooth, peachy shoulders. It was tucked into a full skirt that fell to the ankles of her moccasins.

She looked much more civilized than when she wore her beaded leather pants and tunic. But, surprisingly, it was always her Apache presence that appeared in his dreams at night.

"Will you be back?" She didn't want to see him again. It was just necessary for her to be prepared.

"Yes, I'll stop by this afternoon." His brows dipped together as he noticed her shoulders relax in resignation. "It really is important that I get in touch with your . . ." He hesitated. She had seemed about to say something, but evidently changed her mind. ". . . father as soon as possible."

She felt the blood drain from her face. "Is something wrong?" She had never considered the possibility, but had she made a mistake on the requisitions? Had someone figured out her scheme?

Her eyes went cold and hard. Did the soldier know more than he was letting on? Was he luring her into a trap of some kind? He'd seemed so genuinely disappointed when she told him her father was out, though. Surely her instincts weren't *that* far wrong, yet.

Brent flushed. Why would she assume something was wrong? Was there something to hide, or was he just overly suspicious for some reason? He shook his head. "If he should happen to come back, just tell him I've called several times." So be it. He had business to conduct. "I'd appreciate it."

He and the lieutenant walked to their horses. Brent slanted the wide-eyed officer a warning look, daring him to comment on the strange exchange he had witnessed. When Brent was mounted, he looked back and found her watching. He gave a mock salute, then rode toward the blacksmith's.

Meadowlark slumped against the doorjamb. He'd only given her a few more hours. What next?

Meadowlark propped the door open so she could look out and be warned of Brent McQuade's arrival. She didn't want him to find her making out requisitions and signing them. If she could just make this charade last another couple of days, or maybe even a week, the murderer might make a mistake and reveal himself.

She had thought of another possibility once before, but refused to allow herself to believe it could be true. Yet every once in a while, when there was nothing to keep her mind occupied, the niggling suspicion came to the fore. And her blood turned ice cold.

What if the killer were right there on the reservation? What if he watched her, laughing at her feeble attempts to entrap him, waiting for an opportunity to . . . to what?

A rustling sound in the doorway caused Meadowlark to leap to her feet so fast she almost sent her chair crashing over backward. With one hand, she wrestled the tottering piece of furniture, while using the other to shuffle the form she'd just filled out to the bottom of the pile of papers.

"Just a moment, Captain."

"Little pigeon, why you jump like rabbit?"

Her head snapped up. Scorpion. Air hissed from her lungs as her legs suddenly buckled and she fell once again into the chair. "It's you."

Scorpion scowled and stalked into the room. "*Si*. Who else you look to?"

"*For*. Look *for*." She placed a hand over her heart and took a deep breath.

The warrior crossed his arms over his chest and stood quietly. "So? Who for?"

Gradually, she informed him of Captain McQuade and how she had put off explaining about her father. "I don't want anyone to know about the murder until I know why they're here and what they want."

Scorpion's dark features turned rosy brown. "I stop you from burning building. I help with burial. I wait, but you no tell me what happen."

She admitted that she felt a little guilty about that, but still didn't trust *anyone* with her plans, not even her best friend. There was a chance it could put him in danger. When she found out what she needed to know, maybe then she could share her doubts and fears.

Walking around the small, rickety desk, she placed her hand on Scorpion's forearm. "I *will* tell you."

"When?"

"Soon. I promise." Her eyes dropped from his tense features to the bare expanse of his chest. Bare? "Scorpion? Where is your crucifix?"

The man's brown eyes flashed. His free hand automatically reached up to grasp at nothing. The muscles beneath Meadowlark's fingers tautened. "It is in wickiup."

She looked puzzled. “But you never take it off. It’s all you have left of your mother’s things.”

From behind them, a rich, sonorous voice joined the conversation. “What’s that? Have you lost something besides your father?”

Chapter Three

Brent ducked his head and entered the small room. Once inside, he stood with his hands on his hips, looking intently between Meadowlark and the strange man.

The concern he had first seen on her face altered immediately to what he could only describe as consternation. The guilt he had detected on the man's face transformed in an instant to a scowl of displeasure.

Aw, hell, he thought agreeably, he must have interrupted something.

He hadn't intended to come back by the office so early, but had seen the mustang tethered outside and couldn't seem to stop himself from drifting in that direction.

The horse looked a lot like the one he'd noticed that first afternoon when he had seen the two riders entering the compound. He was curious to know the other person's identity and his relationship to Lark.

His mouth quirked. Lark. During quiet moments alone, when he found himself thinking of her, he imagined her as the small, dainty bird, who easily had her feathers ruffled.

As silence echoed throughout the room, he smiled and said, "Thought I heard you say you'd lost something. Perhaps I can help find it."

"Nothing."

"Nada." Meadowlark and Scorpion answered at the

same time, then looked to each other with smug expressions. But Meadowlark sighed and turned back to Brent. She had told enough white lies during the past two days that she couldn't live with another when it really wasn't necessary.

"I thought Scorpion had lost his crucifix, but he just wasn't wearing it. So, nothing is lost."

Brent studied the smaller, darker man and noticed distastefully the proprietary way he stood close to Meadowlark. "Scorpion, huh? I'm Captain McQuade."

He held out his hand. Though the other fellow seemed to consider it a little longer than was comfortable, he kept his arm extended without a waver.

Finally, the gesture was acknowledged as the man put a cold hand stiffly forward. But the acceptance failed to reach the hard, brown eyes, and Brent mentally advised himself to never turn his back on this Scorpion fellow. His bite might be as deadly as his name.

Meadowlark moved back against the desk. Since the soldier had come into the office, the room had become cramped and stifling. Who did he think he was, always sneaking up on her like he did? Worst of all, what had happened to her well-honed senses? He'd had to walk across sand and gravel to reach the door. Why hadn't either Scorpion or she heard his approach?

And she'd gritted her teeth to keep from cursing out loud when his mouth had made that funny little quirk, displaying that dimple. It was the easy, friendly kind of expression Apaches only shared with trusted friends. But she knew white men revealed their thoughts and feelings more carelessly and with less sincerity.

In fact, the more she was around the captain, the more she disliked him. There was just *something* about him she did not trust. Her body suffered strange and unusual disturbances when he was near. Her mind refused to function rationally. She couldn't control the restless energy he so effortlessly created within her.

Brent felt the varying undercurrents emanating from the two individuals, but couldn't seem to bring himself to leave. He needed to know more about this Scorpion. "Well, it looks as if my trip over here was in vain, again."

Meadowlark nodded. "You can tell me what you want. I might be able to help. You could be on your way much sooner."

Sidling over to lean his hip against the opposite edge of the desk from where Meadowlark stood, Brent took off his hat and reshaped the brim where the heat had caused it to curl. "Why, Miss Russell, I'm beginning to get the impression that you'd like to get rid of me."

She sniffed. "You misunderstand, Captain. I'm merely . . . curious."

Brent thoughtfully considered his options. What would it hurt to go ahead and tell her? It didn't appear Maurice was going to show up any time soon, and he needed to start to work tomorrow morning at the latest.

"All right. I wanted to speak to your father first, to avoid hard feelings, but . . . I've been sent to replace him as the agent here at San Carlos. General Crook is returning to Arizona, and has assigned officers to that position on *all* of the reservations."

Scorpion stared, without changing expression or making a move, other than to lean closer to Meadowlark.

Meadowlark's face paled. "I-I don't understand. Hasn't a good job been done here? The Apache will not easily respect a man they do not know. What right has the general to do such a thing?"

Brent sympathized with her. He'd had the same questions. "It's nothing personal. No reflection on your father at all."

Meadowlark's head throbbed. She paced to the center of the room, then swung back to face the captain. "Nothing personal? What do any of you know? We have gone through hell for the past two years. There have been threats and . . . and . . . attempts of . . . murder. Yet always my people have been dealt with fairly. *I* consider this a *very* personal matter."

Brent swallowed a groan. That was exactly the reaction he had feared receiving from Russell himself. "The general is well aware of your father's honesty. But how would it have looked if all of the agents, *except* your father, were dismissed? Wouldn't that have caused even more trouble for him? General Crook wanted to do what was best for *all* concerned, and this was the only way he found to carry out his plans."

Meadowlark fisted her hands. At the mention of "plans", she realized that the captain's presence would ruin everything she had set in motion. It would be much more difficult now to trap her father's killer, if not impossible. And this handsome cavalry soldier could know nothing of an agent's responsibilities. He would destroy everything her father had implemented.

Her dreams were dissipating faster than mist beneath the heat of a summer sun.

"W—when will you take over?" She was proud of how even and controlled her voice sounded, since every nerve in her body was vibrating with tension.

Brent settled himself more firmly on the groaning desk. "There's a lot to be done. This afternoon wouldn't be too soon."

Her eyes widened with horror. Not today! She had expected him to say tomorrow, or next week, not this very moment. "What's the matter, Miss Russell?" Brent glanced down at the clutter covering the top of the desk. "Surely you wouldn't begrudge some help?"

When she saw the direction of his gaze, Meadowlark hurried around and plopped into the chair. She picked up the stack of papers beneath which she had hidden the last initialed requisition order. Her eyes shot daggers at the white man. "I've been doing quite well by myself, thank you."

"You'll do even better now, then."

Suddenly, Meadowlark tilted her head and eyed the officer. "You mean you want me to stay?"

Brent glanced toward the stoic countenance of the silent warrior. For some reason, the hairs on the back of his neck prickled. But he concentrated on Meadowlark's question. Until that very moment, he hadn't realized what he had said.

Damn! He should make a clean break with the Russell family. His initial idea of making an arrangement with Maurice seemed to be just another method of prolonging agony, especially if it meant keeping his daughter underfoot.

"Will you? At least until your father returns?" Good God! That wasn't what he meant to say at all. He had wanted to tell her to take whatever was hers from the office and leave. The ambiguous feelings that assailed him whenever she was near were more than he could stand.

"Is *no bueno,* little pigeon. Better you come with me."

Meadowlark jumped at the sound of Scorpion's voice. She had forgotten he was in the office, so intently had she been concentrating on her problems.

Her friend was probably right. It was stupid to think she could stay without "someone" finding out what she was doing. And it could be dangerous.

But she had a responsibility to her people. They would need her now more than ever. Besides, the thought of seeing how the captain would handle the job was something she didn't want to miss.

Brent glared at Scorpion and hoped Meadowlark wouldn't listen to the other man. He watched her face, looking for the expected play of emotions crossing mobile, feminine features. But if anger or fear warred with relief or anticipation, he found no evidence of the struggle on her delicate face. Was she going to accept his offer, or not?

He couldn't take the risk of her not. Couldn't? Fool! "I'd appreciate your showing me what your father has been doing here. My barging in and making a mess of things isn't what I had in mind for your . . . people."

Ah, yes, that was the look he wanted. Her expression of pride and fierce protectiveness for the Apache. He had correctly read her complete devotion.

Meadowlark turned pleading eyes to Scorpion in the hope that he would understand how she felt. What the captain was offering was more than she ever imagined. "All right. I'll help you."

Brent tried to control the elation numbing his common sense. The best thing that could happen would be for Maurice Russell to walk through the door that very moment. Unconsciously, he darted a glance in that direction.

Hell, even if it meant leaving her alone with Scorpion, he had to get away. "That's real fine. Well, I've got things to do. Be back later."

As soon as the soldier had left, Scorpion rounded on Meadowlark. "Do not trust the soldier. He is like cat who teases prey to prolong kill. Better we go Mexico. Tonight."

The temptation to go to Mexico was almost overwhelming. Meadowlark longed to live in the mountains, to see what was left of her family again. "I cannot. The captain has offered to let me show him how my . . . how to make San Carlos more comfortable for our people."

Scorpion snorted, but Meadowlark doggedly continued. "We can't turn our backs now. We have an opportunity to be useful." And to herself, she added, "And now I can keep my plan working."

The warrior looked through the open doorway. His eyes were dark and unreadable when he glanced back to Meadowlark. "All right, little pigeon. We wait. But *soon* . . . must go to Mexico."

Meadowlark sighed and nodded. Her fingers rubbed against the bottom page of the stack of papers. "Yes. Soon."

Brent's feet were killing him. His toes were cramped, his heels felt blistered and his soles ached. He sat down in the meager offering of shade provided by the thick branches of one of the few cottonwoods growing near the reservation headquarters.

With a relieved groan, he removed first one boot,

then the other, and laid them aside with a baleful glare. That's what he got for walking in high-heeled riding boots.

But he'd had no idea it would take so long to get his thoughts and priorities in order when he'd left that office.

Rubbing one tender arch, he sighed and leaned back against the rough bark of the tree trunk. He felt better after the walk. Knew what he needed—had—to do.

For as long as he was at San Carlos, his first priority was to the Apache being forced to make their homes there. *All* of the Apache, which included one tiny little woman of mixed blood, Miss Meadowlark Russell. She would be dealt with the same as the others.

Yes, he had asked for her help, would probably need it, be grateful for it. It had been good strategy. She was trained in the basics of running the agency, and was well acquainted with the people he would need to know.

So, it was wise to keep her around for a while, at least until Maurice could take her place. It might be difficult in the beginning, but he, the knowledgeable Capt. Brent McQuade, could handle *her*—and the job. And it was high time he quit making a jackass of himself.

Wouldn't Elizabeth get a great kick if she knew that less than a month after jilting him, he was back at it again, begging for more pain and heartache? Damn it all, what was wrong with him? Elizabeth was still too fresh in his mind, although there were times when he could barely visualize her features.

He shook his head. Apaches. Food. Clothing. Location of the various bands. Teaching them to integrate into the white world. *Those* were his priorities. Right? Right!

Meadowlark melted into the shade. She had finally convinced Scorpion to return to their village so she could come down to the cottonwood grove, her favorite place to be alone and think.

But who should show up? The person most responsible for her state of mindless confusion. The soldier, Brent McQuade. Why couldn't the man leave her alone?

She had finally found a few minutes of peace, staring at the distant horizon, dreaming of walking the tall peaks, imagining the fresh scent of pine and piñon and the amusing antics of squirrels and chipmunks playing in the branches. She could almost hear a gurgling brook, or feel the impression of a snowflake as it melted on her skin.

A sob caught in her throat. Sometimes, the despair of her people was more than she could bear as they languished and died in the harsh, unforgiving desert. Their dignity was gone. Hope destroyed. The warriors were no longer free to hunt for food to feed their starving families. Those who tried the white man's farming were destined to failure because there was little enough water for humans and animals, let alone fragile plants which wilted in the severe heat.

She swiped at a lone tear tracing a path down her cheek. A million of the droplets would not be enough to allay the thirst of one lonely flower.

Then the captain had to come along and invade her hard-won solitude. She watched as he limped into the outer edge of the shade and collapsed onto a flat boulder, struggling to remove his high-topped boots. His sigh of pleasure as he held his feet out and wriggled his toes almost coaxed a smile from her compressed lips. Then off came his bandanna. He unbuttoned his coat.

Her heart beat an incessant rhythm against her rib cage as the heavy material sent up a small cloud of dust when it hit the ground. He stretched his arms over his head, causing his corded muscles to bunch and ripple down his broad back. She wiped her palms down the seams of her skirt.

One thing she could never deny—he was quite beautiful—for a white man. His body was as well honed and sculpted as hard and virile as any Apache. It was funny, though, the way the flesh on the back of his hands and neck was burned darker than the rest of his body. Yet his back and shoulders were a rich tan, like the grains of sand squishing between her toes.

As he slowly turned his head, the sun shone between the branches and caught the pale blue of his eyes. Her knees went weak. His were smiling eyes, although she sensed, and had seen, deep sadness and pain in their depths.

"Hello. I didn't know you were out here."

His voice was deep and vibrated the air like thunder during a summer shower. She sighed and merely inclined her head in greeting.

Brent ducked his head when he saw she was gazing at his naked upper body and quickly shrugged back into his blue coat. It was embarrassing enough to think he hadn't noticed her presence when he first entered the trees. "Ahem, what were you doing out here alone?"

Because of the sincere interest she detected in his voice, Meadowlark decided to tell him. "Looking at the mountains."

"I used to live at Fort Apache." He also gazed longingly toward the deep purple ridges outlined on the northern horizon.

"I know."

A deep sense of satisfaction pervaded Brent. Evidently she was interested enough to find out something about him. But how, or why, he had no idea. Nobody here knew him. Her father had been gone . . . Wait! He *had* come back that first night, but then left before Brent could catch up with him the next morning. His shoulders slumped.

Funny, how learning that should be so disappointing. "I know a little something about you, too." When her head snapped around and her eyes narrowed on him, he admitted, "I only asked your name. Meadowlark. It's very pretty."

She slanted those whiskey eyes away and his throat

went as dry and scratchy as a dead mesquite bush.

"Thank you. My . . . the Meadowlark's call was a favorite of my—"

"I bet your father named you. Seems I recall him mentioning—"

She cringed and quickly corrected him. "I was named by the one who bore me."

Although defensive at first, her voice had turned all soft and throaty. Brent's insides turned as bubbly and liquid as hot lava. "I'd like to meet her someday."

"It would not be possible."

There was such an expression of desolation on her face, that Brent almost went to her. He had a sudden compulsion to give her comfort, to hold her in his arms and . . . "She died?"

Meadowlark shrugged and lowered her gaze.

"I'm sorry."

"Why?"

The question caught Brent by surprise. Why? Why not? "Because . . . I am."

Meadowlark stared at the soldier's solemn features. She nodded when she decided his words rang true. Why should it be so hard for her to accept the fact that he might care, one way or the other? Thanks to her father, she knew that not *all* white men were dishonest or evil.

Silence settled about them, until Brent scooped up his boots and moved to sit beside her in the sand. "Look, I know you have no reason to trust me, but I intend to do my best to help the Apache. Your people . . ."

He didn't know why he kept referring to the Indians as "her people." She was half white, too. Perhaps it was because she seemed to go out of her way to deny it. "Your . . . *they* know General Crook and know he's a fair man. He's going to do everything possible to right the wrongs that have been done, and to keep the Apache on the reservations so no more will feel the need to leave and join Geronimo."

Meadowlark thought of Scorpion's, and even her *own*, dreams of escaping the reservation. General Crook might *think* he knew what was best for the Apache, but then *he* didn't have to look forward to spending the rest of his days at San Carlos.

"Anyway, I'm glad you've agreed to help me."

Suddenly shy, she lowered her eyes and ran her fingers through a hill of sand. "I-I'll try."

Since she didn't see it coming, Meadowlark nearly tumbled over backward when Brent leaned forward and gave her a swift, butterfly-light kiss on the mouth. Then she quickly sprang to her feet and stood, poised, ready to take flight if he dared intimate the desire to touch her again.

She pierced him with an accusing glare, then gasped when he had the audacity to wink and grin. She reeled off a string of Apache curses as he also arose, but turned and walked gingerly through the hot sand, still carrying his too-well-polished boots.

Slowly, she traced her lips with trembling fingers. The next time he tried such a thing, he'd feel the bite of her knife.

The next time? Would there be one?

Brent stopped midway back to the agency and tugged on his boots. He winced as the leather grated over his tender heels. Several limping steps later found him resting in the shade of the condemned building, thinking of the foolhardiness of his latest encounter with "Meadowlark."

No matter how determined his mind, his body prompted him to do the craziest of things. He had no more intended to kiss her than he would purposely ride his horse off a cliff. But he had done it. Oh, how he had done it.

Her gasp of surprise, or was it outrage, still echoed in his ears. In fact, he could still hear . . .

Brent straightened, fully alert. What he'd heard wasn't a faint, breathy intake of air, but the sound of something grating—like a rusty hinge, or a foot over gravel.

He edged around to the side and carefully made his way to the back of the building. The palm of his right hand rested on the butt of his pistol as he quickly stepped around the corner.

A shadowed figure straightened from the window and spun to face him.

"Scorpion? What the hell are you doing?"

Chapter Four

The blade of a deadly, double-edged knife reflected a ray of sunlight, nearly blinding Brent with its brilliance. Scorpion stood poised on the balls of his feet, glaring back at him. Brent's fingers twitched around the pearl handle of his army-issue Colt .45, but he hesitated in drawing it from the holster.

The warrior's muscles quivered and flexed as he slowly relaxed. He took a deep breath and shrugged his shoulders. "White soldier move with stealth of puma."

Brent noted the compliment, but continued to grip his revolver. Though the man's nostrils had ceased to flare and most of the challenging glitter had faded from his eyes, Brent remained cautious until the warrior sheathed his knife.

His attention focused on Scorpion's right hand, he nevertheless caught the sound of a faint, muffled crinkle. Then from the corner of his eye, he saw a rumpled paper flutter to the ground near the Indian's left side.

Scorpion suddenly stepped away from the building. "I be rest in shade."

But even as Scorpion was speaking, all the while edging farther away, Brent noticed the covert glances he directed toward the window.

"So, you were just sitting in the shade for a spell?"

Scorpion nodded.

"Seemed to me you were looking for something." Brent rubbed his chin. "Must have been mistaken."

Again, Scorpion inclined his head.

"Thought you might've been hunting that necklace. But I remember now. You didn't lose it after all, did you?" The warrior's eyes narrowed, causing the hair to prickle along the nape of Brent's neck.

"No!" Scorpion snapped. The Indian's eyes took on a glazed, almost mad, expression.

Brent shifted the gun inside the well-oiled holster. "Hey, take it easy. I only intended to help, is all. Miss Russell seemed mighty concerned about it."

The muscles along the side of Scorpion's neck leaped spasmodically. "No lost. I get." With one last glare in Brent's direction, the warrior turned and stalked toward his tethered mustang, which stood hip-shot in front of the smaller adobe office building.

Brent watched him ride away, then casually searched the ground until he spied a crumpled sheet of paper. He picked it up and smoothed it out, then frowned. There was one name and something else that looked like it had once been a list of figures, but it was smeared and unreadable, splotched by a dark, rusty stain. He had no idea what it was, or what Scorpion had been doing with it, but he folded it neatly and stuck it in his breast pocket.

Tracing Scorpion's steps, he walked over to the little building. It was late, but maybe he could get things ready for an early start tomorrow morning. The room was surprisingly bare except for two stacked crates that had been pressed into service as a makeshift desk, one chair and a pallet against the far wall. His brows drew together. Meadowlark was evidently using the room as an office and a place to sleep. Why?

Maurice Russell had built a small, but comfortable, home a little less than a mile from the headquarters. Brent had ridden by the house once on his way back to Fort Apache. It was set off by itself, away from any particular relocated band, which to Brent's way of thinking was as it should be if the agent was to remain fair and impartial in his dealings.

So why was Meadowlark living here? The question continued to plague him as he sat down in the rickety hand-hewn chair. However, his mind soon became enmeshed in the documents stacked on top of the desk. He read through lists of items that needed to be ordered before the next week's allotments were passed out.

The more he perused the columns, the more puzzled he became. Surely the amounts listed were not enough to feed and clothe the number of Indians reported to be living on the reservation. Scanning through the pages more closely, he flipped to the bottom of the stack. His eyes narrowed. Two requisition orders stared him in the face. Both were initialed by Maurice Russell.

Brent leaned back in the chair. The elusive agent must have reappeared. He steepled his fingers atop his chest. No, someone would have informed him of Russell's return, as per his instructions. Perhaps the orders had been signed before the agent left early the other morning. That had to be the explanation.

He massaged his aching neck. His shoulders sagged. The aging chair creaked a warning as he settled more comfortably. What was wrong with him lately, thinking the worst, becoming so suspicious? There was always a logical explanation for everything.

Knowing that, why was there still a restless, nagging doubt clouding his mind, insisting that things were not as they appeared? His instincts usually proved reliable, and he detested these ambiguous feelings which suddenly assailed him. What was there about the goings-on at San Carlos that left him feeling like he'd been raised on sour milk?

Was it the warrior, Scorpion? Heaven only knew Brent didn't like the fellow. His dislike had been instantaneous, which was in itself unusual, for he hardly ever made snap judgments of persons he didn't know.

Or was it because of Meadowlark Russell? She had certainly thrown him for a loop. There was something about the woman—something indefinable and . . . intriguing. He sighed. More than likely he was suffering nervous reactions to being unable to get the unpleasantness concerning Maurice Russell over and done with.

A hangman. That was what he felt like. A hangman about to place a noose around an innocent man's neck. He was not pleased with that image of himself.

Stretching, he got up and walked toward the door. There were a lot of questions for Miss Russell to answer come morning. He hoped she was an early riser.

Flashes of a sleep-tousled, dark-haired woman caught his breath in his throat. He quickly closed the door behind him, turned the corner and stared into a fiery sunset. Red. Orange. Amber. Whiskey eyes. Damn! Couldn't he do anything, look at anything, without being reminded of that one little lady?

He grimaced. Work. Lots and lots of work. Starting first thing tomorrow. Then he could relegate her to her proper place. A sudden half smile changed the direction of the curve of his lips as thoughts of another "proper place" for the woman took control of his mind.

No! Damn it, no. It had been a long time, was all. Too long since he'd had a woman. *Any* woman would cause him to respond now. *Any* woman.

Meadowlark scrubbed a shaking hand across her eyes. Images blurred, focused, then blurred again as she gazed out of the window. The brilliant early morning sky reminded her for the hundredth time of the color of *his* eyes.

Captain McQuade. Would she never again have peace from the man? She had detected his presence in the office even before discovering the disturbed papers. His scent was unmistakable—a hint of leather, a touch of spicy soap and the allure of that special something that was his alone.

She shivered and wrapped her arms about herself. His scent was extremely pleasing, yet somehow threatening.

Suddenly, her eyes narrowed. There he was, as if her thoughts had mixed bits of dust and particles of bone to mold his image from the earth. The shudder that shook her small frame was indeed disturbing.

She tore her gaze from the tall captain, only to notice several Apache girls standing in front of the commissary also casting glances in his direction. Although Brent McQuade seemed totally oblivious of the appreciative stares being stowed upon his perfect, muscular form, Meadowlark felt shamed by the women's none-too-subtle ogling.

Sudden heat inched up her throat and suffused her cheeks. How could she condemn her fellow maidens? Wasn't she just as guilty, maybe even more so, of casting furtive, appraising glances? The affirmative truth was an embarrassment in itself, but by the time the captain arrived at the office, she had pulled the closed expression over her features that her people reserved for outsiders.

He would never know the power he wielded over her senses. He would not.

Yet as she stood beside the desk and looked down at the shuffled papers, fear crept up on her like a cat in the night. Had he examined them all? Had he seen the requisitions?

She hurried and sat down, refusing to react when he barreled into the office. But, as it had the first time he entered, the air became stifled. The amount of space seemed to diminish considerably. She was aware of his imposing stature, heard his every breath, inhaled his essence. She could almost reach out and touch the aura that invariably surrounded him—and her.

"Morning, Miss Russell."

She slanted him a glance through lowered lashes and nodded.

Brent stood with his shoulders slightly hunched before realizing that if he took off his hat, he could stand without bumping his head on one of the round beams traversing the ceiling. When she looked up through long, spiked lashes, he caught the hint of dark gold hidden beneath the fanlike layers. His gut tautened, but he quickly admonished himself. She would not get to him today. She would not.

He cleared his throat. "Glad to see you like to get started early, too. We've got a lot to do."

She just stared. Brent glanced uneasily around the room. There was only the one chair. He couldn't very well hover over her shoulder all day. "Excuse me a minute. Be right back."

He spun on his heel and left the office, striding with decision and purpose across the compound to the condemned building. No sense in letting that good oak chair go to ruin. Returning to the smaller adobe, he placed his chair at the opposite end of the desk from Meadowlark, then hunted an empty nail for his hat.

Brent sat down, steepled his fingers and sighed. His eyes darted toward Meadowlark and he frowned. He could have sworn there had been an uneasy, almost frightened, expression on her piquant features when she saw his choice of chairs. "Is something wrong?"

Meadowlark choked. Wrong? The perturbing man had just taken her father's position—and in *that* chair. She could still see the slick spots on the arms where her father had rubbed his palms along the smooth surface when agitated. There was the knick on one leg where, as a little girl, she had tested the sharpness of a new knife—a gift from Scorpion.

Giving Brent the kind of sickeningly sweet smile she

had seen white women employ, she purred, "What could be wrong?"

He frowned. "Nothing, I guess." He reached over to take some of the papers from her stack and nearly jumped when she yanked them away. "Look, Lar . . . Miss Russell, you've probably been a big help around here. You've evidently shouldered a lot of responsibility, which I'm sure everyone is grateful for, but . . ." How did he put this delicately? Or should he even try? "I'm the one in charge now. In reality, this is *my* office." He lurched from the chair and latched hold of the bottom four or five papers. "I need to see what you're working on."

When he plopped back down, he held the sheets in his hand. His neck and cheeks pinkened beneath her condescending scrutiny, but he glowered back, proud of his accomplishment. There should be no question now as to who was in authority.

Flipping quickly through the first couple of pages, he read the lists of food and supplies that needed to be inventoried. He turned the next page. His eyes narrowed. A prickly sensation burned along his nerve endings. He raised his head and found Meadowlark studying him. Her intense gaze was disconcerting, but before he could comment, she hastily averted her eyes.

He shook his head and went back through the papers. They fell into his lap as he pinched the bridge of his nose. Crazy. This was absolutely, overwhelmingly crazy. "Miss Russell? Have you heard anything, anything at all, from your father?"

She sucked in her breath. "No."

"You haven't seen him for two days?"

"No."

He had known what her answer would be. What else could it have been? Crazy was a mild description of the way he felt. "Excuse me another minute, will you?"

In a blurred flurry of motion, he was on his feet and out of the door, leaving Meadowlark staring in his wake. As soon as he was gone from view, she snatched up the papers, wondering what he had seen that was so upsetting.

Inventory lists. Three requisitions. She had barely initialed the one for blankets and slipped it into the stack before he'd come in that morning. Everything was there.

She stood and walked to the door, fully intending to follow, but he was already on his way back, carrying a satchel at his side. The look in his eyes dared her to speak a word as he reentered the office and plunked the case onto the desk. So she stood to one side as he pulled out several pieces of paper and appeared to be comparing them to those he'd been reading.

Brent raised his head and pierced Meadowlark with his sharp gaze. He held out the papers. "Are these your father's initials?"

She took the wrinkled sheets and studied the orders she had sent out two weeks ago. Meadowlark nodded. Yes, those were her father's initials. M. R. The captain hadn't asked who wrote them.

Brent shook the papers he had just gone through that morning. "Last night, there were two requisitions. Today, there are three. Did you put that third requisition in here?"

Meadowlark fidgeted and meandered around the room until the desk separated them. "Uhm, well, yes. I-I found it in another stack of papers."

"And you just slipped it in with the others?"

"Yes." She looked him in the eyes for a second, then glanced out the window.

Brent inhaled a deep breath. See? he told himself. There was a logical conclusion. The orders needed to be placed. What did it matter, really, who signed them? "Well, we'd better add a few more to these. The Apaches will be here three days from now for their allotments and I'm afraid we aren't going to have near enough supplies on hand."

As the captain sat back, his mind seemingly on other matters, Meadowlark's knees trembled so badly that she dropped into her chair. She hid the rapid expulsion of her breath beneath a cough. They were past one hurdle. He was suspicious, yes, but it would keep her alert and on guard.

She cocked her head to the side as she studied the young soldier. What was he up to? Why was he acting concerned and ordering more goods? He would bear watching, this white man.

Meadowlark watched Captain Brent McQuade as he walked toward the mess hall at noon. She rubbed her palms up and down the side panels of her skirt. This had to be the most horrible day of her entire life. She hadn't been able to move a muscle without drawing his attention. It had only been one half of a single day and she already envied the coyote that could flee the dangerous white man so swiftly.

How many days until the moon was full again? Could she make it that long—or longer? Her flesh still tingled and he wasn't even near. She had survived the morning's ordeal, but there was still a murder to solve and the captain's suspicions were more likely to blossom than to fade.

Despair clouded her vision as she raked her eyes over the compound. Where was the killer? Why hadn't he made himself known? The captain had copies of the requisitions she'd sent. They had arrived at their destinations. She had expected someone to come snooping around by now, asking questions, looking for her father.

Her throat constricted. There had been one person. The captain. A shiver ran the length of her spine despite the welcome warmth of the day. Oh yes, he was certainly nosy enough, but there was no real reason to suspect him . . . Was there?

He *had* known her father. He *had* been to San Carlos on occasion. She shook her head, angry at the direction of her thoughts. If Brent McQuade had been around San Carlos before, during or after the time of her father's death, she would have either sensed his presence, or one of her friends would have mentioned something of the handsome captain.

She suddenly snorted with disgust. Several of those same friends were now swishing their skirts in a most brazen fashion as they "accidentally" stepped in front of the poor man. Even from the distance of her office, she heard their coy giggles and the deep rumble of his apology.

Silly white man. Didn't he realize they were flirting? Her eyes narrowed. Or maybe he knew full well their intent and was enjoying their wanton display. Curling heat wound through her insides. She would never be so bold. She would despise the white soldier's solicitations. Her only interest was in finding and catching a killer.

Meadowlark swiped an unsteady hand across her eyes, silently cursing that part of her own self that was white, when Scorpion emerged from around the side of the building. She was surprised to see him.

"I thought you returned to our camp, my friend." She noted with pride the band of red clay painted across Scorpion's face. It was a clear sign that he belonged to the *Chihinna,* Red People, the Warm Springs band of Apache.

"I stay. No trust white soldier."

She smiled. At least someone else had misgivings about the captain. But she spoke in Brent McQuade's favor. "I think he means well. He is generous to our people."

Scorpion's nostrils flared, as if he detested hearing

anything good about the soldier. "No white man means well for Apache."

Meadowlark nodded, then shrugged. "I have felt the same." Her eyes stole a glance toward the mess hall. "Yet, things have changed."

"Little pigeon no have *eyes* for soldier."

It was not stated as a question, exactly, but Meadowlark read the wariness in Scorpion's expression. "I—I could never *like* a white man."

Scorpion nodded, but leaned close to her and said, "You belong to Scorpion. It always so."

Her eyes rounded and she backed up a step from the vehemence in his voice. "You have not spoken for me."

His eyes suddenly softened. He clasped her fingers in his hand. "Mexico. We go now."

Looking over Scorpion's shoulder, Meadowlark saw Brent McQuade across the compound. He had turned and was walking in their direction. From the fluttering sensation enveloping her insides, she thought a hasty flight to Mexico held certain appeal.

But then she remembered the plan she had set in motion, recalled the promise she had made to herself to look after her people. Many responsibilities held her rooted in San Carlos. She freed her hand from Scorpion's and sadly shook her head.

The warrior noted the direction her gaze had taken and turned. He spat, "No forget what Scorpion say. Meadowlark Russell *mine*."

She sighed as Scorpion stalked away. Then her nose turned up with distaste as the unsuspecting captain continued to approach. Trouble. He was nothing but trouble. Scorpion doubted her. He would probably ruin her plans to trap the killer. Why, oh why, had he come here now? Or ever?

By the middle of the afternoon, Brent could hardly sit still. Every time Meadowlark breathed, he pictured her firm little breasts thrusting against the thin cotton blouse. Whenever she wriggled in her chair, he imagined a round bottom and long, silken thighs. He wiped a bead of perspiration from his forehead and slid from his chair. His voice was low and hoarse as he explained, "Gotta stretch. I'll be outside if you need me . . . for anything."

Meadowlark nodded and then sighed with relief. She had tried to think of a good excuse to leave the steamy confines of the office herself.

Outside, Brent breathed a deep draught of cool air. He'd never endured such torture. His body ached, especially one part in particular. He shook his head, unwilling to think about it . . . her.

Drawing a thin cheroot from his breast pocket, he shook loose a match and stared across the desert toward the distant mountains. His brother was there somewhere, with the White Mountain Apaches. He missed Brandon. It had only been a few months since they'd been together, but it'd been a twenty-some year separation before that. He wanted to see the boy again—soon.

Boy? Ha! Only a few years separated them in age, but Brand had lived two lifetimes during his years with the Apache. The Indians raised him well, and Brand had believed himself to *be* Apache until he attacked a certain stagecoach and met Brent's own intended, Hillary Sue Collier. She'd been the one who'd had a taming influence on the White Fox, thank God.

Brent sighed, vowing to visit his brother and Hillary. Theirs would be a tough lot in life, but Brand's only interest lay in helping the Apaches survive their transition into the white man's world. And miracle of miracles, Hillary agreed.

Thinking of helping the Indians brought back to Brent's mind the little half-Apache woman inside the office. She was every bit as determined as Brand to accomplish that monumental feat.

Well, Brent couldn't stand outside forever. He started to toss down his cigar, and then realized he'd forgotten to light it. Must be losing his mind after all.

He turned and would've pushed open the door, except he happened to glance through the window. Cautiously, he stopped and backed against the adobe, then craned his neck to see inside without being detected.

Meadowlark was bent over the desk, pen in hand, marking a requisition. She made two fast movements. Initials. Forgery. Suddenly the mystery of the initialed papers was solved. But why? What was her purpose?

Damn! He ran his fingers through a lock of hair that had fallen across his forehead. He had to think. So, she was filling out the forms. No real harm had been done. That he knew of. But how long had this been going on? And again the question cropped up, why?

Why was she desperately hiding her actions? Where was Maurice Russell?

Squaring his shoulders, Brent entered the office. His eyes riveted on Meadowlark. "Well, have any luck with those papers while I was out?"

Chapter Five

Meadowlark gulped. Her gaze became entrapped by Brent's incredibly blue, exceedingly shrewd eyes. Icy splinters pierced her stomach. He *was* just making polite conversation, wasn't he? He couldn't have seen . . .

Brent thought he caught a flicker of guilt, or could it have been defiance, in her gorgeous eyes, but any expression disappeared so quickly that he couldn't be sure. Damn it, every time he looked into those shimmering, golden pools, he had the craziest sensation that he was sinking and sinking, deeper and deeper. Into what? he couldn't say, and wasn't all that anxious to find out.

He sighed and sat down. "Well, is there anything in those papers you'd like to talk about?" He wasn't surprised when all he received for his trouble was a negative shake of her black curls. Any dialogue a person got out of an Apache, even a half-Apache, had to be dragged out with a fifty-foot rope.

Meadowlark was a trifle flushed as she intently studied the captain, wondering just what he was up to. She did not believe his questions were as innocent as he tried to make them seem. Her mind raced to dredge up something *real,* important, anything to focus his attention from the latest requisition she had slipped into the pile of papers.

She blinked, breaking off the lengthy staring game

they both employed. "Maybe there is something you should check into."

He sat forward. "Oh? And what is that?" Was she finally going to explain her reasons for forging Maurice's initials? He was as curious as a cat with a closed box.

"The last herd of beef was short twenty head. And no one will talk to me about it." A certain smugness settled over her features. Let the would-be agent see just how difficult it was to pry answers from the Bureau of Indian Affairs or any of the contractors they hired.

Of course, the fact that she was a woman, and an Apache woman at that, probably hadn't aided the struggle to have her complaints taken seriously. That was just one more reason she wanted them to believe her father was still active in the agency.

Brent rested his elbows on the desk and supported his chin with steepled fingers. "I wondered about that when I checked the herd yesterday. Who has the beef contract?"

The name was emblazoned in Meadowlark's mind. "Efren Frye." In fact, the man controlled several important contracts, and most of the problems in receiving goods and supplies traced to him.

Brent wrote down the name. For some reason, it seemed familiar. "Will there be enough beef for this week?"

"We will make it enough."

Brent closed his eyes, lost in thought. An idea was brewing in the back of his mind. It might be a solution that would benefit both the government and the Indians. Could he make it work?

Meadowlark took the opportunity, while he was not glaring at her, to surreptitiously examine the captain's handsome, expressive features. At least with his eyes closed, he could not provoke the usual confusion in both her mind and body.

She sighed at the sight of that stray lock of blond hair that fell across his high forehead every time he took off his hat. His hair looked so clean and soft that the tips of her fingers tingled, but she gallantly resisted the urge to reach over and comb it back in place.

Her gaze shifted to his straight, narrow nose. It was a dignified nose. Neither too long, nor too short. Just right. She smiled at the faint flush on his cheeks. He was the first man she had ever known who blushed when embarrassed. If he was not a hated white man, it would have been quite endearing.

She sniffed and straightened her back. Endearing? Indeed not! Not even that little quirk to his lips, or that dimple . . .

Sudden heat suffused Meadowlark's face. Her eyes shot up to his. They were open. He had been watching *her* watching him. She gritted her teeth, hoping her own jaw became as hard and stubborn-looking as the captain's. "What are you looking at?"

Brent started. What was *he* looking at? *She* was the one who'd been staring, no devouring, him. Hell, he still felt the sensations from the top of his scalp to the tip of his toes. He couldn't remember a woman ever looking at him that way before. Had she liked what she'd seen, or not? he wondered. "Guess I was probably looking at you." What else could he say? It was the truth.

So, she *had* been caught. But she wasn't embarrassed—much. White women stared at men. She was half white.

Brent got up and reached for his hat, deciding that whatever work was left would have to wait until he was better able to concentrate. He brushed back wayward strands of hair before settling the Stetson on his head. His belly knotted when he looked back and surprised Meadowlark, catching an indefinable gleam in her amber eyes. Damn, but what he wouldn't give to know what was going on inside that pretty little head.

He retrieved his satchel and called, "See you tomorrow."

Meadowlark inclined her head, all the while wondering why? Why now? Why me?

Early the next morning, Brent stood near the window of his room in the officers' barracks, yawning and stretching and generally berating himself for allowing dreams of golden-eyed vixens to haunt his nights. He turned his head and inhaled sharply. That same elusive vision was passing within ten feet of his window.

His eyes were adhered to her straight, regal form as she straddled the bare back of the horse. He attempted, rather unsuccessfully, to squelch another visual image of two bare bodies, locked together just as elementally, as he fastened the last of a long row of buttons. He was still watching the well-matched pair when she reached the outskirts of the compound and kicked the thoroughbred mare into a dead run, as if the hounds of hell were close on their heels.

It was tempting to follow her, to get away from San Carlos and breathe air that wasn't choked with wood smoke and dust. But a more urgent errand came to mind, and he hurriedly struggled into his pants and boots.

Scant minutes later found him in the office, bent over the desk, marking out numbers and writing in new ones. He mentally patted himself on the back. Two could play at her little game. He wondered how long it would take for her to discover *his* secret.

At the thought of the fireworks that were likely to erupt, a flame kindled and ignited in the center of his being. He could hardly wait.

By the time Meadowlark returned from her ride and hesitantly entered the office, Brent was innocently ensconced in his chair, leafing through more paperwork, which fluttered onto the desk when he glanced up to find her standing in the doorway, cheeks flushed, eyes shining, wisps of fine hair curling around her shell-shaped ears. His breath literally stuck in his throat, and he nearly doubled over during a coughing fit.

Meadowlark eyed him distrustfully, then realized he was really choking. Two long, graceful strides carried her to his side where she pounded his back with surprisingly strong blows.

Brent lifted his hand and gasped, "Enough. Please."

She stepped back. He straightened in his chair. Her fingers twined together as she resolutely refused to allow them to reach out to reassure herself that he was all right. He might misunderstand.

"Are you . . . all right?" she asked, suddenly aware that she had forgotten to scold her mouth into obedience.

He gasped, "Yeah." When she had bent over like that, her breasts had swayed provocatively before his eyes. The tickle in his throat was real, and raw. He lurched to his feet. "I need to visit some of the camps. You know, to get a head count before we hand out the allotment day after tomorrow.

She continued to stare as if he had grown two heads. He cleared his throat, determined to stop his damned babbling. "I, uh, won't be back tonight."

How could she go so long without blinking? he wondered. His hands fidgeted with the buckle on his holster. "Think you can handle things here?"

Meadowlark jerked her gaze from his long, slender fingers and the strap of leather encircling his flat belly. Her answer to his question was a faint curvature of her lips. She had "handled" things long before the white man made his grand appearance.

For several minutes after he turned and left, her mind attempted to convince her body that she should return to work. But she continued to stand and stare, watching his graceful, swinging strides as he crossed the compound.

Once he stopped. It appeared that he might turn back, but his body quivered and his back stiffened. She sighed when he finally resumed walking.

What was it about the white soldier that caused her no end of confusion and turmoil? Sometimes it felt as if she walked a dangerously narrow path and, at any moment, it might crumble and she would fall. Where to? She didn't know. How far? She had no idea. To safety? Or to destruction?

The next morning Meadowlark exercised her mare earlier than usual. She wanted to leave the reservation headquarters before the soldiers finished their breakfast. This was to be a private outing. The fewer who knew her whereabouts, the better.

She laughed and the mare's ears flicked back. Who was she kidding? There was only one soldier she wanted to avoid. Because of him, she needed time away to think, to breathe the frosty morning air and to absorb the soothing rays of sunshine.

Riding bareback, wearing the leather britches and tunic, she felt Apache again. She shook her head, felt a little ashamed, but then reveled in the feel of the breeze as it rifled through her short curls. Soon, it would be long enough to braid, and she was almost sorry.

The beauty and mystery of nature loomed all around her. Though she loved the mountains best, there was a quiet serenity in the desert. A dangerous, forbidding serenity at times. But if one were respectful and grateful for what one was given, it was nevertheless something wondrous to behold, of which to be a part.

She gave the mare its head and they followed one of the narrow creeks until reaching a larger stand of cottonwoods than the one at San Carlos. Though the trees were bare of leaves, the trunks and branches yearned toward the sky, offering a crisscrossed maze of shade.

Meadowlark guided the horse through short clumps of creosote and swaying salt cedar. Arriving at the sandy bank of the creek, she slid off the mare, tethered it to a low branch and sank onto the cool ground.

Her hands dug into the loose soil. It sifted through her fingers and fell back to the earth where she was unable to tell one granule from another. She thought of the Apache and how they disappeared one by one, handful by handful, much as the grains of sand toppled from her palm. Was there no one who would miss them? She stretched full length on her back, supporting her upper body on her elbows and forearms. A shudder quaked her slender form as she squinted into the sky, though once again the day was unusually warm for winter. Blue. Pale blue. Transparent. The color of the captain's eyes. Why? Why was she constantly reminded of him, no matter how hard she tried to escape?

Closing her eyes, she came to a decision. One she had worried over the entire journey. She would not go back today. Most of the work was done until the wagons arrived tomorrow morning. Besides, Brent McQuade had been a fast learner and could handle any business that arose.

Happy for the first time in days, she lay down and soaked up the sun. A whole day. A beautiful day. All to herself. No captain. No worries. What more could an Apache maiden ask?

Brent also rode away from San Carlos that morning. He cast wary glances toward the tiny office, hoping Meadowlark would not see him leave.

There was no possible way he could spend another

entire day in the little lady's company. She was driving him crazy. That was all he could say. While he'd visited the Mescalero and Coyotero Apaches yesterday, the only thing he could concentrate on was *her.* He'd ridden for hours, and finally convinced himself that he was *not* attracted to the woman.

Protective. That's what he felt. She was such a little thing. Small, dainty, fragile. Those were the reasons she had so profound an effect on his body and senses. It was a logical and sensible explanation. And again he had to wonder how her father could go off and leave her all alone in a forlorn, desolate, dangerous place like San Carlos.

He was looking after her until Maurice returned. He was *not* attracted. But he spurred his mount into a ground-eating lope at the image of whiskey-colored, almond-shaped eyes. Gorgeous eyes with long, lustrous lashes. Eyes that glowed in his dreams. Cat eyes. Determined, wary, suspicious eyes.

Perspiration beaded his upper lip, though the rush of air created by the horse's pace was cool. He denied his earlier thought. Small? Yes. Dainty and fragile? Hardly. His imagined image of Lark and the woman he knew her to be were like comparing a cottontail to a mountain lion. But he couldn't ignore those "protective" feelings that cropped up every now and then. It was only natural for a man to look out for a woman.

He pulled the gelding to a leisurely trot. Then with a grin and a nod, he slowed it to a walk. Why be in a hurry? He wasn't really needed at the agency today. Meadowlark would probably enjoy the time alone. Think of all the requisitions she could secret into the piled stacks of papers.

The path followed a small stream. Brent sighed and glanced about at the seemingly barren, lifeless desert. But he knew better. Beneath that creosote bush a person would probably scare up grasshoppers and crickets. Snakes and lizards might be denned under the thorny mesquite. No matter how hot and dry, the desert teamed with life, if only a person knew to look for it.

In the distance, Brent noticed the top spines of a few cottonwoods. Since the trunks were concealed, he figured they were growing in a depression along the creek. Stifling a yawn, he decided it would be a good place to rest the *horse* awhile before going on to more of the Apache camps.

Meadowlark came swiftly and suddenly awake, alerted to something amiss by the nervous shifting of the mare's hooves. She lay still another moment, feeling the slight vibration of the ground beneath her. Someone was coming.

She reluctantly arose and went to stand beside her horse. Although she thought the rider was probably Apache, the different bands held little love for one another, and it was prudent that she be prepared—for whoever, or whatever.

Brent approached the wash with caution. Being just a little bit careful could mean the difference in life and death. Topping the rise, he looked down into a shallow basin. A sorrel mare contrasted immediately against the varying shades of grays and browns of the surroundings. Recognition was instantaneous, along with the contraction of his lower belly.

Of all the damned luck! What was *she* doing here?

Despair and anger fleetingly warred for dominance of Meadowlark's features. But as she regained control, a mask of indifference was the face she presented to Brent McQuade.

Brent also feigned nonchalance as he leaned his forearms on the saddle horn. "Howdy. Wasn't expecting to run into *you* way out here."

She muttered, "We are of the same mind."

Since he thought it might appear cowardly to leave

right away, Brent swung off the gelding and tied it next to the mare, all the while silently arguing that he didn't *care* what she thought, anyway. But he stayed.

When he turned around to face Meadowlark he found an expression of what he could only describe as resignation on her face. He smiled.

Meadowlark could not believe her misfortune. The spirits plotted against her. She had been lulled into a false sense of well-being, only to have her greatest nemesis intrude upon her solitude. A sudden, awful inclination to throw her hands in the air and stomp her foot nearly overwhelmed her. It was definitely not her usual calm Apache acceptance of the fates taking precedence today.

Brent gingerly eased his back against the rough bark of a cottonwood. He patted his pockets until he found a lone cheroot, which turned out to be somewhat bent and crooked when he pulled it forth. Pretending to be absorbed in lighting the smoke, he watched Meadowlark from beneath hooded lids.

It was almost comical to watch her pace. She took a step toward him, then turned to her horse. She stopped and turned to face the huge cottonwood, and turned again. Actually, he sympathized with her dilemma, for he felt just as torn. Meeting up with her was the absolute last thing he needed, wanted, to deal with. His intention had been to *escape* the little lady.

Meadowlark breathed deeply and finally faced the captain. Her eyes narrowed and she inwardly seethed at his calm and collected appearance. O-oh-h! Where had he learned such Apache control? The more she had to be around the man the more she despised him.

Her chin tilted upward. She stiffened her spine. *He* would never know his ability to undermine her confidence. Never. Determined and purposeful, she marched over and sat down a short distance from the soldier. She didn't want to sit too near, yet didn't want to advertise her aversion.

She darted a glance at his face. Her chest suddenly constricted, causing her to take rapid little breaths. There was something in those eyes that sent the blood sizzling through her veins.

"You feel it, too, don't you, Lark?" His voice was as soft as a caress, and as electrifying as a bolt of lightning.

Meadowlark was frightened, but not of Brent McQuade. It was Meadowlark Russell, the woman—not the Apache, not the white—just the *woman* who responded so spontaneously to the *man* sitting barely out of arm's reach.

And when he said her name, Lark, the word seemed to float from his tongue. Lark. It sounded nice. It was short. It was oh-so-sweet. What a silver tongue he had.

Those thoughts all roiled through her mind while she put off answering his question. Surely he hadn't meant . . . Or had he? "I feel nothing."

Brent carefully laid his hat aside and tunneled his fingers through his hair.

Meadowlark warded off a shudder when the errant lock gradually drooped onto his forehead. It amazed her that something so simple could devastate her senses. What was so special about the man's *hair?*

"You may be an expert at hiding your feelings, but I know damn well you're as aware of . . . whatever . . . it is between us."

She was staring toward the lazily meandering creek. A feather-light touch caressed her lips. Her head whipped around. He was leaning toward her with his callused hand a bare inch from her face. Her mouth trembled. The air became stifling. Her palms were damp. She felt as if a blazing July sun burned her flesh and seared clear through her insides.

Their eyes locked. She knew what a mouse must feel just as a giant hawk swooped it from the field.

"Tell me you don't feel *something.*"

His voice vibrated over her like thunder rolling over the empty plains. She gulped. How could she deny it? He had seen the effect of that one gentle touch.

Too? penetrated her muddled brain. He'd said, "You feel it, too." Yes, she saw his reaction in those too-blue eyes. The confusion. The question. He was as troubled as she.

She rubbed a finger over her lips. "Maybe there is . something. But it is of no matter."

Brent shook his head. Damn, but she was hard. Two weeks ago, he'd have sworn he was, too. Cold, bitter and disillusioned. Today, everything had turned topsy-turvy. He was hardly certain of his name. There was a warm, mushy sensation in his chest and belly that was anything but hard.

She was right. It meant nothing. He would not become involved with another deceitful female. "I only asked if you were aware of it. Neither of us want to acknowledge it, but it is there."

Meadowlark ruefully nodded.

They sat in the sand, in silence.

Finally, surprisingly, especially to her, it was Meadowlark who asked, "And now?"

He frowned. "I wish I knew."

Minutes drug by. Brent rolled to his feet. Meadowlark watched his graceful movements with wide eyes. His actions were lithe, soundless, sensuous and athletic. It was not the first time she had compared him favorably to an Apache warrior.

"I've got to ride—"

"I need to—"

They spoke at once. Brent blushed and finished, ". . . to some more of the camps."

Meadowlark couldn't finish. She wasn't sure what she needed to do, just that she *needed* to.

When they reached the horses and Brent remembered that she hadn't ridden a saddle, he offered her a hand up. Rather than the haughty acceptance she wanted to demonstrate, Meadowlark instead cast him a shy smile, and lifted a dainty foot.

Brent cupped his hands. She stepped into them. He lifted, then suddenly shouted and let her slip. The sting from the handful of goat heads that had been stuck in the bottom of Meadowlark's moccasins quickly faded from Brent's mind as she flew upward, then started to fall. His gut tautened.

Meadowlark was too far from the horse's back. She missed clutching at the mane, but wide shoulders suddenly filled her palms. Her small body slid the length of his. Then large hands spanned her waist and she felt the heat from the impression of his fingers as if she had been branded with a white-hot iron.

Brent's groin quickened and swelled. Lord, he thought, this was more temptation than a mortal man could handle, or refuse.

Meadowlark's feet dangled in the air. Her breasts were pressed flat against Brent's chest and underwent the strangest sensation when her nipples hardened from the unexpected friction.

Nose to nose they stood. Or, at least, Brent stood. Waiting, barely able to breathe.

"Well, hell." Brent's head dipped forward. He kissed the tip of her pert little nose. A deep sigh hissed through his teeth. Then his lips molded to hers.

Chapter Six

Meadowlark's toes curled when Brent's lips touched her nose. He claimed her mouth and a thousand cactus barbs seemed to prick her body. She was hardly aware of her arms curling around his neck, or her fingers ravaging the hair against his collar. The strands sifted in thick layers and were even softer than she imagined. A ribbon of fire curled through her stomach.

The kiss transformed from pleasant, to deeply arousing, to . . . frightening. She pushed back, bracing her palms against his muscled shoulders. Taut tendons rippled beneath her fingers and her instinct was to jerk away, only she would then have no leverage to hold her extremely sensitized upper body back from his broad, broad chest and those dangerous lips.

"Please, put me down." Her voice was a husky whisper.

Unconsciously, Brent's arms tightened about her rib cage. He was on fire. His body ached for her—a deep, gut-wrenching sort of pain, and a sort of yearning that he had never experienced before.

He gazed into her eyes and sucked in his breath. Her lids drooped. He found only a narrow band of amber and white, but what he did see caused him to set her down and back away so quickly that he was tempted to brush nonexistent sparks and smoke from his jacket.

Shuddering, he prayed his own eyes had not held the same faraway, dreamy expression. It was insane. He couldn't be falling for the half-Apache wildcat. Not Brent McQuade. Not the sensible cavalry officer who came all the way to Arizona Territory to forget and discard the female population altogether.

He didn't need a woman. He certainly didn't want . . . Brent gulped. She was staring at him. And she had left the shutters open. He could read what was going on behind those usually expressionless eyes. There was question, and hurt, and some of the same dismay he was suffering.

But when he moved toward her again, she stepped back. Then her eyes went blank.

Meadowlark couldn't believe what had just happened. Her body throbbed all over. Her mind—it couldn't seem to function. She should have had the sense to get away *before* the kiss. Held so close in his arms, she had known it was coming, yet had been unable to speak the words that would have made him release her.

She was as responsible for what happened as the captain, if not more so. At least she had *finally,* through great force of will, summoned the sanity to beg him to let her go. The backs of her eyes burned and she felt a momentary panic at the empty ache in her chest. Goosebumps prickled her flesh where their bodies had touched.

Suddenly, she was afraid she would disgrace herself and burst into tears. Choking back a sob, she untied her mare, grabbed a fistful of mane and swung onto its back.

Brent snatched up the reins. Worry etched his features as he noted her pinched expression. He didn't know what to say. He was also stunned and confused. "Will you be in the office . . . tomorrow?"

Looking down, she could have drowned in the blue pools staring up so intensely. The pit of her stomach sunk even lower. She wanted to shout, "No! I'll never go back," but it would be a lie. She would be there for her people, for her father, for herself.

She nodded, though her mouth was the barest of white lines on her face. Her heels drummed the mare's sides. The horse raced away, coating Brent with a cloud of dust and sand.

He gritted his teeth, hating the surge of elation that erupted in his gut with her affirmative answer. Damn it! Damn! Damn! Damn!

The next day was the coldest since Brent's arrival at San Carlos. Wind kicked up miniature dust devils in and around the compound. Yet from all directions other small clouds of dust could be seen hanging in the air, getting closer as the minutes passed.

Apaches were coming for their government handouts.

Brent and Meadowlark and a few buffalo soldiers who had volunteered their help, unloaded supplies from the wagons just arrived from Tucson. They separated the boxes and crates and put together parcels of food and clothing to be distributed to each Indian.

Meadowlark's bland expression seemed chiseled from stone, so set were her features as the unpacking progressed. Every now and then she stopped and massaged her temples, but uttered not a word.

Brent tore open a crate, cursed and yanked open another. When the last wagon was finally empty, and the drivers had turned their vehicles back toward Tucson, he flung aside his crowbar and demanded, from no one in particular, to everyone within hearing, from God and then the devil himself, "Where in the hell is the food I ordered?"

He reached into a box and pulled out a handful of beads. They trickled through his fingers and buried with one *plop* in the dust. He kicked at a nearby crate.

Two flimsy boards broke and several hymnals slid to the ground. "What good are those when a man's belly is empty?"

Brent swung to face Meadowlark. His eyes beseeched hers for an explanation.

She met his gaze with an I-could-have-told-you-so smugness written across her face, but—inside—her heart was breaking.

Still fuming, obscuring the lower half of his legs with fine sand and silt as he paced, Brent asked softly, too softly, "Does this happen every damned time they come here?" His arm swept the compound, indicating the various groups of Indians making their way toward the agency.

A line of women and children was beginning to form. Here and there a warrior made an appearance carrying a bottle of cheap, rotgut whiskey that the soldiers even refused to buy. Brent felt sick to his stomach.

He turned to the three Negro soldiers. "We're goin' to see that these people get somethin' to eat. If we have to use army rations, we'll do it."

Two of the buffalo soldiers grinned. The other only nodded. "Major Taylor ain't gonna like that, no sirree!"

Brent asked Meadowlark, "Will the rest of the wagons get here this afternoon?"

"There will be no more." There was almost pity in her eyes.

"What!"

She shook her head.

"But I sent for twice, three times this much." He stopped pacing and stood still. Heat rose from his chest to his neck and finally tingled in his cheeks. "What happened to it?"

Meadowlark wasn't sure if he really wanted an answer or if he was still ranting, but he *had* asked. "Your order left Tucson, but there is a fork in the road to the reservation."

Brent was incredulous. "Are you sayin' that supplies intended for San Carlos are directed elsewhere? Why? Where do they go?"

She lowered her eyes. "To the mines."

He stomped back and forth, clenching and unclenching his hands. "They sell the supplies to the miners and pocket the money. Meanwhile, it shows on their records that the shipment was delivered as directed. They collect twice for the same goods."

Meadowlark was impressed. He was smart, for a white man.

He was thinking back to an earlier conversation they'd had in the office—days ago. She'd said then the contractor out of Tucson was . . . Frye. Efren Frye. "Does the head honcho in Tucson know about this, or do you suppose the drivers do it on their own?"

Her eyebrows rose as she shrugged.

From the men he'd met on the wagons today, Brent didn't believe any of them were smart enough to come up with such an elaborate scheme. One way or the other, though, he would find out who was responsible.

Disgruntled, needing to vent his outrage on something, he spied the broken crate of hymnals. He kicked at it, and then kicked again until it lay in splintered pieces. "No wonder the Apaches run away from San Carlos. Who in their right mind would stay here and starve?"

Hours later, the end of the line of Indians was finally in sight. Brent sighed with relief, only to gulp it back at the sight of a determined Major Vincent Taylor walking briskly in his direction. He saluted. "Afternoon, Vince."

The major threw his hand up, briefly flicked his hat brim with stiff fingers, then yanked it down, all the while piercing Brent with a baleful glare.

He pointed to the empty crates at Brent's feet. "What's the meaning of this, Captain McQuade?"

Brent straightened his aching shoulders. "Handing out food to the Indians, sir."

Major Taylor sputtered, "B-but that's absurd. You can't do that. Those are army rations."

"Don't worry, sir. As soon as I get in touch with General Crook, you'll get more supplies."

"But, I'm—"

"The general will be most appreciative of your kind cooperation. Especially since he's doing his damnedest to keep the Apache happy and on the reservation. Don't you agree?"

"Well, I—"

"I'll tell him firsthand how you found out we were short of supplies this week and graciously volunteered to help out. Your generosity probably averted a full-scale uprising . . . sir."

"Oh? Oh! I—"

Brent held out his hand. "The general and I truly thank you, Vincent, Major Taylor. Excuse me, would you? Got more work to do."

He wasn't being deliberately rude. Brent really needed to get busy. The job was long and tiring and the brunt of it was falling to Meadowlark. His chest swelled with pride for her diligent efforts. He couldn't help but wonder how long she'd been doing this job on her own. And he still hadn't learned how long Maurice had been gone, or when he would return.

Brent hadn't realized he'd been holding his breath until the major *harumphed!* and turned and walked away. Then it all rushed from his lungs in one giant *whoosh.* He happened to glance at Meadowlark. She cast him a shy smile and he suddenly felt as spry as a teenager. Then he scowled and tried to tamp down his excitement. He didn't need her approval. He would do the same thing again if it became necessary. But he couldn't get rid of that little *glow* warming his insides.

Later, after the last of the Indians had left, Brent slumped onto the commissary steps. He was exhausted, but felt good. Every single person had received *nearly* enough food for the next week. Yet he was bitterly concerned over what he'd seen that day.

The Apache were starving. Their eyes were as blank and expressionless as Meadowlark's, only more haunted. And he detected an underlying hatred, whether for him personally, or the army in general, or just because they degraded themselves by having to be *given* food, he didn't know.

And he guessed what really bothered him was the listless, almost utter hopelessness from a group of people who were normally busy every day just surviving. It seemed to him that they just didn't care anymore. They'd accepted that they were going to die, whether eluding soldiers, or starving on a reservation.

Well, by damn, he would not allow that to happen. He didn't know how, or what, but he would do *something* about it. General Crook had sent him to San Carlos for that very purpose.

All of a sudden, Brent felt better about his job. It was important. There was a chance he could make a difference by helping the Apache.

He inhaled, then started when he caught a hint of lavender in the air. Meadowlark had collapsed on the step below and he'd been so lost in thought he hadn't noticed. Reaching out, as if it were the natural thing to do, he squeezed her shoulder. "We did it."

Again he was taken by surprise when she glanced up and he saw where a tear had streaked her face. He was left absolutely speechless when she rose to her feet, leaned over and placed an all-too-brief kiss on his cheek. Then, like a delicate butterfly, she stepped back and darted off toward the office.

He gently rubbed the skin where her lips had touched, and could have sworn he heard a faint, tinkling, "Thank you, Captain," drifting on the breeze.

* * *

The next morning, Brent sat across a huge, polished oak desk from Major Taylor, in an office quite different from the one he and Meadowlark shared. He glanced admiringly at whitewashed walls, framed paintings, a cupboard of bound books and the smooth hardwood floor.

Certainly it was grander than a small hovel with two stacked crates, bare adobe walls; except for one tiny landscape and a cracked mirror hanging at a precarious slant in Meadowlark's corner, and hardened dirt. The major's office reminded him of the one he'd occupied at Fort Apache. He could learn to adjust to one like it again.

The major looked up from a map spread across the lower half of the desk. "All right, Captain. What can I do for you today? Is there a stray tribe of Indians outside my door that would like to share my sweet buns?"

Brent chuckled, grateful that the man had a sense of humor. When the major offered Brent a sticky roll, he regretted the big plate of ham and biscuits smothered with gravy that he'd devoured not an hour earlier. The mess cook had once been some kind of fancy baker in New York, before circumstances dictated the man leave town in a hurry, from what Brent understood. And the soldiers at San Carlos looked after the man as if he were ten bars of gold bullion.

"No, Major, no one wants your breakfast. And I may just have a solution to keep from repeating yesterday's problem."

Major Taylor licked a flaky piece of pastry from his thumb. "I'm certain both myself and *the general,*" he cocked a wary brow at Brent, "will be interested in any idea designed to keep our troops in rations."

Brent shifted in his chair. "Yes, well, sir, yesterday we received less than half of the supplies I'd ordered from Tucson." He waited to see if the major had a comment, but the man only nodded. Then Brent chided himself for his stupidity. Of course, Meadowlark had said she'd complained before. She'd been told that it wasn't an army matter, that matters such as this were to be handled between the Bureau of Indian Affairs and the contractors in Tucson. So, it was nothing new.

"I've been told that the goods all leave Tucson, but that some of the wagons split off and go to the mines. In short, we're being cheated."

Major Taylor popped the last morsel of roll into his mouth and cleaned his fingers on a spotless white cloth. "I've heard that accusation myself. I assume you have a plan."

Brent leaned forward. "I'd like to take a troop down to Tucson next week and personally escort the wagons to the reservation. I guarantee we wouldn't be short supplies then."

"Sorry, Captain. I wish I could help. I really do. But I cannot."

"Why not?" The fine lines on either side of Brent's mouth deepened into well-defined grooves as he contemplated the major.

"We do not have enough soldiers to spare at this time, especially when it involves being gone overnight. The Apache are restless as it is, and I will not take the risk."

Brent sighed. He understood the other man's reasoning. The reservation could be placed in a good deal of danger. But another idea came to mind. "What if I borrowed just two or three men, say, the ones who helped me yesterday?"

"Could you handle the situation with such a small force?"

"I could."

Major Taylor scratched his fleshy jowl. "Just this once. If it works, we'll talk about it some more."

Brent asked the major about another issue that had

bothered him, and when the conference was over, stood and shook his hand. "Thank you, sir. I'll inform the soldiers I'll need them in five days. And thanks again."

Walking briskly across the compound, Brent hunched his shoulders and began to whistle a jaunty tune. Things had gone better than he expected. There was no doubt in his mind but what the full issue of supplies would be handed out next week.

The leather straps, serving as the door's hinges, creaked as he entered the little office. He made a mental note to one day replace the thing and mount a proper door. Disappointment gripped his chest when he found the room empty. He'd been anxious to tell Meadowlark the good news.

To keep from dwelling on the woman, and why he'd allowed her to get to him like she did, he rechecked the requisitions he had filled out last night while the numbers were still fresh in his mind. Turning to the last page, he shook his head. She'd slipped in another initialed sheet.

Damn it! A muscle leaped in his jaw. What was her game? And after all the trouble and secrecy, she never ordered near enough. He picked up a pen and studiously changed her figures. Wrapped up in what he was doing, he failed to see the shadow hovering at the window.

Meadowlark stood silently, watching the soldier mark on *her* paper. A sudden pain stabbed her heart. She should have expected something like this to happen. He was a white man. No matter that her body betrayed her at times. It was of no consequence that she had even begun to *like* him. He was a white man. If the Apache had learned only one thing over the years, the hard way in most instances, it was that the whites were not to be trusted.

She chewed on her lower lip. It would take tremendous effort on her part, but she would have to suffer his presence a while longer, just to find out what he was up to. Yesterday, she had believed he was genuinely concerned for her people's welfare. Now, as she watched him work on her requisition, she knew better.

This time, when the door squeaked open, Brent was the one who guiltily shuffled papers. A sickly grin dimpled his cheek when he looked up and found Meadowlark silhouetted in the doorway. "Uh, mornin'. I've been lookin' for you. Have some good news." Holding the papers, he backed to his chair and plunked down so hard that it groaned in protest.

She sauntered over to the desk and stood, looking down at him. It was one of the few times she'd had that opportunity, and it lent her an air of superiority.

He straightened the already tidy lapel on his jacket. Why did she have to stand so close, staring at him like . . . like a spider about to spin him into her web? He tugged at his collar. "I-I talked to the major this mornin' . . . Why don't you sit down where I can see you?" He waited, but it seemed to take an inordinate amount of time for her to walk three steps to her chair.

"That's better. Now . . . Oh, yeah, the major is giving me three men next week and I'm personally escorting the wagons from Tucson to San Carlos. By damn, we'll just see if any of them try to pull out on *me.*"

Meadowlark smiled at his exuberance. She was surprised and happy that the captain had taken it upon himself to see to it her people were fed, especially after what she'd just seen, but . Ice cold fear clutched her stomach. Fear. She hadn't experienced the sensation since finding her father. The killer was still loose. Doubt as to his whereabouts tormented her constantly.

If the captain carried through with his plans, it could be another means of forcing the murderer into the open. It could also mean that Brent McQuade would place himself in jeopardy. The crooked politicians in Tucson would do anything to keep from losing their easy money—*anything.*

She blinked and looked out the window. Why, after she had just condemned the man barely a quarter of an hour ago, did the thought of the captain being hurt, maybe even killed, upset her so? And why did her heart throb painfully at the notion she might never see him again?

"Hey, why so sad? I thought you'd be pleased."

She snapped her shoulders back and mentally cleared her head. "I am."

"Oh. Glad you told me." Disappointment gnawed at his gut. He didn't know what he had expected, but it wasn't this indifference.

"Maybe it will be dangerous."

A spark flared in his eyes. "I don't doubt it."

Meadowlark seethed. Stupid man. He sounded just like a young Apache brave. The excitement of the raid, the fight, was everything. It was proof of manhood. In this one instance, she concluded, the male of every race was the same.

"What's wrong, Lark? Would you worry about me?"

She sniffed. "Worry about a *white* man? Why should I?"

"Don't know. Why would you?" Impulsively, he reached across the crate and cupped her cheek in his palm.

Dreaded moisture burned the backs of her eyes. Her father used to touch her like that. When she had been upset or worried, he would caress her cheek and lie, "It'll be all right, sweetheart. Everything's going to be fine."

Before she knew what was happening or could lift a finger to stop it, she was being cuddled to the soldier's hard body. His embrace was strong, yet incredibly tender. She buried her face into his chest and allowed him to hold her. Just for a moment. That was all. She felt so warm and safe in his arms. It was good to savor the feeling—just for a moment.

Brent was shocked. This was the last thing he'd intended to have happen. All he'd done was touch her cheek. Then such a pained, tortured expression had darkened her eyes that he was afraid he'd somehow hurt her.

His guts had been torn asunder. An incredible surge of emotion erupted throughout his body. He would give his life to protect this woman. If it ever came to that, he would. Whether she liked it or not.

The solemn interlude was interrupted by a knock on the door. Brent gave Meadowlark a gentle squeeze and reluctantly set her away. She stood, wonderment blazing in her eyes. He had held and comforted her. Nothing more. It was the kindest, sweetest thing anyone had ever done for her. Yet she was disappointed.

Brent cleared his throat and opened the door. "Come in, Corporal. What can we do for you?"

The young black man saluted, then nodded respectfully to Meadowlark. "Pard'n the intrusion, Cap'n. The major wants ta know if'n yore gonna replace them provisions ya borrowed."

"Yes, Corporal. The major already knows that." Brent shook his head. Vince was worse than a coyote with leg bone once he got his mind set on something.

The corporal's Adam's apple bobbed in his throat when he swallowed. "Yes'm, sir, but he says ta tell ya I'm on my way ta Tucson, an' if'n ya got them papers ready—"

"All right, Corporal." Then he realized it wasn't the young soldier who was pushing him, he was only following orders. "I've got them right here."

The buffalo soldier tentatively reached for the requisitions, then hastily saluted and made his getaway once they were in his hands. "Thank ya, Cap'n, sir."

Brent was scolding himself for thinking unkind thoughts of the major choking on the damned rations, when he turned back to Meadowlark. She stared at him in such a way, though, that his poor body went on alert. Aching in places he didn't want her to know about, much less see, he also made excuses for a quick departure. "Look, I've got to, uh, go out. Be back later." Much, much later, he silently declared, hurrying toward the stables.

Meadowlark still stood beside the desk, eyes unfocused, her hand covering her cheek, when Scorpion entered the office a few minutes later.

"Hola, my pigeon." He stopped in front of her, staring curiously at the unusual gleam in her eyes.

"Hi." She hardly recognized the low, whispery voice as her own, so disassociated was she from her surroundings.

"You not well?"

Touched by Scorpion's concern, and having just registered his possessive tone of *my* pigeon," she forced herself back to reality. "I am fine."

Scorpion nodded, though he continued to be watchful. He walked over to the window, then back to the door. "You work hard past day."

Strange, she thought, she hadn't really thought of being tired until he mentioned it. Must have had other things on her mind. All of a sudden, though, energy seemed to drain from her body. She rubbed her eyes and slumped back in her chair.

"White captain work hard."

She watched Scorpion prowl the room, amazed to hear him say anything good about a soldier.

There was a long pause before he added, "Plenty food."

Meadowlark nodded. Sudden excitement coursed through her veins. Yes, there had been enough for a change. Thanks to Captain Brent McQuade.

"Plenty beef next time?"

She shrugged, wondering why Scorpion was asking so many questions. He'd never acted concerned before, not even when the allotments were short. But she answered truthfully, "I don't know." Brent had wondered the same thing.

"Soldier check herd. Count noses."

"Heads. You count *heads.*" Ducking her own head, she was immediately sorry for snapping at her friend. She was tired and irritable. That was all.

"Our people wonder. There be more next time?"

Worry etched her brow as she thought of what the captain planned to do for the Apache. "Yes. Tell them there will be more. Much more."

Chapter Seven

Meadowlark yawned like a young coyote feline who had chased his first mouse and looked longingly toward her pallet in the corner. Scorpion followed her gaze and frowned. He sounded like a child left out of his favorite game when he said, "You rest."

She smiled and forced herself from the chair. "I will," Meadowlark said, touching his arm. Instantly, Scorpion flinched and she drew back. His brown eyes glinted fiercely, but she was too exhausted to try to figure out why and didn't ask.

Together they lifted the sagging door closed. Meadowlark remained inside. Scorpion was left out as she dropped the bar in the slots. She rubbed the back of her neck and started toward the pallet but happened to look out the window. Her friend was still there.

Guilt welled into her heart. Scorpion could be her husband one day. Why did she continuously reject *him*, yet allow the captain to touch her, even to kiss her?

Scorpion turned back to scowl at the small building. She gasped and quickly stepped into the shadows. Had he perhaps guessed what she was thinking? Unworthiness pushed her shoulders into a slump as she stared down at the floor and wondered why Scorpion had asked about the captain.

Her footsteps dragged as she made her way to the pallet. Sinking onto the soft blankets, she brushed away two tears and silently cursed the confusion and weakness that had allowed them. Life had never been easy. She had never expected it to be. The Apache way was to endure and to accept what befell them with stoic calm.

But, sometimes, *feelings* built up inside until she was afraid she might scatter on the wind and eventually float into nowhere, like a cottonwood blossom in the spring.

She was changing. Twisting onto her side, she pounded the blanket with an ineffectual fist. *The Apache way; endure the change, accept the change.*

But that did not mean she had to like it.

The next morning, Meadowlark and Brent attempted to find enough to do to keep them so busy that they wouldn't have to look, or hardly speak to each other. Once in a while, one would yawn and the other would soon repeat the gesture.

Finally, after Brent had checked a column of figures and made a trip to the commissary and back, he leaned forward in his chair and asked, "Have the Apaches had any luck growing crops?"

Meadowlark's eyes literally snapped. "Of course. Have you not seen our beautiful cactus gardens?"

Brent grimaced. "Look, I . . . Have they tried?"

She took a deep breath. "Yes." When he cocked a dark blond brow expectantly, she continued. "General Crook helped to teach the Apache many years ago."

"How come there're no fields now?"

Defensively, she scooted up in her chair. "There are a few. The time is not right to plant." The last sentence was added with the tone a disgusted squaw might use to scold a naughty child.

Brent's chest deflated. There she went again. Her eyes had taken on that familiar feral gleam. Lord but she was an obstinate female. "I know it's winter. But if we started now, we could ready things before it *is* time."

"Can you turn the water?"

"What?"

There was shrewd speculation in her eyes. "Can you change the flow of water?"

Now Brent understood. "You're talking about irrigation. Well, no, but I could learn."

"I know the . . . irrigation."

"You do?" Besides the question in his voice, there was more than a hint of respect.

"General Crook's men taught my . . . taught us how."

"So, the Apaches know what to do."

She shook her head sadly. "No. Those that did learn are gone or . . . dead. The warriors lost their spirit. Even with water, the land is sandy. Too hard to work. My people are hunters."

There was nothing Brent could say. He knew how he would feel if he was suddenly informed that he would no longer be responsible for providing the food for his table. He'd lose his spirit, too, if he had to stand for hours in the hot sun hoeing rocks and dust and cactus. And no man could feel pride standing in line, holding out his hands for meager rations.

He slapped his palm on the crate. Papers rustled. With a startled expression, Meadowlark watched several float to the floor. Brent knew his decision would surprise both Apaches and whites. Whites, especially, since it would mean going against some of the most powerful men in Washington and Arizona Territory. But if it was the last thing he did, he'd help these people make a decent life for themselves. He would do it for his brother, for Meadowlark, and because it was the only right thing to do.

He glanced again at Meadowlark and noticed with amusement that she'd once more hidden her reactions behind an Apache mask. He tried to see through those luscious thick lashes, found it impossible. "Lark, who are your people? I mean, to what band do you belong?" He was also tempted to ask why she refused to claim her white heritage, but decided to save what could possibly be a lengthy and heated discussion for another time.

Warily, she replied, "The Warm Springs. Your people know us as Mimbres."

He cocked his head. "Victorio was Warm Springs, wasn't he?"

Tremendous pride exuded from her finely sculpted features. She nodded, then lowered her head.

Brent understood her dignity and spunk. Victorio had been a truly peaceful man until he was pushed, prodded and provoked into defending himself and his people. From that point on, he waged one of the longest and bloodiest wars the soldiers had ever fought.

The old warrior had been killed by Mexican troops in 1880, but Brent still wondered if trouble with the Apaches could have been avoided altogether if someone had taken the time and patience to heed Victorio's words. He'd even argued the point.

"Don't I remember something about Victorio and Loco both being praised for the good crops they grew?"

Meadowlark looked up. "That was when we were allowed to live in our homeland. Before we were herded to *this place.*" She literally spat the last two words.

"Why can't you do the same here?"

She snorted. "We were the last to come. Other Apaches have the best land."

He leaned forward and stared into her eyes. Becoming immersed in their whiskey depths, he almost forgot what he intended to say. He mentally shook himself. "We can help your people. It'll mean a lot of hard work. They'll have to be shown that the effort will be worthwhile."

Her eyes went blank. Her features settled into a

hard, uncompromising mask. He grabbed her hands, squeezing her fingers hard. "You and I. We can do it."

It was impossible for Meadowlark to ignore his plea. He was talking of *her* people. If he was willing to try, could she do any less? She blinked rapidly and nodded.

Brent lifted one of her hands and fervently kissed the backs of her knuckles.

She jerked her hand free, fisted her fingers, then began to collect the pages that had drifted to the floor earlier. She had to occupy her mind and forget her body's urging to reach over and hug his lean, beautiful body.

Closing her eyes, she prayed for the spirits to lend her strength. She was beginning to like this white man. But could the rabbit and the coyote be friends?

The rest of the week flew by as Meadowlark and Brent discussed irrigation and crops. Soon, it was the day before the weekly rations were distributed. Brent had to leave for Tucson. He took his hat from the nail and settled it firmly on his head.

Meadowlark closed her eyes, desperately fighting a deep, dark demon. When she finally looked up, she stated flatly, "I, too, will go." His expression changed to a mixture of surprise and disbelief. She scowled and resolutely rose to her feet.

Brent wondered if he'd heard correctly. Lark, go with him? Never! She'd said herself it could be dangerous. Why, if anything happened to her . . . It wasn't going to happen, and that was that.

But, knowing the woman the way he did, or thought he did . . . His mouth twitched. What a joke. He'd never really known a woman's mind—ever. Anyway, he couldn't afford to get her dander up by insulting Apache maidens in general, and Meadowlark in particular, so he tried reason. "Someone needs to sort through the supplies we have on hand. I'd sorta counted on you to do that for me."

Her mouth opened, then snapped shut. He actually depended on *her* to take over? Although she knew she had been a help to the captain, this was the first time he had admitted it.

Yet she couldn't discount the unsettling feeling she had that something was going to happen to him. Something awful. Her instincts for danger were sharply honed. For some reason, the thought of his being hurt, maybe even . . . If there was even a slight chance that she could prevent any harm, she would. "No, I will go."

Exasperated, Brent rubbed at the back of his neck. "I guess because I'm *only* a white man, I'm stupid. I won't be able to lead a bunch of wagons back to San Carlos."

His manhood had been challenged. She felt as if a prickly pear had lodged in her throat when she tried to swallow. Men, it seemed, were universal in their reaction to a woman's defiance. "No, I do not believe that," she answered, as her lips twitched.

"Then please do as I ask and stay here. The work needs to be done before I return. Please?" He could tell she was wavering. Maybe if he begged—maybe another *please*.

She stuck out her chin and looked at him through thick, concealing lashes. "I will stay."

Brent hadn't realized how tense he'd become until he heaved a huge sigh of relief at her capitulation. Without even thinking he walked over, wrapped his arms around her and gave her a big hug, swinging her off her feet. He was about to put her back down when he thought he heard a giggle. Giggle? From Miss Meadowlark Russell? Surely his imagination played tricks on him.

Then he became aware of her firm little body pressing against his. The softness of her breasts. Her flat belly. Long, tapering legs. He did what came naturally. He captured her pink, moist mouth and his body exploded into flames. As he traced the outline of her delicate lips, he came to the realization that he wanted this woman. *Really* wanted her. In the worst way.

His hands splayed across her back, massaging the taut muscles. She gasped. His tongue slipped between her teeth, dipping, diving, incessantly probing the honeyed recess.

Her fists knotted in his shirt as she pulled him closer. Her hips moved tightly against him. Brent thought he would die with pleasure.

The sound of horseshoes striking stone and the jangle of a bit brought Brent instantly back to reality. He lifted his head but continued to hold her close as he gulped droughts of air.

Meadowlark's body felt sluggish, as if she'd had too much mescal or peyote. Her eyelids drooped. Her breasts felt swollen and heavy. There was a moist heat between her thighs she had never felt before. Her entire body was warm and languid and she felt as if she did not have a care in the world—until he set her away and smoothed the wrinkles on her tunic and his jacket.

"Sorry. I probably shouldn't have done that." He felt like a stammering schoolboy who'd just kissed his first girl. And as he staggered backward a step at a time, it dawned on him how appropriate was the image. Sensations rocked his body. He'd never experienced such a *kiss*. Lord, what was happening to him?

"Cap'n? You ready? We done brung yore horse."

Brent glanced nervously out the slanted door. He could barely make out the shadows of three riders. "Y-yes, Corporal. I'll be right there."

He took a deep breath and looked at Meadowlark. "I'll be back. With *all* of the supplies."

She had barely regained her wits enough to manage

a nod, but it evidently pleased him. He grinned, and that little gesture turned her heart upside down.

But as she watched him ride away from San Carlos, her own lips curved into a smug smile. She told him she would stay. She just failed to mention how long.

Captain Brent McQuade signaled his men off the road a few miles outside of Tucson. To the right lay a narrow arroyo with a trickle of water flowing amid piles of driftwood and large, rounded boulders. Both sides of the deep cut were bordered by tall, gray-brown trunks of denuded sycamores, starkly contrasted against the reddish-orange streaks illuminating the western horizon.

Brent shivered. On the desert, whether it was during the dead of winter or the hottest day of summer, once the sun settled the temperature plummeted.

Briefly scanning the area, he noticed a gradual slope leading to the top of a ridge and rode up to investigate. His horse climbed the rise easily, and Brent reined it to a stop atop the narrow crest. The arroyo opened into a flat, open vale before the land rose into another, steeper ridge. Water pooled in a rocky depression. He signaled his men forward and rode down the rocky hillside.

"Corporal, we'll camp here tonight. Assign each man a three-hour watch tonight, saving the last one for me. If we're lucky and intercept those wagons, we'll make damn sure they get to San Carlos."

"Yes, sir." The corporal saluted, then turned and began to issue orders to the remaining troopers.

Brent remained on horseback, taking careful note of the countryside. Surprise would be his best weapon, and he wanted to insure against the possibility of a driver escaping and alerting the Tucson contractor of what was happening. Of course, there was no proof that the contractor was to blame. It could very well be a conspiracy on the part of the drivers.

A grim smile etched Brent's features. Either way, it was his duty to find out the truth. In fact, he damned well looked forward to it.

Meadowlark caught her horse at first light. Heavy wagons would travel at a slow speed. Using her thoroughbred, she had no doubts about reaching the general area of the turnoff to the mines well ahead of Brent and the caravan of supplies.

Unless it was absolutely necessary, she would not make her presence known. But she patted the stock of her Spencer rifle. It wasn't that she worried about the captain taking care of himself. He just was not aware of the type of men he would encounter. They were greedy and ruthless and would stop at nothing to achieve their goal—money.

If there was trouble . . . She would be ready.

She took a cutoff and rode across country. Almost two hours later, she approached the rutted wagon road. She caught a movement from the corner of her eye. It was only a flicker. She stopped, listened and waited.

Suspicion and fear warred for dominance in her mind. *If* she had really seen something, it had come from the direction of the mines. What if the miners had learned of Captain McQuade's plan? Would they rally together to assure they received *their* portion of the supplies?

Her more rational thoughts battled to the surface. It could have been an animal, or even an innocent traveler. Or, maybe, only her imagination.

She turned the mare and continued to ride atop the ridge rather than risk jarring stones loose by descending the slope. Reaching an area where three huge soapweed yucca grew close together, she slid from the horse and tried to conceal the horse and herself behind the high, thick, grasslike blades that spread in circles from the grayish-brown, waist-high trunks of the plants.

Once, when the mare threw up its head and flared its velvety nostrils, Meadowlark quickly covered its nose. "Easy, Paloma. Easy." She clucked softly, reassuringly, when the horse continued to fidget.

She stood poised, eyes surveying each direction. Then she spotted him. One man on horseback riding off, yet parallel with the road. He was dodging cholla cactus, Mormon Tea shrubs and the taller yucca, evidently in a concentrated effort to remain unseen and inconspicuous.

As the horse and rider approached her position, Meadowlark grinned and stepped out of concealment. "Hola, Scorpion."

There was no need to raise her voice. He had seen her immediately, so alertly was he studying his surroundings. For a moment, though, she thought he scowled, but if so, it was quickly replaced by a broad grin. Well, she guessed if he was upset with her, she could not blame him. He would not appreciate being startled by a mere woman, and doubtless she would never get away with it again.

Scorpion rode up to meet her. "What you do here?"

Her eyes narrowed. He was hardly ever so impolite. "And you, Scorpion? What are *you* doing here?"

When he just stared, she knew no explanation from the mighty warrior would be forthcoming. But, whatever his disposition, she was glad to have run into him. "Will you stay here and wait with me?" Although she hoped there would be no trouble for the captain, one could never be certain.

Scorpion's gaze turned wary. "For why?"

She glanced down the road and followed its winding trail in the direction of Tucson. In the distance, she detected a cloud of dust large enough to be the wagon train. Quickly, Meadowlark reached out and touched

Scorpion's arm. "Captain McQuade plans to escort the wagons to San Carlos. None will go to the mines today."

A sparkle of excitement lit her eyes. "He does not expect trouble, but . . . I . . . we . . . could keep watch."

Scorpion turned and looked down the road. His mustang sidled away from Meadowlark and pulled the warrior's arm away from the pressure of her entreating fingers. "No *bueno.* Es no *bueno* we be here."

"No one will know. Unless there is danger."

Scorpion shook his head, his eyes intent on the distant wagons. "Best we go."

Meadowlark pleaded, "Please, Scorpion. The captain is helping our people. He must succeed. Stay. For me."

The only movement from the warrior was in his eyes, yet he refused to look at her. He appeared to scan the road and the surrounding countryside, but would not look at her. Tendons in his neck stood out and quivered. His hand jerked the reins as the mustang pawed the ground.

"Please?" Meadowlark had never begged in her life. The words tasted bitter in her mouth. Surely he would not leave. Why did he seem so . . . fearful? Scorpion was the bravest warrior she knew. Why would he not protect their supplies?

Finally, Scorpion dipped his head and nodded. Her sigh of relief was audible and he grinned. Just a flicker of his lips, to be certain, but it *was* a grin. All she needed to build her own confidence was to have Scorpion at her side.

Just past daybreak, Brent and his three troopers heard the unmistakable rumble of approaching wagons. "All right, soldiers, you know what to do. Corporal, wait until the last wagon drives by and fall in behind. No one gets by you. Understood?"

"Yes, sir!"

All three men solemnly expressed their understanding of the order. Springfield carbines rested across their thighs as they waited.

A total of seven wagons jostled past the concealed soldiers. Brent scowled. Only four had unloaded at San Carlos last week, which meant that almost half of the goods had gone to the mine. If the same thing happened *every* week . . .

The captain stood in his stirrups and watched the last canvas top bounce from view. "Let's go. And remember, we just happened to catch up with them on our way back to the reservation."

Brent's palm rested on the butt of his .45. Damn them! How long did they think they could continue with such blatant deception? How long had Meadowlark known? Did it have anything to do with the extra requisitions?

The corporal held his horse in check and reined in behind the last wagon. Brent and the other two soldiers moved on along the line of wagons. As he rode by each in turn, he looked at the driver, smiled and flicked the brim of his hat.

The remaining two troopers fell in near the middle of the line while he rode to the front. That driver glanced in his direction, started to look away, but snapped his head back around.

"Mornin', Gen'r'l."

Brent favored the man with a mock salute. He had no argument with being mistaken for a general.

The driver flicked his reins on the mule team's backs. "On yore way ta the reservation?"

"Yep." Brent searched his pockets for a cheroot.

The mules tugged into the harness as the man slapped the reins again, unnecessarily hard. "Well, ya have a safe trip, hear?"

Brent nodded and carelessly struck a matchhead

down the seam of his trousers. He puffed, slowly, until the tobacco glowed red, then pointed his thumb back over his shoulder. "These Indian rations?"

"Uh, sure. See ya at San Carlos, huh?"

"Oh, I don't know. Might just mosey along with you a ways."

The driver mulled that over. He shot a glance over his shoulder toward the wagons behind, but merely shrugged at the question on the next driver's face. "Suit yorese'f, Gen'r'l."

Another hour passed, uneventfully. Conversation between the drivers and the soldiers was stilted and almost nonexistent. As one mile fell behind the other, the lead driver spat and cursed and darted sly glances over his shoulder. The mules became obstinate. The more he fought them, the more unruly they acted.

Apaches were starving or running off to Mexico in droves, costing innocent lives and the government thousands of dollars because of these bastards, Brent thought. It was a distinct pleasure to watch them squirm.

All in all, he could think of nothing he'd like better than to take these men and whoever paid them, and lay the sharp end of his pistol up the side of their heads. Or perhaps to turn them over to the Apaches, and let the Indians dole out fitting justice. Now that would be sweet . . .

Coming in sight of the fork in the road, Brent's mount began to prance and pace, sensing the tension in its rider's body. Brent eased the horse up next to the wagon box. A surge of emotion heated his veins—the same surge that he'd felt just before his first battle, or the first time he'd made love.

Brent studied the driver. The man was an ugly brute with matted whiskers and a mustache that hadn't seen water in who-knew-how-long drooping beneath a scarred, bulbous nose. Beady little eyes, barely visible beneath thick slabs of dark brows darted everywhere at once. He was the type of man Brent would hate to meet on a dark, stormy night without a trusty gun or extra sharp knife in his fist.

But when they reached the fork, the driver turned the mules toward San Carlos with hardly a flick of an eyelid. Brent mentally laughed at his needless worrying. It had all probably been a misunderstanding. The mistake could have been made last week, and today they were making up the difference.

He was about to slip his carbine back into its sheath when one of the privates called out, "Cap'n? Better get back here."

Brent yanked on the reins, pressing his calves into the animal's sides. *Crack!* A shot reverberated behind them. Midway through the turn, the horse lunged forward. Brent settled deeper into the saddle, struggling for control of the horse and maintaining his grip on the unwieldy gun.

"Watch out!" someone shouted. Brent managed to turn his head and saw the driver standing in the wagon box, holding a bloody hand. A pistol thudded to the ground near the front wheel, causing a small explosion of dust.

Brent's head spun in every direction. Who had shot the driver?

Chapter Eight

A small battle was taking place toward the rear of the train. Men scuffled on one of the wagons, knocking a crate to the ground, catching Brent's attention. Another gunshot sent him riding in that direction.

As he passed the second wagon, the driver was kneeling in the box, sighting his rifle on a trooper. Brent brought up the barrel of his carbine, shouted for the man to throw down his weapon and waited until the ruffian had done so before urging his prancing mount on.

The two soldiers he had stationed in the middle of the train seemed to have the next three wagons and their drivers under control. He nodded in the troopers' direction and spurred his horse to the rear of the train. The last two wagons were stopped at the fork in the road. He found Corporal Bent holding a gun on one driver, while another leaned against the spokes of a wheel, holding his bleeding shoulder.

"These gents seemed mighty inclined to travel that other road, Cap'n. But Henrietta," he indicated the smoking carbine, "an' I, we talked 'em outta that notion right quick."

The man on the ground moaned as he raised his head. "Ya made a big mistake, Captain. We were supposed to take that road."

Brent stared the man down. "Tell you what, when

we get to San Carlos and it turns out there's more in those wagons than what I ordered, I'll let you take it on. How's that?"

The driver couldn't meet Brent's eyes. Instead of answering, he grimaced and looked down at the blood soaking his shirt.

Brent called up the line. "There's a wounded man back here. Someone come take care of him."

One of the privates answered his summons on the double. He was the oldest of the troopers, with seventy-year-old eyes peering out of a twenty- to thirty-year-old body. "I'll handle him, Captain. Plugged up a lot of bullet holes, I have."

"Thanks, Private." Then Brent reined his horse back toward the lead wagon. He zigzagged between the first two conveyances and came face to face with Meadowlark Russell.

His eyes widened. He jerked his mount to a sudden, sliding stop. She sat bareback on the thoroughbred mare. A Spencer repeater dangled from her hand, the barrel pointing toward the ground. Wearing her buckskin tunic and breeches, she looked every bit an Apache warrior, and seemed quite comfortable with the role.

Brent turned beet-red as an uncontrollable anger spread throughout his trembling body. She was not a warrior, for God's sake. She was a woman. A very attractive female who didn't belong where bullets flew and danger lurked behind every scraggly bush.

"What are you doin' here?" he shouted. When she flinched, he regretted his outburst, a little. For all he knew, she had saved his miserable hide, and his yelling was the thanks she got.

Meadowlark sat in stunned silence. She had not thought what his reaction might be, but had never expected such anger. Fool white man. Who was he to nip the hand that saved his life?

She tilted her chin in defiance, realizing the answer

was obvious. He was a typical male. The thought of being protected by a mere *woman* was probably more than his pride could acknowledge.

Actually, she was as surprised as anyone about how quickly she had come to his rescue. As she sat beside Scorpion, watching the wagons approach, deep in the back of her mind lingered a nagging doubt that maybe the captain would renege on his promise to help her people. That everything he had said was only pretty words containing little substance.

But she knew that was wrong. From her vantage point, she'd had a bird's-eye view of the whole thing. The first wagons had taken the turn off to San Carlos. The last two attempted to keep going to the mines. The soldiers had been ready.

One of the troopers had shouted for the captain. He had turned his back on the first driver, who had then pulled his gun. She hated to admit it, but her heart had fluttered wildly against her breast, and even now continued to beat at an abnormally rapid rate.

She had hardly been aware of lifting her rifle. The only evidence—the ringing in her ears and a throbbing bruise on her shoulder where the stock had bucked against her. Her first instinct had been to protect the handsome soldier.

Meadowlark's stomach churned at the implication of her actions. She consciously willed her body not to quake as she looked into Brent McQuade's taut features.

"Damn it, woman, answer me! What do you think you're doin' out here?" Silently, he admonished, "Don't you realize you could have been hurt?" He gulped. Maybe even killed.

Meadowlark stared impassively at the aggravating man. "I was here to spare your worthless hide. Maybe I made a mistake."

Brent sputtered and stammered and finally snapped his jaws shut. She didn't mince words, did she? He choked out, "Thank you for that, but, damn it, you shouldn't have come all this way alone. It's too dangerous."

"But . . . I was not . . ." Meadowlark swiveled her head. Scorpion had been right behind her. But now he was gone. Why?

Her train of thought and Brent's anxious tirade were brought to an abrupt halt when the first driver, cradling his injured hand in the crook of his other arm, stomped over to the rest of the assembled drivers and troopers.

"What's the meanin' of this, Gen'r'l? There'll be hell ta pay. Just you sit back an' watch."

Brent shrugged. "Like I told your friend, when we tally up the goods, and *if* there's been a misunderstanding, you'll have my apology. But not before. You understand *that,* mister?"

The bluster quickly faded from the man's obnoxious demeanor. He added only a few choice curses as the private examined his broken fingers. Private Colquitt clucked his tongue. "Well, well. Looks like you were lucky. Someone's a hell of a shot."

All eyes turned to Meadowlark, who also, but silently, cursed the heat she felt suffusing her face. So, she was good with her rifle. Why were they surprised? The Apache had fewer weapons than the whites, but they struggled to become proficient with anything at their disposal.

When the driver's hand had been adequately tended, Brent ordered everyone back to their wagons. "Private Colquitt, drive the last wagon so you can keep an eye on our friend's shoulder. Wouldn't want anything to happen to him before we get to San Carlos."

Most of the drivers recognized the underlying threat and muttered obscenities as they walked back to their teams. The lead driver glared hard at both Meadowlark and Brent. "There'll be hell to pay. Mark my words."

* * *

The wagons and their escort arrived at San Carlos well past noon. Some of the Apache women and children had already formed a ragged line. Several warriors held half- to three-quarter-empty whiskey bottles in their hands as they staggered through the dust muttering and calling for their supplies.

Brent's stomach sank to his toes. He darted Meadowlark a glance. From the staunch line of her jaw and set, hard features, he guessed the scene wasn't a new one. And from her white-knuckled grip on the mare's reins, she was more upset that she would ever allow anyone to see. His heart went out to her.

It was tough, trying to appear casual and unaffected when something was literally ripping your guts apart. He knew. He'd felt despair. He'd felt rejection.

And he had to admire the little lady. She had guts.

Once the wagons pulled up in front of the agency office, Brent immediately ordered the corporal to *escort* the drivers to the doctor's quarters, and to assign someone to keep an eye on the whole lot. He then joined the other troopers in going through the wagons, taking a rough inventory.

As he'd suspected, the last wagons contained the same blankets, clothing and items of food. But when all of the items were totaled, the numbers were less than he had ordered. Why the drivers had taken the chance of making the mines, surrounded by soldiers, was a mystery. Either greed had overcome them, or they assumed the soldiers were gullible enough to believe their stories. And of course the obvious reason, if the men were not acting on their own, was that whoever ordered them to make the run to the mines, had threatened them with their lives.

Brent shook his head. At least the agency would have enough supplies to distribute today.

The same volunteer buffalo soldiers who had helped

the past week soon relieved the exhausted troopers. Brent and Meadowlark began to sort through and stack the goods to be allotted each individual.

As the Apaches filed through the line, Brent received a shy smile every once in a while from the older squaws. Sometimes a young woman would cast him an appraising glance from beneath lowered lashes and he felt himself flush.

Even when the warriors filed past, he sensed a lessening of hostility in their greetings. He was gratified.

Then one older, extremely dignified Apache man stopped directly in from of him. Brent squirmed beneath the cold, black-eyed scrutiny. He smelled liquor on the old man's breath, and the warrior's arms trembled slightly under the weight of the supplies. Decidedly uneasy, Brent was stunned when a deep, well-articulated, "Thank you," rumbled from the scarred chest.

Other Indians in line behind the old man let down their guards enough that Brent sensed their own astonishment. His gaze followed the stately figure's back until Meadowlark snapped, "Here! People are waiting," and thrust another bundle of goods into his startled grasp.

During the next half hour, he found himself wondering at Meadowlark's suddenly aloof manner and remote features. What had he done to offend her now?

Meadowlark was grateful when the last warrior lumbered through the line. If she had to stay in the captain's company one more minute, or observe while her people groveled at his feet, she would certainly be physically ill. Already, her chest felt as if it could cave in at any time, and her eyes burned.

How could the Apache take to the man so quickly? How dare them! Her own poor father had broken his back for over a year before they acknowledged his existence. Then along strolled this blond, ruddy-complexioned white man. Within three weeks' time, he had garnered the approval of several of the wisest and most respected chiefs.

It was not fair.

The minute the captain turned his back to confer with a black soldier, she quietly backed away from the wagons and disappeared behind the office. Hurriedly, she scurried through the compound, wishing she were any place but San Carlos, working with anyone but Captain McQuade.

Before she became aware of her surroundings, she stopped and took a few long breaths. When she looked about to see where she was, she was horrified to find herself behind her father's old office building. Panic easily seized control of her. She hurried to get away and suddenly collided with a tall, solid figure.

Strong fingers bit into her upper arms, holding her upright. Her eyes were unable to focus in the building's shadow. But she recognized the odors of wood smoke and leather. "Scorpion." The name floated on a breathless whisper.

He seemed just as startled as she. "What you do, little pigeon? No more hand aways?"

"Outs. Handouts." Suddenly she remembered that she had hoped to find and speak with the elusive warrior. "Never mind me. Where did you go this morning?"

His eyes ranged from her face to the cracked window, to the band of Indians slowly parading through the dust down the center of the compound on their way to a distant campground. "I . . . I be close . . . following." He shrugged. "Maybe more men come. Maybe need ambush."

Meadowlark smiled. "I think you mean you were ready to surprise them."

He nodded.

Pain radiated through her upper arms when Scorpion released them, reminding her of his powerful grip. Rubbing her palms up and down her tender flesh, she glanced to one side. "Why are you here, Scorpion?"

A shudder raked her spine. She imagined ghosts of the dead stalking the shadows, looming, hovering . . . In a flash, she moved away from the building and into the reassuring sunlight. Scorpion followed, though less quickly. Her eyes narrowed. He appeared to be at war with himself, searching for answers, unable to look her square in the eyes.

He mumbled, "I go for hand . . . out."

Meadowlark's eyes were inexorably drawn to the empty building. A deep feeling of sadness, of being alone in the world overwhelmed her. Another shiver caused her to draw herself together. She was being silly. Her thoughts were those of a white woman, not an Apache. There was always Scorpion. Her aunt lived, as far as she knew.

Slowly turning, she stared fixedly toward the wagons parked in front of the agency office. Her gaze had settled on a familiar blue, double-breasted jacket that denoted an officer of rank. The captain. Her stomach tightened. Deep, deep in her soul, she harbored the insane notion that, if the need arose, she could count on him to help.

The only white man she had ever trusted was her father. Now, all of a sudden, a particular captain entered her life, and she no longer relegated her beliefs and emotions to their strict orders of priority.

No longer could she insist that she hated *all* whites. No longer could she assert that all soldiers were determined to destroy her people. No longer did she have absolute control over her actions and reactions.

"Little pigeon?"

Meadowlark blinked. She flushed beneath the concern in Scorpion's voice. What would he think if he could read her thoughts? She cleared her throat and pretended to be busy studying the wagons. "You better go soon. The line is gone."

Then she scanned the compound, noting that most of the Apache were gone. At least those that were sober enough to walk on their own. Silently she cursed the white man's whiskey. They knew the Indians' systems could not tolerate the strong spirits. Yet the whites freely—even happily—sold it or traded it. And the Apaches often parted with goods of much greater worth to pay for the poison.

There had to be something she could do. Maybe Brent McQuade was right. Maybe he and she, together, *could* make a difference.

As much as she dreaded spending even more time in the captain's company, it might be worth a try. *Anything* was worth a try.

Each day that passed seemed a week to Meadowlark. It was easier to fill out her requisitions, because the captain was seldom in the office. Yet she continually amazed herself by standing at the window, staring outside, watching for him.

When she realized what she was doing, she busied herself with something time consuming. She liked the time alone. She did. Her days were spent much the same as they had been *before* Captain Brent McQuade.

One day, deciding she needed even more time to herself in order to put her mind on the really important things in life, she rode to the Warm Springs camp. The thoroughbred covered the miles in a ground-consuming lope. Meadowlark's black curls fluttered softly with each rocking motion. Her eyes searched the road and the manzanita-covered hills. And she hated herself for being disappointed because she couldn't find a sign of the captain.

Her stay with the Apaches was disheartening. She constantly checked the sun's position. The Apache women's busy-work of grinding seeds and nuts into flour, gathering firewood, washing and cleaning, seemed dull and boring. It was a disturbing revelation because, always before, she had known this was the way she wanted to spend her life. But now, something was missing. The work was not as fulfilling. The camp less appealing.

She enjoyed a long visit with her favorite cousin, Angelita, but the content of their conversation kept returning to the restricted way of life their band was forced to endure. When she caught her mare to take the horse, and herself, out for cleansing exercise, her heart was more sad than when she left San Carlos.

Her emotions in turmoil, she rode the thoroughbred hard. Finally, lather from the animal's sweaty hide soaked into her breeches. Labored heaves for air grated on Meadowlark's usually sensitive ears and she guiltily drew her horse to a walk. Shame filled her soul. What had gotten into her to behave so irresponsibly? She had always taken good care of *any* animal entrusted to her keeping. And yet she could have just destroyed the last possession belonging to her family of any real value.

She kept the return pace to camp slow, reveling in the stark beauty of her surroundings as the horse cooled. They topped a low ridge. Meadowlark gazed down a gradual incline. The slope eased into one of the small creeks, which in turn looped around an unusually large area of flat surface.

As she sat there, unconsciously gazing at the shrubs and weeds, the peace and quiet of the place allowed unwanted images to fill her senses—of Apache warriors stooped from aching backs, tilling rocky soil, of Apache women, fingers cut and bleeding, providing hay for army livestock. Indian men and women drunk and staggering across the reservation, falling, passing out, freezing in the winter, or parched from exposure to the harsh sun in the summer.

Tears traced crooked paths down her cheeks. Sad.

So sad. Yet, to survive, her people had to do these things.

She and Brent had helped to solve an immediate problem by bringing enough rations each week. But food was not enough. What of the real problem? The loss of pride. Handouts were only a temporary solution. The Apache needed to feel they were useful, that they were capable of fending for themselves. But how? In the past, they couldn't even raise a decent crop. If only the captain's questions about irrigation . . .

Meadowlark blinked. She shook her head and focused on the incline. An idea took root in her fertile brain. She saw a canal above the field. Water diverted from the stream flowed freely through the ditch. Used for irrigation, excess water that did not soak into the ground would return to the stream.

All of a sudden, she began to think in terms of corn and potatoes and squash, rather than sage and cactus and gila monsters.

She became so engrossed on the subject, that she failed to turn back toward the Warm Springs camp. Hope and excitement brightened her features. She had to get back to the office—and Brent.

It was afternoon of the next day when she turned the mare into the corral. They had approached the office from the back, and had been unable to see if it was occupied. Humming to herself, she gave the horse a good rubdown while wrestling with thoughts of how she would coerce her people into giving farming another try.

Her footsteps were light, her moccasins padding soundlessly past the cracked adobe and the small window. She was dreaming of rows and rows of green sprouts growing from the desert when a movement caught her eye and she stopped to peer through the dusty pane.

She must have unwittingly made a noise of some kind, for the captain's head jerked around. The tip of the pen he'd been wielding slipped and marked a line straight up the requisition. His jaw dropped open when he saw her watching. Too late, he tried to hide the order.

A few seconds passed as Meadowlark rid her mind of farming and registered what she had just seen. The captain's guilty expression confirmed that her eyesight was perfect. The bastard! How long had he been going behind her back, changing her forged requisitions?

It never occurred to her that *he* might have discovered *her* deception. The most important thing on her mind was *his*. Anger surged through her taut little form with all of the force of roaring flood waters gnashing slabs of earth from a narrow arroyo.

She rushed to the door and stormed inside. "What were you doing?"

Brent shoved the papers behind his back, then shrugged and held his hands out to his sides, palms up, in a kind of helpless gesture.

She marched forward. "I asked you a question, white man."

Her belligerent attitude struck a raw nerve. Brent had been tense, walking on eggshells for weeks because of the little minx. His eyes narrowed dangerously. She had gall, challenging him like a full-grown she-cougar defending her cubs. Who did she think she was, anyway? Who'd started the entire mess by sneaking around with those damned requisitions in the first place?

He stepped toward her. "All right, I'll give you an answer. I changed a few figures. Now tell me why you've become an accomplished forger."

She conveniently ignored all but his admittance of guilt. "You . . . you . . . pile of horse . . . horse . . . droppings. My people are starving, yet you would deny them the food from their mouths."

Her eyes rounded. She did not truly believe her

own accusation. Confusion tore at her. Had he not proven in many ways how he cared what happened to the Apache? But . . . she had seen . . .

The captain took another step forward. She stood nose to chest with the man. The top buttons of his jacket were loose and light wisps of hair curled from the open vee. He poked *her* in the chest and she felt as if he doused her with icy water. She was pushed backward, but managed to hold her own and only lost one step.

"You best hold your tongue, woman. Don't go chargin' me with somethin' you know nothin' about."

"You are a sneak and a thief. You have gone behind my back. And it is not the first time." And through the red haze that glazed her eyes, she picked up something subtly different about Brent McQuade. Most men, when angry, spoke very fast, running their words together. The captain slowed his speech, making his words long and lazy. It could almost be described as soothing—at any other time and volume.

Then he poked her again. She scowled at the warmth his touch ignited in her breast.

"Just how stupid do you think I am? Did you really think you had gotten away with addin' requisitions, initials and all?"

They both took a breath and stood glaring at one another.

"A long-eared donkey is smarter than you," Meadowlark spat.

"You're more stubborn than a jackass." He lowered his head until he looked her in the eye.

She fisted her hands.

He stood spraddle-legged, vying for a decent foothold, preparing himself for whatever she threw at him next, whether it be as blistering as her heated words or as punishing as bare knuckles. She was more unpredictable than a wildcat and, God, how he admired her spirit.

From out of nowhere he chuckled. He lost control. The entire situation suddenly struck him funny.

Meadowlark almost jumped up and down in her fury. She shifted her weight to the balls of her feet. "You dare mock me? As you mock all Apaches?"

Brent wiped his eyes and dared to turn his back on the termagant. He searched through the scattered papers until he found the one on which he'd been working. His voice cracked with mirth as he held it out to her. "Look at this. Then tell me if I'm mockin' *your people.*"

Wary suspicion darkened her eyes. She read over the changes, and read them again. Her eyes remained downcast. Her mouth opened and formed a round, "Oh."

Brent leaned forward. "What? I didn't hear you."

She gradually lifted her head until her chin jutted out. She swallowed, hard, when his blue, blue eyes trapped her gaze. It felt like she had a mouthful of sand. "Oh."

"Just *oh?*"

She tore her eyes away. He was laughing at her. What he found humorous in the situation was beyond her comprehension. She felt humiliated. He smiled. She felt two inches tall. He towered over her, flaunting his strength and power and . . . And she couldn't seem to think straight. "I was wrong. You are not cheating my people."

"I'd have thought you'd known that by now." Brent crossed his arms over his broad chest and gazed down his nose at her. The statement had been uttered grudgingly, but she *had* admitted her error. That was something in his favor.

"I do."

She sounded so contrite that he bent his head to get a closer look at her face. Traces of resentment glittered from her eyes and carved her normally stoic features.

"Now I want *my* answer. What've you been up to these past weeks? An' why?"

Meadowlark went over and slouched into her chair. She felt safer there, away from his magnetizing body and alluring scent. Maybe then she could concentrate and decide what to do.

Small white teeth gnawed at her lower lip. He knew she had forged the initials. He was in a position to ruin any hopes of catching the killer. His suspicion concerning her father's absence was almost palpable as she sucked in a calming breath of air.

What should she do? She could lie—again. But instead of becoming more comfortable with each falsehood, she became more convinced the spirits would punish her wrongdoing. And surely he would find her out.

But if she told the whole truth, would he not report her father's death and inform the world of her deceit? Yet it was impossible to think up more believable excuses concerning her father's continued absence.

The captain watched her too closely as it was. How could she stand his breathing down her neck for who-knew-how-long?

Her fingers relaxed. The crumpled paper wilted in her hand. She looked up. Their eyes locked. She had the strongest urge to get down on her knees and beg for his help. But she could not, would not, stoop to such an undignified posture.

"It is a long story."

Chapter Nine

Brent McQuade slid into his chair across the desk from Meadowlark. "Go ahead with your story. I have nothing but time."

Grimly, she noted the anger was gone from his voice. Once again his words were clipped and precise. "I need your promise."

He frowned. "To what?"

"Th-that you will keep what I say . . . private . . . between you and me."

"You mean confidential?"

She nodded.

He hunched his shoulders. "All right. If I can."

It was all she could hope for. "I have used those . . . initials . . . because I must trap a murderer."

The silence after that statement drew on almost interminably. Finally, Brent sighed and rubbed his hand over his eyes, pushing his hat onto the back of his head. "I think I understand. Your father . . . hasn't been able to meet with me because he's . . . dead."

A moist sheen coated her eyes. Brent's heart lurched into his throat. The poor kid. It explained a lot of things that he'd wondered about lately—why she never spoke her father's name—the move to this tiny building.

"Does anyone else know?"

She nodded. "Scorpion. And probably most of the Apache."

Come to think of it, Brent mused, during his trips to the various camps, he'd never heard a soul mention the agent. The Apache were terrified of ghosts and were deathly afraid that to speak the name of a dead person would bring forth the spirit. He shivered. As far as he was concerned, there could be something to their beliefs.

"You've tried to lure the killer out using those . . . initials. Do you think he's connected to the Tucson contractor?"

"Maybe." She held her council. The murderer could very well be on the reservation. The captain had enough to worry about, and she would keep a close watch.

"What about your mother?" He remembered mentioning her once and Lark had said . . . Suddenly it struck him. She had said it would be impossible for him to meet the woman. Her mother wasn't living at the house. Good God!

His eyes voiced his question. Her eyes lowered.

He recalled her mother. Estrella Russell had been a diminutive, beautiful woman. "When? Where?"

"Last year. In Mexico."

He sucked in his breath. "She left with Loco's band when Geronimo raided San Carlos." It wasn't a question. He'd been at Fort Apache then, following the elusive Geronimo and half of the Apache nation, it seemed. Even in country as rough and impassable as the Salt River Canyon, it was impossible to imagine how so many Indians could disappear so completely.

He'd been relieved of duty when word came that his mother was deathly ill. But he'd heard about the Mexican massacre, even in Washington. "I'm sorry." It was little enough to say. The attack had been an outrage.

She shrugged. "It was a long time ago."

Brent leaned back and stretched his long legs to the side of the crate-desk. "All right. You can have more time. But I'll have to make a report—soon."

Meadowlark sprang to her feet and ran around the desk to kiss his cheek. Then she stepped back, horrified. What had gotten into her lately? She had never been impulsive. She was the one who always carefully considered her actions.

Yet she needed to express her appreciation, to show in some way how happy she was that her trust had not been misplaced. He understood and would allow her time, if only a little. Brent McQuade was a good man, for a white man.

All of the emotions that had knotted Brent's gut when he'd glimpsed her loneliness and vulnerability came rushing to the fore. He couldn't stand it. In one fluid motion he rose to his feet and captured her in his arms. But he held her loosely, giving her a chance to pull away even as he prayed she would allow him to hold and comfort her.

The fierceness of his reaction surprised him. This instinct to touch and caress, with no thought of what her body could do for his, was new to him.

Meadowlark clung to the captain. He was so stable and strong. She felt safe and protected in his embrace. How she would love to stay there forever. What? She blinked. Had that thought come from her? It was impossible—could never be.

Yet as his hand roamed the length of her spine, massaging the tense muscles along her shoulders and ribs, she found herself pressing closer rather than pulling away.

When he sat back down and settled her onto his lap, she wrapped her arms around his neck and rested her head on his broad shoulder. His thighs were hard, yet supple, beneath the backs of her legs. His chest was warm and corded with muscles that rippled and flexed with each movement. His lips were tender as they kissed her cheek, his breath hot against her ear.

Liquid fire coursed through her veins as she instinctively turned her head just enough that his mouth brushed hers. He felt good and tasted even better. She allowed the words of her inner, warning voice to be swept away. She had never before felt like this—had never before wondered what would happen next.

Brent's hand rested on her rib cage. The heel of his palm supporting the curve of her breast. He hadn't intended for things to go so far, but when her bottom shifted on his lap, his manhood responded accordingly.

Her mouth opened like a spring blossom beneath the gentle probing of his tongue. He sighed with both pleasure and pain as she strained against him. He cupped her perfect little breast. It nestled into his palm as if it had been made just for him to fondle and arouse.

Meadowlark was hot and cold, excited and frightened. Her head spun. Wisdom warred with desire. Butterflies attacked her insides and an ancient voice of caution fluttered through her. "W-we m-must not. S-someone will come."

Brent groaned. His head snapped up. Damn! What had he been thinking? Too quickly, he set her from his lap, then caught her as her legs refused to support her and she almost toppled back. "I'm sorry, Lark. You're right. I'm behaving worse than a stupid jackass." Without another glance in her direction, he got up and staggered from the office.

Meadowlark blinked, confused by his sudden and quite hasty departure. He had sounded hurt and in pain. What had she done?

Scorpion lounged on the back step of the small saloon on a rare cloudy afternoon, several days after the skirmish with the wagon drivers. He flipped the coin he held into the air, caught it, flipped it again. Should he spend the shiny new silver dollar on whiskey? White man's whiskey would rot a man's innards. Or should he put the coin back in the bag with the others?

"There ya be, ya damned Injun."

The loud voice startled Scorpion and he bolted to his feet, slipping the dollar into a leather pouch tied beneath his breechclout. His head turned in the direction of shuffling footsteps. A big white man made an unsteady approach.

The disgusting Anglo raised a bandaged hand and stuck his stubby finger at Scorpion. "Come 'ere, redskin. Wanna palaver with ya."

The warrior hissed and backed against the rough adobe building.

"Ain't no place fer ya ta run, if 'n ya be the one called Scorpion. That be yore moniker, don't it?"

Scorpion's eyes narrowed. His hand went to the knife sheathed at his waist.

Captain Brent McQuade rounded the corner and saw Scorpion, the Apache's eyes slitted dangerously as he watched big-nosed "Slaughter" Ryan weave toward him, down and out drunk. Brent hesitated only a second when he realized the warrior stood with his back to the wall but prepared to defend himself against the tremendous bulk of the other man.

Rushing forward, Brent blocked the path of the wagon boss. He winced when the man belched in his face, but steadfastly stood his ground. "Look, Ryan, if you're having a problem, take it up with someone else. Leave the Indians alone."

Ryan hiccuped and scratched his gut. "Oh, I got a problem a'right. An' you, an' that Injun there. We all got problems. But yourn be lots worse'n mine." He laughed and stumbled off a step or two. After he steadied himself, Ryan glanced back at Brent. "How long we'uns gotta stay in this hellhole, Gen'r'l?"

Brent looked over to make sure Scorpion's hands were well removed from any weapons. "Far as I'm concerned, you and your friends can crawl back where you came from any time."

Ryan leaned forward, almost overbalanced and tottered backward. "Shee here, Gen'r'l, ya ain't got nuthin' agin us. We's onliest waitin' aroun' on poor ole Mac ta mend."

A grimace marred Brent's features. No, there wasn't any real proof of their wrongdoing, but if he intercepted any more wagons loaded with Apache supplies headed for the mines, they'd think torture was a picnic next to what *he* had in mind.

He waited until the driver staggered away, then turned to Scorpion. "What did he want?"

Scorpion scowled and shook his head.

Brent stared at the warrior, trying to find anything at all in his features or actions to refute the bewildered gesture. There was none. Scorpion seemed genuinely baffled. As was Brent himself. Ryan had been after something, had indicated Scorpion was involved. But what?

He kept watching the warrior. Over and over he had studied Scorpion, wondering what it was about the man he didn't like. In Lark's eyes, Scorpion was wonderful, could do no wrong. The warrior was quiet, didn't cause trouble. Yet, there was . . . something.

"You like Meadowlark?"

The question came from out of nowhere and caught Brent completely off guard. His eyes flew up to Scorpion's. The warrior's gaze was penetrating. "I, uh, sure. I like her. Who wouldn't?"

Had he sounded as casual and disinterested as he hoped? Would Scorpion sense the upheaval of emotion that he felt at the mere mention of her name?

"She *my* woman." Scorpion thumped his chest. His expression smug and threatening at the same time.

Brent swallowed a painful gouge of jealousy and shrugged. "You're a lucky man." Deep down, his gut ripped in two. It was what he'd feared all along. But

Meadowlark didn't seem . . . Hell, he chided himself, when had he ever asked? Every time she came within reach, he kissed the poor girl until she could hardly tell him her name, let alone if she was promised to another.

She was as innocent as they came. He had known that. He had *probably* taken unfair advantage of her. But damned if she hadn't seemed to like it. She certainly responded willingly enough.

He coughed and queried, "I take it you're planning to marry Miss Russell?"

Scorpion nodded once, emphatically.

Brent's stomach turned over. "When's the big event?"

"We go . . ." Scorpion stopped abruptly. "Soon."

"Well, that's real fine." Brent guessed he'd hidden his own feelings pretty well, for Scorpion slanted him a last considering glance, nodded and then swaggered away.

Brent slouched down on the step the warrior had previously vacated. So, Scorpion had spoken for Lark. He propped his elbows on his knees and rested his chin atop his steepled fingers. Damn! He should feel happy. But, instead, he felt depressed and empty inside.

She was taken. Now he wouldn't have to suffer all of those ambiguous emotions where the infuriating woman was concerned. He didn't want her. Not really. There was no room in his life for a woman. Hadn't he told himself that same thing repeatedly since leaving Washington?

Yes, by God! Scorpion had just reaffirmed his position. Meadowlark Russell was not a consideration. He stood up and dusted off the seat of his trousers. Taking a deep, deep breath, he stretched his arms over his head and loosened the tension in the muscles cramping his shoulders.

Ah, he felt better than he had in weeks. Whether he

liked the man or not, Scorpion had done him a good turn today.

Meadowlark snuggled deeper into the blankets. She took a soothing breath, and another. Then she turned onto one side, lay there a moment, and flipped to the other. Her legs tangled in the cover. She threw an arm over her eyes to block out the cheerful brilliance of the moon shining through the one blasted window.

Tap. Tap.

She held her breath.

Tap. Tap.

Someone was at the door. Since she had moved into the little building, no one had ever come by at night.

The rapping became more insistent, yet was done lightly, as if whoever it was did not want to be detected.

She reached for a long, white blouse whose tail reached almost to her knees and slipped it over her bare body. Quietly, she crossed the open space between the pallet and the door, staying close to the wall. The Spencer was propped just to her right, and she wrapped her hand around the narrow barrel.

A sharp whisper broke the silence. Several dogs barked and a chill went up Meadowlark's back. Dogs had begun roaming the compound—hungry dogs.

"Scorpion?"

"*Si.*"

Sighing with relief, she replaced the rifle, climbed to her feet, and removed the bar securing the door. Cracking it open, she peeked out, just to be sure it actually was her friend. "Come in," she invited, and fully opened the door.

Scorpion looked back over his shoulder before slipping inside.

"Why are you here?" she asked with a frown and stepped to the window to peer around the curtain.

Coming to stand beside her, Scorpion glanced outside before turning to her. "Come to Mexico. Tonight," he implored, taking her hands.

"What?" With dismay, she realized she had let the surprise she felt be heard in her voice. But she thought this had been settled. Slipping on her instinctive mask, she asked flatly, "Why tonight?"

"*Muy importante.* Time be run out."

He squeezed her hand until she finally winced and pulled free. "Go if you must. I thought you understood. I cannot."

Scorpion paced in a half circle from the door to the window and back. "You must."

Meadowlark shivered. She stood with one bare foot covering the other. The grim determination on Scorpion's face and the vehemence in his voice was almost frightening. There was something about her friend tonight that was extremely disturbing.

"What has happened? Why your haste? Things are better for our people."

The warrior snorted. "Still not free."

She shook her head sadly. "We will never be again. We Apache must accept the fact that our life will never be as it was."

Again he pleaded. "Come. No leave without you."

She tried to explain, for the last time, she hoped. "There are reasons to stay. If I am here, the captain will continue to make sure there are enough rations. He had plans to again try to teach the Apache to grow their own crops. But he needs my help." He needs me. Her insides glowed with warmth. It was true. Brent McQuade *did* need her. And she would stay.

Scorpion leaned against the door with his shoulders rounded in defeat. His brown eyes were hooded in the shadows and she did not know what he was thinking until he straightened, once again becoming the proud warrior. He nodded at her.

Inwardly she sighed, knowing he would make the request again.

Needlessly, Scorpion told her, "One day you *will* come."

Meadowlark stood wide-eyed in the center of the small room and stared at the bronze-skinned man who was so determined to leave San Carlos. What good would it do to run to Mexico when Crook was preparing to go after Geronimo and Loco and the other renegade leaders? The general would search until he found the Apaches, she had no doubt. And then what? Those left alive would be returned to San Carlos.

What was the use of dreaming? As she had told Scorpion, they would all have to learn to accept life on the reservation. It was either that—or die. And she wanted to live. Now more than ever. She covered her face with her hands. How could her visions and beliefs have changed so in such a short time?

Suddenly Scorpion was beside her. She sagged against him. His embrace was gentle and warm, but she found herself comparing the warrior's embrace to the captain's. There was no urgency, no consuming heat, no irrational security. Scorpion was solid, like a boulder. Brent McQuade was a sheer granite cliff, able to withstand the test of time and the forces of nature and humanity.

"Little pigeon, you are my woman. I need you as much as the Apache."

She could feel his chin resting on the top of her head. An intense pang of remorse gripped her soul. Yes, he probably did need her. Times were hard, especially for the warriors. They were no longer free to hunt at will, to roam the vast deserts or high mountain ranges, to battle among themselves or their age-old enemies, the Mexicans, for the true test of manhood.

But if her choice was to be made between the

Apache people, or Scorpion, she had to choose her people as a whole. It was hard, because she truly cared for her friend, but it must be done.

"I am sorry. You must leave me behind."

His guttural, "Never!" prickled her body with goose bumps as he slammed from the office. He was angry, and she was sincerely sorry.

During the next week, Meadowlark became more and more exasperated with herself. Every morning, she went to the creek to wash. She pulled her hair into tight, short little braids and tied them with bright ribbons. She wore her best calico skirt and the white blouse with her newest moccasins.

Why she wanted to look her best for the captain, she had no idea. She just did. But her efforts were wasted. He acted as if she hardly existed.

Every once in a while, however, she caught him looking at her. Like the Apache, there would be no change in his features, but there was something in those eyes—something that set her insides on fire. Yet the expression disappeared so quickly she almost believed that it was only her woman's imagination that had seen it in the first place.

Yet try as she might not to think about it, she would have been willing to bet her thoroughbred mare that if Brent McQuade had been the man who came to her late at night, and she was dressed in nothing but a short blouse, *he* would have desired more than a hug. . . .

Not that she wasn't glad Scorpion had not demanded more of her. Maybe if he had not been so distracted by wild thoughts of Mexico . . . Yet, if she was glad, why was she also disappointed?

Lately she had felt too many unfamiliar and contradictory emotions. Since Apaches rarely acknowledged their feelings, there had been few opportunities to observe how to handle herself in such a situation.

With a sigh and a shrug she looked at her hands. Hands that had once been held by an Apache mother—and a white father. Hands that now helped a white captain do white man's paperwork. Was it time for her Apache-self to acknowledge the side of her heritage she had always denied?

Brent leaned his chair back on two legs and propped his heels on the edge of the wooden crate. He was also going through a state of confusion, attempting to convince himself that Lark belonged to Scorpion. He tried not to watch her every movement, tried not to notice how pretty she looked and how even the loose-fitting clothes she wore did little to hide her figure.

She was more sensual than a lot of women with voluptuous curves. Her flesh was soft and firm and well-toned and vibrant and . . . Hell, it was happening again. He was going mad. His body was as taut as a too tightly strung wire. One brush of her thigh or round little bottom and he would snap in two.

He heard a loud rustle of papers. He looked up. She smiled. That did it! He staggered to his feet. "Oh, I've got to take a trip. Probably be gone two or three days."

"Why?" She was surprised and frightened. What if something happened to him? What if the killer was waiting for just such an opportunity?

Brent cleared his throat. "After yesterday's rations, there's only enough beef for another week. I've talked to the major about an idea I had. Now I just need to see if it will work."

"What idea?" He hadn't mentioned anything to *her* about a solution to the problem of cattle. "I will go, too." Maybe she could be of some help if he had to work with the Apache.

"Lord, no! I mean, I'd rather you not, this time." Sweat prickled between his shoulder blades. That would be all he needed. He remembered too clearly the one afternoon he had "escaped," only to run right into *her* by the . . . Huh-uh. Not this time. He needed those few days—alone.

Meadowlark frowned. Was he trying to get rid of her? Did he think it would be that easy?

It was almost dark the next evening when Brent located Brandon's home. He rode along the Salt River until he reached a new logging mill and several sparkling fresh houses.

He sniffed the air and sighed with contentment. There was something invigorating about the aroma of newly cut pine. He stopped his horse and soaked in the cool mountain atmosphere. How wonderful it had felt to ride through trees again. Juniper, piñon and the big Ponderosa. And the breeze contained a fresh January bite that was missing on the desert.

He watched the river rush over large boulders and smiled at the splash of water roiling against the bank. Finally, he nudged his gelding forward. He would sit and compare and daydream another time. Right now, he was anxious to see his brother.

A coal-oil lantern illuminated the last house, which sat farther away from the others in a natural clearing amid the trees. Instinct insisted it was Brand's, but if he supposed wrong, the inhabitants would doubtless know his brother's whereabouts.

He hitched his horse to the rail, then brushed the trail dust from his clothes. It seemed unusually important that his bandana be straight and that his hat sit just right. Then he shook his head. What was there to be nervous about? It was just his brother. But then again, they hadn't known each other all that long.

Would Brand resemble the well-bred city boy he had waved good-bye to, or would he have reverted to the feared White Fox, the fierce Apache warrior who'd confronted Brent after twenty-three years of living in two distinct and separate worlds? He gave his sleeve another brush and took a deep breath. Well, there was only one way to find out.

Brent sidled up the rock walkway. He raised his hand to knock on the door, but hesitated. With one more deep breath, he rapped firmly. A muted rustling sounded from behind the door before it was suddenly pulled open. Facing him was an attractive woman possessing brilliant auburn hair and the most peculiar navy-blue eyes he'd ever encountered. Eyes which widened with surprise and joy.

"Brent? Is it really you?"

The first thing he knew, he was wrapped in a warm hug and pulled inside.

"I can't believe it. Brand will be so surprised." She stopped fussing long enough to lean back and look through the door. "Elizabeth didn't come with you?" Then she shouted toward the kitchen, "Brand! Brandon, come here. We've got company."

Brent waited, smiling. Hillary had always been impulsive. Soon she'd settle down and he'd be able to answer her questions. However, his attention was quickly drawn to a tall, blond man with streaks of hair so sun-bleached as to appear almost white. He wore a plaid flannel shirt tucked into buckskin leggings.

Brent chuckled as they shook hands and then awkwardly embraced. He should have known. His brother was always going to reflect a little of both worlds. Brent looked up several inches and quipped, "How've you been, little brother?"

Brand laughed. "Perhaps you should say younger brother, no?"

Hillary clucked impatiently and shooed them both into the kitchen where she and Brand had been eating supper. She set an extra plate on the table and told Brent to help himself to roast beef, beans and fresh-baked corn bread. Brent licked his lips, wondering if he really had to go back to San Carlos and army chow.

Brand asked about Elizabeth, causing Brent to choke. Finally he swallowed and told both of them, "She went to London with her father."

"Wouldn't it be grand?" Hillary rolled her eyes and sighed. "How long will they be gone?"

"I don't know. Several years."

Everyone became suddenly serious about their food.

"How long have you been in Arizona?" Brandon poured more coffee into his cup and cocked his brows, silently questioning if Brent were ready for more.

Brent declined, sending his brother a grateful look for so adeptly changing the subject. "I've been at San Carlos for three or four weeks. Was going to send you a wire, but I kept thinking I'd get up here before now."

"You came with Crook?"

Brent shook his head. Nothing much escaped his brother, or any of the Apaches, for that matter, regardless of the distance and poor communication. "In a way, I guess. He assigned me to be the San Carlos agent."

Brand nodded. "That is good. They have needed someone like you to help the Apaches there."

Brent wondered if Brand had heard anything about Maurice Russell, but decided against asking. His brother was Apache enough to be made uncomfortable by the questions. So, he flushed at the commendation and said, "Yes, well, that's kind of why I'm here tonight. The agency's lost a lot of supplies and come up short several head of cattle on every drive. I've discussed an idea with Major Taylor, and he sees no problem . . ."

Brand prodded, "Yes?"

"Well, I'd like to buy our beef from you and the White Mountain Apaches. Kind of help each other. What do you say?"

Chapter Ten

Brandon McQuade's mouth opened, then closed. He looked at his wife. Their expressions of disbelief turned to smiles.

"What can I say?" Brand shook his head as if still unsure he had heard his brother correctly. "Yes. It would be a perfect arrangement. For all of us. But . . ."

Brent frowned. "But?"

"Our herd is small. Most of them only arrived last month. It will be many more months before we can fulfill a contract."

A long, drawn-out sigh deflated Brent's enthusiasm. "I hadn't thought of that. The agency needs beef in two weeks."

Hillary squirmed in her chair. Finally, when it seemed neither brother was going to add to the conversation, she reached over and grasped Brand's knee. "What about the rancher near Holbrook where you purchased some of the cows? Would he be willing to sell more?"

Brent forced his gaze from Hillary's intimate touch when her hand continued to rest on his brother's leg. His gut wrenched painfully when Brandon looked at his wife with an expression of adoration and utter contentment.

Brent harbored no feelings for Hillary, but he was envious. Envious of the love and intimacy they shared. Maybe he would find that someone special, someday.

Almond-shaped eyes and black curls suddenly danced in his mind's eye—real enough to touch. Hell and damnation. It was true. He was going crazy. Sure enough.

"Brent? Are you all right?"

He blinked when the soft, feminine voice brought him back to the kitchen table. Hillary was leaning forward, her eyes filled with concern. It unnerved him a bit. "Huh? What?"

"You looked like a mule kicked you between the eyes, brother."

"A mule?" That was for certain. But it was his chest that pained him. "No. I'm fine. I was worried about the beef. That's all."

Brand's lips quirked to the left. "Give me a week. Your trip may not have been wasted."

Brent was still shaken, but held out his arm. The two McQuades clasped hands.

Hillary stood up and tossed her long, sienna-colored hair over her shoulder. "Now that you've taken care of the beef," she said with a twinkle in her eye, "who wants gooseberry pie?"

The trip back to San Carlos went faster than Brent had expected. Of course, all he'd been able to think about was the extra day he'd spent with Brand and Hillary, and the improvements Brand had helped the White Mountain Apaches implement on their reservation.

San Carlos had no timber, so a lumber mill was out of the question. But there was no reason, sometime in the near future, why they couldn't raise a few head of their own beef and maybe even breed a good line of horses. Once the San Carlos Apaches learned to cultivate crops, they could plant fields with grass or alfalfa seed for better forage.

It would all take time. Lots of time. And he'd been bothered lately by the desire to be around at the end of that time to see if his suggestions worked. But he'd only reenlisted for two years because of a promise he'd made to his recuperating mother to return to Philadelphia soon. According to her latest letter, though, she was up and around and visiting friends and shopping as if last winter's near-fatal illness was forgotten.

Oh, well, by the time his two years were up, he'd probably be sick to death of the desert and the gnats and bugs and heat.

It was nearing dusk as he rode into the San Carlos compound. Lanterns had already been lit in most of the army quarters and amber spots of light flickered down the rows of tents like well-ordered columns of fireflies. He rode past the little office building. The door and window were closed, and the interior was darker than the ace of spades. Only the mare whickered a greeting, and Brent's U.S. Army mount responded in turn.

It was tempting to stop and tell Lark what his trip had accomplished, but he resolutely spurred the gelding on. Three days. Three nice, peaceful, carefree days he'd spent without one moment of torture from that little, half-Apache . . . woman.

Brent grimaced. No, he hadn't been tortured *once*. It was more like a *hundred* times. Every night. All night. In his dreams. As he lay awake staring through a window at the inky darkness beyond. Every day when he talked about San Carlos and "his" Apaches.

Damn it! He might as well admit it and get it over with. Miss Meadowlark Russell had gotten under his skin. It was true. There was nothing he could—or would—do about it, of course. But now that his dilemma was acknowledged, he could work on exorcising her from his soul.

It would be a task, all right. It would take strength of character and the willpower of a wolverine. Heaven-only-knew it took a lot of both to get as far as he had in the United States Cavalry. With confidence and perseverance—and a little luck—he would one day wonder, "Lark who?"

Hell, he might as well start distancing himself from intimate thoughts of her right now, beginning with the pet name he'd given her. No more *Lark*.

Brent was surprised to find he'd reined up in front of the deserted building. Funny, he'd spent a good deal of time staring at or walking past the place before he left for Fort Apache—almost as if it beckoned, luring him to approach a forbidden object.

He hunched his shoulders and urged his mount toward the barn. A good night's sleep. That was what he needed.

Meadowlark awoke before daylight. As had been the case for several days, she was tense and restless. Captain McQuade had left San Carlos before she had a chance to mention her discovery. She had found a perfect location to start their irrigation project. But the tenseness and restlessness was not just because she was anxious to share her news. There was something else—a sense of . . . foreboding. She huddled beneath the blankets, willing herself to sleep another hour. Unfortunately, her eyes refused to stay closed.

Finally, she threw the covers back, levered her nude body to a sitting position and wriggled into her leather breeches and tunic. For days she had taken great pains with her appearance in an effort to look nice for the captain. Then he left and she had continued the effort with the hope of looking especially attractive on his return.

Tucking a wayward curl behind her ear, she grimaced. The vain tendencies she had suddenly developed galled her to no end. Well, today she just did not care. If he came back to San Carlos now and found her looking as pathetic as a staked-out deer hide, that was fine. She had indulged her foolish whims long enough.

She started a small fire in the ancient wood-burning stove hidden among the shadows in the far back corner. Using a flour ground from piñon nuts, she stirred up biscuits and topped them with thick, sweet clover honey.

Breakfast was eaten and cleared in only a few minutes. She stared outside. The sun had been up almost an hour, and since there was little to do in the office, she decided to take the mare out for exercise. It had been several days because she had been . . . waiting.

The morning air was crisp and cool and Meadowlark took several deep breaths. On the way to the corral, she picked up a braided horsehair hackamore. But when she stepped inside the pole enclosure and started to whistle for the thoroughbred, she stopped abruptly. The corral was empty. The mare was gone.

She stood dazed, incredulous. The horse had been there, in fine condition, when she fed it last night. Then her stomach turned nauseous. Had she forgotten to close the gate? No! She had just opened it on the way inside.

So what could have happened? Sadness clutched her chest. The thoroughbred. The last living extension of her father. And now the mare was gone.

Meadowlark drew another deep breath and forced herself to regain control of her emotions. Look around, she commanded herself. Calm down. Search for a sign. The horse could not have just disappeared.

Quietly, methodically, she searched in and around the corral. Within five minutes she had learned all she needed to know. Scorpion. He had taken the mare. His moccasin tracks were inside the enclosure. And his own mustang left clear prints in the dust where Scorpion had tethered it.

She shook her head and stared at the ground. If he

were going to steal her mare, why had he left so many clues to his identity? Any Apache child could recognize Scorpion's mustang. It had one white hoof, and since a white hoof was softer than black hooves, it had a tendency to dry out and crack in the desert climate. Scorpion's mustang had a crack in its right hind hoof, just like the one in the tracks she found leading south, away from San Carlos. And following the mustang's tracks, were those of her mare.

Her heart throbbed in her ears. Her eyes clouded. The warrior had said he would go to Mexico. Had claimed she would follow. And he was right. But she would only catch up with him and retrieve her mare. Then she would return to San Carlos.

She tightly laced her moccasins and checked to be sure her trusty pouch was tied about her waist. Sticking her arm through the hackamore's headstall and pulling it up to rest on her shoulder, she walked back to the office. A cavalry canteen hung from a beam on the side of the small building. She yanked it down and filled it. Then, chin out, head held straight, she followed the clear imprints of the two horses.

Brent was late. He'd overslept. Yes, for the first night in ages, he'd actually gotten some sleep. Probably because he was bone-tired from his trip and mentally exhausted from hours spent figuring what could be done to help the Apaches survive the next few years.

Then again, he'd been content to be back. To know that this morning he'd see Meadowlark.

He slapped his hat against his leg. Lord, but he was every which kind of a fool. He possessed no gumption or determination to adhere to a vow.

As he berated himself, he noticed one particularly scraggly member of the pack of stray dogs that had taken up residence nearby. It growled and scratched at a loose piece of bark hanging from the old office building. Hound must've cornered a rabbit, Brent figured.

His steps slowed. The next thing he knew, he'd turned and walked over to the door. He reached out, hesitated, then pushed inside.

If he'd expected the office to look the same as when he had first entered over a month ago, he was sadly disappointed. The desk was now overturned. More papers littered the floor. A busted chest of drawers that had served to hold Russell's files blocked the doorway to the next, smaller room.

Suddenly, a sharp yip sounded behind Brent. Startled, his hand dropped to his gun. A frenzied rush of gray cottontail and brown mongrel almost upended him. They plowed through the rubble and raced into the second room. With a bit of a path cleared, Brent followed.

He couldn't explain why he was there, or what he was looking for. A gut instinct told him that there was something pertinent to be found. But for what? He didn't know.

The hound whined at an overturned box. The crate scooted backward and the rabbit took off again. Papers flew in every direction as the room was suddenly vacated by the four-legged critters.

Brent chuckled at their antics and released his hold on the gun butt. Replacing his hat on his head, freeing both hands, he then hunkered down and picked up several of the wrinkled papers. The sun shone directly through the one window, and he held them up to the light one at a time. Most of what he found was dated two years past. Damn! There *had* to be *something.*

He ran his hands beneath scattered leaves and twigs. Nothing. Disgusted, he sat back on his heels and stared at the dust motes dancing in the warm rays. He tilted his head and a bright flash caught his eye. He glanced to the right. The sun shone on a dark lump of something near where the dog had moved the box. Junk. Debris. Everywhere. All evidence that someone else had been interested in the office. Had the person found whatever he—or she—had been searching for?

Brent shrugged and rose to his feet. Gently prodding and lifting papers with the toe of his boot, he started to leave the room. But for some reason he stopped and looked back at what he could now discern as a piece of wood with a long, leather thong attached.

Curiosity got the best of him. Hadn't he examined almost everything else in the room? He couldn't leave without at least looking at the thing.

Bending to one knee, he picked it up and turned it over. It was a carving of some kind. A crucifix. And a rusty stain had soaked into both the wood and the leather. He rubbed it between his fingers. The stain cracked and crumbled from the thong. Blood!

Brent rubbed his forehead with the back of his free hand. A crucifix. There was something familiar about a crucifix. Something he should know. He thought until a dull, throbbing pained both temples. Maybe Lark would know . . .

And then he remembered an interrupted conversation between Meadowlark and Scorpion. She had noticed something about the warrior's crucifix . . . That it was missing! She'd been concerned because it was missing.

Brent's eyes narrowed. He'd found Scorpion snooping around this building, several times. Had the warrior been searching for something? Perhaps the crucifix?

Could the cross have been lost in a struggle? Maybe with Maurice Russell? Did Scorpion know more than he was telling about the agent's death? Or had the adornment been innocently left behind at some earlier date?

Brent paced across the littered flooring. No, Scorpion hadn't even admitted it was lost.

A growing sense of urgency directed Brent's path from the old building toward the one now housing Meadowlark and the agency. When he came to the door, he didn't pause, but pushed directly inside. The office was empty. Everything appeared normal, except Lark's pallet. It was unmade. That was unusual. She always had the room neat and spotless long before now.

He went outside and checked the corral. Empty. He breathed a sigh of relief. She had probably gone for a ride.

Brent still held the exquisitely carved crucifix in his hand. His fingers gripped the object until his knuckles turned white and he grimaced with pain. What would he say to her? He had no proof, but Scorpion's behavior had been strange recently. Possibly, Lark's friend—or lover, or whatever Scorpion was to her—had *something* to do with Maurice Russell's death. It was only another of Brent's instincts—but they seldom failed.

His chest ached as if someone had reached inside and crushed his organs in one giant fist. He was afraid. Afraid of her reaction. Of course Scorpion would deny any guilt. So, who would she believe when it came to choosing between the warrior's word or his? Brent sighed. The answer was simple enough. Scorpion. Who was Brent McQuade, after all, but just another *white* man?

Hell!

Perched on the top pole of the corral, he waited. And waited. About midmorning, he walked over to the corporal standing duty near the guardhouse. The man saluted smartly. Brent returned the motion.

"Mornin', Cap'n."

"At ease, Corporal Bent. Have you been on duty all morning?"

"Yes, sir."

Brent nodded. He'd thought the corporal was there

when he'd first left his quarters. "Have you seen Miss Russell?"

The soldier scratched his head, tilting his cap to the opposite side of his head. "Yes, sir, I have. Real early, it was." He hesitated, then added, "It was funny, Cap'n."

A sinking sensation emptied Brent's stomach. "What was funny?"

"All the goin's-on over there." The corporal shook his head and pointed toward the little office.

Brent strangled on a groan. "Tell me what happened, Bent. Everything. And hurry." There was that tension in his gut again. His "instincts" were working overtime this morning.

Corporal Bent rubbed his chin. "Well, first off, that 'Pache they call, uh, Snake, or Lizard, or—"

"Scorpion?"

The corporal grinned. "Yeah, that's the one."

"Go on, Corporal."

"Uh, yes, sir. Anyway, that Scorpion fella was messin' 'roun' fore daylight over there an' rode off with that there good-lookin' mare." Bent clicked his teeth together. "Sure would like ta have a horse like that'un some day."

"Cor-por-al!" Brent impatiently ground the word out.

The soldier's Adam's apple bobbed in his throat as he nodded. "Well, I would. So would half the reservation. All right! I didn't think anythin' much 'bout it at the time, bein' they's friends an' all, an' ride together a lot. Anyway, a little later, Miss Russell comes out, carryin' her hackamore an' all. She stops real sudden when she see the mare's gone, like she wasn't expectin' it, an' she's all surprised, an' all." He stopped and swallowed.

Brent tapped his foot in the loose sand.

"Well, she bends down an' looks all aroun' the ground an' walks all over the place like that. Real funny, it was. Then she grabs down a canteen an' takes off on foot in the same direction as that 'Pache. That way. South. Ain't that funny, Cap'n?"

"Hmmm." Distracted by the disturbing information, Brent started toward the barns. Suddenly, he stopped and called back, "Thanks, Corporal. Keep an eye on the agency, will you?"

The soldier beamed. "Shore will, Cap'n, sir."

By the time Brent reached the barns, he was almost running. Fear gripped his heart. But the faster he tried to hurry, the more clumsy he became until he finally stopped and took a deep draught of air.

Stupid woman! What was her idea of going off across the desert afoot and alone? When he caught up with her, and he *would,* he was going to tan that golden hide of hers, but good.

Something bit into his palm. He looked down. The crucifix. Quickly, he stuffed it into his saddlebag and ordered a private to fetch him a fast gelding. He saddled the horse himself, then rode back to the office where he picked up Lark's barely visible tracks and those of Scorpion's mustang and the mare.

He waved at the corporal and thanked the Lord for busybody soldiers around a quiet headquarters who had nothing better to do with their time than watch after everyone else's business.

Meadowlark plodded on. The sun shone down from straight overhead. She was hot, yet the air was cool enough for the breeze to dry her perspiration. Opening the canteen, she washed a sip of water around her mouth, then let it trickle down her throat. It was tepid, but tasted wonderful.

She closed her eyes and thanked the spirits of the desert and the sky for giving her the strength and power to continue. Although she did not appreciate the circumstances of her outing, she was nonetheless grateful for the opportunity to escape the oppression of the reservation.

After replacing the canteen, she started forward and tripped over a partially buried root. She laughed. Were not the Apache known for their grace and agility? The slight tingling in her big toe reminded her how glad she was to have been wearing her high-topped moccasins.

The Apaches had adapted their footwear for desert use. The sole was one thick, hard piece of leather, curled up in the front to protect the toes in case of such clumsiness, or for when they were caught in really rough terrain. She had to admit that the moccasins made her feet look large, but they were very practical.

The sun moved farther across the sky. She stumbled up and down rolling hills, through thick mesquite and chaparral. Perspiration trickled down her neck and back and between her breasts. Cactus needles tore at her breeches.

Twice she stopped to rest. Each time she drank one mouthful of water and spit out enough in her palms to dampen her cheeks. Her skin was dry and sunburned and tingled painfully when she touched it.

Sunflower seeds and piñon nuts assuaged her hunger. She did not wish to stop long enough to build a fire or search for more filling food.

Traveling across fairly clear spaces, she would increase her pace to an easy, ground-covering jog. Most of the time, though, she dodged gangly ocotillo and avoided the shade of huge boulders, especially now, during the heat of the day. That was another Apache artifice. Wherever there was shade on the desert, that was where one would find an enemy.

Thinking of the desert and the means to survive kept her mind off Scorpion and her growing anger toward the warrior. He had intended that she follow him, and to her ire, she was doing exactly that. But when she caught up with the man, which she expected to do by early morning, he would be one very surprised Apache. He was about to learn the error of stealing from Meadowlark Russell.

The sun dipped toward the horizon. A muted reddish-orange glow permeated the western horizon. Her feet ached. Every muscle was sore. It had been a long time since she had punished her body to such an extent—probably since the last time she and Scorpion had played as children.

A grin crinkled her flushed face as she sat atop a narrow ridge and leaned her back against a flat-surfaced rock. She had driven her mother crazy begging to learn the exciting ways of the warriors rather than a woman's drudgery.

It did not matter to her that the woman was the most important unit of the family and owned the most possessions. She still wanted to be a warrior, to experience the thrill of the raid.

Meadowlark's stomach grumbled. She searched the pouch strapped around her waist and sated her hunger on beef jerky, wild onions and more nuts, washed down with another sip of precious water. Oh, she knew where to find the lifesaving liquid if necessary, but wanted to travel quickly, avoiding the detours Scorpion would have to take because of the horses.

She had finally figured out where he was headed. To a bend along the Gila River. There was a glade where grass grew thick and plentiful. Few bushes had thorns. The sycamore and cottonwoods were stately and tall.

Curling against the rock, she watched the twinkle and glitter as more stars became visible. The night was so clear that even a quarter moon enabled her to make out the varied shapes in her surroundings. She loved this time of evening, when the day creatures retreated to safe havens and the denizens of the night began to make their presence known. She had been taught to know the sounds and movements of the desert at night and was not afraid.

Soon, her lids began to droop, her breath deep and even, blending with the soft soughing of the breeze. Yet even as sleep claimed her, her last thought was to wonder if Captain McQuade had returned from his mysterious trip.

Brent nodded in the saddle. He caught himself and wearily dismounted to lead the gelding a ways, but it was too dark to see the trail well.

He felt a distinct queasiness in his stomach every time he thought of Lark on the desert—alone. For the past hour he'd been able to tell she was tiring. Her tracks were deeper, scuffing sand as she took each step.

And he was amazed, horrified, and proud as hell of the little lady. He'd been horseback and had yet to catch up to her. Every hour he'd expected to top the next rise and see her below, unconscious, suffering from sunstroke and exhaustion. She would awaken in his arms, smiling and grateful that he had come to her rescue.

Then his dream would vanish like the desert mirage. The closer he came, the farther away it seemed before it disappeared into nothingness.

He'd purposely kept his horse to a sedate pace to be sure he didn't lose her tracks. Also, if he happened upon her and she needed medical attention, the animal would have to be rested enough to carry them both—quickly, and for a long distance. But he'd never thought he wouldn't overtake her by now.

A short time ago, the tracks he'd been following had divided. The two horses had turned onto a dim trail heading south. Lark's moccasin prints had angled more to the west. He'd chosen to follow Meadowlark because of fear for her safety. Some good it had done.

There was no use in beating a dead horse. He had to stop.

The first thing he did before settling into camp was to share a portion of his sparse water with his horse. The gelding was the most important part of the team to keep fit right now. Then he hobbled the animal so it could feed on nearby clumps of grass.

A fire would be risky since he didn't know the situation with Scorpion or other renegades in the area. So he made a dry camp and ate jerky and hardtack for supper. Reclining on the hard ground, he chewed the tough repast and came to the conclusion that it was a lousy way to spend the night.

Just before he dozed, a star fell. He made a wish, then smiled, wondering if it would ever come true. In his dreams, maybe. Only in his dreams.

Meadowlark arrived at the glade about midmorning the next day. The Gila River flowed lazily between cottonwood trees and salt cedar bushes wearing their winter colors of grays and browns. In another month, the weather would warm and green buds would begin to appear, making the spot a summer wonderland of thick grass and tall trees, compared to the beige sand and thorn-spiked shrubs of the desert.

The analogy caused her to think of the changes in her relationship with Scorpion and the budding feelings taking root in her heart for Brent McQuade. Like his name and the desert, Scorpion had lain waste to her trust with one swift decision to go completely against her wishes. Yet she could never imagine such an occurrence with the captain. He almost tried too hard to please and to make others happy.

A sudden gust of wind blew sand in her eyes and she blinked, bringing her thoughts back to the clearing. She scanned the small area, watching for signs of an approaching rider.

She had expected to arrive before Scorpion, and sighed with relief that she had. After all of the hours spent walking and thinking and cursing, she needed time to figure out just how to confront the man she had always considered her best friend. Until now.

What ghastly revenge should she extract? He had been unusually cruel, leaving her afoot. She was determined to let him know how deeply she resented his childish behavior.

Meadowlark sat on the edge of the riverbank, dangled her aching feet in the cold water and waited. She sniffed. All she really wanted was to get her mare and go back to San Carlos.

Suddenly, a warm breath huffed against her chest. Her muscles tensed. Her eyes flew open, but she did not move. She realized she must have drifted to sleep, but what had startled her? She was ready to bolt until she saw that the interloper was the big thoroughbred.

And then she saw Scorpion. He sat on his mustang, grinning like a triumphant warlord she had once read of in one of her father's books. Her anger flared to rage. The gall of the man! She slid away from the mare so as not to startle it and leapt to her feet. She yanked the horse's lead from the warrior's hand.

"You have done a foolish thing."

A smug expression blanketed Scorpion's face. "You come. We go Mexico."

She pierced him with a look as sharp and dangerous as the knife he always carried. "No! I will not go with you. All I want is my horse."

Suddenly Scorpion scowled. His eyes narrowed to dangerous slits. "I make you go."

Meadowlark's pride would not allow her to back down, though she knew it would be futile to fight the taller, stronger warrior. "Where is the honor in forcing me to go? But try if you must." She hoped she had been successful in keeping her hurt and surprise from showing in her voice.

What was wrong with Scorpion lately? He had never behaved in such an aggressive, intimidating manner before. Her beloved friend was beginning to frighten her.

Scorpion slid off the back of his mustang and started toward Meadowlark. Despite herself, she backed up a step.

He sneered, "You would fight me?"

She held her chin high and met his eyes. "Yes."

"Well, well. Looks like the lost is found."

Scorpion and Meadowlark both jerked around at the sound of the voice. With a sense of the familiar, Meadowlark's wild gaze fastened on the tall captain limping into the clearing and leading a lame horse. She heard Scorpion's hissed intake of air, but could not budge her eyes from the dusty, beautiful Brent McQuade. His was a commanding presence, straightforward and honest. . . .

Her heart literally felt like it jumped up and down. The stiffness that had held her body erect in front of Scorpion's threatening countenance now deserted her to leave in its stead a weak, trembling sensation. Despising such frailty, she shook her head and demanded, "Why are you here?"

Brent hunched his shoulders. She sounded angry—at *him.* He wasn't the one who stole her damned horse and made her walk all those miles. It was he, Brent, who'd spent the last two hours tromping on foot, after his horse had bruised the sole of its hoof, to make sure her little hide was still in one piece.

Well, hell, Brent thought, so much for the care and concern. "I came after you. That's why."

She grimaced. He was angry. His voice was low and soft, yet she detected the underlying steel resolve. And then it occurred to her—he had followed her. Again she asked, "Why?"

Unable to admit to one truth, Brent thought up another. "To keep you from makin' a big mistake. Get on that horse. We're all goin' back. Now."

She'd had every intention to return. Was even going to risk Scorpion's friendship to do so. But that white soldier had the gall to order her around like she was a mindless infant, as if she belonged to him, or something. "I will not go back to San Carlos with you." All the while she spoke, an undeniable thrill tingled along her spine. Belong to *him?*

Both men eyed her suspiciously. She had turned them both down. Just what did she plan to do?

Brent dropped the reins and stalked forward as well as he was able with a foot full of blisters. "Oh, yes, you will."

Scorpion grumbled so deep that it resembled more of a growl. He stepped forward to block Brent's path, but Meadowlark stopped him with a touch of her hand. "No. We will go."

She chanced a glance in the warrior's direction and was surprised to find his face registering the astonishment he must be feeling at her sudden change of mind. Her declaration had stunned Scorpion and she knew he would feel weakened for revealing his emotions. She softened her expression and tried to communicate her understanding to her Apache friend before turning to glare at Brent, warning him to keep his distance. Maybe if she and Scorpion left and ignored the pesky soldier, he would go away—disappear—give her some peace.

But Scorpion was not ready to leave. "White soldier interfere too much."

Sensing Scorpion's perilous frame of mind, Meadowlark held onto his arm. "No. Please. There is no need to fight."

To Brent, she pleaded, "Go away. We do not want trouble."

Some of Brent's initial rage had cooled. He thought more rationally. "Trouble's all you'll get if you run now. The government doesn't take kindly to renegades these days."

Meadowlark sucked in her breath. It had never occurred to her to think of what her leaving the reservation so suddenly would look like to the soldiers.

Brent's eyes narrowed on the warrior who stood straight and still as a wooden statue beneath Meadowlark's restraining hand. "Scorpion can go to South America for all I care. But *you,* little lady, are comin' with me."

Meadowlark bristled. There he went again. Throwing around orders. And he called her "little lady." Little lady? The captain might just as well have stepped on an angry rattlesnake. "No." She said the word quietly. The challenge lay between them like a honey tree between two starving bears.

Brent scowled. Damned stubborn, hardheaded shecat. He should turn around and leave, right now. It would serve her right. Why should he care if she ruined her life with Scorpion? Disgust welled in his chest because he wouldn't let her go. He couldn't.

Meadowlark was so furious she was incapable of movement. Brent stood with his hands fisted on his hips, glaring at her. Scorpion took advantage of the captain's distraction and drew his knife. Two long strides carried him close to Brent's right side.

Brent only saw the flash of white teeth in a snarl more feral than any wild animal's. Before he had a chance to go for his gun, a sharp blade stabbed deep into his shoulder.

Instinctively, he jerked back, wincing as the knife wrested free of his flesh. His muscles tensed and flexed. He crouched and lunged, levering his left shoulder into Scorpion's midsection. Scorpion was knocked backward, but not off his feet, as the air was blasted from his lungs.

Blood dripped from Brent's useless arm. He blinked, focusing on Scorpion. The warrior danced in and out of Brent's line of vision as his own movements became too slow, too cumbersome. He shook his head to clear the perspiration from his eyes. Suddenly, a blurry shadow loomed in close—too close. He raised his left hand. The descending blade knicked the flesh of his palm before he grasped Scorpion's wrist. His dwindling strength channeled into his left side as he pushed and strained to keep the knife from plunging into his chest.

Suddenly Scorpion's weight shifted as he hooked the back of Brent's knees with his leg, forcing the captain onto his back. The deadly point of the knife hovered over Brent's chest.

"No!" Meadowlark screamed and threw herself between the captain and the blade. "Do not kill him!"

Chapter Eleven

Meadowlark fell to her knees and placed her own body across Captain McQuade's chest. "No! Do not kill him!" Her eyes met Scorpion's. "Please!"

Startled by her impassioned plea and by how narrowly he had missed putting his knife in Meadowlark's delicate back, Scorpion hesitated. The glazed lust to kill gradually faded from his eyes.

Angered as much by his own weakness as by Meadowlark's dangerously impulsive act, Brent struggled feebly, attempting to remove her from harm's path. "Get up, woman," he panted. "This . . . is . . . t'ween me . . . an' . . . him."

Meadowlark's heart beat faster than a hummingbirds's wings. Those blue eyes were so pale it was frightening. Instead of glowing with mischief, they were dull and glazed with pain. Something warm and wet tickled her arm and she looked down to see blood steadily pumping from his wound.

She gasped. Unbearable sorrow knifed through her chest. Scorpion leaned over her shoulder, ready to finish what he had started and she savagely shoved him aside. Quickly, she untied the captain's bandana and folded it, then pressed it to the wound. In no time at all, it seemed, it was stained brilliant red. She jerked out her own knife and began to loosen Brent's belt.

Scorpion hissed a guttural response to her action, but she ignored him and pulled out the captain's shirttail.

Cutting a wide strip of material, she held it over the already saturated bandana.

She leaned her weight into the compress and was eventually gratified to see the bleeding diminish. The captain's eyes blinked closed, then opened again. The dimple to the left of his mouth was prominent for a fleeting moment and her heart constricted. The backs of her eyes burned and she blinked rapidly.

Suddenly, she was jerked to her feet. Scorpion's fingers dug painfully into her shoulder. He bent his face close to hers. "Now, we go."

Meadowlark shook her head. She could not leave the captain like this. Yet she could not bring herself to admit, or even acknowledge, the reason why. It delved into emotions much stronger than those needed to stay and tend a man's wound.

When she remained silent, Scorpion's eyes narrowed with venom. He moved toward the captain, the bloody knife held menacingly in his hand. Meadowlark cried out, "All right! All right."

But when she glanced back down to the captain, she was dismayed to find him trying to rise. She leaned a hand on his chest and forced him to lie back. Then she looked to Scorpion and demanded, "Give me your headband."

Scorpion stiffened. He glared at the downed soldier. "Best white man die now."

Meadowlark sprang to her feet. She swung on Scorpion. "I have said I will go. But first give me your band to tie the pad in place." Acknowledging the captain's earlier words as truth, she hissed through clenched teeth, "We will have enough trouble without answering for his murder."

Grudgingly, Scorpion unwound the red cloth from his head. It had been doubled around and tied with the ends dangling down the back of his long, brown hair.

Meadowlark held her breath as she lifted the captain's shoulders, praying the cloth would be long enough to wrap around his broad width. She shuddered when the movement elicited a muffled groan from the injured man. As gently as possible, she bound his right arm, pad and all, to his chest and then lowered him back to the ground. A moan of thanks cut into her heart and she quickly turned her head. If either man saw her expression just then . . .

Brent's good arm lifted slightly. His fingers curled around her wrist. "Don't go."

His voice was the barest of raspy whispers and Meadowlark feared she would keel over with despair. How could she leave him so weak and helpless?

In one fluid motion, Scorpion took the decision from her control. He flipped his knife, caught it by the blade and suddenly bent down and rapped Brent on the side of the head with the heavy bone handle, knocking him unconscious.

Meadowlark cried out and flailed at the warrior with her fists. He easily held her at bay with one hand while he sheathed his knife, then caught both of her arms. His glance raked the white man. "Best this way. He no follow."

Her head fell back and she gazed into the cloudless sky that so reminded her of the eyes now hidden beneath closed lids. Yes, in one respect, Scorpion was right. It was best that the captain did not see them leave.

At least he lived. She could see the uneven rise and fall of his great chest even as she walked to her mare.

Resignedly, she mounted the horse and reined in next to the warrior, a friend who had become a stranger. She looked back once at the inert form of Brent McQuade, then turned her head and followed Scorpion away from the river.

She did not look back again. If she did, she knew she would never leave. And it would cost the captain his life. Her eyes darted quickly to Scorpion's tense features.

Brent McQuade blinked. He tried to completely raise his eyelids, but opening them to the bright sunlight caused excruciating explosions to reverberate through his head. But there was something important in the back of his mind prodding, urging him to remember.

Again he tried to open his eyes. Somewhat successful this time, he was shocked to discover that he lay flat on his back, on the ground, peering through the criss-crossed branches of bare cottonwoods, or maybe sycamores. Suddenly, the trees began to dip and sway. His forehead felt as if someone was taking an ax and chopping the bone into a million tiny fragments.

He forced his eyes closed. Who cared what kind of trees they were? His head hurt. His body ached. It felt as if he were being held down by a thousand-pound weight.

Taking short, even breaths, he tried to think, to remember. His mind might as well have been swimming through a muddied pond. Where in the hell was he? Why was he lying on the ground? And why couldn't he get up? As hard as he tried, he could not force his muscles to respond.

He blinked again. A moist sheen coated his eyes. He'd never felt so helpless or lost or vulnerable in his life. Damnation!

Drifting in and out of wakefulness, every once in a while he heard noises. A jingle. Sometimes a snort. And an eerie sound of something slurping water. He licked his lips. Water. It was so hot. He was so thirsty. Burning up. Water.

His lids crept open over eyes that felt like sandpaper. He started to turn on his right side. A sudden pain stabbed his body. He almost cried out. Stabbed. Then he remembered. Everything.

Fear for Meadowlark's safety. Trailing her. The unbelievable anguish of finding Meadowlark and Scorpion together. Scorpion's attack. Meadowlark's body protecting his. The two of them riding off together. Hell!

Oh yes, he recalled everything.

But still, there was something else. Another reason he'd driven himself to find her. He maneuvered around until he came up against an old tree stump. Nausea churned his stomach. He felt faint from the pain. Finally, he managed to raise his upper body to a sitting position.

Something sticky trickled down his rib cage. He'd reopened the wound.

Then he heard a noise. A jingle. A soft thud. He tried to reach his gun belt. Couldn't. A vertebra in his neck popped when he jerked around to see what, or who, was there. He sighed and slumped against the stump. The gelding. It was a wonder the horse hadn't followed the others when they left. Thank the Lord it must've been more concerned with filling its belly, he thought.

Lord! The crucifix! Damn! And Meadowlark! He had to warn her.

Brent struggled until he got to his feet, unmindful that the trickle of blood increased to a rivulet.

How long had he been out? How far could they have gotten? Why'd she go with Scorpion? Did she love the warrior *that* much?

Concentrating on placing one foot in front of the other, he started for the horse. The animal stood near the river. It wasn't far. Just a few more steps. If he just wasn't so light-headed. And if whoever was using his head for a war drum didn't quit beating on it soon, he'd go insane.

Crazy, all right. Look at that crazy horse. Why was it looking at him as if he were some kind of monster? Had to catch the horse.

Brent staggered. His knees buckled. It felt as if he fell through layer after layer of thick clouds as he descended into total blackness. Down. Down.

The last thing he saw was the horse shying away. Damn.

Scorpion rode hard and fast. He followed arroyos and kept to depressions whenever possible. Meadowlark trailed behind, her mind and body numb. Once, when they had stopped to rest the horses, she had asked Scorpion why he had attacked the captain without warning. He had looked at her as if she were foolish to think he could have done anything else.

Her eyes now bored into the warrior's narrow back, burnt the color of ironwood. It made her sick at heart and stomach to even look at the man—the man she had so admired and adored, thought to someday wed. He had performed a coward's act. Brent McQuade had fought like the true warrior, though he never had a chance.

Meadowlark's spine stiffened. The captain had never quit trying to survive, even in his weakened condition. He had been magnificent. Her chin dropped to her chest. Surely by now he was dying. With no one to tend the wound, it would become infected. He might even have reopened the wound and could be bleeding to death.

She pulled her mare to a halt. No matter what she had promised Scorpion, he no longer deserved her loyalty. She had to go back. Somehow, she would keep the captain alive. A man that strong and with such a will to survive could not die. And Scorpion would never threaten Brent McQuade again.

Riding a few yards ahead, Scorpion suddenly stopped. He turned to stare at her, probably wondering what was holding her back.

Meadowlark stuck her chin out, determined to confront him. Then her eyes widened. Scorpion had gone pale as a ghost. His mouth gaped. But he was not looking toward her. His gaze was directed over her shoulder, to the edge of the narrow gully.

The hair on the nape of Meadowlark's neck stood on end. Slowly, she turned her head. Mounted above and behind them were two Apache scouts and a troop of soldiers. It appeared that, for the moment, they were just as surprised at encountering the two riders as Meadowlark and Scorpion were to see them.

Calling for Meadowlark to follow closely, Scorpion bent low over his mustang's neck and kicked the horse into a run. A bullet whizzed past Meadowlark's ear and she wasted no time in sending the big mare in swift pursuit. The soldiers meant business. Deadly business.

As they raced down the arroyo, Meadowlark's mind worked furiously, planning a way to escape Scorpion *and* the army. The arroyo opened onto a narrow plain that literally disappeared in the distance. A cliff? Had the spirits recognized her dilemma and come to her aid?

Scorpion reined his horse off to the right. She heard the clatter of shod hooves striking stones and gravel, coming fast behind. Taking a deep breath, she kept the mare traveling straight. The gallant animal never faltered, never balked, though it must have sensed what was ahead. Meadowlark began to feel more confident about her decision.

She risked a quick glance over her shoulder. Only one scout was on her trail. The rest followed Scorpion.

All at once, the mare stumbled, but gathered its legs under it again as the ground became more uneven. Meadowlark gulped, hoping that what lay ahead would not kill them both.

Then the earth disappeared. Meadowlark sucked in her breath. For a few seconds, it seemed they floated on air and Meadowlark imagined what an eagle must see, soaring high on spread wings. But her wings collapsed quickly. The mare's hooves struck ground with a bone-jarring impact. Over and over, they bounced and careened down an almost perpendicular incline. Cactus and creosote tore at the mare's legs and sides and scratched over Meadowlark's breeches.

Behind her, she heard an oath and a grunt. A small avalanche of stones caught up with them and rolled faster and faster down the slope. Dust swirled beneath the mare's feet and clogged Meadowlark's eyes and nose. She literally clung to the horse—her fingers curled so tightly in the red mane that the coarse hair cut into her hands; her legs clamped so tightly around the horse's barrel that her thighs and calves cramped from the unfamiliar pressure.

Then she looked up and caught her breath. In front of them, looming like a forbidding monster, rose fallen stalks and spines of several soapweed yucca that formed a barricade three or four feet high. It was too late to turn.

The thoroughbred's body trembled. Hard muscles bunched beneath Meadowlark's legs. The mare sat on its haunches, trying to slow the rapid descent. It was impossible.

Meadowlark closed her eyes, doubled over and buried her face in the horse's sweaty neck. She gripped the huge animal as a puma would sink its claws into prey to keep it from escaping. Yucca blades sliced at Meadowlark's leather-clad legs and the horse's tender belly. The mare snorted and Meadowlark felt the hide flinch and ripple from its bowed neck to its tautly stretched flanks as the great thoroughbred lifted its magnificent body high in the air. It seemed they hung suspended for hours, only to land on the other side amid a series of teeth-rattling bounces, and before racing across the rolling hills.

With no direction from its master, the mare snorted and shortened its strides and its pace. Meadowlark sighed and straightened. She took several deep breaths that seemed to coincide with the droughts sucked in by the horse.

At last, reining to a stop, she slid from the foam-flecked, trembling animal. She looked behind and up the face of a canyon wall that appeared so steep and rough as to be impossible to climb, or descend. Several hundred yards away stumbled a riderless mount that acted as if it were as dazed and surprised to be alive as she. There was no sign of its rider. Elation trembled through Meadowlark. She had escaped.

Meadowlark looked northward, in the direction of the Gila River and the glade they had left behind. She turned her back on the mountain, willing herself not to think of the past few minutes and began walking. When the mare cooled, then she would ride.

Her insides quickened. What would she find when

she reached the river? Would Brent McQuade be alive? Or dead?

Meadowlark muttered Apache curses under her breath as she neared the little vale where she and Scorpion had left the captain. Sundown was fast approaching. Two hours. It had taken two hours of constant riding, watching the trail ahead and glancing over her shoulder to make certain she was not being followed. Two hours from the bottom of . . . She shuddered and patted the mare's neck. Their rapid descent down the cliff seemed more and more like a horrid nightmare.

She tried to swallow, but found it difficult. Brent McQuade had been living his own nightmare—if he had survived. Had he called upon some power to . . .

A horse nickered. The captain's army gelding limped from a row of salt cedars. The horse's bedraggled appearance and gaunted flanks were not reassuring. Her eyes shot directly to the spot where she'd left the wounded man. She choked down a gasp. Her heart attempted to take flight.

Rust-colored sand denoted where his body had lain. Otherwise, the ground was bare. Scanning the area like a long-horned owl, she looked over her left shoulder and examined the ground in a sweeping gaze that ended over her right shoulder. Letting her eyes sweep back again, she searched desperately for some sign of the captain's whereabouts.

Sliding from the mare's back, she bent low, looking for a track, a drop of blood, anything. The hairs on the back of her neck prickled when she discovered two drops of blood beside the imprint of a white man's boot.

The tracks led her through a clump of sage, around a prickly cholla and onto the sandy river bank. Her chest caved toward her spine, crushing her heart. The captain lay still as death, awkwardly sprawled with his face down alongside the river, one side of his long body submerged by water.

His ghost-pale face was turned toward her, his long, callused fingers clutched limply around a piece of driftwood. But was he alive? Years of being taught to fear the dead slowed her steps, but something else, some unknown force drew her cautiously forward. A sudden burning sensation blurred her eyes. Her heart cried to find such a strong, vital man lying so still and lifeless.

Still, several feet away from the body, she sank to her knees. Was life itself not strange? She had known the captain but a short while, had only been able to abide him less time than that—much less. Yet she felt a sense of loss—of heart-stopping grief—of timeless emptiness. Why? He was a white man. A white *soldier* at that.

Ripples of water lapped against his side, washed over his pant leg, covered most of his right side. Alive, or dead, she had to get him out of there.

Reluctantly, she rose to her feet and crept closer. Flies scattered before her. Shudders racked her body. Images of her father hovered overhead like hungry buzzards. She gulped, choked, and bent to take hold of his jacket.

"Lark."

Instantly she dropped the stiff material. Scared breathless, she rubbed at her fingers as if she had touched hot coals and scanned the sky. Who had spoken? Afraid, yet curious, she studied the river and the brush-lined bank. The voice had floated softly around her, not seeming to have come from anywhere.

"Oh-h-h, Lark."

She felt her eyes widen. She scrambled backward, caught her heel on a root and sat down hard on her backside. Her eyes scoured every barren branch, every bush. Satisfied she was truly alone—no owls, no ghosts—she turned her gaze to the only person who had ever called her *Lark*.

He lay motionless. His eyes were still closed. His lips did not appear to have moved. But there was a scary bluish tint to his skin. He must be dead. Yet there had been a voice. What if the sound . . .

One of his eyelids flickered. She gasped and scooted

back, digging into the sand with her feet. It had flickered. Just barely. It was an almost imperceptible movement. But she had seen it. She had.

Joy and excitement bubbled through her veins. She quickly crawled over and very gently raised his head off the cold sand. His skin was cold and clammy, yet the fact that he was alive at all was a veritable gift from the spirits. The river had taken his body and returned it to her.

Meadowlark dragged his inert body as far as the salt cedars. She carefully removed the pads and binding she had improvised earlier and was shocked to find the wound was not as red or angry-looking as she had expected it to be.

When he had fallen, his right side had landed in the river. Evidently, the cold water had kept the wound from becoming inflamed and had helped to stop the bleeding. She figured that was the only reason he had survived.

But right now he was shivering from the effects of his wet clothing and the cool breeze. He needed warmth and something to treat the gaping gash in his flesh. And they both needed shelter. The night would be cold and she already felt an unnatural flush in his forehead and cheeks. A severe fever in his weakened condition could be deadly.

A sudden chill rioted down her spine. She had to quit thinking in terms of "death." He was alive, and if it was possible, she would see to it he remained that way for a long time to come.

She rose to her feet and brushed her palms together. There was a lot to do before darkness settled in.

First, she should get him out of his uniform. Her hands were gentle, but quick, as she removed his boots, loosened buttons and peeled off articles of his heavy, scratchy clothing. Raised to feel there was nothing unusual or out of the ordinary about a naked body, she was not shy about touching him.

Yet, as she stripped the captain, she found herself admiring the perfection of his lean form. His muscles were thick and prominent, but not as bulky as those of

Apache warriors. And surprisingly, she even found his pale flesh attractive.

Continuing to work quickly and efficiently, she tried, but could not keep from becoming distracted, especially by the fine, curly mat of blond hairs coating his chest and tapering down his flat belly. Heat suffused her breast and rose up her neck to fill her cheeks. He was very, very masculine. Especially in a particular section of his anatomy. She blinked, unable to believe she was actually blushing.

Laying his clothing aside, she hurriedly fetched his bedroll and smoothed it out. By gently lifting and prodding, she finally coaxed him onto one half of the tarp. Satisfied, she used the other half to cover him before gathering twigs and limbs to build a fire.

She found a tin cup and small but deep pan in his saddlebags, filled them both with water from the river and set them on flat rocks next to the flames. Then she untied the pouch from her waist and searched through various pieces of leather which were carefully wrapped and folded around their precious contents.

From one packet she extracted dried safflowers and added them to the water in the cup. From the next she took a piece of root and dried leaves. She found another flat rock and a smaller round one, and began to mash the jimsonweed until it made a thick poultice.

While the safflowers steeped, she used the warm water in the pan to rinse the wound, then smoothed on the poultice. The gash seeped a small amount of blood, but his flesh appeared clean of fragments of material and dirt.

Her own flesh suddenly prickled. She glanced at his face and found his eyes open. The usual deep blue was murky and his pupils were dilated with the glassy sheen of fever. She smothered a curse.

"Lark." His uninjured arm lifted slightly.

She instinctively sensed the effort it cost him to move and bent closer to him. His fingers caressed her cheek. A tear burst through the invisible dam her heart had been diligently constructing ever since she had found him.

His finger captured the small droplet and she caught her breath. Together, they stared in wonder at the evidence of her emotions. His touch had been so gentle that it reached way down inside of her, drawing out feelings she had been taught since childhood to keep hidden away.

Silently, her mind screamed, No! He was a white man. She was Apache. His skin was light, hers dark. He was a man—she a woman.

His eyes closed and did not reopen. She was able to breathe again. She was frustrated and angry with herself. He was a very attractive white man, almost irresistibly so. She could not take her eyes from his face.

He had a kind face. Tiny, pale lines circled the edges of his eyes and mouth, indicating he was a man used to squinting through bright rays of sunshine and laughing at whatever adversities or pleasures the spirits saw fit to place in his path.

In repose, he had a definite manly quality about him. There was nothing boyish about Capt. Brent McQuade.

Suddenly, she blinked and scooted back as if he had reached out and seared her to the soul. She remembered the haunted look that entered his eyes now and then. More often than not, when he touched her, or seemed to be getting close . . . What—or who—could have caused him such pain?

Meadowlark shook her head and moved away from the man's disturbing presence. She checked the safflower mixture, nodded, and carried it to where he lay. "Captain? B-Brent? Can you hear me? Open your eyes."

He did, barely, and grinned. She sucked in her breath at the sight of the dimple. Her free hand shook slightly as it sifted through the thick layers of soft hair at the back of his neck. She gulped a quick breath of air and offered him the cup.

"You must drink this for your fever." Her voice

sounded clipped and harsh, even to her own ears. She frowned when his features hardened.

"I'm . . . fine. Can't . . . drink."

He tried to turn his head away, but her fingers tightened on his neck. She concentrated on making her command more gentle, coaxing. "You can drink. Do not act the baby."

He blinked. His eyes opened wider. There was a new spark of life in them. She smiled and held the cup to his lips, then winced when she noticed for the first time how parched and cracked they were.

Brent gagged and sputtered, "Ugh!"

She was relentless. "Drink it all."

It took several repetitions of the process, but she managed to get the entire cup, minus a dribble or two, past his clenched teeth. When she laid it aside, she also removed her hand from the back of his head. Then in an oddly compulsive gesture for her, Meadowlark brushed that one enticing, irresistible lock of hair from his forehead.

Brent's lids drooped in an unconsciously seductive manner as he gazed at her. He caught her wrist in his left hand and tugged her close. "Th-thank . . . you-u-u."

The last word was a whispered puff of breath that blew the fine strands of hair from in front of her ear. She shivered, but sat quietly, allowing him to hold her hand until his fingers relaxed and she pulled free without waking him.

She stood looking down at the captain, torn by a pain in her chest so strong that it felt like her heart was being ripped from her body. One part of her yearned to cradle his poor injured body to her breast, the other longed to sprint to the mare, leap upon the broad, powerful back and ride like an army of ghosts was on her trail.

The last thought was so appealing that she drifted in the horse's direction until she happened to notice the angle of the sun. She could not leave. Her conscience would not allow it. And she had only a short time to construct a shelter and take careof the animals for the night.

Since the horses were foraging nearby, she decided to use the fading light to build a makeshift wickiup close to where Brent lay. Luckily, there was a rounded area bare of growth that could comfortably fit two people. Standing in the center of the cleared space, she pulled the young, slender branches of the salt cedar trees toward her and wove them together, leaving a small open space at the top. The effect was a crude, dome shape that she reinforced by winding through smaller, thinner branches to close the open places. She also left a narrow doorway, facing the east.

Once the shelter met with her satisfaction, she entered, remaining slightly stooped as the roof was not very high. Again she moved to the center and knelt to scrape a hole in the sand which she lined with rocks and filled with kindling. The opening she had left at the top would allow smoke to escape and she and Brent would sleep in warmth during the night.

Suddenly uncomfortable with the thought of spending the night in such close proximity, even though the man was nearly unconscious, Meadowlark exited the wickiup. The sun was gone except for a few remnants of orange and lavender that tinted the clouds along the horizon.

She sat by the fire and watched the rest of the sunset. All of a sudden her body began to tremble. Adding more sticks to the small blaze, she scooted closer to the warmth. She had been so busy seeing after the captain and setting up camp that the magnitude of everything that had happened in such a short space of time was just beginning to seep into her consciousness.

It seemed she had only sat down for a few minutes, but when she glanced back toward Brent, a shiver raced along her nerve endings. She cursed her weakness and stupidity for not checking on him sooner. Sometime during the past hour he had tossed off the tarp and now trembled with violent chills. A grimace turned down her lips as she wondered how she was going to get him inside the shelter. She bent down and gently shook his shoulder. "Brent, wake up. I need help."

She sensed that pleading for his help was the one certain way to focus his attention. And she was right. His eyes popped open, though she could tell he actually saw very little. "Stand up, Captain. You have to move to the wickiup."

His head lolled to the side and he looked toward the brush hut. She thought a glimmer of surprise darkened his eyes. He licked his lips and nodded. She nearly bit through the inside of her cheek at the agony flickering across his already strained features. But he did not complain. She felt a glow of pride for him.

It took time and some patient maneuvering but, finally, Brent got to his knees. He felt sweat drip from his temples and his clenched jaw. The pain in his chest and arm he could stand, but having Meadowlark see him so helpless and weak was agonizing.

He struggled, but no matter how he tried, could not get to his feet. Swallowing his dignity, he crawled on his knees while she supported his left side and dragged the bedroll along behind.

In front of the entrance, it still seemed a hundred yards remained before reaching the interior. It was only six feet, but what little energy he'd been able to muster was fast draining away.

Meadowlark felt his fatigue. "Rest," she ordered, and disappeared inside with the sleeping bag.

Brent drew in ragged gasps of air. A cold breeze ruffled the fine hair on his body and he shivered. Slowly tilting his chin, afraid that even that small movement would be more than he could handle, he looked down to see that he was as naked as the day he was born.

Dear God in Heaven! How humiliating. Not only had he been embarrassed in battle, but he was crawling around on his hands and knees, bareassed naked. And all in front of Meadowlark Russell. Could anything worse happen?

A rustling movement near his side caused him to

move his head too quickly. As everything began to blur, he saw her. She smiled, or was she laughing—at him. He swayed, mortified to the roots of his hair.

Then he fainted.

Chapter Twelve

Meadowlark saw what little color there was left in Brent's face turn chalk white. As he slumped into her arms, she wondered about how easy it was becoming to think of him by his given name. It felt good on her tongue and comfortable in her mind. Brent—stalwart, solid.

His inert weight strained her shoulders and began to pull her toward the ground with him. With a giant breath, she heaved herself up and tugged until she finally had him inside the shelter. He groaned several times before she was able to position him on top of the bedroll, and another trickle of blood escaped the wound.

Each pitiful sound he uttered ripped through her. She sat with him until he was quiet, then reluctantly left to tend the horses.

Pausing in the doorway, she looked back. He was so still and lifeless, so different from the obstinate, hard-headed man he'd been before Scorpion . . . A scowl puckered her forehead. Scorpion. She had tried not to think of him since her frantic flight down the mountainside.

She had never seen her friend, or the man she used to think of as friend, in such a frenzy to kill. And for what reason? Brent had been nothing but kind and generous to their people. What could Scorpion have against the captain?

Shaking her head, Meadowlark went after the horses. As she looked for the animals, her mind could not be still. The entire situation, starting with Scorpion taking her mare, was highly unusual behavior for the easygoing warrior. No Apache killed just for the sake of killing. They were too fearful of the ghosts of the dead.

A deep sigh shook her weary frame. There were too many unanswered questions. An injured man needed her care. She had to conserve her energy for him.

Once she found the horses and hobbled them near the wickiup, she returned to discover that it would require every ounce of strength she possessed to handle the delirious captain. The fever seemed to give him the power of two men and she literally had to sprawl across him to keep him from hurting himself or reopening the wound.

A while later, during a rare quiet moment when his thrashing would not spill the concoction, she coaxed him into taking a sedative of horse nettle root. As soon as he quieted, though, his teeth began to chatter. Chills shook his large body. She watched with growing concern, knowing she had a decision to make.

His head rolled from side to side. He whimpered. Her breath grated her throat. What had lurked in the back of her mind, causing her to hesitate, was instantly obliterated. He needed her.

Her clothing was discarded in seconds. She pulled back the tarp and slid inside the heavy layer of cover next to his left side, careful to avoid disturbing his injury. She whispered in his ear, "I am here."

"Liz'beth?"

Meadowlark stiffened.

"Liz'beth . . . thought you . . . loved . . . me."

A woman's name. A white woman. Who was Lizbeth? What was this Lizbeth to Brent? And why did she feel so hurt and suddenly unsure of herself? Yet when his body shook, she held him tighter. A fine mist coated her eyes. She sighed, "I do," and her eyes closed as she nestled his head to her breast. A surge of tender emotion like nothing she had ever known sang inside her awakening body, causing her to wonder just what were *her* feelings for the white soldier.

"Liz'beth . . . *thought* . . . I loved . . .you."

A gigantic pain knifed through Meadowlark's heart. His declaration of love for the other woman was all she heard. Again she silently questioned, Who was that Lizbeth person? Meadowlark did not believe she had heard Brent mention the woman before. But he loved the unknown woman. He loved Lizbeth.

A tear meandered down her cheek. Another soon followed, then another. She sniffed and ordered the tears to stop. They seeped faster. For a woman—an Apache woman—who never cried, she was fast recognizing her vulnerability where Brent McQuade was concerned. It was no one's fault but her own. When she had first seen the captain, she had discovered a weakness, a gap in her defenses she had never noticed before.

Brent shuddered. Meadowlark held him close and softly chanted an Apache song in his ear. His head turned. He snuggled his cheek to her breast. Their legs entwined. She cried harder.

Who had insisted all along that there could never be anything between the white man and an Apache? Who had known from the beginning the trouble such a relationship would cause? Why was the truth suddenly so unbearable?

For twenty-four hours Meadowlark alternated between warming Brent's shuddering body and sponging away the fever with cold water from the river. When he thrashed and attempted to turn over, she cuddled him and sang to him. He would instantly calm, as if he listened to her every word with diligence and care.

If Meadowlark had been confused before, her emotions were now in total disarray. Not only had he called to a woman named "Lizbeth," he had also cried out for a "Hillary." Meadowlark cursed her own stupidity. She thought only Apache males were allowed to have many women. Evidently Captain McQuade kept a string of ladies, like the extra mules for a pack train, just in case he wanted one in a hurry.

Her face flamed, an annoying habit of late. She had almost allowed *herself* to fall for the big coyote. She could imagine him now, bragging about his conquest of a naive half-breed. Even her ears burned with embarrassment. She scrubbed the cold cloth she was using to wipe down his heated body across his broad chest.

"Ouch!"

Meadowlark jerked, dropping the cloth in the middle of his stomach. She found it impossible to look him in the eyes, so she watched the muscles on his abdomen harden and ripple up his rib cage and down his . . . Uh, oh. Quickly, she tilted her head back and stared through the smoke hole.

"Lark? What're you . . . doin'?"

Goosebumps prickled her flesh. His low, rumbling voice vibrated down her sensitive spine. "N-nothing."

Brent licked his lips and slowly glanced around the small enclosure. "Where . . . are we?"

"In a wickiup. By the river." She covertly watched him from the corner of her eye, wishing she could cover him again without appearing obvious.

"Wh-what happened?"

She frowned. "You do not remember?"

His brows slanted together. He took a deep breath and winced when the muscles across his shoulder were stretched. "Can't lift my hand." A look of genuine puzzlement settled over his drawn features.

Meadowlark was pleased to see that the glassiness had disappeared from his eyes. Their blue color now held just a slight grayish tint. Soon they would again rival the brilliance of the sky.

Her own eyes narrowed. She was doing it again. Finding him attractive. No doubt Lizbeth and Hillary would be heartened to know he was improving, too.

"Damn," he croaked. "My head hurts, an' . . . muscles. Why can't I . . ." He stopped and stared at Meadowlark. Clouds billowed in his eyes. She was wearing his shirt—and nothing else. And a jagged tear near one shoulder exposed the barest hint of a bare breast.

He closed his eyes. For the first time in his life, such a delectable sight caused too much discomfort. Too much? He could hardly believe it. He must be sick or . . .

Frowning, he cracked his eyelids, then began to squirm. Meadowlark was kneeling over him, a knife in her hand, reaching toward his shoulder. He tried to sit up. Suddenly his vision blurred. A horrendous buzzing began in his ears.

Memory rushed over him like a swarm of angry bees. A knife. Scorpion. They'd fought. He'd tried to save Meadowlark. Then a dark fog had rolled in, lifting only when a sweet, soothing voice and a firm, warm body wrapped around his nakedness.

Hell! He swallowed as best he could around the cotton in his throat and squinted up at the bright light shining through the opening in the roof. Meadowlark. She'd forced wicked tasting brews down his throat. Had lain naked against him . . . What a time to not remember clearly.

She'd undressed him. His already flushed body could hardly pinken any more, but he felt embarrassed to his bones. What had she thought as she took off his clothes as if he were no more than a baby? When she lay with him, did she compare him with Scorpion?

Damn! He cleared his throat. "Water . . . please."

He wanted to beg for his clothing, too, because he'd just felt the barest stirrings of a breeze over his skin. Only skin. No blanket. No tarp. Nothing covering him. Yet she seemed to pay his nudity no attention at all. Was she not as uncomfortable as he? Or did he not measure up enough to arouse her interest?

When she held a cup of cool water to his cracked lips, he gulped it down, spilling some down his chin. She dabbed at the liquid with the hem of her—his—shirt. "Thanks."

She started to move away. He forced his muscles to obey and managed to feebly lift his left hand. He sighed when it was enough to stay her departure. "Why . . . did you . . . come back?"

It was troublesome, to know how important her answer was to him. But if she were truly Scorpion's woman, wouldn't she have followed the warrior? Was there a chance, any chance, that she might care just a little for a certain cavalry captain?

Meadowlark's mind raced in frantic circles, searching for an answer she could voice. It was out of the question to admit she had been concerned, scared silly, that he would die and that she might never see those incredible blue eyes or that adorable dimple again. And she could never tell him that for a few precious minutes, she had imagined she cared for him. Her, and how many *other* women? No, she would never allow him the opportunity to gloat over Meadowlark Russell.

"I *had* to come." True enough. "I could not risk your death. As you said, we were in enough trouble."

Brent hadn't realized he'd been holding his breath until it hissed through a puncture in his heart. What a hell of a relief. Wouldn't it have been a sticky situation if, indeed, she had cared for him? He would've had to let her down gently, of course. Wouldn't have wanted to hurt her. Poor little lady. It was a big weight off his shoulders. O-oh-h yes.

He glanced toward the fire. There was a moistness in his eyes he couldn't explain and didn't want her to see. "You saved my life. I'm . . . grateful."

She gritted her teeth. Now he was being humble. Noble and humble. The man would have made a great Apache. Even Victorio would have liked this soldier.

But when she noticed him wince, and his lips compress so tightly that they turned white, she mentally shook herself and bent back to the task of placing a fresh poultice on his wound.

Brent watched her pulverize an ugly mass of . . . whatever . . . and felt a bead of perspiration pool in the indention above his upper lip. "Wh-what is . . . that?"

Her lips curved with amusement. So, the big, brave soldier was afraid of something after all. Her chest swelled with power. At least she held control over this one part of his life. He had no choice but to trust her—if he were to survive.

"It will heal the wound." And as she smeared it over the injury, she was proud to note that the wound looked as good as it did. Other than the loss of a lot of blood, nothing vital had been damaged. A few days of rest and he would be fine.

Brent sighed and closed his eyes. He was too tired to worry about her witch-doctoring. Whatever it was, he was still alive. And he could think of no one else he'd rather have taking care of him.

His Lark was one of a kind. It was a shame he hadn't met her a long time ago.

Meadowlark gently prodded Brent awake. She had let him sleep for over eighteen hours, but it was morning and he needed nourishment. Dark circles ringed his eyes. His cheeks were sunken and his lips so chapped that it hurt her to look at them.

Last night she had set a snare and this morning had prepared a thick broth with tender rabbit and wild onions.

She lifted the captain's head and rested his shoulders on her thighs before shaking him again. "Wake up, Brent McQuade. You must eat."

Brent struggled from a deep sleep. He sniffed. His stomach grumbled in protest to pressing, empty, against his backbone. One eye at a time, he peered up to find Meadowlark's sweet, round face hovering above him.

"Did . . . you mention . . . food?" He tried to swallow, but found it almost too difficult. His throat felt like it was lined with gravel. And damn but he was weak. He could hardly summon the strength to hold his eyelids open.

Then he felt Meadowlark's small hand at the back of his neck and sighed as she tilted the rim of the cup to his lips. He winced. It was hot. His mouth was tender.

Meadowlark lifted the cup away and smiled when his head followed the motion. She blew on the broth to let it cool before trying again. When she held him like this, it was hard to remember that she was angry with Brent. Even hurt and sick, he was the most handsome, masculine man she had ever known.

Brent's eyes rolled up to meet hers. "I'm sorry, Lark."

Her hand trembled. "For what?"

"I'm sorry you have to take care of me like this."

Something warm and tender fluttered insistently inside her belly. The distress dulling his eyes and tautening his features tore at her heart. "Try again." She held the cup to his mouth.

This time Brent was able to take a sip of the savory liquid. He tried to rise, to take the whole cup at once, but Meadowlark held him down. "Only small sips. Your body will tell you it is so."

He swallowed another taste and felt the full sensation in his stomach. "I know." Another sip trickled down his throat, easing the parched lining. "This's good."

She glowed. No one besides her father had ever complimented her on her cooking before. It was nice to know Brent appreciated her efforts.

Brent drained the cup and smacked his lips. "More?" he begged.

Shaking her head, Meadowlark laid his head back on the tarp, regretting the absence of the heat from his body and the sudden cold that encompassed her flesh. "Later."

"Please?"

She turned away from his engaging grin and dimple before he could change her mind. "No."

"You're a cruel woman, La . . . Meadowlark."

His pitiful sigh surrounded and squeezed her heart. "No!" she practically shouted, and quickly left the wickiup, dutifully reminding herself that he was accomplished at getting his way with women. No wonder, she fumed, as she rinsed the cup in the river. Who could resist him when he turned on the charm?

When she returned to the shelter, he was sleeping. Thankful that the spirits smiled on her, she added a few twigs to the fire and sat cross-legged on the edge of the sleeping bag. Though he appeared to be recovering, she felt better where she could keep an eye on him. Just to be sure the fever did not return, she told herself, that was all.

Brent awoke with a start. Something heavy lay across his thighs. *Something* warm and moist teased his manhood. His eyes blinked open, but closed again. He concentrated on his left hand until he was able to move it slightly. It came to rest on the sleeping bag. That was what trapped him? The sleeping bag?

He suddenly felt it again—that tickling sensation on his groin He took a deep breath that strangled in his throat and felt himself growing hard and full. His eyes flew open. Managing to lift his head, he peered at his lap. Good God!

Meadowlark lay stretched along his legs, her upper body resting atop his thighs, her head nestled in his lap. Her lips were slightly parted, allowing her warm breath access to his most sensitive flesh. And her open hand was there. If it moved half an inch, he would fill her palm.

He was consumed by the most intense yearning to squirm and do just that. For weeks, he had dreamed of touching her, of her touching him.

Restlessly, she snuggled into him. He stifled a groan, wondering how he would ever get out of the situation without embarrassing them both. Then he saw her lashes, spread like thick black fans across her peach-tinted cheeks, flutter open.

Quickly, he closed his eyes and let his head fall back onto the tarp. He tried to take deep, even breaths, though it felt as if every nerve in the lower half of his body was twitching out of control. If he could just remain still, he could leave it to her to wriggle out of this mess with discretion.

Meadowlark sighed. Something beneath her head jerked. She yawned and slowly opened her eyes. When she inhaled sharply, she felt another jerk. Something chaffed her cheek. Shifting, her hand encountered warm male skin. She twisted her head and saw the tarp. She had fallen asleep on the tarp.

The smooth flesh, muscled and hard, moved beneath her hand. Her eyes slanted up, then down. She jerked upright, pulling her hand away. Liquid fire throbbed through her veins and scorched her cheeks. She stared at the place her head had rested. The place her hand had rested. What had she done to the poor man, and in his condition?

She darted a swift glance to his face and exhaled the breath she had been holding when she found him still asleep. What on earth had she been thinking to doze like that, *there?* How awful. How embarrassing. How . . .

Her mouth quirked. Her skin tingled from the top of her scalp to the soles of her feet. How interesting.

She had appreciated his manly physique earlier when she had bathed his feverish body. But from what she now saw, she had not *fully* appreciated all his assets . . . or . . . his finer points.

Sighing, pleased that she had not been discovered, she shook her head and left the wickiup to reheat the broth. She had a suspicion the captain's appetite would be even greater. She grinned, then chuckled at her wayward thoughts.

Brent groaned with heartfelt relief when she was finally gone. She was torturing him—using cruel Apache torture. His lips lifted into a mischievous smile. It wasn't Apache at all, it was feminine torture. She would pay. Oh yes, he would exact his revenge.

—

In the middle of the afternoon, Meadowlark made one of her now infrequent trips inside the shelter. She had avoided Brent's company except for times when it was necessary to feed him or change the dressing on his shoulder. He had yet to say a word and his silence was suspicious. It was not like him.

And though he had slept through the morning's mortifying experience, *she* could not forget it. Every time she looked at him, she remembered the feel of . . . how she hated the familiar heat creeping up her neck.

But there was something disconcerting in his eyes now, something that had been absent before. A new glint—a devilish glint—that she did not know how to interpret.

Well, she was stalling. Meadowlark took a deep breath and tightened her grip on the cup. No matter how uncomfortable he made her feel, she had vowed to the spirits that she would see to it he regained his strength—quickly. The sooner he recovered and they returned to San Carlos, the better.

"Ah, Miss Russell, I thought you'd forgotten me."

If Meadowlark thought there was a hint of devilment in his words, she found no sign of it in his earnest expression.

"I'm a starvin' man."

Her eyes narrowed. After what happened this morning, there could be another meaning to his statement. But she knelt beside him and once again lifted his head so he could use her thighs for support. She had purposely changed back into her leggings, now that she would not have to keep crawling into bed with him. Yet it was as if the leather was no thicker than a spider's web. She could still imagine the soft, springiness of his hair when he nestled his head into a more comfortable position.

"You are feeling better?" He certainly felt wonderful beneath her fingers. Her eyes lowered so she would not have to look into his face. The way his eyes bored into her, following her every movement, caused her to feel like a mouse stalked by a swooping owl.

Brent smiled to himself when she immediately stuck the cup to his lips and looked out the small entrance. Evidently she didn't expect an answer to her question. She'd been like this every time she'd come into the wickiup today—nervous, fidgety, hardly able to look him in the eyes. Good.

He choked on the last swallow and almost banged his head on the ground when she scrambled from beneath him. He grabbed her wrist before she could run away. "Do somethin' for me?"

"Wh-what?" Her eyes were wary and distrustful.

"Help me outside." His eyes pleaded, implored.

"No. You need more rest."

"I've rested so much there isn't a part of me that doesn't ache." His lips quirked when she flushed—again. She definitely knew what she'd done that morning. For a while, he hadn't been sure, had thought maybe she was inexperienced . . .

"You will have to ache." She jerked her hand from his, unable to look anywhere but at the pale light filtering through the doorway.

"Please."

Her insides melted like snow in July. She had been taught the value of the word "please." Besides the sun was shining. It was fairly warm if he stayed out of the wind. Inside the shelter, the air was stale, smothered. "All right," she snapped, then indicated the ground sheet covering his lower body. "But keep a tight hold on that."

His eyes literally danced. "Yes'm."

He sobered quickly when he discovered just how weak he really was. Even with her help he couldn't stand. It took the two of them working together to scoot him out the small opening, keeping his dignity and the sheet intact. A three- or four-foot stump stuck up from the sand just a few feet from the wickiup and Meadowlark quickly guided him to where he could lean back against the smooth bark.

The air smelled so fresh and clean that he took several deep breaths and exhaled in a long, contented sigh. One more minute in that small space and he wouldn't have been responsible for his actions, especially cooped up with the delectable Miss Russell.

Meadowlark busied herself about the camp, finding any excuse to remain out of close proximity to Brent. But all at once, she swung around to stare at him. A strange sensation had assailed her, as if he had called her name, yet she knew he had not spoken aloud.

Brent sucked in his breath when Meadowlark turned. Behind her was the glow of the setting sun, the horizon broken only by the silhouettes of a few tall yuccas and mesquites. The greater the brilliance of the reflected colors, the more striking became the woman.

A rosy radiance surrounded her, like a silver lining around a cloud, he thought. Her skin looked all soft and silky, with a peaches-and-cream quality. And her dark hair, with the sunset in the background, flamed with sparkling red highlights. The coal black pupils of her eyes appeared to swim in an orange haze, reminding him sharply of cat-eyes—intense, knowing eyes.

He could look at her forever.

Meadowlark's hands trembled as she knelt and cut more meat into the simmering broth. Whatever had just happened had completely unnerved her. She warily looked around the campsite. The spirits in this place were powerful. She would have to be on her guard.

Then she slanted Brent a glance from beneath the shadow of her lashes. He had to have felt the same sensations or he would not be looking at her like that, like she had suddenly sprouted horns or grown two noses.

She added more sticks to the outside fire and went to check the smaller one inside the shelter. When she once again emerged into the clearing, she watched Brent clumsily adjust the sheet around his shoulders.

"You're beautiful." His words came as a surprise.

Halting in midstride, she tilted her head to one side. "What?" She studied him closely. Had the fever returned?

"Guess I said you're beautiful. And you are." And he meant every word, although he certainly hadn't intended to say it out loud. There were too many reasons he shouldn't have said *anything.* Most of the time the woman acted as if she couldn't stand to be near him. And there was no room in his life for any kind of entanglements. Yet he had come out and said something as provocative, and asinine as, "You're beautiful." Hell, he'd end up in an asylum yet.

Meadowlark did not know how to respond—if she should say anything at all, or if she could. His seemingly casual statement had caught her off guard, after she had just admonished herself to be careful. But she wondered if she was—beautiful.

Heat spiraled through her body until her limbs felt as weak as watered mush. Finally, afraid she might embarrass herself further, she just nodded and went to check on the broth. She licked her lips and darted a glance back toward the captain.

He was staring at the river. She shrugged off the tension in her shoulders and gazed into the black, moonless sky, begging for the patience and strength to survive the next few days—and nights.

But as she scooped out a cupful of broth, she hoped to get through just the next few minutes. "Can you hold the cup?" she asked, walking carefully to his side so as not to spill the hot liquid.

Brent had to consider the question. His right arm was useless, but he was so anxious to prove that he wasn't completely helpless anymore that he turned loose of the sheet, which immediately slipped down around his hips, and held out his left hand.

The more of his broad expanse of muscles and bare flesh that became exposed, the quicker Meadowlark's heartbeat accelerated. Instead of handing him the food, she reached down and jerked up the cover. "You will catch a chill. I can help tonight."

"I'd like to try," he protested.

"Tomorrow, maybe." She shoved the cup at his mouth.

He wasn't expecting the sudden movement. The edge of the cup hit his lower lip. "Ow!" Part of the liquid sloshed over the side and dribbled down his chin and onto his chest.

Meadowlark muttered a string of expletives, but realized the captain had to understand at least a few words of Apache when his eyes widened with shock. She picked up Scorpion's clean head band, which she had scrubbed in the river, and patted it over the red splotches on Brent's skin.

Suddenly, his left hand wrapped around her wrist in a surprisingly strong grip. "What're you so angry about?"

His face was only inches from hers. She could smell his freshly washed skin and caught a faint hint of safflower on his breath. "I am not angry."

"You are."

Yes, she was, but could not admit to *him* that she was mad because she could not keep her eyes from him, that she ached to smooth back that lock of hair falling into his eyes, that her body experienced unexplainable, unimaginable sensations from his just holding her wrist, or the sultry way he was looking at her right now.

Maybe she should give him more sedative. The sooner he slept, the better she would feel. She could use an evening alone, to think. "I will not be angry if you eat. Then I will take you to bed."

Brent's body stiffened. His eyes shot blue smoke.

Meadowlark realized the implication of what she had said and swallowed, dropping the cup to the ground.

Chapter Thirteen

A smile tilted Brent's lips. "You mean you're goin' to take me inside an' have your way with me?"

Meadowlark gulped and shook her head.

"Aw, shucks." Real disappointment tinged his voice. But maybe? Some day? A wave of dizziness suddenly set his ears to buzzing and he closed his eyes. Tired. So tired.

Cursing herself for allowing the captain to overdue himself, Meadowlark quickly took control and helped him back into the shelter before he completely passed out. Trying not to look at his finely sculpted body, she took the sleeping bag and shook it out before spreading it and settling him as comfortably as she could.

A strange sensation crept over her body when she hastily glanced up and found him doing it again—staring—as if she were a prime, tender mouse and he a rangy lobo. "Are you hungry?" She bit down on her lower lip, understanding and regretting her unintentioned innuendo. Would she never learn?

But he did not tease her, or take unfair advantage of her second slip of the tongue. He just shook his head and rolled from one side to the other. She frowned and felt his forehead. It was warm. As was the flesh around the wound when she examined it. Maybe she should make a new poultice.

"Do not leave. I will be back soon." As soon as she

ducked through the opening and took a fresh breath of air, she felt better, safer, now that she was back in control of the situation. She could handle him like this.

"I'll be waitin'." The soft sound of his voice tugged at her conscience. What did he mean by that?

Brent floated in and out of consciousness the next few hours. When he awoke to find Meadowlark cleaning and changing the dressing on his wound, he reveled in her tender ministrations. But it had hurt. He'd tried to hide the pain, yet she had evidently heard his sudden intake of breath, or had seen something in his eyes when he darted a glance in her direction. She'd forced more of that awful tasting stuff down his throat.

The next time she intimidated him into swallowing that hellacious brew, he'd . . . he'd . . . given the way he'd, more or less, let the minx have free rein lately, no telling *what* he would do next. Roll over? Beg?

He must have fallen asleep again, for when he opened his eyes she was sitting cross-legged, absently staring into the fire. How un-Apache of her. But then he guessed she wasn't used to living like the renegades who had to stay on guard and alert every minute, who knew that looking into a fire could night-blind a man, making it impossible to search out enemies in the shadows.

Brent grimaced. There it was again—that gut-tightening wrench which always accompanied thoughts of Lark alone and on her own, with no one to care for or look after her. Well, as long as he was garrisoned at San Carlos, she had him. With a silent, magnanimous nod of his head, he accepted responsibility for her safety.

He shifted his weight and groaned, wondering how he could look after a beautiful Apache woman when he could hardly see after his own needs.

Suddenly, he looked up to find her bending over him, concern straining her features as she demanded, "Are you still in pain?"

Too quickly, he answered, "No!" No more of that sedative. He was a grown man. He would withstand torture rather than swallow one more vile mouthful.

Her hand on his forehead was cool and soothing. He smelled the sweet scent of lavender and wood smoke and woman as she drew even nearer. Involuntarily, a shudder worked down his spine.

"Are you cold?"

"Oh-h-h, no . . . yes-s-s." Though he'd been racked with fever, he had distinct memories of a naked body pressed to his—a slender woman's body. Had he been hallucinating? Or had Lark crawled under the blankets to warm his chilled flesh? Gooseflesh covered every exposed inch of his skin.

Meadowlark sat back on her heels, worried. He did not seem feverish, but he was chilling. Had she taken his strength for granted, jeopardized his health by allowing him out of the wickiup for even that short time?

Guilt flushed her cheeks. If anything happened to him . . . She glanced at his face. His eyes were closed. His features pale and still. Had he passed out again?

Immediately, she shucked her clothes, lifted the edge of the tarp and slid in beside him. She was rewarded with almost violent jerks and a tooth-jarring trembling that vibrated his body as she gathered him in her arms.

She sighed with relief, though, when his skin did not have the same icy, clammy feeling it did before. Maybe this was just a minor ailment. He would be all right. He *had* to be all right.

Brent hadn't been prepared for the myriad of sensations that rocketed through his body when Meadowlark's naked, satin flesh eased against his own. He'd thought about—dreamed about—her willingly lying with him. But to actually experience her skin warming his . . . A million needles jabbed him everywhere at once. It was awful . . . wonderful . . . excruciating.

Every hair on his body stood on end as she snuggled against him. With every press of her firm, young flesh he thought he would expire from the worst possible agony and the greatest of pleasures. He twisted his lower body slightly away from her, praying she wouldn't come in contact with the one healthy part of him throbbing with life and desire. Yet deep down he wished she would. Her touch would probably . . .

Damn, but he wanted this woman with every fiber of his being. Sure, he had wanted women, but he'd never been on fire before, never felt that he might wither and die without that one special someone—not *any*one. Except Lark.

How many other women would've known how to set up camp, build a shelter, or mix ugly healing concoctions as if it were an everyday occurrence? God, what a woman.

Her arms curled around him and he ached to be able to feel her in both of his. He blinked. His lids grew heavy. What little energy he'd drummed up seemed to evaporate. He could have literally wept. Later. Later, he would hold her, touch her, love her.

Brent awoke to a familiar tenseness in his body. He hoped it was an indication he was healing, because he felt much better. Yawning, he gazed through the smoke hole and saw that the sky was just beginning to lighten.

He sighed and closed his eyes, content to sleep another hour. Lying there, all warm and cozy, cuddled up to . . . his eyes shot open. A soft feminine form lay the length of his left side, head nuzzled into his good shoulder, the fingers of her right hand twisted through the wiry coils of hair on his chest. When he shifted his lower body, he found her belly and thighs curled around his hip, her right leg thrown across his.

A groan welled from deep in his gut, but he managed to choke it back down. He was feeling good all right. Every little bit of her felt downright wonderful. His manhood was so tight and swollen that he was afraid to move. If she were to awaken suddenly and move her knee . . .

He closed his eyes and decided to enjoy the unfamiliar sensations. It had been a long time since he'd just *held* a woman. And he *was* holding her. His left palm was filled with a firm little buttock. His right thumb and index finger toyed with a turgid nipple.

A slight movement on his chest caused him to lift his head high enough to see that her mouth had curved into a grin. Aha! he thought. Was this the opportunity he'd been searching for? He would demonstrate what happened when one enticed a person to the edge of control, wittingly or not.

Then his eyes narrowed. *He* was the one who lured her into bed last night, pretending to be more sick than he actually was. But who would have known she would just shed her clothes and climb in buck naked? She had done it so naturally, so . . . unselfishly.

A frown wrinkled his brow. She had done it for *him,* and here he was, feeling suddenly angry and jealous, wondering how many other feverish men she'd helped. She sure knew what to do, didn't she? Such a little bit of a thing. Some men would definitely take advantage of that kind of trust.

Of course, *he* wouldn't. But she didn't know that for certain. A curse drowned in his throat as he mentally kicked himself for lying there talking himself into teaching her a lesson. He was a lecherous ingrate.

And he was incredibly lucky to have a woman like Lark curled so sweetly in his arms. He couldn't *not* touch her. His hand gently massaged her bottom, then ever so slowly smoothed over her silken hip and up her rib cage. Up and down, slow and easy. His confined hand lay across his stomach, and the tip of his index finger tickled her breast and brushed her nipple. He felt the change as it peaked into a hard little nubbin.

She unconsciously squirmed. With each move she made, every sensuous slide and bump, his flesh burned. It took every hard-won ounce of his willpower to keep from crushing her to him. If he didn't have the damned wound . . .

Subtly, oh-so subtly, he moved his left leg until she straddled it. He lifted it and rocked against her in short, gentle motions. His hand continued its path up her back until his fingers brushed through her hair and teased the tiny lobe of her ear. Tracing the delicate shell-shape, he then concentrated on the nape of her neck.

Meadowlark dreamt she lay in a grassy field of wildflowers. Wispy, colorful butterflies surrounded her, their delicate wings fluttering against her body, here, there, everywhere. One even batted the end of her nose as she took a deep breath. Slowly she stirred, reluctant to open her eyes and lose the serene peacefulness and beauty of her dream world.

But a deep, restless heat began to build, radiating throughout her body, stimulating every nerve. Even as she awoke, the butterflies continued their fanciful forays. Each time they nudged against her, exquisite sensations assailed her—concentrating in her most secret feminine core. Hot. So hot.

She tingled all over, yearning for . . . something . . . she could not put a name to, yet so basic and elemental as to be instinctive. Becoming aware of the presence beside her, she turned into his warmth, knowing, without knowing, that he was the one to assuage her tender, budding ache.

Her hands sought and found a supple foundation and clung with all her might.

Brent sucked in his breath. His sensuous game suddenly backfiring. She wasn't completely awake, but Meadowlark was responding to his light touches like a tigress demanding a hearty caress. Her hands were everywhere, stroking, feeling, until he groaned with his own intense response. He was on fire. At any moment he would burst into a million tiny sparks, like a pine knot exploding into blue-white flames.

His manhood pulsed with a life of its own. He wanted this woman like he'd never wanted a woman before. Yet his mind shouted, "No!" Actually, making love to her had not been his intent when he'd started this lesson. If he took her now he would be no better than . . .

Meadowlark opened her eyes. She twisted her head until her chin rested on Brent's chest and she gazed into his eyes. The bright blue color had turned to the shade of a hazy mist. Sweat beaded his forehead. A sudden pang of fear knotted her stomach. Was he sick again? Had the fever returned?

She shifted to rise. Her hips brushed a stiff hardness that jerked with her touch. Her eyes widened. A muscle leaped in his jaw. Cords and tendons roping his iron-hard body strained with her every movement.

He raised the thigh nestled between her legs. Her body spasmed. Liquid heat pulsed at the core of her womanhood. Her legs clamped tightly about his. Intense pressure coiled in her belly and expanded her chest. The captain's face became slightly unfocused.

Brent became lost in the depths of Meadowlark's eyes. The rich amber hue seduced him. He imagined himself sipping a smooth aged bourbon when he lifted his head and sampled her inviting lips. She tasted good, felt good. He wanted to absorb her into his flesh and make them one.

Meadowlark's fingers tunneled through the shaggy hair at the back of his head. The pads of her fingers massaged the knotted muscles at the base of his neck. She shifted further atop him when he rolled his hips. Her belly lay flush to his. The wiry hairs on his chest taunted her breasts.

His head fell back. His fingers dug into her flesh. His body screamed his frustration and he unconsciously moaned. If he didn't stop now . . .

Meadowlark started. She had become so finely atuned to the pleasurable sensations sparking inside her body that she had completely lost herself to Brent's lovemaking—until his hands gripped her almost painfully. And his low, guttural moan sounded as if it had been ripped from the very heart of him. She was frightened. "Did I hurt you?"

Brent breathed deeply and expelled the air from his lungs in a long sigh before answering. "No-o-o."

Meadowlark was skeptical. The tendons in his neck stood out. His voice was strained. Worried that there was something really wrong, she insisted, "You sound pained. Please . . ."

His head popped up and he kissed her into silence. "Hush, Lark. If I'm hurting—" Her look said, "I thought so," and he quickly rushed on. "It's not because of . . . you had nothing . . . well, maybe a little. Damn it! You're so soft and beautiful and soft . . . and . . ." He couldn't resist. His hands explored her satin flesh with a will of their own.

Meadowlark gulped a ragged breath and rested her forehead on his broad chest. She could not think when he touched her so—did not *want* to think, or do anything but lie with him for the rest of her days.

It was not an easy admission for her to make. But as she had cared for and lain with the man over the past few days, she had realized she had strong feelings for him. Misplaced they might be, but she had them. He was a decent, honorable man. A brave man.

Still, she searched her soul. The Apache were a strict society. Like the white man, they frowned upon a man and woman coupling before marriage. She could, should, get up and run like a deer from the cozy shelter.

But something held her back. No longer would she consider marrying Scorpion. There was no other man. This white man, Capt. Brent McQuade, instilled emotions in her soul as deep as time itself. She had felt them from the first moment their eyes had fused.

Finally, having regained some control of his own rampant emotions, Brent suffered feelings of guilt for his assault on her virginal senses. He steeled himself to let her go—now.

He cleared his throat. "Honey, you better get up. Real quick."

Beneath her body she felt the tension in his muscles and sensed the control he fought to wield. Her heart caught in her throat. Though she had never lain with a man, she had slept in a family wickiup as a small girl. She knew about coupling, knew the gift he was bestowing, giving her the chance to leave. "What of your shoulder?"

Brent's jaw worked. "My shoulder? What about it?"

"Is it painful?"

He gritted his teeth. At that particular point in time, his shoulder was the *least* painful part of his tortured body. "No. Really. You go ahead—"

She slid up his long form, inch by tantalizing inch, until she looked him in the eye. "I will stay, Brent."

His eyes closed. "Say that again."

Exasperated, she huffed, "I will—"

"No. My name. Say it again."

Heat quickened her body. "Brent?"

He nodded, knowing he was being childish. There was nothing that special about his name, it was just the way she said it. The way she puckered her lips and the slight hint of roses that pinkened her cheeks. Roses and lavender.

"Do you not desire me?"

He heard the uncertainty behind the quiver in her voice. His left arm circled her back, pressing her hard little nipples into his chest. Muscles rippled beneath his flesh as if he'd been branded with a red-hot poker.

He swiveled his hips, allowing the full length of his manhood to press into her belly and thighs. He growled, "What do you think?"

A tentative grin curved her lips and she wriggled against him.

He laughed.

Meadowlark held her breath. She had never heard him really laugh before. It started deep in his chest and rumbled like thunder. His entire face changed as the muscles there relaxed. And *there,* on his right cheek, was another slight indentation. Not as large and deep as the one on the left side of his luscious mouth, but it was a dimple, nonetheless.

She touched it with a fingertip.

Brent stifled another moan. All she had done was move her arm. Lord, every nerve on his body was sensitized to this one little woman. She might be slight and slimly made, but her curves were lush and generous, all satin and silk. Perfectly made just for him.

He raised his head. She bent hers down. Their lips met and melded. Though his body ached and throbbed, his heart beat serene and content, as comfortable as an old rocking chair in front of a warm fireplace.

Meadowlark's body seemed to melt into a pulsing mass that engulfed his strength and masculinity. His power became hers. She had given him life. He was giving her more. She would treasure his loving in her memories.

She was a realist. She would enjoy this moment and keep it dear to her heart in the days, weeks or years ahead. White man or no, she had chosen her first man well. Physically handsome. Spiritually good. She did not care if there was never another.

Slowly, reluctantly, Brent cupped her face in his palms and held her there as he gently disentangled their mouths. He gazed at her through narrowed eyes. After several attempts to catch his breath, he asked, "Lark . . . are you sure?"

She hesitated, bit her lower lip, then nodded.

He sighed and curved his lips into a rueful grin. "I'm afraid you'll have to do a lot of the . . . work," he said, slanting a rueful glance over to his injured shoulder.

Her eyes blazed. She puffed out her chest. Good. She wanted to be an equal part of the coupling. Pride, and Apache custom, would not allow her to receive more than she gave in return.

Brent was lost the moment she thrust out her chest, pointing her coral-tipped nipples toward his waiting lips. He did not refuse the invitation, knowing that if she hadn't granted her assent, he could've hardly stopped himself anyway. His body was consumed by a desire as barbaric as a raging prairie fire.

Meadowlark's bones and muscles melted to the consistency of molten lava. The only thing she could concentrate on was the sensation of his lips on her breast. Her legs parted to envelop his hips. The soft roundness of her stomach settled into the hollowed planes of his flat belly. She started to brace her hands on his shoulders, remembered his wound, and placed them on either side of his head instead.

She looked down into his face. Their eyes locked. The heat reflected there shocked Meadowlark clear to her toes. She briefly wondered if smoke seeped from her pores when Brent laved her nipple with his tongue. Her back arched. A low moan escaped her parted lips when he suddenly released her.

Brent's right hand found her knee and braced it near his hip. "Sit on me, Lark. That's right. Let your legs take your weight." He raised his hips.

She sucked in her breath as she felt the tip of his manhood nudge the damp entrance at the apex of her thighs. For an instant, doubt tugged at her conscience. But his eyes, which had never released her gaze, darkened. He smiled. She was mesmerized. She was sure.

"Can you feel me, honey?"

She gulped and nodded.

"I can feel you, too. An' you're ready. Tell me you

want me, Lark."

Moistness burned the backs of her eyes. She blinked. She had not realized that he might experience hesitation or insecurity. If anything could have endeared him any more to her, it was his tentative words. "Yes, Brent, I do want you."

Her husky voice enveloped him. His chest constricted as his breath came in erratic gasps. He held both of her knees, arched his back and teased her nether lips. His teeth ground together when she instinctively wriggled her bottom and settled lower, easing his quest.

God, she felt good—warm and tight. He bucked his hips and slid deeper. Bucking higher, he encountered an unexpected resistance. He reined himself to a stop faster than if he'd run headlong into a granite boulder.

Left helpless and wanting, not understanding why, Meadowlark rocked up and down. An intense ache blossomed in her lower belly. That part of him inside her pulsed with life, igniting small sparks that flickered, then blazed and flickered again. Why had he stopped? She throbbed. Her inner muscles spasmed around him.

Her body gradually took control of her mind. Little explosions erupted as she moved. She wanted more—had to feel more of him deeper inside of her. Up. Down. Up. And this time she came down hard, gasping when she felt a slight tearing sensation. But it was immediately forgotten beneath the power of a yearning, burning need.

Brent was mindless with desire. His hips moved in rhythm with hers until, with forceful thrusts, he took the lead and guided them both through the most glorious moments ever created for human fulfillment.

Meadowlark felt as if she had been taken into the

heavens to touch the moon and the stars. Bright lights flickered behind her closed eyelids. Then she was falling, slowly, drifting gently, only to be plucked from the clouds by the solid strength of Brent McQuade's arms as they wrapped securely around her weightless body.

She latched on to him as if she clutched at a lifeline. He was a safe haven. He was a gentle protector. In one blinding flash, he was everything to her.

Shaken by the realization of how much the captain had come to mean to her, Meadowlark laid her head on his chest. Heart-to-heart, she captured the essence of his being, committing it to her soul for safekeeping.

Brent was overwhelmed. He pulled the tarp over their damp bodies, still entwined, as if clinging desperately to each other for support. He was astounded by the passion and power of their lovemaking. He'd never felt such an intense flood of emotion or wondrous satisfaction.

"Lark, are you all right?" His voice quavered with concern. She hadn't moved or hardly taken a breath.

Nuzzling her nose into the fine down coating his chest, she answered, "I think so." Then she lifted her head and gazed into his eyes. "Are you?"

Brent felt as if he'd been kicked in the chest by a locoed mule when he stared into her sparkling amber eyes. She had to be the most beautiful woman in the world with her flushed cheeks and kiss-swollen lips. Black tendrils of hair clung to her face and he tenderly brushed them behind her ear. Was he all right? He needed time to think before he could answer that question. "I don't know, honey. I don't know."

It was true. After the experience they'd just shared, he wasn't sure he'd ever be the same again. Making love to Meadowlark Russell was both immensely pleasurable and terrifying, both at the same time. He hated losing control, and that was all he'd done since meeting the minx.

Meadowlark was thinking, not of what she had lost, but of what she had gained. Moments spent with Brent McQuade were the most beautiful of her life. Of course she was wary and distrustful of *any* white man, but the captain had so far proven to be an exception. She looked forward to and enjoyed being with him. An air of excitement and expectancy now filled her life. That had been missing for a long, long time.

Maybe that was another reason she had balked at leaving with Scorpion. Maybe that was why she had chosen to defend Brent with her life. She had searched her mind for an explanation of her behavior for days. The answer had so far eluded her. A *truthful* answer anyway.

Suddenly uncomfortable with the direction her thoughts had taken, she sighed and glanced awkwardly toward his shoulder. "Did we . . . I mean . . . you . . . hurt . . ."

Some of the tension drained from Brent's body when she broke the silence that had seemed to enfold them in a shroudlike atmosphere. Why was he hunting for the negative side of something that had been so good?

He interrupted her embarrassed mumbling. "My shoulder's fine. A little sore, maybe. But we, *you,* didn't harm it."

She shyly raised her eyes to his and found he was smiling at her. Her own lips curved into a grin as a coil of heat unwound in her stomach. She darted her gaze away lest he read too much in her expression.

Brent cupped her cheek and turned her face back to his. There was an important detail of their lovemaking they needed to discuss, and his chest swelled with possessive pride. "I know I hurt you, honey. I just didn't know . . ." Oh God, how should he say this without stomping his big foot in his mouth? "I thought you and Scorpion . . ."

Meadowlark tried to duck her head, but his hand kept her chin up. A deep inhalation of breath hissed back out through her teeth. He thought she had lain with another man. Why? "There has been no one before . . . you."

"I know that now." He also knew from what his brother had told him that Apache women did not make a habit of giving away something as important as their maidenhead. His manhood surged with renewed desire as he thought about the fact that she had allowed *him* to be her first. Arms tightening reflexively about her, he squeezed her hard against him.

There was something he needed to know. Sure she had wanted him, had been on fire for him, he'd seen to that, but . . . "You don't have any . . . regrets . . . do you? I mean . . ."

She placed a finger on his lips. After her wanton response, how could he think such a thing? "No. No regrets."

"But your people? Scorpion?"

"Scorpion has not spoken for me. Now he will not." Anger laced her words.

"I just don't want to be the cause of hard feelings, or make trouble for you."

Hard feelings? She sniffed. She did not know if she could ever forgive Scorpion his actions. But in a teasing tone, she added, "No one will slit my nose." Suddenly, she became pensive. Now that she knew Brent and had tasted his lovemaking, her life would be sad and terribly lonely when he left.

Brent's eyes widened. Slit her nose? Damn! "Is that what happens to an Apache woman if she's not faithful?"

She somberly nodded.

He was curious. "What happens if a warrior cheats on his woman?"

A mischievous gleam reflected golden in her eyes. Brent held his breath.

"A woman has the right to kill a disloyal husband."

"You've gotta be kiddin'."

She shook her head. "There is one hardship. The woman may never find another man who will have her."

Brent looked incredulous. Then, when she grinned, he realized the humor of her statement, even if it were true. He laughed.

When Lark forgot herself and laughed, Brent thought he'd never heard anything so moving. The throaty sound was soft and musical. He longed to hear it more often.

All at once, he cocked his head. He'd heard a horse snort. His arms squeezed a warning to her. Now a bit jangled. "Surrender your weapons," someone barked. "Come out slowly. You are surrounded by the United States Cavalry."

Chapter Fourteen

Saddle leather creaked. Brent and Meadowlark froze, taken completely by surprise. He muttered an explicit oath. Meadowlark's eyes rounded larger than an owl's as she scrambled from beneath the ground sheet.

Brent motioned her to hurry and dress at the same time the leather tunic slithered over her head. Carefully patting the cover around him and watching Lark's progress from the corner of his eye, he called, "Hold your fire. I'm Captain McQuade from San Carlos. I've been injured and can't come out."

Whispered commands and a muted scuffling of troop boots sounded from the entrance. A saber tip cautiously thrust aside the flap just before the white-eyed, tight-lipped countenance of a very frightened private poked through the doorway. The rest of a gangly body crept inside a foot at a time.

"Well, what did you find, Timmons?" was barked from a few feet beyond the opening.

Another private followed the first and the four bodies compacted the limited space of the small wickiup. Four sets of eyes warily scanned each other. The first soldier scooted backward as far as he could without shoving his friend from the enclosure. "They be two of 'em, Sarge. A woman, an' de man, he be down, jes' like him says."

Meadowlark picked up the captain's jacket, which

she had rinsed in the stream, dried and neatly folded. She handed it to the private who seemed to be in charge. The amount of white visible around his eyes, promptly diminished as he held the piece of uniform outside. "He be a so'jer a'right. A cap'n."

Soon, a pair of knees and a grimy face squatted in the doorway. "I'm Sergeant Ahern, sir, with a scouting detail from Fort Thomas. Can we be of assistance?"

Brent struggled onto his left elbow and immediately felt the fan of Lark's rapid expulsions of breath on his bare shoulder, so closely was she hovering behind him. "Actually, Sergeant, I think I'm going to be all right now, thanks to my friend." The direction of his nod indicated Meadowlark, and he could have shot himself for drawing the attention to her when he sensed the tension emanating from her slight form.

The sergeant crawled inside as far as possible and peered intently at the two strangers, especially the woman. "We've been on the lookout for a buck and a half-breed squaw who jumped the reservation at San Carlos. You know anything about that, or happen to have seen 'em, sir?"

A muscle in Brent's jaw spasmed. His skin quivered beneath the slight suction of Lark's indrawn breath. His voice was low and deceptively calm as he replied, "You've just insulted a *lady* who saved my life, mister."

The long, weathered face became more indistinct as the man shifted his weight backward. "Beg your pardon, sir, ma'am. Didn't mean any disrespect."

Brent glanced back and gave Lark a reassuring grin, but could tell from her pinched features it had little effect. Her eyes shone like two gold coins when flames from the fire suddenly blazed higher. Shadows flickered and ebbed, casting her in an eerie, almost haunted light.

He turned eyes of blue steel on the two privates. "Help me out of here, will you? We can't talk like this."

Moving was awkward, but the short journey was managed quickly and only jostled Brent's injured shoulder twice. Outside, Brent was brought face to face with a wizened older sergeant who appeared to have spent his entire life out-of-doors. The skin on his face, neck and hands was tanned a deep brown and wrinkles creased the flesh like age lines on fine leather.

Twelve troopers ringed the camp, appearing, in age and state of crispness of dress, to range from new recruits to old veterans. They had all dismounted and loosened their girths, allowing their horses a drink and a little rest.

Brent nodded to himself, glad to see them taking good care of their animals. In his time, he'd seen soldiers steal oats and even gather sparse grass for their horses. He, and most good cavalrymen, shared precious water from their canteens with their mounts. In Indian warfare, a poor horse could put you afoot. No one wanted to think about those consequences.

"How long have you and your detail been out, Sergeant?"

The older man pulled a plug of tobacco from the top of his boot and offered it to Brent, who declined. Biting off a good chaw, Sergeant Ahern settled onto a flat rock near the injured officer. "Near two weeks now. Met up with troops from Fort Bowie and Fort 'Pache." He spat and moved the lump of tobacco to the other cheek. "With so many patrols out, shouldn't be too many more Injuns trying to make a run for it."

Brent merely cocked a heavy brow. It was typical soldier superiority speaking. Funny how they all seemed to forget that a year ago, with little more than a few sightings and small skirmishes, Geronimo and seven hundred Apaches had fled in the midst of over five thousand strategically deployed troops.

Sergeant Ahern pointed to the wickiup where Meadowlark remained hidden. "She fits the description of the . . . woman we're looking for. What happened to the buck? We were told the two of 'em were headed south and in a hurry."

Brent yawned and stretched his good arm, stalling as he tried to think. "Don't know if he's the one you're after or not, but I had a run-in with a mighty touchy warrior. Would've died if Miss Russell hadn't come along when she did. She's been here ever since, so don't figure she had plans on leavin' the country." He rubbed his sore arm. "You say the two you're lookin' for are travelin' together?"

From inside the shelter, Meadowlark's insides turned all hot and mushy. Brent McQuade had just repaid the gift of his life with that of hers. Although not in as drastic a sense, he was saving her the embarrassment of returning to the reservation as a prisoner and the humiliation and degradation of being kept under guard. *If* the sergeant believed what he said.

She clasped her hands and bowed her head. Thanks to the captain, there was a chance she would retain the freedom to ride her mare and travel over the reservation. It may be little enough in itself, but was far better than the alternative.

"Well, there's always a chance I'm mistaken," the sergeant reluctantly admitted. "A couple of my scouts are ranging to the south. We'll take extra precautions to find the renegade who did this to you."

The sergeant's voice was rough, his words skeptical, but they were a balm to Meadowlark's ears. Scorpion would be well beyond his reach by now, and the man appeared to have accepted Brent's account of her actions. She wondered why he had chosen to disregard the fact that she may have been one of the reasons for Scorpion's attack?

The pain of Scorpion's viciousness continued to literally double her over. Although victorious, he had acted the coward. No honor involved. No daring feat to boast about around a camp fire. If she had not seen it with her own eyes, she would never have believed her longtime friend capable of such shame.

However, thoughts of Scorpion evaporated like puffs of gray smoke in a swirling dust devil as she listened to Brent and the sergeant talk about the officer who had taken over as agent at Fort Thomas. The captain had been telling the truth about Crook's replacing civilian agents with officers. The revelation came as no surprise. The more she knew of Brent McQuade, the more she respected him.

She leaned back on the ground sheet and listened to the men's conversation drone on. She loved to listen to Brent's voice. Its low, rumbling tones. The way he softened the crispness of his words when he was upset. It reminded her of the softness of his hands and their ability to entice her body to experience the most pleasurable sensations.

A slow warmth seeped throughout her bones until she slumped down on her stomach and peered out to the circled men. Her gaze darted at once to Brent's prone figure. Pride wriggled through her constricted chest. Of all of the men, he was the most handsome. His body the most beautifully sculpted. Though she knew *only his* intimately, it *had* to be, because his was the tallest, leanest, broadest . . .

She had to tear her eyes away. Although it was impossible for him to see inside the wickiup, he had turned his head to look in her direction. Caught. Trapped. He knew. Her mind raced and she wondered if he had the power to know her thoughts. It was not possible. Was it?

Sergeant Ahern noted the captain's evident distraction. "Would you like us to escort you to San Carlos, Captain McQuade?"

"What?" Brent snapped around to stare at the sergeant. Though he didn't want to appear overly anxious, he hoped the troop moved on soon. He was concerned about Lark.

"We could build you a travois." The sergeant

glanced around the open countryside. "It's dangerous to stay out here alone for too long."

A flash of heat ignited Brent's lower belly. "God, I hope so."

The sergeant cocked his head. "What was that?"

"We, uh, won't be stayin' much longer. I'll be up to ridin' real soon." Sweat beaded his forehead and upper lip. He had been ready for ten minutes. Why didn't the damned soldiers leave? She was inside, waiting. He sensed her watching. Wondered what she was thinking.

Was she remembering their lovemaking? Did she want him again as much as he wanted—needed—her?

Would she be grateful he had kept her out of the troops hands, or would she be angry that he had interfered? She was so complex and unreadable. He never knew from one minute to the next what to expect. And it was wonderfully exciting. He enjoyed a good challenge.

Brent swallowed a groan of relief when the sergeant rose to his feet. But the soldier just stood, staring down at him. Brent glanced nervously around the fire. No one else seemed to have suspicions about his story.

Sergeant Ahern placed his hands on his hips. He couldn't force his help on the officer, but Captain McQuade was definitely not in his right mind. His eyes held a faraway look and perspiration had suddenly broken out on his upper body. Probably still had a touch of fever. "I hate to go off and leave you, Captain, but we've got to move on. I'll wire San Carlos if we catch up to that renegade."

Brent nodded. "Thanks." Leaving. Finally. Why didn't they go ahead and just *do* it?

The sergeant shook his head and walked over to the wickiup. He hunkered down and whispered, "Ma'am, the captain seems feverish. You need some medicine?"

Meadowlark was surprised by the man's solicitous

tone. “N-no. Thank you. I will see to him right away.”

“Yes, ma’am, you’d best do that.” He ducked his head and held out the double-breasted jacket. “From the looks of that hole, he had a right nasty wound. Seems you’ve done a good job of patching him up.”

She nodded, then doubted he could see her in the darkened interior. “I did what I could.” Satisfaction softened her voice.

After a short silence, Ahern added, “Sorry ’bout what I said earlier, ma’am.” Then he shot to his feet and returned to his troopers. “Check your saddles. Prepare to mount.”

In less than a heartbeat, it seemed to Meadowlark, the soldiers were gone. She sat stunned, wondering at the sergeant’s change in attitude, as if she deserved a medal for her actions. The captain had been hurt. All she had done was come back and . . .

The scene beside the river replayed in her mind. Realization dawned on her. She had stepped in front of Scorpion’s blade to save Brent. The cliff she had ridden down to escape both Scorpion and the soldiers could have killed her. Fear had consumed her every moment until she found her way back and discovered that he still lived.

Hours spent forcing medicine down his throat. Holding him when he chilled. Letting him touch her. The ways she touched him. Their lovemaking.

No other man had affected her heart like the captain. It was wonderful. It was sad. There would never be another man to take his place. The years ahead loomed lonely indeed because there was no place for *him* in her life.

“Lark?”

She tensed. When he called her that, something inside twisted.

“Can you help me?”

He had managed to make the doorway. The sheet had slipped down until it barely covered the lower half of his body. Every muscle flexed as he tried to enter the shelter. Meadowlark focused on the broad expanse of his chest. Then her gaze followed the mat of light hair down, down . . .

Her pulse quickened. She couldn't catch her breath. Her lower belly and that central core of her pulsed with heat and . . . excitement. No! It could not be happening again. She tried to mentally ignore her traitorous body.

Slowly, as if treading over a bed of sharp thorns, she crossed the few feet separating them. Her hand trembled as she reached out. His eyes turned up and she melted at the sight of his pained embarrassment and . . . what was that she saw? Eager anticipation? Did he feel the same as she?

She jerked back. He caught her wrist. "Help me. Please."

"I-I—"

"Please?"

She could not do otherwise. Resigned to her fate, knowing it was useless to fight him when he so desperately needed her. Her own desires were another matter. She would resist. She had to.

Taking a moment to bolster her strength, she hooked his good arm around her shoulders and supported as much of his weight as she could. The sheet fell from his hand. She tried to keep her eyes on the dying fire, anything within her line of vision, but failed miserably.

His flesh was vibrant and supple beneath her fingers. Warm puffs of breath teased her temples and neck as he leaned over her. Every fiber of her being was set aquiver by the time they reached the center of the wickiup. She looked at the packed earth, the loosely entwined branches. Gently she bent down on her knees and lowered him to the ground.

"The tarp. I will get it." She had to take her mind off of him, divert her thoughts to something besides the special passion they had shared, the feelings that still clamored in her body.

But his hand was still curved around her shoulder. He pulled her close, so close. His lips tasted the lobe of her ear. She shivered and allowed her body to sag against him. No! Of their own volition her arms lifted to push against his chest. Or were her fingers curling in the soft mat of hair?

He trailed kisses down the side of her neck. No! She writhed, trying to escape. Or was she only arching nearer? Through the supple leather tunic, her nipples hardened as they brushed over his solid strength.

No! She kicked out, desperately seeking a foothold, anything to give her enough momentum to move away from his embrace. But his hand thrust beneath her tunic. His palm slid gently, resolutely up her back, down her rib cage, up the smooth flesh of her belly. Her muscles contracted as her body came to life like a bud opening to the warmth of the sun.

Brent cupped the silky underside of her breast. His thumb rubbed across the point of her nipple until it puckered and throbbed with sensation. "Love me, Lark."

She choked on a sob. "No!"

"Then kiss me."

"No."

"Just one little kiss?"

"No-o-o!"

"Please."

"I-I—"

"Please, Lark?" It was as close to begging as he'd ever come.

She lay sprawled across his chest. He had no hold on her now except where his palm warmed the fullness of her breast. All she needed to do was ignore the sound of his voice, the tender way he said "Lark" . . .

He shifted his hips until she lay across his lap. Her eyes flew up to his and she had made a mistake. His eyes were the color of indigo—deep, beckoning, pleading. They were magic and magnetic. They tempted her lips to just brush his.

"Yes, honey."

Thunder crashed. Lightning streaked the sky. The greater forces of nature consumed her soul as surely as they consumed the heavens. Her body thrilled as each rumble vibrated her senses. Each explosion of light ignited an inner blaze that devoured her capacity to think.

Her clothing might have evaporated for all that she was aware that it was gone. His lips burned a fiery trail down her neck and chest. She nearly screamed out with agony and delight when he suckled at her breast.

The storm outside the wickiup raged. Inside was just as devastating a disturbance. Blood surged through Meadowlark's veins. Every pore became flushed and sensitive to his touch. Her legs parted as a flower petal would spread to absorb the rain when his manhood quested between her thighs.

He thrust suddenly, deeply. It felt as if he were the driving force of her power and it was centered in her femininity. Each movement of his hips was met with one of her own until she could take no more of him into her.

Lightning struck a tree across the creek. Seared bark sizzled and popped as their flesh melded, mated. Their bodies were one. The current of the lightning might just as well have coursed through Meadowlark as she rode and reveled in his possession.

With each driving thrust of Brent's body, she felt the pressure and heat increase. Like the stricken tree, she felt as if she could fragment into a thousand splinters. She gripped his hips with her hands and her thighs, holding onto the last secure vestige on earth as the heavens finally erupted and overflowed.

Brent gasped for breath, plunging, straining, spilling his seed in short, hot bursts that drained part of his soul. Her body stretched to receive him as she met his thrusts and answered with spasm after spasm of her own fulfillment.

He surged upward, his eyes intent on Meadowlark's enraptured face. His pleasure had been doubled by watching and feeling the naked passion of the woman straddling his lap. She had literally taken control, but he knew if he ever mentioned it, she would deny the truth.

Spent, he caught her in his good arm as she leaned down onto his chest. He didn't think he had ever taken such satisfaction in seeing to a woman's gratification. Had never been so concerned that she attain the most from what he had to give.

The storm outside gradually abated, along with their heavy breathing. The air was still, almost static. Water dripped between the woven branches and cooled their too-warm skin.

Her nose nestled into the hollow at the base of his throat. A tiny hand spread across his chest. An answering warmth filled his heart. Such a tiny little thing. She needed him. He needed her. Lightning exploded in his brain. *He* needed her? Denial reverberated throughout his body. But he held her tight. So tight.

Meadowlark sat outside the wickiup, facing the western horizon. Silvery highlights outlined impressive gray masses, setting apart the clouds from the brilliant, varying shades of maroon and lavender and orange and red, staining the newly washed sky.

She inhaled the fresh evening breeze, so pungent and clean after the sudden storm. Her lids drooped lazily to cover her eyes. Her limbs felt heavy and sluggish. She could not seem to overcome the unfamiliar sensation of total lethargy.

Earlier she had rebuilt the fire and snared another

rabbit. The soldiers had left jerky and hardtack, which she had discovered just inside the entrance of their shelter. She thought the sergeant must have left it when he came to bid her good-bye.

Good-bye. A shiver raced down her spine. She wrapped her arms about her waist and watched a thin, dried twig shrivel and curl before bursting into flames. Would that be her fate when Capt. Brent McQuade left Arizona Territory and returned to his home? His real home. Would she wither away without him?

Straightening her back, she sniffed and thought not. Oh, she would miss him. Her life would never be the same. And she knew there would never be another man whom she would . . . love. Yes, she had thought long and hard on the subject and she did love the handsome, daring captain.

It seemed as though the spirits had directed him to her, proving that she had a chosen mate in the world. He had touched a part of her that she had never known existed. He would have a special place, a little nook tucked away in the recesses of her heart. He would occupy that space for all time. If only . . .

"Meadowlark? Where are you?"

She smiled at the note of panic in his voice. He would miss *her,* too. He cared for her, whether he would admit it or not. It pleased her to know that.

She took one last, longing look at what was left of the sunset and gracefully rose to her feet. Bending low, she reentered the shelter.

Brent smiled when he saw her. For some reason, when he'd awakened and she'd been gone from his side, he'd been frightened. And then he'd become angry at himself for that unaccustomed *needy* feeling suffocating his chest.

Strange things were happening to him—to his body and mind—since crossing Meadowlark Russell's path. The emotions were not always explainable, defied logic and were, therefore, startling and somewhat fearful. He liked order in his life and nothing about Lark was routine.

When she sat down beside him, he reached out and took one of her hands in his. Her fingers were small and so fragile, yet were lined with calluses. He wished her life could have been easier, that he could give her everything . . . Damn!

"Ahem, I've been wondering why you left San Carlos." He groaned. Just because the question had been on his mind for days didn't mean he had to blurt it out like a curious fool.

Meadowlark did not even blink. She had wondered when he would ask for explanations. It was the white man's way to worry an old bone. "Scorpion took my mare."

"Why? Why'd he do something so low-down and sneaky? I thought you two were . . . uh, you know."

Meadowlark's mind was filled with images of Scorpion—the Scorpion of her youth. Her friend. She did not really pay attention to Brent's last statement. "He knew it was the only way I would leave San Carlos."

Brent frowned. "He wanted to leave, but you didn't?"

She nodded.

Thinking of the horrible, squalid conditions of San Carlos, he was genuinely looking for answers when he asked, "Why didn't you want to go?"

"My people need me. You and I, we talked of ways to make life better on the reservation. Yes?"

"Sure, I remember."

"And then there is the matter of . . . a killer."

With everything else that had been happening lately, Brent had almost forgotten about Maurice Russell's murderer.

Suddenly his pulse beat erratically. A lead weight crushed his chest. She hadn't returned just because of him, or because she was worried about whether he lived or died. She would have gone back to San Carlos one way or the other. He just happened to be on the way.

Funny, he thought—although it wasn't really—how much that realization hurt.

"Well," he sighed, "I'm glad you weren't running to Mexico."

She cocked her head to one side and studied him. He blinked and looked away, unable to hold her intent gaze.

"Would you have followed me to Mexico, Brent?"

Damnable heat rushed up his neck and he squirmed beneath the cover. He wished he could pull the ground sheet over his face and hide. He'd asked himself that same question and still had no reasonable answer. He kept trying to tell himself he'd only started the trek because she had taken off into the desert on foot. He'd just been worried for her safety.

So, when he'd seen she had her horse back and that she was safe, he guessed, with Scorpion, why hadn't he turned around and made a run for it back to San Carlos? Instead, he'd stayed and made an ass of himself and almost gotten them both killed.

He glanced over at her smooth, peach-tinted face. His mouth opened. His jaw worked. He croaked, "I don't know." Being able to admit to *that* much, rekindled some of his courage and he met her eyes. "Why did you throw yourself between me and Scorpion's knife?"

"Because half of the United States Cavalry would be hunting us once your body was found." She did not have to think about the answer. It was the one she had rationalized over as she had left with Scorpion.

But that was *before*. Before she recognized the depth of her feelings for Brent McQuade, the good, honest, decent man. A man who cared enough to come a long distance after her to, perhaps, save her from herself. A man who *would* have followed her to Mexico.

Brent thought his heart had been rended in two.

How could she be so callous? Surely there was more behind her actions than just concern for the army's retribution. Yet she had never given any indication that she cared for him, more than maybe as a friend, or a person who could be of use to help "her people," as she so often stated.

Sure, she had been passionate beyond belief when they made love, but that was a part of her nature. He'd known her responses would be hot and wild. Had done his damnedest to assure it. But that was no reason to think she *cared.* Hadn't she just given him all the proof he needed that any relationship they had was perfunctory on her part at best?

Disheartened, he swallowed the bile gorging his throat. "Well, I'll always be grateful you came back for me."

She nodded, doing her best to hold back the frown that threatened to crack her stony features. Was that all? Would he not ask her anything else? *Say* anything else?

"Guess we can leave tomorrow." He flexed his right arm. "My shoulder is better."

Meadowlark just stared. Had she been mistaken? Did he not care for her after all? Should he not have asked a few more questions? At least tried to worm out her deepest secrets?

Yet now he was in a hurry to leave. Anxious, maybe, to get back to his responsibilities. Back to his life.

She reached across him to check his wound. Her eyes narrowed. A scab had begun to form on the outer edges and had stuck to the cloth. She yanked it off.

"Ouch! What the hell're you tryin' to do, skin me alive?"

As she quickly hurried from the wickiup to fetch a fresh dressing, a contented sigh escaped her clenched teeth.

Chapter Fifteen

Brent crawled from the wickiup and straightened his back, grateful to be leaving the close confines of the shelter. Yesterday's storm and this morning's high winds were taking their toll. Dried leaves and twigs shook and rattled and tore free. There were bare spaces now between the sturdier branches. But it had served its purpose and Brent would always harbor fond memories of the little refuge.

A horse snorted behind him and he turned to find Meadowlark holding her mare's lead. His gaze reluctantly slid past her, though not before he noted the dark circles beneath her eyes. Good. He hoped she'd spent as miserable a night as he. They had both huddled on a corner of the sheet, straining away from each other, knowing that one touch, just one light brush of flesh against flesh and they'd . . .

Buckling his gun belt around his waist as best he could using his left hand, he said, "Guess the gelding's enjoying his freedom. I'll fetch him up in a minute."

Meadowlark looked at the ground, then to the naked treetops and back to the small limbs tumbling end over end from the shelter with each wicked gust of cold air. She held her hair out of her eyes and watched Brent struggle to dress. He was so tall and slender, yet his authoritative demeanor gave the impression of a man of much greater bulk. Muscles bulged in his uninjured arm as he tried to hold the flap of his holster together and flip the buckle at the same time.

With a shake of her head, she handed the lead to Brent. She stood directly in front of him, her nose within inches of the curly blond hair peeking from the open top buttons on his jacket and shirt. She grasped the thick leather with both hands and breathed deeply in an effort to calm her suddenly raging senses. The opposite occurred, though, as she inhaled his musky, masculine scent. Her knees began to tremble.

One good yank drew the belt together and she quickly closed the buckle. At the same time, the movement had thrown Brent off balance and he stumbled into her. Fancy footwork ensued as they gingerly sidestepped and managed to avoid touching each other.

"Excuse me."

"Sorry."

"I'll go get the horse."

"It is gone."

"What?" Brent halted in midstride. At first he thought she might be joking, but then remembered that he'd never seen Lark kid or joke with *anyone.* And her expression was dead serious. He gulped and wiped his hands down his trouser legs. "Where'd he go?"

Her dark, perfectly arched brows drew together just before she gave him that all-too-familiar shrug.

He cursed the stupid question. If she knew, she'd have the horse, wouldn't she? If she was anything, she was efficient. He swallowed another curse. Now he was jealous of her knowledge and experience. Yet as she stood so close in front of him, he had to smother an irresistible urge to plant tender kisses on both of those tempting almond-shaped eyes and her rosy, wind-burned cheeks.

Instead, he cast a woeful glance toward his boots, sitting neatly in a row off to his right side. He sagged to the ground. Maybe leaving wasn't such a good idea. What good did it do, going to the trouble of dressing, when he didn't even have a damned horse to ride, or the energy with which to mount it if he did?

Meadowlark sensed his dejection and noted the direction of his gaze. She recognized the battle warring inside her captain. He was used to caring for himself and anyone else who needed him, but felt helpless and inadequate when it came to the situation being reversed.

Since he still held the mare's lead, she walked over to his boots, picked them up and brought them to him. She looked from his wriggling, stockinged toes to the high-topped footwear. Getting his feet into these could not be easy with two *good* hands.

As clearly as she had seen the tracks of a sidewinder in the sand while gathering her horse earlier, she knew there was no choice but to help. A shudder racked her tiny form as she knelt at his feet.

She sensed his smile. Her insides turned wrong-side-out. Not daring to look into his face, she held out the left boot. He stuck his toes inside the narrow stovepipe upper and slid it up his leg as far as it would go before the arch of his foot prevented further easy access. She put her hand on the sole and pushed. He used his left hand and pulled. It moved *maybe* another inch.

Shooting him a why-do-men-wear-such-confounded-contraptions look, she climbed to her feet. A grimace curled her lips as she stood with her hands on her hips, trying to decide the best course of action. His expression was so sheepish and hangdog, that she sighed with exaggerated exasperation. As calmly and nonchalantly as possible, she stepped one moccasined foot over his legs and settled her posterior in his lap.

Her teeth ground together when he audibly groaned. She gave an extra-hard wriggle as a warning and leaned forward to grab the top of his boot. She yanked. It slid up a fraction. She pulled. It stopped moving altogether. Her bottom ground into his crotch. She dug her heels in and jerked again.

"My God, woman! You're goin' to unman me."

Meadowlark's eyes glinted devilishly. She settled in to give the boot a yank. He leaned forward, his chest curving around her back, his chin resting on her shoulders. His breath was warm and moist on her neck. She shivered.

From that position, he reached down with his good hand and took hold of the boot, too. Together they pulled. His toes wriggled down. They tugged on the heel and pulled again. A muted *whummphh* gave proof to their success. She looked over her shoulder. He smiled. A grin spread across her face as she ducked her head.

Then they turned to the right boot. She wriggled to get a better seat. He groaned. His breath taunted the sensitive spot at the base of her neck. "I can't do this, honey. Honest, I can't."

Grim satisfaction was replaced by tender concern. She had not meant to hurt him—well, maybe just a little. His arm was around her waist. She liked the possessive, protective feel of it there. But slowly, reluctantly, she moved away and went to stand behind his back. Better. Much better.

Brent saw her intent and bent his leg. She reached around his shoulders and could just barely grasp the slick leather. He was too big and broad. Too . . . She closed her eyes and pulled. Her feet slipped. Her breasts smashed into his back.

Brent moaned, pitiful, mournful, like a hound with a nose full of porcupine quills. Her breath came in ragged gasps. They both sighed when another *whhumphh* sounded.

Meadowlark fell back onto her bottom. The sudden movement caused the mare to shy, but Brent had a death grip on the rope. He'd had to hold onto something, or he would've filled his hands with ripe, luscious Lark. After the thoroughbred was under control, he gazed into the heavens. What had he done to deserve such prolonged torture?

Maybe once they returned to San Carlos and things returned to a semblance of normal, he could put this interlude out of his mind forever. For a while there, he'd almost had a change of heart. A woman like Lark could make a man happy, raise a good family . . .

But since something had caused her to hardly abide his touch, it was a good thing he hadn't said anything foolish. And something else puzzled him. If she was so determined to dislike him, why had she let him make love to her? Twice.

Heaven only knew they had a certain "something" between them. Like fire and ice. Their lovemaking raged like a wild fire, and afterward they acted as cold as sleet in a winter wind. It was true. He was as guilty as she. And now? He wanted her worse than ever.

Confused by the absurdities of life, he struggled to his feet and stamped them securely into his boots. The lead rope still dangled from his hand. He looked curiously from Lark to the horse. Although he was weak and his wound throbbed after the effort of pulling on the boots, he did the only gentlemanly thing. "You ride an' I'll walk. It might take longer to get back, but I guess it won't matter."

He sounded as disappointed as a dog whose bone had slipped into the river. Only this dog, she thought, had an injured shoulder and useless forepaw that she had spent days nursing. Meadowlark fought the urge to wrap her fingers around his thick throat. "You are hurt. I will walk," she insisted. "Apaches are used to traveling quickly on foot."

Brent's eyes narrowed. She had deliberately insulted him, challenging his rights as a man. Yet, in the back of his mind, he couldn't rationally argue the point. The minx had kept ahead of him for a day and a half after she'd left San Carlos to retrieve her mare.

Still, it was not a woman's place to walk. He took a

step toward her, his hands clenching and unclenching at his sides. "I'm walkin'."

"I will walk."

Stubbornly, mutinously, they set out, both walking. The mare trailed happily behind. Suddenly Brent stopped, slanted a look at Meadowlark and grinned a little-boy grin. She saw that dimple and shyly smiled back. Soon they were both laughing.

"You're more hardheaded than *two* jackasses."

"A mule is less stubborn than you."

They spoke at once and broke into more giggles and deep rumbling chuckles. Brent offered a suggestion after they sobered somewhat. "Why don't we both ride a ways, and then trade off."

Meadowlark consented and he coiled the rope until the mare was at their sides. His face fell. No saddle. Then he remembered the one he'd used on the gelding.

Brent walked back to the camp. He searched everywhere. No saddle. "Somethin' funny's goin' on. The horse I can see wanderin' away, but a saddle?" He threw his good arm in the air. "Hell, the damned horse had to've been stolen." Yet as he looked over to the thoroughbred, he knew if anyone had wanted a horse that bad, he'd have chosen the mare.

Meadowlark did not say a word. She had noticed that the horse's tracks cut more deeply into the sand as they left the picket area and was sure that a fleeing San Carlos Apache had recognized her mare and only taken the army mount. A glimmer of pride reflected in her eyes. It had been a good raid.

Still fuming, Brent picked up his jacket and tried unsuccessfully to shrug into it. His imploring eyes riveted on Meadowlark at about the same time a strong gust of wind toppled the remnants of the wickiup. They both stared at the spot, quietly thinking their private thoughts, undeniable sadness dimming both pairs of eyes. Something important in their lives had disappeared like sand drifting from dune to dune.

Meadowlark tensed when she looked to Brent and saw him still struggling to get into his coat. Pretending that he had no effect on her was going to be hard for the next few days. There were going to be times, like now, when she would have no choice but to help him, to touch him.

Her hands barely trembled as she held the coat. And when he decided that it would be too painful to put his injured arm in the jacket, she calmly helped him into the left sleeve and buttoned it around him as far as she could. Then she suggested that he bend his right arm and rest his wrist over the last button, like a sling.

Loose items she wanted to take with them were rolled into the ground tarp and tucked under her arm. The bundle was heavy and hard to hang on to, so she led the mare to a nearby boulder that was a perfect stepping-stone to swing onto the horse's back. She held the lead rope and motioned for Brent to mount.

While she waited for him to make up his mind whether to climb on first or not, she contemplated the man and how easily his name came to mind lately. It was a strong, solid name, like the soldier himself.

Shaking her head, she stifled another smile as Brent shrugged and tried to appear unconcerned as he awkwardly climbed aboard the mare. Meadowlark handed him the ground tarp and also clambered up the rock. But when it came time to mount, she was faced with a momentous decision. Should she sit in front of or behind him?

After the fiasco with the boots, she prudently chose behind. But they had traveled only a few miles when she became exhausted from trying to keep from sliding into him. Now she knew why he had wanted that saddle. There was no way to avoid close contact—real close. From her nose to her knees, her body was one solid nerve—feeling, experiencing, reacting.

Brent kept his eyes straight ahead. He concentrated on the countryside, watching for dips and swales, guiding the mare around prairie dog holes. All the while he told himself the horse couldn't find its way without him, that he *had* to pick the way, to do *anything* besides think about the two round globes brushing, nudging, flattening against his back.

Sensations shooting along his spine, butt and thighs from the thrust of her body rolling and rocking into his was enough to drive a man to an early grave. Heart trouble. That was what it was. She was putting a terrible strain on his old ticker. If it beat any faster or harder, it would pound a hole through his chest.

They rode in silence. The mare's long-legged gait evened out to a steady walk. Now, Brent thought, while they were together on the horse, would be the perfect time to broach a subject that'd been bothering him. The rope reins suddenly slipped between his damp fingers. He brushed his forehead with the back of his sleeve. "Ahem, Meadowlark?"

She had finally tired of the useless chore of trying to avoid his lean, virile body. She allowed herself to shift wherever the horse's motions carried her. "What?" She could have slid under the mare's belly when her voice came out a breathless whisper.

"Uh, about what happened . . . back there." He clamped his teeth together when he thought they were going to start chattering as if he were a quaking coward.

The muffled shuffle of horse's hooves scuffing sand was the only sound for miles. They had ridden quite a ways and it seemed Lark wasn't going to comment. He inhaled deeply, wishing he had a cheroot stuffed in a pocket somewhere. "Meadowlark?"

"Hmmm?"

He sighed. She felt so good, pressing her body into his. Too good. He should never have . . . "I know a little about you . . . that is, the Apache beliefs. And I know . . ."

The mare stumbled. Meadowlark wrapped her arms around his waist to keep from rolling off. "You know *what?*" His rambling was making her skittish.

"You, had never been with a man."

Her eyes narrowed. "No-o-o." Was that what was wrong? She had thought he would be happy.

"There's a chance you could be . . . well, when a man and a woman . . . I'll be around San Carlos a good while yet. You know, if you need me . . . for . . . anything."

He tried to turn when he felt her sag into him. Her body was trembling. He twisted as far as he could, but still could not see her face. "Aw, damn. You aren't cryin', are you? I'll . . . we'll . . . oh, hell!"

His throat constricted. He'd offer to do the honorable thing. His lustful urges had gotten the best of him. It was his responsibility. Whether he wanted one or not, it looked as if he was going to have a wife at San Carlos after all.

"Wh-when we get back, I'll look up the chaplain. He . . . I . . . we . . . can be . . . m-m-married, ahem, right away." God help him!

Once she grasped the gist of Brent's meandering conversation, her inner tension was replaced by open-mouthed wonder. Then a curious sense of hilarity overwhelmed her. White men were funny. At least this one white man.

He talked as if she were a child, uneducated in the ways of coupling. It was worthy of him to offer, what sounded to her to be his grand sacrifice, but she was affronted by his superior attitude.

She had allowed him the rights usually reserved for a woman's husband. Because she had no family near, she felt right in making him *her* choice.

In reality, he was her husband; would always be. She had no intention of taking another man. But she would *not* marry the white man. Not now. Not ever. She would not suffer the humiliation of being left behind, alone, perhaps with family, when he took the notion to leave the reservation.

He would leave. Burdened with a half-breed wife and brats he had no use for, he would be embarrassed to take them with him. She had seen it happen before—to her cousin Pilar and two of her mother's dearest friends. No white man, or Apache, would have Pilar, other than to lay with her and toss her a few pennies for the service.

Meadowlark was too proud to allow that to happen to her. It was an insult that he did not know she would never have given herself to him if she had thought it would cause him remorse. Listening to him, hearing the concern, the fear, the anguish and what sounded like the resignation of thinking he would have to wed her . . .

Have to? She swallowed a sad chuckle. Felt an uncontrollable fit of giggles crowding into her throat. The poor captain. It might serve him right if she *did* take him as her man. How would he explain her to . . . what was her name? Lizbeth?

Brent cocked his head. There! That sound. His brows nearly touched. That wasn't her sobs he heard. She was laughing. Laughing. He was pouring his guts out, offering to do the right thing by her and she had the nerve to laugh.

He stopped the horse, threw his leg over its neck and slid to the ground. Curses erupted when the sudden jar sent a jolt of pain through his shoulder. Angry enough to spit nails, he looked up and demanded, "Listen to me, woman. This is serious. What if you're carrying my child. What if—"

"I will tell you, if it is so." Her lips continued to twitch suspiciously, though the backs of her eyes burned with unshed tears.

"Well, I . . . damned right you will. And I . . . we'll

still . . ." To his consternation, he couldn't quit sputtering. Her forthrightness was entirely too disconcerting.

"There is no hurry to wed."

"I don't know . . ."

"Neither of us wishes to join with the other."

Brent's eyes went wide. She'd made a poor choice of words as far as he was concerned. Looking at her, sitting proud and straight on the mare's back with rays of sunlight playing across her dewy fresh skin, he wanted nothing more than to "join" with her then and there.

What would be so bad about waking up every morning with her supple little body pressed intimately to his, their limbs and breaths entwined? The image of her sleep-drugged whiskey eyes and tousled black curls framing her flushed features caused an instant contraction in his groin.

He shifted his stance and pointedly argued, "I think I know what's best here. As soon as we get to San Carlos, we'll—" His tirade stopped abruptly. Meadowlark's gaze followed his and they both watched the approach of two warriors, three women and a passel of children, ranging from infants in cradle boards to toddlers and young teens. When the Indians became aware of Brent and Meadowlark, they hesitated, then began to run, weaving and dodging until they reached the top of the nearest ridge.

With just the use of his good arm, Brent deftly swung up behind Meadowlark. He grabbed the reins and drummed his heels into the mare's sides. They took off in the direction of the ridge, with Meadowlark doing her best to thwart his pursuit.

A bullet hissed past Brent's head and he pulled the horse up at the bottom of the hill. He tried to set Meadowlark down so he could ride on and not have to worry about her safety, but she refused to be discarded so callously and clung to him like cat claw.

"Damn it, Meadowlark, get off the horse. I've got to stop those Indians." He felt like an ass, climbing up behind her like he'd done, placing her in such danger. If the Apache's aim had been any better . . .

Her hand covered his on the reins. "They are causing no harm. Why must you stop them?"

"Meadowlark, let go," he ordered, trying to free his hand from her surprisingly strong grip. She was pressed so tightly against him that he found it difficult to move. Finally, he released the reins and scooted back until he could drop from the horse. She could have the damned animal. He would go after them on foot.

But Meadowlark had guessed his intention and followed after him, flinging herself off the mare in front of him. Another bullet kicked up the dust at their feet. He grabbed her arm and pulled her behind the protection of a large boulder. The mare shied, dragging the rein out of both of their reaches.

Brent glowered at Meadowlark. "Now see what you've done?" He scowled at the self-satisfied twist of her lips. Shards of stone fell about their heads as more bullets peppered the rock. Instinctively, Brent pulled her close, bending his upper body, sheltering her as best he could.

Flinching with each echoing report, he pictured the damage one small piece of lead could inflict on Lark's beautiful, sensitive body. He would take the bullet himself before he would allow her to be injured.

Meadowlark gasped for breath. The big bear was smothering her. No matter how hard she struggled, she could not budge the steel barricade of his shoulders or evade the strength of his grip. At last she was able to turn her head enough to gulp in some air. Another spurt of gunfire caused her to grasp a handful of his coat and she buried her face in his neck.

Tears blurred her vision. Brent McQuade was protecting her with his body, his life. She blinked rapidly to keep from breaking down and crying like a child just presented with an extra-special gift. She inhaled deeply and reveled in the scents of creek water, horse hair and sweat. Oddly enough, even among the danger and fear, her body responded with a quickening of her pulse rate and a warm tingle between her thighs.

As her arms crept around his slim waist, she hoped her friends on the ridge would keep them pinned down for a long, long time. For once the standoff was over, she had no doubt things would return to the cold, stiff distance they both seemed to work so hard to sustain.

Brent pulled his revolver from his holster and sighted it toward the ridge. Nothing moved. Wherever the marksman was hidden, he had a good view of their position. Several long minutes passed and no more shots were fired. He relaxed slightly and heard a muffled sigh. Hell, he had to be crushing Meadowlark!

He immediately lifted the pressure of his upper body, but she continued to cling to him. Fear crept along his spine. He took his eyes off of the ridge and scoured Meadowlark's tiny form. "Meadowlark, are you all right? Did I hurt you? God, I never meant to—"

"I am a little frightened, is all," she lied. A moment like this might not present itself for a long time and she was determined to take advantage of it. At least she knew he cared for her enough to defend her with his life. She needed to savor that knowledge, if only for a while.

Brent eased his good shoulder against the stone. Keeping his eye on both the ridge and the woman in his arms, tried to settle her more comfortably. "How could they have gotten hold of a rifle? Their weapons should've been confiscated."

Meadowlark shook her head. "You soldiers. You treat the Apache like children. Mindless children. We have learned to cache guns and food that will not spoil for times when they will be needed." She did not mind sharing that secret. She could not explain her feelings, but she *knew* he would not use that information against her people.

Brent rested his chin atop the silken softness of her hair. Strange, but he was almost relieved to know the Apaches had some means of feeding and defending themselves.

Then he mentally reprimanded himself. He couldn't feel sorry for them and still do his duty. They would not be allowed to leave. He scanned the hillside again and admitted to being surprised at finding more Indians, especially families, running south. They were getting plenty of rations now.

His brows furrowed. "Hell, Meadowlark, this is ration day at San Carlos. You don't suppose . . ."

They stared into each other's eyes, stricken expressions on both of their faces. Suddenly, Brent put Meadowlark to one side and crawled to his knees, then his feet. Stepping into the open, he holstered his gun, then unbuckled the belt and let it drop to his feet. With his uninjured arm held out from his side, he started up the hill toward the ridge and the waiting Apache marksman.

Meadowlark called for him to come back, but he ignored her and kept walking, slowly, determinedly. "Don't shoot. I'm the San Carlos agent. You're making a big mistake."

He had no idea if the Apaches would understand a word he said. But he continued to talk, attempting to appear confident and unafraid, though his knees quaked so badly he tripped every other step. As he climbed, he explained why he and Meadowlark hadn't been at the agency to hand out supplies.

A clatter of rocks sounded behind him. He jumped and spun, nearly losing his footing. He scowled at Meadowlark. "Go back. There's no call for you to get shot." All the while, he expected a bullet to tear into his back. Surely the Indians wouldn't pass up that good a target.

The only indication that Meadowlark had heard a word he said was reflected in the narrowing of her eyes. He contemplated stopping long enough to paddle her deserving behind, but decided from the impudent tilt of her chin that it would be a waste of time. Her bottom was probably as hard as her head.

Knowing better than that, his mouth quirked and he turned around to continue the climb. His thoughts were distracted, though, by the thought of soft, smooth flesh that almost fit into his palms. Flesh that he was going to enjoy giving a proper tanning once this was all over.

But when he neared the top of the ridge, he shook his head and concentrated on keeping himself and Lark alive. He called, "Come on out. If you go back to San Carlos with me, I promise you won't be punished. There'll be food to go around. Blankets and clothing for everyone. Come out. Now."

Studying the rocks and shrubs, he hurried from one to the other, but there were no shots, no sounds, nothing. Atop the ridge, he stopped and caught his breath. A trickle of sweat rolled down his side. They were gone.

Meadowlark came up beside him. She noted the wan pallor of his cheeks and the rapid rise and fall of his chest. Gently, she took his hand to give him support on the trek back down the hill.

She set him down beside the boulder and unbuttoned his jacket. She clicked her tongue. "Stupid white man . . . better sense . . . start wound bleeding . . ."

Brent heard only a few of her words, but realized she was scolding him for being foolhardy and careless. And she was right. But he was in a hurry now to get back to San Carlos. What if something had gone terribly wrong in their absence? What if the wagons had gone on to the mines? He had let the Apaches down.

Damn it, he wasn't getting off to a very good start on his new job. Not good at all.

He winced when Meadowlark checked his wound. Scowled when she announced that they would have to stop where they were for the night. "Oh, no. Gotta go on. Gotta get back." He tried to get up.

Meadowlark put a restraining hand on his chest. He couldn't seem to gather the strength to fend it off.

A wicked grin bared Meadowlark's even white teeth as she rolled out the ground sheet. "Lie down, Captain. You will follow *my* orders this night."

He wearily tried to argue even as his eyelids fluttered closed. "But . . . my brother . . . cattle."

Chapter Sixteen

Brent and Meadowlark rode into San Carlos two days later, just as the sun sank on the western horizon. The journey had taken them longer than expected and Brent was shamefaced because of his weakened condition.

His arms tightened instinctively around the slender form perched in his lap. During the past week, he had come to respect and admire Meadowlark Russell more than any woman he'd ever known, excepting his mother, of course. Lark was soft and gentle, intelligent, resilient, capable . . . A thousand apt adjectives came to mind, but the one that recurred most often seemed to be . . . lovable.

Even now, especially now, she fit perfectly to his body. Her softness molded to his hardness. Her ripe curves filled his flat planes. Without his realizing, she had stealthily crept into his heart and his mind until he couldn't imagine going through the rest of his life without her.

He swallowed hard, unsure of what to do with that knowledge. It was unclear which thought was the more terrifying—that of keeping her, or somehow fooling around and losing her. And there was still the question of whether she would accept his decision that they become husband and wife. One thing for certain, he wouldn't be responsible for causing her embarrassment or ruining her reputation.

As they approached the agency, his arms squeezed

tighter about Meadowlark. Yet as they rode through the compound, there was such a bustle of activity that no one seemed to pay them any mind. Soldiers stood in front of the cantina and lounged in whatever shade was available. The "tent" city had increased in size by another row. Corrals were filled with horses and mules.

They rode up to the office and Brent was puzzled as to why no one had bothered to greet them and question their whereabouts or comment on any nefarious activities in which the two of them—alone—might, or might not, have participated.

Disappointment turned down the corners of his mouth. He'd thought the gossip, sure to be circulated, would be a means of forcing Lark to accept his wishes. He frowned when she slipped off of the mare without waiting for his help, and then had the audacity to shoot him an I-told-you-you-were-worried-about-nothing glare.

Brent shrugged, unconsciously adopting her annoying gesture, and stiffly slid his leg over the horse's uncomfortable back. He felt permanently bowlegged and decidedly tender in certain unmentionable parts after riding bareback for so long. He was glad when Meadowlark took the mare to its corral, leaving him free to limp into the building.

He had barely lowered his aching bones into his chair when a courier stomped through the open door and into the room. The man was so tall that he had to remain stooped as he saluted. "Captain McQuade?"

Brent nodded and wearily slumped against the chair's hard back. He was more tired than he'd thought after the long day's ride, but was happy to be back where his life and libido would return to normal.

He glanced toward the young, buckskin-clad man still standing at attention a few feet away. "Yes, I'm Captain McQuade. What can I do for you?"

"Gen'rl Crook wants to see you right away, sir."

Brent snapped erect. Crook? "The general's here?"

"Yes, sir. He arrived two days ago."

Brent now understood the extra tents. The general was making his preparations. Soon, the detachment would leave for Mexico. Brent's pulse throbbed. His throat went dry. But there was no use in *his* getting excited. The general had made it clear that San Carlos was to be his assignment.

"Tell General Crook I'll be there in just a few minutes."

"I'll do that, sir. Thank you."

When the courier was gone, Brent sat, scratching his chin. He had fully intended to have it out with Lark once and for all about marrying him. Now the discussion would have to be postponed. He sighed and wearily forced himself to his feet. The sooner he saw the general, the sooner he could collapse onto his bed and the sooner he would feel like tangling with his little Apache wildcat. A short grin curved his lips as he left the office.

Meadowlark was relieved to see Brent headed toward the huge tent encampment. Maybe he would find something to keep him busy and give her a chance to collect her thoughts. Her heart jumped into her throat, though, when he staggered once and looked like he was about to fall.

She forced herself to remain where she was and not go running after him. It would be his own fault if his stubborn refusal to admit his weakness caused him more injury. Any normal man would have gone directly to the infirmary, but not Brent McQuade. He would never deign to do such a sensible thing.

At least while he was gone she could have a few minutes of peace without him spouting all that nonsense about her marrying him, she thought, and stalked to the office. It was a nice thought, an honorable idea, and sounded like something he would do. *She* could not. Sitting back in her chair, she looked up at the cracked vigas lining the ceiling. There was no harm in daydreaming, was there, of being Mrs. Capt. Brent McQuade?

Life with a white man. Now that would be interesting, would it not? A warm fluttery sensation tickled her insides as she thought of having to endure his attentions, especially his lovemaking, every day and night.

She shook her head. There were just too many reasons why their union could never be, not the least of which was her refusal to wed a man who did not love her. She wanted a man to look at her the way her father had looked at her mother. Their love had been special and survived the worst obstacles two prejudiced races could place in their paths.

No, she had just enough white blood in her veins to know what she wanted and to insist on getting it. Although many white couples and Apache, too, married for other reasons, she did not presume to believe she could be happy with less than the total joining of two hearts and souls.

If the captain were the only man with whom she experienced that strength of emotion, then so be it. She did not need a man to fulfill her life, although someone like Brent could certainly enhance it. Her life before Brent McQuade had been reasonably happy. She could be content once he left. She hoped.

When they talked again of marriage, she would have to convince him it could not be. He did not *really* want her. *She* would not be a burden to tie him down. He had to understand.

And he would. She knew many ways to insure that he did.

An orderly met Capt. Brent McQuade at Gen. George Crook's tent and disappeared inside. A moment later, Crook himself called out for Brent to enter.

Brent ducked under the flap and stepped aside to allow the orderly to pass. He then saluted his commanding officer. The general returned the salute and gestured toward one of the empty chairs lined up in front of a solid mahogany desk.

About to take his seat, Brent hesitated and suddenly turned his head. He found himself staring into a pair of intent gray-green eyes. The other occupant had pulled a chair to one side and into the shadows of the tent. Slowly, a tall, slender man unfolded his body from the seat and walked into the center of the enclosure so as not to have to bend over.

Pale shaggy hair hung to the collar of a plaid flannel shirt. Stylish cowboy garb and high-topped moccasins clothed the leanly muscled frame of Brandon McQuade. Brent laughed and engulfed his brother in a one-armed grizzly bear of a hug.

"Brandon, what in the hell are you doing here?" Brent cast a wary glance to the general and fought back images of Brand, or the White Fox, standing blindfolded before a firing squad, or with a black hood over his head and a noose tightened around his neck.

However, the general was smiling with no hint of suspicion or sign of recognition marring his genial features. Brent was not convinced and stood tensed, silently cursing his brother for daring to challenge his luck.

Brand, on the other hand, appeared disgustingly relaxed as they exchanged the welcome. "The general and I have been discussing whom he should assign to the post of San Carlos agent since the captain he appointed seems to be missing more often than not."

Though he was teasing, Brand's eyes narrowed with concern at the sight of Brent's ill-fitting jacket and the one empty sleeve which had been turned away until then. "Perhaps the most important questions are, 'Where have you been?' and 'What happened?,' is that not right, General?"

Noticing for the first time the young captain's strained features, General Crook came around the desk and insisted that Brent sit down. He then called for the orderly, who appeared to have been waiting just outside the closed tent flap. "Jonathan, send for the troop surgeon, quickly."

Brent held up a defensive hand. "No, please. Don't worry about me. I'm fine. Really."

General Crook nodded to the orderly, who ducked back out of the tent. "We were told you'd left the post quite mysteriously, about the same time two renegades were reported missing. Were you in pursuit?"

"Yes, sir, I guess you could say that." Brent grimaced as he digested the word "renegade" and thought of it being applied to Lark. "But there was only one warrior who could be termed a "renegade." The other was a woman caught up in something beyond her control." He took a deep breath and indicated his shoulder. "The warrior and I fought. When I lost, the woman saved my life."

Sighing at the sudden glint in Brand's eyes, Brent knew he was due for a good tongue-lashing, or even teasing, for coming out on the worst end of the battle. He gritted his teeth. Not everyone was a super human like the great White Fox.

But his resentment lost out, as usual, to respect for Brandon's indomitable spirit to both survive and flourish during his life with the Apache.

He was saved from having to answer to himself or the others when a commotion at the entrance preceded the arrival of the camp surgeon. A short, wiry little man, wearing a pair of spectacles that nearly obscured his narrow face, blew in like a whirligig.

Brent was tempted to just leave, but at the doctor's clipped orders and Brand's hard glare, finally shrugged out of his jacket, suspenders and shirt. He winced and glowered at his brother when the doc's competent fingers poked and probed his shoulder.

"Uhhmm. Uhhmm huhhmm."

Brent looked pleadingly at Brand, then the general. Both were steadfastly concentrating on what the little man was doing to Brent's puckered flesh.

"Uhhmm. Uhmmm huhhmmmmm."

Unable to stand the hummed litany any longer, Brent craned his neck until he could see the surgeon's face. "Well?"

"Uhhmm. Uh—"

"Doc, how bad is it?" Brent gulped down a shout of pain as his shoulder was lifted and lowered and twisted.

The wound hadn't hurt like that since about five minutes after the knife plunged into his flesh. Was there something wrong that Lark hadn't told him about?

His eyes darted to the doctor's face. The little man looked down his nose through the thick lens of his glasses and winked. A sigh rippled through Brent's taut frame. He'd panicked. His arm would be all right. He trusted Lark. She wouldn't have let him come back to San Carlos if she hadn't thought his wound was better.

Yes, he trusted her, had come to rely on her during the hours she'd spent caring for him. And, maybe, she'd learned she could trust him, too.

While the doctor continued to examine his shoulder, and Brand and the general seemed caught up once again in conversation, Brent had time to wonder if he'd done the right thing by not telling Lark about the crucifix and his suspicions about her friend, Scorpion.

When he had some real proof, that would be the time to mention it. Right now she didn't need that kind of burden with everything else on her mind. His spirits lifted. The decision of just what to do had been weighing on his conscience.

Finally the doctor pushed his spectacles more firmly onto the narrow bridge of his nose. "Shore an' you're a lucky lad. Whoever treated your wound did as fine a job as I've seen."

Pride in Lark's feats swelled Brent's chest.

Brand looked over the surgeon's shoulder and inquired, "Just who is this woman who saved your scrawny hide?"

Brent bristled. For some reason, he was loathe to mention Lark to Brand or to the general, yet knew he would have to explain about her sooner or later. Reluctantly, more surly than he intended, he said, "Her name is Meadowlark Russell. Her father was the agent before he was mur . . . before I replaced him."

His eyes flickered away from Brandon's intent scrutiny. Damn his brother for being so perceptive. Then he stifled a groan when even the general's interest was piqued.

"How did you get along with Russell when you took over as agent? Some of the other officers had trouble."

Brent became very interested in a tuft of grass poking through the tarp floor. "Ahem, there was . . . nothing to . . . speak of." Other than an irate little wildcat of a daughter who nearly skewered him with her sharp words and obstinate attitude.

"Good. Good." Crook pulled at one side of his forked beard.

Brent shifted uncomfortably beneath the gaze of blue-gray eyes that were never still.

"So the man you fought, did he get away?" The general's keen mind had forged ahead to another pressing matter.

Brent grimaced. "Yes, sir." Then he paused to thank the doctor, who had finished binding a fresh dressing to his shoulder and pushed a bottle of pills into his hand. He was concentrating on the surgeon's brusque exit when the general asked, "And the woman?"

His breath caught. Ah, yes, the woman. What was he going to do with her? "We . . . she . . . returned with me."

No one seemed inclined to immediately respond. Brent attempted to change the subject. "You never said what brought you to San Carlos, little brother."

Brand's eyes sparked with suppressed amusement. Brent seethed. That "knowing" look reminded him much too much of a certain little whiskey-eyed woman. What was it about those two and their superior attitudes that made them more Apache than if they had one hundred percent Indian blood flowing through their veins?

"I drove down a few head of cattle in case your beef supply was low." Brand tugged uncomfortably at the bandanna around his neck.

Brent vaguely remembered dreaming something about his brother on the way back to San Carlos. "But . . . I thought it would be at least a year before you would have beef to sell."

"They are not our best or fattest, but cows that did not breed and would be culled this spring anyway. They will still roast well over a camp fire."

Brent held out his left hand. "Thanks, Brand."

Brand smiled and nodded toward the general. "It has been a profitable journey. The general has given us an order to supply beef for the army once our herd is established."

George Crook turned to Brent. "And perhaps the White Mountain Apaches can set an example for the bands at San Carlos. The Indians here need to see that they do things on the reservation to help themselves."

"They've tried before, General. The land is not exactly hospitable, but Meadowlark . . . I mean, Miss Russell and I have given that some thought. We've come up with a few suggestions we'll try to implement."

"Good. When we bring the Apaches back from Mexico, you can instruct them in ways to keep them occupied."

Brent glanced toward Brandon and saw the look of relief on his face. His brother had been worried about the general's intent once he started the trek to the Sierra Madres. Most of Arizona Territory was hoping none of the renegades would live to be returned. And, of course, there was the chance that if the Apaches put up a struggle to remain in their rugged mountains, the general might not have a choice on the outcome.

"When do you plan to go after the renegades, sir?" Brent couldn't keep a slight tinge of wistfulness from his voice. He wanted to be included on the expedition.

"I leave for Willcox in a few weeks. The settlers and townspeople along the border are afraid the Apaches will become bored in Mexico and raid into the United States. I plan to put together a protection force for that area and, at the same time, make inquiries to the Mexican government for permission to cross the border and scout the Sierra Madres. Their answers will determine my timetable."

Brandon straightened in his chair, if it were possible to stiffen such a ramrod-straight back. "When you enter Mexico, how many scouts will you take?"

The general smiled. "Most of my force will be Apache scouts."

Brent's eyes widened. "What?"

"I will take maybe fifty soldiers. The rest of the command will be made up of scouts."

Brandon McQuade's voice became urgent. "May I go with you as a scout? I have been to the Sierra Madres. I might be of help in persuading Geronimo to surrender."

Brent ceased breathing. What in the hell was Brandon doing? Signing his death warrant? Somewhere, somehow, someone was bound to recognize him. The Apaches themselves could inadvertently give away his identity.

Crook thoughtfully studied Brandon while Brent nearly suffocated until the general finally nodded. "I'd be grateful for your company, McQuade. The captain here will contact you when the time is right."

Several minutes passed before Brent changed the subject and asked the question that had worried him all the way back to the agency. "Did you notice if there was trouble when the Apaches came in for rations and found Miss Russell and myself gone?"

Brand smiled. "Why, big brother, do you not believe the world will turn without you?"

Brent frowned.

The general informed the bewildered captain, "Your brother and a Corporal Bent did an admirable job on your behalf. The Apaches were quite satisfied."

"Oh. Well, that's good. I was afraid . . . We ran into a family that was . . ." All of a sudden it occurred to Brent why the Indians were running. Crook's grand arrival had probably frightened some of the more wary Apaches. The situation at San Carlos was volatile and unstable enough without the uncertainty caused by the appearance of more soldiers. No telling how many Apaches had fled during the past few days.

The general seemed to read Brent's mind. "I was afraid some of the people here might be fearful of my arrival. I am prepared to spend the next few weeks visiting the Apache leaders on all of the reservations in the area. I want them to know that I mean what I say when I tell them their lives will improve."

"The White Mountains will welcome your visit, General. You have many friends who remember and respect you." What Brand said was true. His people would feel much more secure now that Crook had returned.

The general's orderly stuck his head inside the tent. "Sorry to interrupt, sir, but you're needed at the corrals. There seems to be some problem with the mules."

Brand stood up and helped his brother to his feet. "We need to leave anyway, General. Our captain looks as if he should have been lowered into his grave hours ago."

Brent would have protested but he was too tired. It was a wonder he hadn't dozed off in front of the general.

Good-byes were accorded and Brandon walked Brent back toward the office while General Crook hurried off to the stables. Brent smiled a crooked smile. "The general still has a thing for mules, has he?"

Brand shrugged. "He does seem to have a way with the long-eared beasts. From what the soldiers tell me, he rode one into San Carlos."

Brent regarded his brother with raised eyebrows. Brand lifted his shoulders. "That is what they said."

"I'll be damned. Guess what I've heard all these years is true." Brent walked slowly, thinking, then cocked his head toward his brother. "When the supply wagons came in, was there a big, ugly bastard in charge?"

Brand hunched his shoulders. "None of the men I saw were exactly pretty, but all five of them were fairly small in size."

Brent took several more steps before he abruptly stopped. "Five? Damn them to hell! How could they have known so fast?"

The air turned blue with the string of oaths that issued from Brent's mouth. Then seeing an inquisitive look on Brand's face, he gave his brother a sickly grin. "There's been a little misunderstandin'. Somethin' I'll need to straighten out before next week, is all."

Brent definitely had unfinished business with Mr. "Slaughter" Ryan. And it would be settled before time for the next rations.

"When're you headin' back to the mountains, little brother?"

Brandon kept a cautious eye on his officer brother, not liking the pallor of Brent's usually ruddy features. "I had planned to return tomorrow, but . . ." His gaze turned longingly toward the north.

Brent had a distinct feeling he understood why. "You miss her that much?"

Brandon nodded. Brent hunched his shoulders. The two brothers continued walking—so different, yet so much alike. And while they walked, Brent wondered what it would feel like to miss a woman so.

Sure he'd been worried and concerned for her safety when Hillary had been abducted, but he'd been able to carry on with Fort Apache business. And when Elizabeth left, he'd been angry and confused, but it hadn't brought his world to an end nor produced the kind of mind-stopping impact he'd just seen on Brandon's face.

Until that moment, Brent had never realized just how much his brother loved his wife. He was glad. Hillary deserved a love that strong.

A niggle of guilt crawled through his gut. Guilt that he'd been incapable of ever giving Hillary, Elizabeth or any other woman that same depth of devotion or commitment. Then whiskey-colored eyes and a gamin grin rudely intruded into his thoughts. Feelings for a certain little woman surged to the surface of his usually well-tempered emotions.

No, he couldn't care that much for Meadowlark Russell. Could he? Not like Brand loved Hillary. No, it couldn't be love. Never love. Love? Naw!

"You have not heard a word I have spoken, my brother."

Brent blinked. "What?"

"Are you sure you will be all right if I leave?"

"Oh, right. You want to go home. I'll be fine." And he would. He just needed rest. Then he'd be able to think rationally again. Rest. In his own bed in the barracks. Away from haunting cat-eyes and whiffs of lavender in the air.

But first he needed to stop by the office. There was a very important reason. Or perhaps several reasons.

"You will let me know when Crook is ready to leave for the Sierra Madres?" Brand stared into his brother's eyes.

"Sure, it's your neck." And damn it! everyone was going to go but Capt. Brent McQuade.

Brandon hesitated, his eyes reflecting wary speculation. Brent sighed. "Sorry, little brother. I'm just tired. Go on home and give Hillary my best. I'll be in touch when it's time."

Relief, and maybe a little emptiness, settled over a subdued Captain McQuade as he watched his brother ride out of San Carlos. He waved once, wishing he were riding out, leaving all of these conflicting emotions behind. But he turned and trudged toward the office.

Inside the tiny room, he sagged into his chair, more exhausted than he could ever remember feeling. It seemed he carried the weight of an ore car on his shoulders. Still, he thumbed through the papers, looking for that name. Tomorrow morning he had business in Tucson.

Returning from a soothing bath at her secret hideaway in the stream, Meadowlark found him slouched uncomfortably in the chair, grumbling in his sleep, one hand covering a portion of a page she recognized—the list of names and addresses of the supply contractors. His finger pointed at Efren Frye.

Now what could he want with Mr. Frye? What had happened now? What mischief was the white man planning?

She shook his shoulder. "Captain? Brent? Wake up."

"Huhhh?" His eyes blinked open. Kind of.

"It's late. You should go to bed." Or to the infirmary, she silently added.

"Yeah." His lids drooped closed.

Exasperated, she tossed her head, flicking drops of water from her wet hair over Brent and the papers. She put her hands under his arms and succeeded in straightening his lax form in the slick seat of the chair, but could not raise him to his feet. "Get up. You have to go."

"Uh-huh." He knew that. But he couldn't seem to get his legs and arms to work together.

Meadowlark noted the glassy sheen to what she could see of his eyes and the warmer than normal flesh on his neck when her fingers brushed his skin. His hat had fallen back on his head, allowing the wayward lock of hair to droop across his forehead. His mouth quirked in a self-conscious grin and her heart melted.

The man was incorrigible and . . . thoroughly worn out. When she pulled his left arm around her neck and attempted to shift his weight from the chair, his body had no more control than if she held a lizard by the tail.

She managed one step, then two, before buckling beneath his superior size. He swayed forward, teetering her along with him. He wobbled backward and she almost tripped over his feet. His momentum carried them both to the pallet, where she took the brunt of the fall in an effort to protect the big beast from reinjuring his shoulder.

Air whooshed from her chest. One of Brent's elbows gouged her tender belly. Her legs became hopelessly entangled with his. Lying on the pallet blankets, gasping for breath, she was still able to support his right arm as long as she allowed him to use her breasts as a pillow.

She felt the cool intake of his breath against flesh already slightly aroused from the brisk scrubbing she had given herself in the stream. Suddenly, she pictured what they must look like, pinned on the pallet, arms wrapped about each other, his head still cradled to her breasts and his large body stretched between her thighs. She hoped no one would take a notion to pay a surprise call.

One thing she knew for certain, the clumsy captain would pay for the abuse of her backside. She would extract her vengeance one day soon.

She struggled and squirmed and finally extricated herself from beneath his dead weight. The big beast had had the temerity to fall asleep immediately upon reaching the pallet and she could not bring herself to try to move him again.

She sat by his side, running her fingers through the wavy thickness of his blond hair. Deep feelings of regret rioted through her insides. It was a shame that her feelings for the young white captain would never have the same joy of innocence of twenty-four hours ago.

And all because of General Crook. The general had returned. Soon he would take his army south to annihilate Geronimo and her Warm Springs family that had been forced to accompany him to Mexico. The captain would, of course, support his commanding officer and they would be on opposite sides of the conflict.

She had to stop General Crook or find some way to warn her people. No one had better get in the way. Not even the handsome Brent McQuade.

Chapter Seventeen

Brent McQuade stretched and yawned. He felt like a new man after his first good night's sleep in ages. When he shifted his back, though, his spine grated on something hard and the mattress didn't give. He'd dreamed of sleeping on his mattress again. He shrugged his shoulders and winced when his stiff muscles complained.

His eyes popped open. The dingy gray walls of the office stared back at him. The office? What was he doing here? His left hand plopped against packed earth. On the floor? Wool scratched his back where his shirt had ridden up. On Lark's bed?

A quick intake of breath caused him to pause and sniff the air. His eyes closed with pleasure at the heavenly scent. His stomach grumbled. Pastry? He could swear he smelled fresh baked cinnamon rolls. Dreaming or not, his mouth literally watered.

Something soft and warm touched his wrist. His eyes flew open. Meadowlark was kneeling beside him, holding a cloth-covered plate just above the portion of chest bared from his open shirt. His brows arched. He struggled to raise his upper torso. "Are those cinnamon rolls? *Real* cinnamon rolls?"

Meadowlark nodded. A smile threatened to curve the corners of her mouth. He sounded like a little boy waiting for a special treat. It had been an accident that she and the major's cook had become friends because of a shared love of thoroughbred horses. But every now and then, during the early morning, he would send her a pan of hot rolls. Today, the pan had arrived at a most welcome moment, just in time to awaken a hungry man with an apparent weakness for sweets.

"You like cinnamon rolls?"

"Hmmm." He licked his lips and reached for the cloth. Lifting one corner, he groaned as the aroma of yeast and cinnamon tantalized his twitching nose. He cocked one eyebrow at Lark, allowing his fingers to hover over one of the gooey buns.

Solemnly, she nodded and then stifled a giggle as the roll disappeared in two huge bites. She watched in fascination as his eyes rolled back and he licked every sticky crumb of sugar and bread from his fingers.

Handing him another, she quickly snatched her hand back and counted her fingers before taking one for herself. The savory morsels melted her reserve and soon she was licking her fingers just like Brent.

She cast a covert glance in his direction. Usually, she ate alone in the little office, but this morning, with the captain lying in her bed, the rolls tasted better than ever. And she was enjoying his company.

She sensed a change in the man. The deep hurt and sadness she had seen the first few weeks after he had come to San Carlos seemed to have lifted. He smiled more now, and the look in his eyes . . . had nothing to do with melancholy.

He looked at her. Her insides went liquid with heat, like the melted butter and cinnamon consumed by the ravenous soldier. He licked at a spot on his bottom lip and she felt her eyes widen as she hypnotically mimicked him.

Brent stared at Lark, wondering at the expression on her face. She was beautiful, and so sensuous, sitting there looking at him with those soft kitten eyes . . . He tore his gaze away. No sense in torturing himself. Since starting the trip back to San Carlos, she had made it plain that they should forget the wonderful moments they'd shared. She'd made him feel like a fool for even thinking she might want to marry him. Hell, he'd only mentioned it for her own protection.

He sighed and took another roll. When he finished it, he cleared his throat and mumbled, "Sorry about last night. I shouldn't have stayed."

Meadowlark shrugged and looked down. It would be better if he did not discover that she liked having him near her. "What were you doing here?" She remembered very well the paper he had been reading and the name he had found. Would he tell her the reason it had been important enough to keep him working until he literally dropped from exhaustion?

"I, uh, had some business to take care of." He hated the evasive answer, but didn't want to get her involved in something dangerous. If he knew his little wildcat, she wouldn't sit idly by if she knew what had happened to her people and their rations—again.

"Did you?"

He squirmed to button his shirt. "What?"

"Did you take care of it?"

Damn it! Why did she have to turn those big, soulful eyes on him like that? "Yeah, I did."

"What do you want me to do, then?"

Brent gulped. Keep your mind on business, McQuade, he thought. "Keep an eye on things, Meadowlark," he said.

"Where will you be?"

He stifled a groan. He usually had to yank words from her. Why was she so curious all of a sudden? "I've, got to go to Tucson."

"Why?"

Brent scrambled to his feet, tucking loose articles of clothing into places they weren't supposed to fit. Her intense scrutiny this morning made him more self-conscious than he'd been when he was wounded—and naked. "I have things to do, that's why."

She leaned against the desk and crossed her arms over her chest. The captain seemed rested. His shoulder appeared less painful. But it was foolish of him to think he could ride that great a distance by himself so soon after his injury. He had yet to recover his strength.

And he was hiding the truth. Why was it such a sudden trip? What was this white man trying to hide from her, the Apache woman who had helped him? Did it have anything to do with General Crook and the plans to go after Geronimo? What was Brent McQuade involved in? Her lashes drooped, concealing her sudden suspicion.

Brent fumed as she continued to stare and not say a word. He'd almost finished dressing, but fumbled with the clip on his suspenders. In frustration, he snatched up his boots and, without even trying to pull them on, stalked toward the door.

"You will not leave looking like a skulking coyote guilty of robbing a hen's nest. Were you not concerned with what people would say about . . . us?"

He stopped in his tracks. Damn a logical woman, Brent grumbled to himself. "You know I can't get the boots on."

She derived an undue amount of pleasure from watching his discomfort. If the man was up to no good, he deserved it. But . . . if he was truly only going to Tucson on business . . . "I will help."

Unbuttoning his jacket, she held it while he struggled into his suspenders. She sensed it would be best to not offer assistance unless asked first. Silly, proud white man. *Everyone* needed help sometime. It did not make him any less of a man in her eyes.

To Brent, the simple task of dressing alone mattered a great deal. During the past weeks she had saved his life, nursed him back to health, brought him back to the agency, put him to bed like a helpless babe, and now this.

He thumped the chair and deposited himself in it none too gently. Dropping the boot to the ground, he positioned his foot as far down in the soft leather as he could without having to pull. He grimaced when Meadowlark knelt down beside him and tugged the front, then the back. She repeated the process over and over until his heel was a quarter of an inch from slipping inside.

She tried unsuccessfully to ignore the warmth of his breath on the back of her neck as he leaned over her, tried not to think about the heat that erupted over her flesh when he put his hand on her shoulder for balance and stood.

He was so tall and usually so strong—yet it felt good to be needed by this one man who so easily overpowered her senses and her will. His presence alone caused her better judgment to evaporate like a snowflake in the summer sun.

Brent touched Lark's shoulder and suddenly a surge of energy charged his body. Before he pulled her down beside him on the rumpled blankets, he stomped and wriggled his toes until, with a muffled *poof,* his foot slid into the shiny black leather. Much to his relief, the other boot went on easily.

He sighed and gazed down into her upturned face. His gut knotted. God, but she was incredibly beautiful this morning, with her hair tousled and loose tendrils clinging to her cheeks. She reminded him of a woman rising out of bed after a good morning's . . .

"Well, thanks. Guess I'd better be goin'." He snatched his hat from the peg and made his exit.

Meadowlark remained on her knees for a while. Brent was definitely flustered and trying to get away with something. He had drawled his words again. To her way of thinking, a sure sign of guilt.

Well, she had better follow him and find out for herself what he was up to. He might be headed for trouble. Besides, if he were to feel weak or feverish on the trail, he might just need her.

Several hours later, after cutting across miles of hilly, rocky terrain, Meadowlark stood beside her sweat-caked horse, wearily watching the road leading into Tucson. From information garnered from Corporal Bent, she was on a ridge near where Brent and the troopers had camped when they had come to escort the wagons to San Carlos.

She was tempted to ride into town and see just what business Brent was conducting. But she had worn her buckskins and knew that her appearance would probably cause a commotion and alert the captain to her presence. So, she hobbled the mare and leaned her back against the stump of a dead sycamore, legs outstretched, gnawing a piece of dried jerky, waiting, watching.

Soon, the sun shone high overhead, warming and lulling her tired body into a relaxed state of bliss. It felt wonderful to soak up the sun's warm rays. All too quickly, within a few weeks' time, those same rays would beat down unmercifully, taking the pleasure from moments like these.

She blinked. No one was on the road. Her head jerked. She blinked again. It was so warm and comfortable . . .

The next thing she knew, someone kicked the soles of her feet. She flinched, but swallowed the panic. Forcing on a mask of calm, she peered through the narrow slits of her ever so slightly raised lashes.

"Get up, Injun, fore we shoot ya like the lazy dog ya are."

Meadowlark's gaze traveled up filthy trousers and over a huge protruding gut to the narrow shoulders and matted whiskers and mustache she would never forget. "Slaughter" Ryan. She would have rather run into a grizzly bear. And there was another man with him she recognized as one of Efren Frye's men.

Fear constricted every muscle in her body. She diligently willed her limbs not to tremble. Slowly, she rose to her feet.

"Looky thar, pard. It's a squaw. We'uns got ourselves a Injun squaw, shore 'nuf."

Meadowlark's gaze was drawn to a short, stocky man, with hair resembling the color of muddy water and clothes that looked as though they had not seen so much as a good sprinkle in years. Her lips curled as she glared into his bucktoothed, pointed nosed and chinless features. She had heard of people who were called "rat-faced" before, but this was her first encounter with anyone deserving of such a description.

Her flesh crawled as the two men flanked her on either side. Mentally, she cursed herself for leaving her carbine in its sheath across the mare's back. But her knife was in the top fold of her moccasin. If only they gave her the chance to get to it.

Meadowlark stood silently, imperceptively shifting her weight on the balls of her feet, slanting her eyes warily from one to the other of the two men.

"This's our lucky day, Zeb. Ain't had me a squaw fore two days. Reckon this'n'll fight like that other'n?"

Ryan was so close that Meadowlark could smell blood and whiskey and rotted food odors, and who-knew-what-else, that had dried on his clothes. She honestly could not decide which man was the more dirty—really dirty. And she found it easier to concentrate on these minor details than to think about what might be about to happen . . . It kept her alert, watching their movements.

The rat-faced Zeb leered at Meadowlark. "All's we kin do is try'er. She don't look like much, though, do she?"

"Woman's a woman, got all the right parts, no matter the size'r color."

Zeb loosed a high-pitched giggle. "That be true, pard. The bitch'll serve my needs good 'nuf."

As the men spoke, they moved closer. Meadowlark tried to back up, but her way was blocked by the stump and two huge cholla cactus. But she continued to balance on the balls of her feet, ready to defend herself as best she could.

Then they came at her. Moving more quickly than she expected for a man of his size, Ryan reached out and grabbed her by the shirtfront. A snarl escaped her lips. She curled her fingers and raked her nails down his fleshy cheeks.

Ryan roared. He dug the fingers of his free hand into her hair, yanking her head back. She felt as if her neck would snap in two. She could not swallow. She could hardly breathe.

"Yore gonna pay for that, bitch, with pieces of purty flesh," Ryan promised, as blood trickled down his face and dripped off his chin.

Brent rode quietly out of Tucson. His features were as dark as a thunderstorm.

So, Efren Frye was out of town, was he? No one knew where he went or when he'd be back. The man was either very busy or had the whole town on his payroll.

Mr. Frye would certainly recognize the name Brent McQuade when he heard it again, because Brent had purposely left his name and the reason for his visit with every man, woman and child who would stop to listen.

He'd even received threats on his life for his trouble. People in Tucson didn't take kindly to soldiers, it seemed. Especially soldiers intent on protecting the "heathens" on the reservations. If Brent's instincts were correct, and he had no reason to expect otherwise, he wouldn't be surprised to find a group of Tucson vigilantes marching on San Carlos, itching to destroy every Apache who happened in their path.

His insides curdled. Didn't those people have any humanity? Did they all live only for their greed? Was a different culture so threatening that they had to have the Indians moved—or better yet, eliminated entirely?

Captain Brent McQuade was a soldier. He respected right and honor and duty. He didn't consider himself an *Indian-lover* per se, but he believed in giving them a fair chance to survive the never-ending crush of the white man.

Of course there were good and bad Indians, just as there were good and bad whites. But most of the Apache warriors and leaders Brent had met were honest and truthful. And to those who earned the title "friend," the Indians were loyal beyond a doubt.

At that particular moment, he wasn't sure he could say the same about any one person in the whole town of Tucson. Bitter and discouraged, he was glad to reach the outskirts of the city where he could breathe fresh, pure air.

The farther he rode, the more vigilant he became, watching the road ahead as well as his back trail. One or two, or even a dozen of those hotheads might decide, after a few more drinks, to string up another "Injun-lover."

He had only ridden two miles when, off to his left, he heard a loud bellow of pain.

Meadowlark took her eyes off the blood-streaked face of the man who held her long enough to see the crazed gleam in the smaller man's beady little eyes. She struggled all the harder, cringing as hairs were torn from her scalp. Zeb grabbed for her legs, but she kicked him in the nose and he fell back screaming.

"Get up, Zeb, damn you! She's only a woman."

This time Zeb avoided her legs and managed to

catch hold of one of her arms. She struck out with the other and he caught it, too. Distracted, trying to free her wrists, she couldn't keep her balance when Ryan hooked a foot behind her knees and kicked her legs out from under her. Soon Zeb had her arms pinioned above her head. Ryan threw a huge trunk of a thigh across her legs. She was helpless.

She burned him with scorn when Zeb stuffed both of her wrists into one of his long-fingered hands and drew his knife with the other. The soft leather ripped easily as he slit her tunic with the cold, hard blade. She felt as if he had sliced her flesh.

Terror seized her. She gritted her teeth. They were stronger. They would rape. They would hurt her. But no white would hear her cry out. And if they made the mistake of leaving her alive . . .

Zeb stuck the knife in the sand next to Meadowlark's shoulder. Then he touched her. Not a gentle, tender touch, but a grabbing, pinching, squeeze of her bare breast. She gasped, even though she had vowed not to utter a sound.

Ryan's rough hands were at her waist, yanking at her leggings. He had to rise off of her legs, and she kicked up, trying to squirm out from under him. He cursed and curled powerful fingers into her thighs. The pain became so intense that she had to stop thrashing.

"That's a good girlie. Maybe ya ain't never had a white man a'tween yore legs, huh? Wal, this white man's better'n ten o' yore scrawny bucks. See if'n I ain't."

Zeb's pants were already around his knees. "Hurry, pard. I'm harder'n a grizzly," the little man bragged.

Shutting out reality, Meadowlark closed her eyes. She prayed to the spirits to let her live, to give her the chance . . . some day . . .

A shot rang out. "Get away from the girl. Now!"

Ryan jumped. His huge member pushed inside

Meadowlark, nearly rending her in two. She trembled with horror and relief and opened her eyes. Brent!

Ryan had withered immediately and pulled out of Meadowlark.

"Aw, fer Crissakes, man. We're jus' havin' some fun. It's only a squaw . . ." Zeb's words trailed off when he saw the officer's gaze was riveted on Ryan and the woman. Though Zeb's trousers were wrapped around his knees, the gun belt was still strapped to his waist. He reached for his gun. The barrel had just cleared the holster when, quick as a heartbeat, another shot was fired. Zeb's pistol fell from slack fingers. He sank to the ground like a sack of potatoes. Dead. A neat hole between his eyes.

"Hey, now, c'mon an' be sociable," Ryan blubbered as he straddled Meadowlark and stared at Zeb's body. "I'll share—"

"Get away from the lady or you won't be a threat to another woman as long as you live."

Meadowlark's chest ached, but she was breathing more evenly. As Ryan rolled off of her, she remembered the knife the man named Zeb had buried in the sand. She retrieved it and slipped it under the edge of her torn tunic before glancing up to find Brent.

Ryan held his hands out to his sides and awkwardly regained his feet, but still remained within a foot or two of the woman. His big belly protruded through his shirttail, his limp and flaccid member stuck out through his trouser flap. His eyes burned red when he recognized the intruder. "So, it's you, Gen'r'l. Sure you don't wanna piece? Or've you already sampled the goods?"

Captain McQuade's gun bucked in his palm. He watched, seemingly unconcerned, as Ryan screamed, jerked his hand up and found nothing but blood where his earlobe had been. "I've told you twice to move away from the girl. You know where the next bullet will go."

Brent's hand shook, though he managed to keep the barrel pointed directly where he aimed to shoot. He wished the bastard *would* try something, anything. One little excuse and he'd carry out his threat. Men like Ryan were a blight on mankind.

His gaze shifted back and forth between the wagon boss and Meadowlark. She was so quiet. His hand started shaking again. What if he hadn't come in time. What if the bastard had killed her? What if . . .

Meadowlark remained crouched on the gritty sand with her eyes hooded. How could she face her attacker? How could she face her rescuer? How could she face living with such shame?

A subtle movement from the vile, two-legged animal just a few feet away drew her attention. Ryan's hand was moving ever so slowly, from the bloody mess of his ear toward his shoulder.

She looked up. Did Brent not see? Suddenly their eyes locked. Even from a distance, she felt the ferocity of his gaze, the hard line of his jaw. But with a nod of her head, she saw the barest softening of his features.

That was the moment "Slaughter" Ryan had been waiting for. He reached across his chest for a hideaway derringer. Even with his fingers slick with blood, he managed to find the grip and jerked it free.

Brent's gaze shifted. Meadowlark seized the knife.

Ryan fired at Brent, heard Meadowlark, and spun around.

Brent raised his gun and aimed at Ryan just as Meadowlark jumped to her feet, brandishing the sharp blade. It was too late to pull back. His finger squeezed the trigger. His voice rang out. "No! Lark!"

Brent's bullet staggered Ryan, but the huge man tottered toward Meadowlark. His lips curled in a malicious leer. "You . . . you an' yore daddy . . . yore gonna . . . join 'im in . . ." He coughed and stumbled. His finger jerked the trigger and fired the little derringer's last round.

Meadowlark felt a rush of air as the bullet whizzed past her thigh to bury harmlessly in the sand. Her eyes blazed. Blood rushed through her body and she swayed dizzily. All she heard were Ryan's hissed words, *"Your daddy."* What did he know about her father's death? He was a rapist. Was he a murderer?

Blinking, she focused on the enraged man. Her pulse pounded. He just kept coming. A mad film glazed his eyes. His lips curled back from his rotted teeth. Frozen with fear, she watched his thick, grimy hands reach for her throat. Instinctively, she raised her arms.

He stumbled again and lost his balance. His fingers harmlessly brushed her flesh. He fell forward. She had forgotten she even held the knife and gasped as the blade caught him in the chest. His momentum careened his body into hers. As she grappled with his heavy weight, his hissed words, "Your Daddy," rang in her ears. Managing to sidestep him, she watched him hit the ground.

Ryan had hardly rolled to a stop before she was there, both hands clenched in his shirtfront, shaking, shouting, "What about my father? Did you kill him? Did you?"

Ryan's eyes gazed straight into the evening sky. His lips still curled and Meadowlark could almost imagine he was grinning. Suddenly, his head turned. She started and sat back on her heels. His face contorted, but he looked right at her and shook his head. She opened her mouth to ask if he told the truth, but his chest lifted in one last gasp and his eyes rolled back in his head. "Slaughter" Ryan was dead.

She sat stunned and shaken to the core of her being. No. Ryan did not murder her father. There had been nothing in his eyes to make her think he had lied. But who else could it have been? Who had a reason to want the agent dead?

The next thing she knew she was being wrapped in

a pair of iron-hard arms. At first she struggled, then Brent whispered in her ear. "It's all right, Lark. You're goin' to be all right. I promise."

She quieted, believing him. She did. But it did not stop her from staring at the big man's body or from darting a glance to his smaller friend's crumpled form. Even in death she could not trust them.

"God, Lark, you could have been killed." The depth of Brent's emotion staggered him. He'd never been so afraid. The thought of losing Lark had been unbearable. And if she'd died by his hand . . . his arms locked about her, pressing her into the muscular expanse of his chest.

Meadowlark shivered when his uniform scratched her bare skin. Only moments earlier she had silently vowed to never, ever, let another man near her. Now she was engulfed so tightly in Brent's embrace that she could hardly breathe, and reveled in the safety and security he offered.

For one of the few times in her life, she had been totally and completely overpowered. Control snatched from her. Those men would have surely done worse than rape her.

But Brent McQuade had charged to her rescue, dispatching the vile whites with all the prowess of avenging Apaches. The thought that he would have done the same for any woman, white or Apache, warmed her heart. But what set her soul aflame was that he had done it for *her*.

Brent shuddered as her arms stole around his neck. He buried his face in her hair and held her, afraid that at any minute she would be ripped from his arms. "Th-they didn't hurt you, did they?" He stroked her back, sliding his hands up and down her spine, reassuring himself that she was safe in his embrace.

She shook her head, snuggling her cheek into the throbbing hollow at the base of his neck. Yes, they had hurt her, but not as badly as they could have.

"God, Lark, are you sure? When I saw Ryan bending over you, and you fighting like a wildcat . . . You went so still . . . I was so scared. I-I . . ."

Meadowlark sniffed. "He *tried* t-t-t—"

Tried was all Brent needed to hear. The throbbing in his temples eased. He glared at the body sprawled only a few feet away. If "Slaughter" Ryan had succeeded in raping Lark . . .

Controlling his murderous need to avenge her pain, he soothingly coaxed, "Shh-h, honey. It's over. They can't hurt you. They deserved what they got."

Again he shuddered, awed by the direction of his thoughts. The Apaches didn't take scalps, but were known for their effective methods of torture. It was their way of warning enemies away. Brent recalled all the horrible sights he'd seen over the years and wished the same gruesome acts on the dead "Slaughter" Ryan. Was he no better than a savage at heart?

Maybe. He couldn't help but wonder. If his own family had been subjected to the same indecision and broken treaties as the Apache, if he'd had to watch his people starve and die, wouldn't he have behaved in much the same manner as the Apaches?

Meadowlark hiccuped. She looked up at Brent with wary eyes. As much as she loved being in his arms, feeling secure and protected, a niggle of doubt swam through her mind. What would the captain have done if he'd been sure that pig of a Ryan had raped her? Would he still have held and comforted her? Or would he have pushed her away, thinking her no better than an Indian squaw who would spread her legs for *any* man?

Suddenly she realized she was not being fair to Brent. Deep down in her heart she knew he was too good a man to let something like what had almost happened rule his emotions.

She sighed and rested her head on his shoulder. Her trust was not misplaced in Brent McQuade—for many reasons. Thoughts of Ryan and his words about her father had also reminded her that Brent could have reported everything he knew, but had held his council. He had placed *his* trust in her. She would not let him down.

Brent felt Meadowlark tense and then relax. He wondered what she had been thinking, but then thought of everything she had just been through. She'd probably have nightmares and bad memories for quite a good while. She'd need a friend.

Slowly, he rose to his feet, still cradling her in his arms. "Let's go home, Lark."

She nodded against his shoulder, then glanced at the two bodies. "What of them?"

Brent snorted. "We'll leave them to the varmints." He scowled at the two men's state of undress. Let Frye wonder what his men were up to when they died.

What *had* they been doing out here, at that particular time? Had Frye sent them after him? What did it matter? He couldn't put Lark through the questions and inevitable hatred that would be directed toward her for her part in killing a white man. No, let people wonder, and worry.

When he reached their horses, Brent took the saddles and bridles off the extra animals and turned them loose. Then he put Meadowlark on his gelding, looped the mare's rein around the saddle horn and swung up where he could position Lark on his lap and hold her firmly against his body.

Meadowlark closed her eyes and absorbed the scent and feel of her captain. He rode silently, wondering at the possessive, protective emotions that had consumed him since meeting Meadowlark Russell. His arms tightened about her. "Lark?"

"Hmmm?"

"Do you have family at San Carlos?"

She snuggled her nose into his neck and smiled when his flesh quivered. "A cousin."

"No closer family?"
"Huh-uh."
Brent grimaced. She sure was a talker. "Damn it, woman, you've got to have some family *somewhere.*"
"Uh-huh. In Mexico."
"Oh, God!"

Chapter Eighteen

Meadowlark paced the floor the next few days. She was baffled by Brent's solicitous behavior, yet was also pleased that he allowed her some distance. She just wished she knew his true feelings concerning Ryan's attack. Her instincts told her Brent was more honest with himself than most white men. Her feminine nature was more cautious and oh-so vulnerable.

Since they had returned to San Carlos, he had hardly touched her—really touched her—other than a few awkward pats on the shoulder or taking her elbow to guide her through a door or up a step. Stupid white man. She was not an invalid. She was a woman. Surely he had not forgotten so soon.

And he had yet to again mention his desire to marry her. Of course, she had refused when he had talked of the subject before. But as adamant as he had seemed, she had not expected him to give up so easily.

She had worked herself into quite a quarrelsome mood by the time Brent sauntered, unsuspecting, into the office.

"Morning, honey. How're you feeling?"

She sighed. As if he *cared.* He had taken to calling her *"honey."* What had happened to "Lark"? She liked "Lark." But she only shrugged. "I am fine."

"Good. Oh, were you able to sleep last night?" He was concerned about Lark. There were dark circles beneath her eyes, and when he accidentally gazed into those whiskey-hued depths, he felt a burning sensation in the pit of his stomach, as if an Apache had piled hot stones in his gut.

He was beginning to care very deeply for the little minx—it was frightening to think *how* deeply. Whenever he thought of her, which was almost constantly, he suffered two conflicting body ailments. His chest constricted and his feet itched. Was he ready yet to make a new commitment? He'd had two disastrous attempts at settling down. He'd vowed to remain a free man for the rest of his life.

Yet, here he was, within just a few months of his latest debacle, thinking of convincing a woman he hardly knew, but couldn't seem to function without, to be his bride. He was torn between the certainty that he was either the smartest man on earth, or the dumbest. And he'd almost deduced the latter was the better explanation.

Now, as he looked at Lark's unusually drawn and pale features, he was glad he'd quit pressing her about the marriage. When Crook returned from Mexico with her family, then he would do the proper thing and ask to court her. In that way, he could prove that he respected her Apache heritage and was willing to make a *real* commitment.

And if it turned out that she was pregnant with his child . . . well, all of his good intentions would be shot to hell. She would marry him right away, whether she liked it or not.

Feelings of guilt nagged him for seducing such an innocent, though devastatingly beautiful, girl. Yet it was because of that innocence and the purity of her awakening passion that he felt responsible for her. Passion? She was the most sensuous, earthy woman he had ever known or made love to. And she was totally unaware of her allure.

He imagined there had been scores of men, besides even Scorpion, who had been chomping at the bit to have her. Suddenly his hands curled into fists. Just the thought of any other man claiming *his* Lark curdled his guts.

His knees went weak and he staggered to his chair and sat down when, for the thousandth time, he pictured Lark lying still and helpless beneath "Slaughter" Ryan. Yet, even images of a man taking her tenderly, lovingly, caused violent eruptions throughout his body.

She was *his,* damn it. He had a premonition that one day soon *she,* and even *he,* would come to terms with that fact and accept it for what it truly was—love.

The word caused his body to tremble. Love? Did he truly love her? His loins quickened every time he saw her, but that could just describe lust. His chest ached whenever he was away from Lark, but that could be attributed to loneliness. He'd just gotten used to having her around during the days, and for a few glorious nights.

What he couldn't put a description to was the way his heart throbbed uncontrollably when he only held or comforted her. He literally hurt all over, but with a need far greater than for just a physical joining. He wanted her to return his feelings. He wanted her heart, mind, body and soul; for he had just now come to realize she had total command over his own.

And even stranger still, was that the emotions he felt were disturbing, yet granted him a sense of peace and contentment.

Meadowlark was so caught up by the expressions flickering across Brent's mobile features that she almost forgot he had asked her a question. But when he turned those cerulean eyes on her, she gulped and said, "I could not sleep."

God, neither could he. Not without her curled at his side. "I'm sorry. Did you have bad dreams?"

If he only knew, she thought. The few nights they had spent together, sleeping side by side, were emblazoned in her memory. Her flesh ached to be pressed to his solid warmth. She wanted to wake up with his shoulder as her pillow. It was a foolish notion, and she knew it. No matter how hard she wished, it could never be.

He would always be a white man. She would always be Apache. He would return to wherever he came from. She would remain on the reservation. Ryan and Zeb's attack had proven what she had already known—she would never be accepted by the white world. Brent could not keep defending her forever. One day he would lose, and she would never be able to forgive herself.

"Yes, I dreamed."

Brent ground his teeth. "Of Ryan and his . . . friend?"

She shook her head.

"Good. You've got to put that terrible experience behind you and live your life, Meadowlark. You know that, don't you?"

She nodded, thinking something like that was easier said than done. Her body still felt dirty where the awful men had touched her, hurt her.

Lark's eyes loomed so large and misty that Brent could hardly swallow. What he wouldn't give to know what was going on inside that beautiful little head. "Oh, everything's about ready for tomorrow. It'll be interesting to see how many wagons drive up, especially with two of Frye's top hands missing."

He steepled his fingers. So far, no one had mentioned anything about any murders. No one had brought news of bodies being discovered. No alert had been sounded. He just prayed no one blamed it on the Apaches, like they did every other assumed depredation against the white community.

His head began to throb. It was the first time that possibility had crossed his mind. He crossed his legs, scooted more comfortably into the chair, then uncrossed his legs. Maybe he had made a mistake, keeping the attack on Lark to himself.

Meadowlark watched in confusion as Brent, agitated, rose to his feet and began to pace. When he stopped abruptly, excused himself and left the office, she gaped after him. Whatever was worrying him had certainly come up quickly. He had seemed so calm and collected earlier, compared to *her* discomposure.

Maybe he would see fit to tell her about it later. Right now, with the myriad of chores needing to be done before her people arrived, she had much to keep her mind and hands busy.

Brent went directly to Major Taylor's office. He had to wait, and was disconcerted upon finding General Crook inside when an orderly finally led him into the room. He hesitated only briefly, then snapped a smart salute.

"At ease, Captain McQuade," the major commanded. "The general and I were just talking about you."

"Oh?" Brent couldn't think of anything he'd done wrong—today.

"Yes, General Crook has visited some of the Apache bands located here on the reservation. Seems they've come to respect and trust you a great deal during the past few weeks."

Brent felt the heat creeping across his cheeks. "Well, I'm glad, sir. But I haven't done anything much. Miss Russell should get most of the credit for showing me what needed to be done."

"That's understood, Captain." General Crook rubbed the tip of his nose with the back of his right hand. "Nevertheless, I appreciate the good job you've done."

Brent glanced guiltily toward the major, thinking of the time he'd "borrowed" army rations. Evidently Major Taylor's thoughts were running in the same direction, for he smiled and winked, then asked, "Now, what brings you to the office? Thought you'd be busy readying supplies."

"Yes, sir, but . . . there's a slight problem I think you need to know about." He launched into the details on his discovery of two men in the process of attacking an Apache maiden and his subsequent killing of the drivers, leaving out only the name of the woman. There was no need for anyone to know Lark was the intended victim. He did, however, mention the possibility that the men were passing the time while awaiting Brent's return to San Carlos.

Brent frowned. "I should have reported the incident sooner, but—"

General Crook spoke very quietly. "I think I'll send a detail to Tucson to pick up the mail. If they just happen to run across any dead bodies—to the right of the road, didn't you say?—they can bury them, all neat and proper. And the girl? Is she all right?"

Brent sighed, "Yes, sir. Thank you, sir."

As he was about to turn and take his leave, the general stopped him. "Perhaps you would accompany me when I visit the White Mountain band next week. Weren't you garrisoned at Fort Apache last year?"

"Yes, sir, I was. And I'd be happy to go with you." And he would. Not only to see his brother, but to have a chance to get away and think.

About midmorning the next day, Brent heard the creak and jingle and crunch of approaching wagons through the open door. He laid his pen on top of the report he'd been writing and sat for a moment, hesitant about getting up.

He wasn't anxious to see what, or how much, had arrived in the wagons. He was feeling guilty because he hadn't gone to Tucson and escorted the wagons to San Carlos, but his heart hadn't been in making the trip. Something was wrong with Lark and he was worried.

He'd refrained from touching her lately, or spending a lot of time with her, knowing she needed to deal with the effects of Ryan's attack. And every time he was near her, he had to fight the desire to literally grab her and ravish her in front of God and the entire post, making him no better than the brute, "Slaughter" Ryan.

So he'd kept a tight rein on his emotions, knowing he was doing the right and gentlemanly thing, for a change. Yet each day she became more distant. It left him feeling frustrated and dejected and entirely out of sorts.

Meadowlark poked her head through the door, shaking him from his musing. "The wagons are here."

"I know." That blank expression, her Apache mask, settled over her features and he silently cursed. He hadn't meant to sound so brusk. But he waved her on and sorted through the papers on the cluttered desk until he found the lists he needed. As he followed her from the office, watching the sway of her enticing hips, he decided that it was best they stay at arm's length, at least for a while.

His eyes strayed to the wagons. Exhaling a long, drawn-out draught of air, he could hardly believe what he saw. The wagons were all there. *All* of them. And with several new drivers who seemed very amenable, in an exaggerated sort of way. But Brent didn't mind. He could stand a little boot-licking, as long as he didn't have to storm up to the mines today.

"Mr. Frye fulfilled his contract today." Lark's voice was low and throaty and rasped seductively up his spine. He swallowed a groan. "Yes, so he has."

Meadowlark leaned toward Brent, wishing with all her might to feel the strength of his arms around her, to see the glint of desire burning from his eyes. Yet he seemed to visibly shy away. His eyes looked everywhere but at her.

Her shoulders drooped. It was true then. His interest in her was gone. The attack, his suspicions, the fact that Ryan "could have had" his way with her—all had lowered her in his eyes.

She sniffed and drew her spine ramrod straight. That was fine with her. It should have been this way all along. She had let herself be drawn into a fantasy world for a short time. And that was fine, too. But now she had come to her senses. They would work together—they seemed to do that well—but no more tender touches or soft caresses or heated looks. No more.

Brent sensed Lark's stiffened form and wondered what was wrong now. She had sent so many confusing signals lately that he felt like a bowstring tied so tight that he would snap in two at the slightest twang.

It had been his decision to keep a reasonable distance to allow her time to recover her composure and confidence. Now he knew he had done the right thing. If she was avoiding him, lumping him into the same mold as those two thugs, then she didn't know him—and he didn't know her.

But, God, it hurt. He had truly thought they had something special between them.

He kept his eyes trained on the paper as he checked off the items being unloaded from the wagons. It was good that he had discovered the truth now, before he'd made an even bigger jackass of himself.

He'd vowed not to touch her, and the declaration only made her that much more desirable. Damn her! Damn women! Damn his ungovernable lust. And damn him for being every kind of a fool to still want her, to the distraction of his job and everything important in his life.

Would he never learn? Was he destined to always fall for women who could never love him in return? A giant sigh heaved from his chest. It would seem so.

Thank God he'd made the commitment to go to the White Mountain Reservation. At least he'd get a few days and *nights* of peace.

Meadowlark watched with mixed emotions as the cavalry troop rode out of the post. On one hand, she was relieved to have a few days' respite from the turmoil of being so physically close to the captain, yet so far away emotionally, as if he stood on one bank of a raging river and she on the other.

Her heart ached from battering it against the dam being erected so sturdily between them. Yet she was mostly to blame.

An emptiness filled her soul that had never been so noticeable, not even when she lost her parents.

Bewildered, unhappy, and at a loss as to what to do about it, she turned back to the desk.

At least with Brent gone she could focus on her objectives—investigating what Ryan might have known about her father and maybe finding a clue that would lead to the murderer, and continuing her quest to help the Apache irrigate and cultivate some of their otherwise useless land before time to plant the seeds for corn, squash, pumpkins and potatoes.

She had met with a few of the older warriors from her band and shown them the location she thought would be good for their first field. They had observed the slope of the land, seen where she recommended they dig the canals and had nodded in approval.

Her knees had felt weak and trembly, her voice cracked and raw, as she walked with them and spoke her thoughts. Though the Apache respected their women, she could not have predicted their reactions toward a woman's suggestions for a man's labor. Her pride had been great when they seemed to accept her words.

Since General Crook's arrival, even the women of the band were earning a little money by following one of Brent's suggestions. They now cut tall grass and sold it to the army to feed the increased number of horses and mules.

The work was beneath what proud, nomadic people would choose to occupy their days, but it was a start. From now on, the older, surviving Apaches would have to tell their children and grandchildren of life and culture as it was before the white man roamed their land. And the younger Apaches would have to learn to live on the reservation, now that there were as many whites as sharp barbs in a cactus patch. Or a hundred cactus patches.

The Apaches could never return to the old days.

As they had so many times before, they would learn to adapt. Like most Apaches, Meadowlark had too much pride to allow the white man to succeed in wiping the Indians from the face of the earth.

Her people were grateful for and respected the land and all things upon it. She truly believed the Apache were the first to practice the words in the white man's Holy Bible, "Do unto others as you would have others do unto you." Yet after years of fighting the Mexicans, other Indians—and now the whites—"do unto others as others have done unto you," had become the way of life.

There was no shame in defending your home and family and honor and dignity. But there was shame when men were denied dignity.

A tear streaked her cheek. She cried for the Apache and a beautiful way of life forever lost.

Brent rode with General Crook and his detail northwest from San Carlos to pay a call to the Warm Springs band. The general presented quite a dashing figure with his broad-shouldered back straight as an arrow and long legs trailing down his mule's sides. Yet he was also a very humble figure, since he had an aversion to wearing uniforms. Instead, he sported a cork helmet and a canvas suit that put Brent more in mind of a cavalryman doing stable duty than an important general.

Brent had to smile when Crook twisted in his saddle to peer back down the column of troopers. His magnificent beard was forked, and this morning each side was braided. The man's alert gray-blue eyes surveyed both men and animals and his kindly mouth curved into a grin when his gaze settled on Brent, riding directly to his rear.

"The scouts tell me the Warm Springs people have been restless of late."

"Yes, sir. All of the bands have. I think it's a good thing you're visiting the individual bands like this. More Indians came for allotments this week than the week before. Evidently some of the renegades would rather take their chances on the reservation now that you've returned."

"I hope you're right, Captain. I surely do."

As the mules and horses slid down a steep, crumbly bank into a dry riverbed, conversation became impossible. Brent sighed unhappily. The country was parched and desolate, punctuated by rolling hills and thick stands of mesquite and chaparral.

No wonder Lark was skeptical about her people working the land. Since the Warm Springs had been one of the last bands moved to San Carlos, the good locations had already been taken by other bands, and they had been relegated to the worst ground on the reservation.

Brent glanced up to check the position of the sun. He guessed it was near two in the afternoon. As he again scanned the riverbed he noticed a Mescalero scout approaching the general. The scout pointed toward the next ridge and Crook called over his shoulder, "Look sharp, men. We're almost there."

There was no trail, but the mule seemed to instinctively and reliably choose the easiest route. The detail followed and when they topped the rise, they looked down into a poor, shabby encampment, inhabited by ragged, hungry-looking Apaches who appeared anything but happy to have their afternoon disturbed by the arrival of guests—especially guests wearing blue uniforms with yellow stripes down the seams.

Brent shook his head in wonder—wonder that these people were able to exist at all. The wickiups were constructed of straw and small twigs and looked as if they would collapse if someone dared to sneeze.

Families stood silently beside their homes, staring, as the soldiers rode to the edge of the village. Brent looked around, noticing the inhabitants were mostly women, small children and older men. Then he recalled that Loco, one of the leaders after Victorio's death, and his followers had been among those literally forced from the reservation by Geronimo. Yes, he remembered Lark speaking of it, and subsequently, of her mother's death.

These people were the *lucky* ones that escaped Geronimo's mass roundup. He snorted beneath his breath. Lucky? Who was to say that dying free in Mexico wouldn't be preferable to this existence?

He straightened his shoulders. He and Lark would have to do something about these hopeless-looking people with their skeletal bodies and blank, almost ghostly, eyes and faces. Things were going to change—soon.

Two of the older warriors approached General Crook. Their leathery faces crinkled into a thousand creases with gap-toothed grins. Brent smiled, surmising they had recognized Crook from earlier years.

He watched as the general somberly greeted the old men. Brent's biggest source of amazement stemmed from the fact that even with the rousing tromping Crook had dealt the Apaches ten years ago, they all seemed to like and respect the man. It was a feather in Crook's helmet, and a testament to a general who saw his enemies as human beings rather than savages.

Brent gave the order to dismount and the soldiers stood by, awaiting their next command. Soon, the general walked over to Brent. "We have been invited to spend the night. Have the scouts pick out a camp at some distance so as not to make our hosts nervous."

"Yes, sir." Brent saluted and turned to find the Mescalero Apache standing almost directly behind him, glaring distastefully toward the scruffy camp. "You heard the general, Tonito. Might just as well get it done."

Black eyes glittered fiercely from the round-faced, high-cheeked visage of the Mescalero, but he nodded once and turned sharply on his heel without making the barest whisper of a sound.

As Brent's eyes followed the scout, he couldn't help but think that everything about this country and these people was incongruous. A person might think that an Apache was an Apache, but the various bands were entirely different, each an entity unto itself. Before the white men invaded their territory, they had warred against each other, and even now Apache scouts helped the soldiers track down other Apaches.

That was one of Crook's biggest assets, his ability to use the Apaches and to train his troops to live and travel and fight like Apaches when he started a campaign against the renegades. One would think the Apaches would unite to fight the whites, but the reverse was true. It was quite perplexing to a military strategist like Brent.

Near sundown, the general and Brent sat cross-legged in front of the central fire in the Warm Springs village. One of the older warriors spoke English, though it was broken and garbled with Spanish. The leader was regaling them with stories of better times and battles won against the hated Mexicans.

A light tap on Brent's shoulder caused him to start and reach toward his pistol, but his hand relaxed when he saw a very pretty young maiden kneeling at his side. She wore a calico skirt and tunic and her long black hair was braided into two plaits that swung gracefully in front of her shoulders.

"You . . . Captain agent?"

Her voice was soft and her eyes wide and adoring. Brent swallowed and nodded, reminded all too painfully of another, even more beautiful woman back at San Carlos.

The girl put her hand on his forearm. "You . . . Meadowlark's man?"

His eyes rounded. He readjusted his tender backside on the hard ground. "Uh, no. Not yet."

She smiled and his stomach bounced. Damn, but she reminded him of Lark. And when she said, "Soon, no?" he choked. Soon? How he wished.

"Who are you?" He recalled seeing the girl when she had come to the post for provisions, but how did she know so much about Lark and himself? And what would it do to Lark if she found out her people were even more curious than the soldiers had been?

The girl's eyes studied his bent leg. "I am called Angelita at the agency."

That was appropriate, he mused. He'd only seen such sweet innocence from one other woman. Someone called Meadowlark. He had to ask, "How do you know Lar . . . Meadowlark?"

"She . . . my cousin."

He sighed, relieved. Lark had mentioned she had a cousin here. "What can I do for you, Angelita?"

Her fingers pressed into his arm. Her knee rested next to his thigh. He tugged at his collar, suddenly very warm despite the cool evening.

"May be . . . when you take Meadowlark for wife . . . you also take Angelita."

Chapter Nineteen

Captain Brent McQuade sat stunned. He was aware of many of the Apache customs, knew that the woman usually made the first overture if she was interested in a man, and then it was up to the man to do the courting.

Well, an overture had certainly been made. Sweat beaded his skin and soaked into his uniform, though the night had turned cold since the sun had set and a slight breeze had become a strong wind.

He stared at the woman-child, then gave her a weak smile as he frantically searched for something intelligent to say, some noninsulting means out of such a sticky situation.

It was permissible for a warrior to take more than one wife, he recalled. And usually the woman was a sister or a cousin from the first wife's family. But, dear God, what man could handle *one* woman, let alone a houseful? He frowned and hunched his shoulders. The Apaches were braver men than he to risk such a combustible and dangerous home life.

Angelita moved closer. Her bottom lip stuck out petulantly. "You no want Angelita?"

"No!" Oops! That wasn't very tactful. A few of the warriors sitting around the camp fire glanced in his direction with glittering black eyes that caused another layer of perspiration to pop out on Brent's forehead.

"I mean . . . No, I really can't make any promises now, Angelita. You see, I haven't spoken with Meadowlark's relatives yet, and she *is* the woman I wish to take as my *first* wife." He gulped. Would Angelita understand, or would she cause a scene and create hard feelings between the Warm Springs band and the soldiers? It was a delicate situation he wasn't sure even General Crook could forestall.

Finally, Angelita smiled and removed her hand from his arm, only to place it on his knee. His muscles jerked and quivered. From the slant of her eyes, he knew she had felt his reaction. Damn!

What would Lark say when she found out he'd been approached by her relative? He had enough trouble already, without something like this happening. Then he grimaced. He probably needn't worry on that count. Meadowlark didn't give a damn about him.

Women! They were man's curse.

He glanced out the corner of his eye and watched Angelita shyly lower her thick black lashes. Oh, she was pretty enough, he had to give her that. Soft, serene and exceedingly feminine. He had no doubt she'd make some Apache warrior a fine wife. So, why'd she have to pick on *him?*

Brent deliberately shifted, scooting away from Angelita and darted a look about the fire. He was brought up short by the eerily grinning countenance of an old man who couldn't have weathered less than a hundred years from the looks of his face and body. Small white marks, healed wounds and forgotten scars, were illuminated with each flicker of the bright flames.

Wind caught the fire and seemed to pull the Apache closer. Without warning, sap exploded, sending out a shower of sparks and pushing the ancient one back again. Brent jumped, then inched even farther away from Angelita as the old man's laughter mocked him.

"White soldier no like Apache woman?"

The raspy voice sounded like sandpaper grating over stone and Brent shivered. The warrior looked like he could shrivel up and disintegrate with the next gust. "No . . . yes . . . certainly I like Apache women. It's just . . . I already have a woman. Waiting. At San Carlos." But did he? Was she waiting?

Waiting for him to disappear and let her life return to some semblance of order, no doubt. He had no illusions concerning Meadowlark. More times than not, she gave him the distinct impression she could hardly tolerate him, let alone miss him. She was beautiful and passionate and constantly reminded him he was nothing but a *white man.*

Brent sighed and looked at Angelita, turning slightly to put a few more inches between them. Why couldn't Lark be more like her cousin? Sweet. Demure. Subservient. Yet wasn't it Lark's independence and fiery nature that had attracted him in the first place? Somehow, sweet and demure seemed incredibly boring when compared to the whiskey-eyed wildcat.

With natural feminine grace, Angelita oozed into the space he'd painstakingly vacated—inch by nonchalant inch. An unwitting smile crept across his face. The corners of her mouth turned up and her eyes danced. Damn! She must've thought the smile was for her.

"The captain will think about what Angelita has said?" Her voice was a husky purr.

He ran a finger under his collar and tugged until the button nearly popped free. "Oh, yes, I'll, definitely do that." Pausing to catch a breath, he quickly added, "But it will be a long, long time before I can ask for Meadowlark. If you, uh, receive a good offer, from a brave warrior, you, better take it, don't you think?"

She pouted, "But you are good man. You help the Apache. You powerful and rich. Afford many wives."

Hell! One wife would be the death of him. "Well, that's kind of you."

As his eyes moved wildly over the small group gathered around the camp fire, he encountered General Crook's amused features. "What do you think, captain? Should we return to our troop? It's been a long day."

Brent was on his feet in a heartbeat. "Splendid idea, sir. Splendid. I need to see to my horse and clean my gear and . . . and . . ."

The general rose and bid his hosts good night, thanking them graciously for their invitation. The Apaches nodded solemnly and extended more invitations for "The Gray Fox" to return.

Brent's eyes accidentally brushed those of Angelita and he felt that embarrassing telltale flush. Though he couldn't help but feel flattered by her interest, he was filled with a desperate desire to flee—and fly back to Lark.

In a way, it was disturbing to find there was only one woman he wanted. Just one. Did trouble and heartache have to follow him everywhere?

The cavalry detail left the Warm Springs camp early the next morning on their way to Fort Apache. Brent was chagrined to see a bright-eyed, eager-faced Angelita standing close by. He grimaced and lifted his hand in a feeble wave. Then he turned his gaze toward the distant mountains and prayed the general's mule would hurry its pace.

Once the small camp was out of sight, the steel rod holding his shoulders erect melted slightly. He released the air that had nearly burst his chest. If he was smart, when he reached Fort Apache he would keep right on riding.

The closer they got to the mountains, though, the more he concentrated on the rough trail. The ground broke into a succession of ascending ridges, and the detail had to ride around and through enormous volcanic boulders amassed in formidable piles. The landscape was unique and interesting, not to mention intimidating.

On one stretch of flat ground where the trail widened, the general guided his mule back to Brent. "We won't reach Fort Apache until sundown, and it will be too late to speak with the representatives of the White Mountain band. Perhaps you wouldn't mind locating your brother and requesting that he organize a meeting tomorrow—say midmorning."

"Of course, General. I'd be pleased to do so."

"Good. Good. Feel free to spend some time with your family. I won't need you until the meeting."

Brent grinned. "Thank you. My time will be put to good use since I seldom get a chance to visit Brandon and his wife."

"Your brother seems to know a good deal about the Apaches. Has he lived out here long?"

Brent's blood turned to ice. "Well . . . yes. He has."

"He must have married into the band since he lives on the reservation."

"Er, no, actually, he didn't. Hillary, his wife, is from Philadelphia. Her family and . . . ours . . . have been friends for years."

"I see."

Brent's gut ached. His brother had better stay as far away as possible from the general and his questions. Crook was a very smart man, and if he heard tales of the famous White Fox and became suspicious . . .

Brent was infinitely relieved when the trail began

to narrow. The general took the lead again and Brent gladly rode alone.

Surprisingly, they made good time on the twisting, winding trail and reached Fort Apache before the sun had begun to set. Brent called out to the general, saluted, and turned off before the detail crossed the stream that led up and into the compound.

The muted golden light of evening cast long shadows from the squat piñon pines and juniper dotting the ridge on which Brand and Hillary lived. Brent rode past several wickiups and mentally patted his brother on the back for making the gesture of building a log and quarried stone home for his wife.

Smoke rose, welcoming, from the chimney as he tied his mount to one of several hitching posts. Before he could knock, Hillary threw open the door and rushed out to greet him. "Brent! What a surprise. I didn't expect you back this soon."

He laughed. "It's been a month, Hillary. To some people, that's a long time."

She took his hand and led him inside. "And it is. I guess I've just gotten used to living out here where we don't see . . ."

Brent cocked his head. "It's lonely for you, isn't it?"

Her cheeks pinkened as she sat in one of the hand-hewn chairs pulled up to the round pine dining table. Her eyes flitted to Brent and then to her hands, which were entwined in her lap. "I must admit that at first, it was. But now I don't mind it so much."

Her face literally glowed when she looked directly into his eyes. "Brand keeps me happy. Very happy."

Brent took the chair across from her. "I'm glad. I've got to tell you, though, I never thought you'd take to living out here, especially on a reservation."

She looked through the kitchen window, searching, as if she expected someone soon. "Anywhere Brand is, I'll be happy. It really doesn't matter where."

His eyes narrowed. "You don't sound anything like the Hillary Sue Collier I used to know."

She smiled and reached out to clasp one of his hands, the one drumming its fingers incessantly against the spotless, polished surface of the table. "You've never met this Hillary before, Brent. This Hillary is a joyously pregnant Mrs. Brandon McQuade."

Brent's mouth gaped open. His heart constricted with pleasure. He rose to his feet and went around the table to give his sister-in-law, the woman who would soon make him an uncle, a bone-crunching hug.

"Hey, what is going on in here? I have worked my poor fingers to nubs today in order to come home early and see my lovely wife, and I find her in the arms of another man."

Brand had barely finished speaking before he, too, was grasped in Brent's arms. He coughed when Brent began clapping him on the back.

"By God, man. I'm goin' to be an uncle. I can't believe it. Why didn't you tell me when you came down to San Carlos?"

Brand draped his arm around his wife's shoulders. "Because I did not know then. We only found out for sure a few days ago."

Brent grinned. "No wonder Hillary's acted so excited. Bet I'm the first one she's had a chance to spill the beans to."

Both men laughed when Hillary flushed and covered her cheeks with both hands. "I couldn't help it. I'm just so happy I could burst."

Brand patted her tummy with his free hand. "It will not be so long before you do just that, my love."

Some of the pleasure faded from Brent's eyes as he watched the happy couple. During the evening, a melancholy ache pestered his insides. Though Hillary served a wonderful meal of roast beef, boiled potatoes, green beans and, later, dried apple pie, he hardly did it justice.

Would he ever find a love like theirs? Did he really want to?

Watching the intimate glances and loving caresses they naturally bestowed on one another, Brent came to a conclusion. Yes! He wanted what they had. He wanted a family, and a woman who glowed with love for him, just like Hillary did for Brandon.

After dinner the brothers sat in front of the blazing fire talking about the things they had missed growing up apart. Brent didn't begrudge his brother and Hillary their feelings for each other, he just hoped he would be lucky enough to have a tenth of the happiness they had found together.

And later that night, as he lay in the spare room that would soon become a nursery, he wasn't even surprised when visions of a black-haired, whiskey-eyed she-cat paraded in all her honey-skinned glory before his closed eyes. He had to admit that Miss Meadowlark Russell inspired gut-warming feelings from him.

A baby. He pictured her holding a raven-haired, blue-eyed little girl, or boy, with golden skin and peach-tinted cheeks.

Suddenly, his resolve intensified. What if she were pregnant now, too, with *their* baby? Would she even bother to tell him?

Well, he would keep his eyes on her. She wouldn't get two feet away from him until he was certain, one way or the other.

If she wasn't pregnant? It didn't matter. He was determined to get General Crook to take him along on the campaign into Mexico. He would speak with Lark's aunt and every other member of her family, if it was necessary.

Oh, yes, Miss Russell would be his. And she

would like it. He would make sure she liked it.

The detail rode into San Carlos three days later, amid gusts of wind that threatened to pluck horse and rider from the shifting land more easily than plucking down from a goose. They passed the little agency office building and Brent struggled to keep his eyes trained toward the stables. He wanted to peek, to chance getting a glimpse of her through the window. But he *didn't* want her to catch him looking, didn't want her to think he was eager to see her again.

It galled him to think she had some sort of invisible hold over him, that even without her being aware of it, she seemed to control his actions, his body, his mind and soul.

No, he couldn't do it. He couldn't just ride past. His right side twitched. His neck burned. His head turned of its own volition.

There she was. He fought to pull his gaze away, but it was drawn back. She stood in the doorway, looking at him. Something caught at the base of his throat. God, she was beautiful. God, he had missed her.

Brent blinked and was past the office.

His chest felt as if a two-thousand-pound bull had stomped across it. He *had* missed her. Like a man missed food, water and air. With an ache that ricocheted throughout his being. It came as a shock, a complete surprise, his sudden reaction to just that one quick glimpse.

Yet he had noticed everything about her. The full calico print skirt. Plain white cotton tunic. Her hair had finally grown enough to tie back and only a few strands blew loose against her cheeks. What a shame. He liked looking at her when blue-black locks framed her ears and hung provocatively against the slender column of her throat.

Well, hell. He'd suspicioned it. Now he knew. He'd done it again. He'd fallen head over heels, heart in throat, ringing ears in love with Meadowlark Russell. It was something he'd heard men talk about, but never experienced before. *Real love.*

But would the woman of his heart ever return his feelings? His stomach liquified. He was a *white* man, remember? The white man who kept her people fed and hid her damned secret about her father, but nonetheless only a white man.

He hadn't even been able to defend himself against her boyfriend, Scorpion. And what had happened to the warrior? The man had told him in no uncertain terms that Meadowlark was *his*. Did she return Scorpion's feelings? Had she really only come back when he was wounded to be safe from the army?

Brent sighed. She certainly couldn't deny there was a strong attraction between them. They made glorious love together. But that hadn't been enough. Afterward, she'd been distant and quiet. In fact, it seemed that anytime she let down her guard and thawed toward him, she felt guilty later. She was never comfortable around him, that was for sure.

So, at least she wasn't indifferent. She was definitely aware of him as a *man.* Once in a while she allowed her passionate nature free rein and he became a very happy man.

A sly grin quirked his mouth. He'd always been hardheaded enough to love a challenge. The harder, the better. And Lark was about as difficult a challenge as he'd ever gone up against. She was stubborn as a mule and tough as a braided rope, but she would be worth the effort.

If he had anything to say about it, and he would, she was going to make him happy over and over again. And he would return the favor tenfold.

* * *

Meadowlark paced the packed earth floor, fretting over whether Brent would come back by the office that evening or wait until the next morning. Her pulse still raced from the fire that sparked from his eyes as the detail passed.

She cursed the spirits for her weak nature. She had not intended to go to the door, had thought to hide in the shadows and peek through the window. But when she had seen him, sitting so gracefully erect in the saddle, his broad shoulders thrown back, his perfectly chiseled features so handsome in the glow of the afternoon sunlight, something had snapped inside her.

Her legs seemed to move with a mind of their own, supporting her unresisting body as far as the doorway. Ice-cold fingers closed around her heart when it looked as if he would ride right by her without even looking in her direction. But then he lifted the reins, slowing his horse. His head turned. His eyes found hers. Those blue, blue eyes. How cold the color sometimes, yet how they had seared through her at that moment, radiating heat waves from her scalp to her toes.

She was so glad he was back. As tormenting as his presence could be, it was better than the past few days spent wondering and worrying about him.

Meadowlark crossed her arms and chaffed the chill bumps that suddenly erupted on her flesh. Why had she allowed the captain into her life so completely? When had he taken control of her senses? How would she survive when he left San Carlos forever?

And he *would* leave. They all did. No one wanted to spend any longer than necessary in "Hell's forty acres." Most of the soldiers requested a transfer after only a few months. So far, though, Brent didn't *seem* anxious to escape the reservation. But maybe leaving was something he was afraid to talk about in front of her. He *had* made that rash declaration about wanting to wed her—which had not been mentioned again.

The rays of sunlight, casting glares across the paper-strewn desk, had long since disappeared. Meadowlark sighed and finally sat down. Maybe it was best he did not come. His return had already ignited a fire in the pit of her stomach and confused her senses.

By morning, she might have enough control to carry on a normal conversation. She might even resist the urge to throw herself at the captain. She hoped.

"Mornin'."

The drawled word perked Meadowlark's spirits. So, he was not as unaffected by their situation as he would have her think, though he sauntered casually into the office. She smiled and inclined her head.

"How're you feelin'?"

Her brows drew together. "Fine."

"Good. Some of the soldiers have come down with malaria. You, uh, haven't been sick?"

She shook her head.

"Not sick at your *stomach* . . . or anythin'?"

Meadowlark scowled. "No."

"Well . . . good." Brent hunched his shoulders and paced beside the crates. He shot her a covert glance. "You look tired. Have you been gettin' enough sleep?"

"Yes." Meadowlark could not believe it. He had been gone for days, and all he wanted to talk about was her health. *She* wanted to hear about his trip. She wanted . . . She wanted . . . him to take her in his arms and kiss her senseless. She . . . Her eyes widened at the sudden notion, and the unbidden image of Brent McQuade naked, holding out his arms, inviting her to come to him.

Inhaling deeply, she turned and closed her eyes for

a brief moment. It did not help. Rippling muscles and smooth male flesh paraded through her mind more vividly than a sidewinder trail in the sand. "H-how was your trip?"

Brent immediately thought of Lark's cousin and felt his cheeks burn.

Meadowlark saw the color suffuse his face and wondered what had embarrassed him. "You saw the Warm Springs people?"

He cleared his throat and looked down at the scuff marks marring the toes of his usually polished boots. "Yes, we did. Even spent the night there."

She nodded, pleased that Crook had seen fit to spend some time with her people. "I have started plans on the irrigation canal. Maybe now the warriors will raise crops."

Relieved that the subject had reverted to safe ground, Brent found his footing and went over to slide into his chair. He gripped the seat with both hands. "They might. They told the general they wanted peace and would stay on the reservation."

"Did you go to the White Mountains? Was your brother there?"

"Yes." Unbidden images of a very pregnant Meadowlark flooded Brent's mind. She was so big she waddled, her belly filled with his child—their child. And she had never been more lovely.

"I would meet your brother one day."

Brent stifled a surprised gasp. Oh, no! That would never do. She would recognize the White Fox. No telling what would happen. "No, I don't think . . . I mean, I doubt he'll come back . . ."

She just stared. Brent fidgeted until his darting eyes stopped on a half-filled sheet of paper. "Are those requisitions?"

She nodded.

"Don't you think we should order blankets? I noticed some of your people needed more for their families." They needed more of everything, he thought to himself.

He finally breathed normally when she turned her attention to the lists. God, how was he going to keep Lark from running into Brandon? And how would he keep them both away from General Crook?

Tension hung thicker than fog for the next few days. Meadowlark edged around Brent, wary and watchful, skittish as a filly around a mustang stud. Her hands shook, her knees quaked, her breath came in short rasps whenever he looked at her. A heightened fierceness shone from the icy-blue depths of his eyes, more intense, yet more subtle than any hungry gaze she had ever seen.

There was something about him now, something different and dangerous—like a puma stalking a newborn fawn. His body was just as lean and muscled, his movements as sure and graceful, his features every bit as intriguing and beautiful.

She caught herself staring out of the window at the firm cut of his jaw as he intently watched her mare cavorting in the corral, when someone stepped into the office doorway.

"Mornin', ma'am."

She inclined her head.

"Cap'n McQuade around?"

A crunch of gravel and flash of navy-blue passing the window answered the question. "He is here now."

The trooper arched his back and looked outside, then grinned at her before backing out of the door. "Thank you, ma'am."

Meadowlark shook her head and walked over to the cracked piece of mirror leaning against the washbasin. She picked it up and peered into the glass. Her skin was clean, with only a few fine lines around the corners of her eyes. Freckles dotted her nose and sprayed across her cheekbones, but other than that, she did not think she appeared particularly aged.

So why did everyone insist on calling her "ma'am"?

She darted a glance through the window and saw Brent gesturing with his hands. The trooper nodded his head and Brent's shoulders sagged before he turned and headed toward the office.

His muscled breadth looked handsome in the crisp, clean uniform. The jacket fit his shoulders perfectly and tapered down his lean torso. A yellow stripe along the seam of his trousers bent and stretched with every lithe stride.

All at once, Meadowlark realized the mirror was about to slip through her fingers. She drew in several deep breaths and carefully replaced it.

Brent walked into the room just as Meadowlark was straightening from her task. He whistled under his breath at the sight of tight leather britches hugging a round, firm derriere and lusciously curved hips.

But it was when she turned around that those amber eyes pierced him to the quick. He shivered as if the sun had suddenly been consumed by a roiling bank of thunderheads. With concerted effort, he broke the spell of their locked eyes and scuffed his toe over a crack in the hard dirt.

He cleared his throat and glanced hesitantly about the room. "The general's ordered me to take a detail up to the mines and investigate the latest claim that Apaches are harassing the miners. I, uh, won't be here to help you pass out the rations."

Meadowlark shrugged. She had handled the rations for weeks before the captain's arrival. She could do it again. And it would give her something to do. Besides gawk at him. Or think of him. She welcomed the chore.

Brent frowned. He didn't know what reaction he'd expected, but he'd hoped for more than just a negligent lift of her shoulders. Thought maybe she'd come to depend on him. Imagined she might even be upset and pitch a fit.

But, no, such a display would never come from Lark. Why she could barely summon the energy to show she didn't give a damn.

When his gaze raked her form up and down, to settling on her midsection, Meadowlark had to force herself to keep from covering her belly with both hands. It was not the first time he had stared at her so, and her stomach muscles quivered. What was he thinking?

"Well, if you have any trouble, get hold of Corporal Bent. He'll probably be nearby, anyway." Brent was proud of his young corporal, who seemed to have made it his mission in life to help load and unload and distribute supplies to the Apaches. Few soldiers had taken such a personal interest in the Indians' well-being. It was a pleasant change.

Meadowlark nodded, yet there was something in her eyes that kept Brent rooted to the floor. He searched their amber depths, trying to read her thoughts. Whatever it was disappeared with one quick blink.

Without another word, he spun and left the office.

Chapter Twenty

Captain Brent McQuade and his detail found no evidence of Apaches causing trouble for the miners. But he was worried about the vehemence with which the men talked of taking matters into their own hands if the army didn't provide them with enough protection.

It was typical, he thought, that because the whites wanted more land, they provoked trouble and talked the government into cutting deeper into the size of the reservation. Five times. Five times the government had allowed it to happen—whenever miners or farmers or anyone else discovered something valuable on Indian land.

Hell, the Apaches didn't stand a chance against such a biased political system.

The detail had ridden as far as the outskirts of the agency when a man on a mule intercepted them. Brent called the detail to a halt and saluted. "General Crook, I was going to report to you as soon as the men were dismissed."

The general looked down the double line of troopers. "Turn the detail over to the sergeant, captain. I'd like a word with you in private."

Brent did as the general commanded, all the while wondering what could be so important as to bring the man out to meet him. Once the soldiers rode away, he followed Crook to the stream where they dismounted, tethered their horses and took seats on two rounded boulders.

"How did your meeting go with the miners, Captain?"

Brent shook his head. "I didn't find any sign of Apaches having been near their camps. But several mines have been worked right up against the reservation boundary. They want that land."

The general nodded. "I am well aware of what the miners want. But this time, they will be disappointed." He rubbed the tip of his nose and then informed Brent, "Captain McQuade, I purposely sent you out today so I could see how well Miss Russell handled herself when given charge of the rations. She did an admirable job."

Brent's chest swelled. On hearing praise for Meadowlark, he felt like a preening peacock. It was irrational, but true.

"And since I know the agency will be left in good hands, I want you to accompany me into Mexico when I take the campaign to Geronimo."

Brent couldn't have been any more surprised if someone had come up and offered him a fortune in gold. He just sat there, stunned, elated, and wary. Surely the general was joking. He'd already made it clear that Brent was needed where he was, as the San Carlos agent. "Are you serious, sir?"

"Dead serious. I'm hand picking my officers, Captain. I've watched you during the past few weeks and I like the way you work with the Apaches. You seem to respect these Indians as individuals, and they return the favor. You're the kind of man, and officer, I want with me when I meet the renegades."

Heat suffused Brent's face. He didn't know how to respond to the general. His treatment of the Apaches wasn't something he'd thought about. They *were* individuals, and human beings, and needed help to survive the challenges sure to come. All he'd done, he'd have done for anyone under those circumstances.

But he'd wanted to accompany the general ever since he'd heard about the mission. Why was he hesitating? "I'd be honored to go with you, General. Do you know when we'll be leaving?"

"I'm starting for Willcox in three days. But I have to see about the troops guarding the border there, and have yet to hear from the Mexican officials regarding the letters I sent last month. I may have to go down in person. Wouldn't want to step on any toes by going into Mexico without permission."

Brent smiled at the general's sly wink, knowing the man would do what he had to do, one way or another. But it was like the general to see to it everything was well thought out in advance and done correctly.

Crook rose to his feet and walked over to his mule, where he patted the animal affectionately on the neck. "Glad to have you aboard, captain. I'll be in touch as soon as I hear from the Mexican side."

As he watched the general mount and ride toward his tent, Brent was proud he'd been chosen to serve with such a man, commanding officer or not. Crook was a leader of few words, and when he spoke, men listened. Brent leaned back and rolled off the boulder onto the ground, where he smiled up at the blue sky. His dream had become a reality.

He and Brandon would be riding together, working for a mutual cause. Blood roared through his veins. He shot to his feet, swung into the saddle and raced his horse to the stable. He slid the gelding to a stop and simultaneously dismounted amid a cloud of boiling dust. Seconds later, he slapped his hat against his thigh, brushed particles of dirt from the brim and headed toward the agency office.

It was late in the afternoon, but he figured Lark would still be at work. Wait until she heard the news. Crook had thought she'd done a hell of a job with the rations today. She'd be pleased, too. It was a special compliment.

Meadowlark stifled a yawn as she finished recording the number of people who had come to the agency to collect rations that day. She was greatly encouraged to see that more and more Apaches were taking heart from General Crook's presence to either return to or remain on the reservation.

The general's return to Arizona Territory had prevented a major Apache uprising, and Meadowlark's own heart was eased knowing that her people's situation was already improving.

Along with thoughts of changes for the better, though, came thoughts of a tall, blond-haired captain. She was beginning to worry because she had not seen him return from the mines. Recalling "Slaughter" Ryan, she shivered. No telling what reception the army detail had received. The miners had been deprived of their surplus, and cheap, supplies.

She sighed and stretched, then rose from the desk to peer through the window. The sun had yet to set, but already lights from the buildings and tents winked in the wind. Few soldiers or Apaches remained outside since the day had turned blustery and cold.

Rubbing the chill from her arms, she pulled the scrap of muslin over the window. Though it was early, she was tired and decided to try to get some sleep. There was little to keep her occupied since the captain had made himself so scarce lately, she thought while readying herself for bed.

She discarded the leather tunic and reached for

the basin of water she had just heated and began to cleanse her upper body. The warm cloth smoothing her knotted muscles was so relaxing her lids drooped and she yawned again.

Suddenly, the door grated open. Her mouth snapped shut and she crossed her arms defensively over her breasts as she turned only her head to see who had entered.

Brent stopped dead on the threshold, holding the door open. His eyes narrowed. His heart thudded painfully against his rib cage as he gazed down the slender expanse of Lark's smooth, naked back.

Meadowlark's blood surged through her veins, making her ears buzz. She tottered dangerously. But she gulped down several quick breaths of air and snapped, "Either come in or go out. The air is cold."

Goosebumps did raise her flesh, but she was not sure if they were from the sudden chill, or blazing desire.

She reached for her tunic, but he stepped forward and took her outstretched hand. Shivers rippled across her flesh. He raised her palm to his lips and brushed his mouth and then his moist tongue, over her sensitive skin. She sucked in a breath of air and stared at her hand.

Brent's knees shook so badly he wasn't certain he could stand, but with a stern admonition to himself, somehow managed the difficult task. Her bare, silken skin beckoned his caress and his willpower deserted him. Her hand trembled in his. Her eyes had darkened, hazy, almost dreamlike. His gut cinched inward as his free hand stroked the nape of her neck and his fingers brushed through thick black tresses, now almost long enough to curl atop her shoulders.

Meadowlark shuddered when his fingers sifted through her hair. His touch so tentative, so gentle that even now she trembled, torn by the desire to run away, to hide where she would be safe—safe from him, safe from her wanton desires and wildly surging emotions. He had become too important, too all-consuming in her life.

But now, with his hands gentling her, it was not in the realm of possibility for her to move even an inch. Her body was responding, anticipating, overwhelming her common sense. She shifted forward until her bare breasts brushed the coarse material of his jacket. Her nipples puckered. Her breath came in shallow gasps.

Brent felt the searing heat from her body through the thick layers of his own clothing. Hurriedly, he reached between them to shed his coat. But his fingers encountered Lark's hands, already working at the task. He drew in a deep breath and tilted his head back, willing himself to go easy, to take it slow . . . It had been so long—too long. Then her hands were on his bare chest, rubbing in circles, teasing his nipples, tickling over his ribs with caresses as soft and light as gossamer. He clenched his teeth. When her knuckles grazed his belly, working at the buttons on his trousers . . .

Brent grabbed her wrists and pulled her to him. His pants fell around his hips as his mouth closed over hers. His tongue probed and pressed until she parted for him and he delved deep into the honeyed recess. Their tongues met, entwined, and dueled. They strained, each trying to get closer to the other. But Brent suddenly ended the kiss, rasped in a draught of air and plucked her off the ground as if she weighed no more than a butterfly.

Taking short, rapid steps because of the precarious position of his trousers, he carried her to the pallet. He knelt and placed her gently on the blankets, but when he would've arisen to finish removing the rest of his clothing, she wrapped her arms around his neck and pulled him down to lay full length beside her. He reached to take her in his arms, but she avoided his hands and sat up to pull off his boots and pants herself.

Brent tried to help, to hurry her efforts, but she tenderly shoved him aside. He fell back, sweat beading his forehead, as she slowly tugged off each boot and then set to work on his pants. Again the backs of her hands brushed his sensitized belly. His muscles contracted. His hands curled into fists.

But then he was naked. Her soft hand closed around him. An agonized groan escaped his constricted throat as she squeezed and slid her flaming fingers up and down, concentrating all of the blood and energy in his body to that one all-important extension of himself.

Meadowlark was awed by her own audacity. Where had she found the courage to take control of their lovemaking? Yet, why should she not? She had yearned to lie next to him like this, to touch him and have him touch her in return. Without releasing his manhood from her grasp, she reveled in the sensations his fingers wrought as they roved every inch of her body.

Her self-assurance soared as she realized she held control over the strong, virile captain. With each tiny movement she gave pleasure or pain, agony or ecstasy. Her design was to please, and from the smoky hue of his hooded eyes, she was succeeding admirably.

She felt ten feet tall, felt like a pampered goddess, as he cupped her face in his palms. He shifted his hips until she sat astraddle him. She met him halfway as he lifted his shoulders and coaxed her head down for the most perfect, loving kiss she had ever experienced. The firm softness of his lips, his tender exploration of her mouth, her eyes, her cheeks and once again her lips, seared her to her soul. Desire melted her bones, along with any reserve she may have harbored.

Then his hands spanned her hips. He lifted her gently. The tip of his pulsing manhood probed the feminine core of her being. Electric spasms jolted through her as he deftly, unhesitantly thrust inside. Her muscles contracted around him creating a friction that sent her rocking to a primitive rhythm older than time itself.

Her head fell back, arching the fullness of her breasts into his waiting palms. He rolled her nipples between his thumbs and forefingers, squeezing so softly, then pinching sharply. She bit her lip to keep from crying out her pleasure. He repeated the motions until her body rose and fell atop him, taking him into her.

His hips bucked beneath her at the same time he grasped her head and pulled her down for a kiss so passionate that drops of moisture squeezed from the corners of her eyes. Her chest felt as if it would also explode from the pressure and intensity of her emotions.

She loved this man more than she thought it possible to love another human being. He could easily become her world, her reason for existing, her very heart.

Brent felt the ferocity of her climax as her inner muscles contracted about him. He purposely held himself, giving her all of the pleasure he was capable of giving, but she clasped him so hard she pulled him over the edge. They came together, giving and receiving every bit and particle of themselves until, spent and drained, they collapsed into each other's arms.

United as one, chest heaving against chest, belly to belly, they inhaled steadying breaths.

Brent nuzzled his lips into the damp tendrils of hair hiding her earlobe and whispered, "I love you."

She sighed and snuggled her head onto his shoulder, too content and sated and tired to utter a sound. Later, they would talk and she would tell him how she felt. Later, after a tiny nap. Later . . .

The moon shone through a hole in the curtain directly into Meadowlark's eyes. She blinked and started to stretch, but found herself wrapped in a warm cocoon of arms and legs and solid, furred chest. She slowly pried open her eyes, only to stare up into Brent's shadowed face.

He was leaning on one elbow, watching her. A glowing heat spread upward from her belly to her chest and neck to finally tingle in the apples of her cheeks. A slight grin curved her lips as she thought of how easily Brent blushed. It was one of his most endearing traits. He was so guileless. Yet so much a man—strong, brave, tender and gentle.

She opened her mouth, but before she could speak, he laid a finger across her lips.

"Sh-h-h. I have somethin' I need to say. An' I'm afraid I'll lose my courage if I keep puttin' it off."

He took a deep breath. She smoothed the hair from his forehead, allowing her fingers to linger in the clean, crisp strands longer than necessary.

"I love you, Lark. I want more than anythin' for you to marry me, bear my children an' grow old with me."

She sucked in her breath.

"Hear me out, please. I know I pressured you . . . earlier, about gettin' married."

Maybe, Meadowlark thought, but then he completely ignored her, as if the notion had slipped his mind.

"I know it frightened you to think I'd seduced you. An' then we had to worry 'bout your maybe being . . . pregnant."

But she wasn't, and was surprised by the sharp twinge of disappointment that squeezed her heart.

"Anyway, I wanted to surprise you an' find a way to talk with your aunt before mentioning it again, but I can't wait, honey. I'm afraid I'll lose you if I don't tell you how I feel an' get your promise to wait for me, at least till I get back." He was thinking of Scorpion and the closeness that had existed between the warrior and Lark.

What if Scorpion returned while he was in Mexico? What if Lark decided she truly loved the warrior? That event would break his heart. He had to get her to promise to give him a chance before making a choice—of any kind.

Meadowlark was touched by Brent's thoughtfulness in intending to speak to her family. She had not expected such consideration from a white man. It served to intensify her feelings for him all the more. She looked into his earnest eyes. "I lo . . ."

The rest of his words filtered through her mind. *Until he got back?* Got back from where? How could he leave after making such a beautiful declaration of his love? "Where are you going?" Her voice was harsh, her words stilted.

Excited and hopeful, Brent ignored the strained tone of her voice. She hadn't immediately refused him, and he'd seen a certain look shining from her eyes, a look that was definitely encouraging. And she'd almost said the words, he knew it.

"I talked with General Crook this afternoon."

When he hesitated, she prodded, "What were his words?"

"For one thing, he bragged on you, an' the good job you'd done with the rations. He was so impressed that he thought you'd get along fine handlin' the weekly chore all by yourself." He waited, hoping to see her enthusiasm and pleasure at being singled out for Crook's praise.

But she was anything but pleased. She frowned. "Why would I be alone?"

Now Brent frowned. He'd expected her to be happy. "Well, he asked me to go to Mexico with him."

She looked away. So it was finally going to happen. "When?"

"I don't know, exactly. He'll get in touch when the time comes." He ran a finger along the line of her jaw and turned her head back until he could look into her eyes. His breath stuck in his throat. "What's wrong, honey?"

Meadowlark felt as if a dull knife had been stabbed into her heart. What was wrong? What was *not* wrong? Crook would soon be off to annihilate her people and Brent McQuade would be at the front of the charge. And he lay there, smiling, as if the thought of murdering Apaches was pleasing to him. Oh, how grateful she was that she had not voiced her feelings earlier.

"Lark? What's the matter? What did I do?"

She stared him in the eyes. "You are a white man. To you, you do nothing wrong. But I cannot marry you. I will never marry you."

She struggled, trying to unlock their bodies and move from beneath him. It was impossible to remain so intimately close and say the words that must be said.

But Brent would not release her. His eyes hardened. He wedged his large body more firmly upon her, until she ceased her efforts to escape. "Tell me, Lark. How did I hurt you? I'd never intentionally do such a thing. You know that."

She choked back a sob. She could not reveal how deeply she was hurting. "No, I do not. And why do you care? I am Apache, after all."

His fingers clenched at the back of her head. "What're you talkin' about, woman? I love you. An' all I've done is try to help the Apache. Whatever you're thinkin', I don't deserve it."

She hiccuped, "You will go to Mexico and murder my people. How can you say you love me, when you can hardly wait to join with Crook and slaughter everyone. How much suffering are we to endure at your hands?"

Brent rolled off Meadowlark and covered himself with one corner of a blanket. She might as well have slapped him soundly and kicked him in the gut at the same time. All he'd ever done was try to help the Indians, and he'd be doing the same in Mexico.

And who did she think *she* was, acting so noble, so high and mighty?

He reached out and took hold of her shoulders, shaking her as he spoke, "How much suffering are *we* to endure? *You* never had to suffer. Not like *your people*. You've never had to live on nothing or been forced to sleep without a shelter or grub in the dirt for your next meal. Whether you admit it or not, Meadowlark Russell, you're half-white, and that white blood has served you pretty damned well."

At her stricken expression, Brent immediately released her. He rose and began to dress. She sat as if struck dumb and terrible remorse filled his heart. He shouldn't have said those things. She was following *her* heart. Because he was angry and feeling rejected, he'd lashed out at her.

He stood in the middle of the room and hunched his shoulders. "Look, I can't promise that some of the renegades won't be killed when we go into the Sierra Madres. Crook won't run from a fight." He stuffed his hands in his pockets and thought back to the general's campaign of ten years ago. Crook had resolutely gone after the Apaches with cunning and skill and the determination to get them to the reservations by whatever means necessary. He showed no mercy until the defeated Indians surrendered and were ready to accept his terms. No, Brent couldn't promise Meadowlark anything.

"Just remember, the general will never wage a war on women and children. He won't be goin' down there to *annihilate* your . . . anyone."

He looked up at the ceiling. All he saw was black nothingness, stretching on and on and on. There was nothing left for him to say. Meadowlark refused to look at him. He'd hurt her, just as she'd hurt him. Maybe it was best that he tuck his tail and slink away. Maybe later, after the campaign was over, he'd be able to repair some of the damage. Maybe they could start again. Or maybe neither of them would want to.

Quietly, regret etched in his soul, he turned and left the office, pulling the door closed behind in a final, significant gesture. Outside, he hesitated, as if he might turn back. Instead, he hunched his shoulders, shivering as the cold night wind seeped through the unbuttoned flap of his jacket and sliced like ice-cold knives down the back of his neck. It was a fitting end.

He'd never loved the way he loved Meadowlark Russell and had never hurt as he did now.

Meadowlark turned when she heard the door close. Tears rolled unchecked down her cheeks. Tears for what could have been, for what she had lost and for what was to come.

What hurt the most was the fact that he had spoken the truth. She had never suffered like the rest of the Warm Springs band. And she had always felt guilty because of it. That was one reason why she was so adamant about her dealings with them and tried so hard to see they were treated fairly.

She had made a difference, too. She and her father, and then alone as she acted as the agent. The Apaches appreciated her efforts, knew she had risked much on their behalf, for they had told her so themselves. But still it was not enough. Because of her white blood, she had never felt like a true member of the band.

It was always there, the deference, the wary looks, as she taught them irrigation and planting, as she handed them their rations.

Maybe that was why she fought so hard to ignore her white heritage, why she fought her feelings for Brent McQuade, why she would do whatever was necessary to keep fighting for *her people*.

Her spine stiffened as she sat cross-legged on the pallet. She absently traced the pattern of a small circle of moonlight.

She would keep a close watch on the captain. When he left for Mexico, she would follow. Somehow, she would warn Geronimo that Crook was coming.

Chapter Twenty-one

Brent stared across the desk at Meadowlark. Funny, how all of a sudden she was Meadowlark, rather than Lark. It fit her now. She was all dignity and poise, cold and remote.

Tension had permeated the room many times before, but was so thick now one could part it with two hands. For days they had each come and gone, saying only what needed to be said concerning requisitions and rations, flinching if one would accidentally brush against the other. He was sick of having to be so careful, like a long-tailed cat in a room full of rocking chairs.

They both jumped when Corporal Bent pushed through the sagging door and into the office. The young soldier saw Brent in the corner and saluted before entering further.

Brent's lips quirked at the excited flush on the corporal's face and the soldier's agitated movements as he waited for Brent's acknowledgment. "At ease, Corporal. Now, what's on your mind this morning?"

"It's the general, sir. He wants that you should come right away."

Brent frowned, then rose to his feet and reached for his hat. Before he left, however, he glanced at Meadowlark. "I'll finish these papers when I get back."

His insides knotted when she barely shrugged and failed to look up. Pretending to be busy, was she? Well, he . . .

"Hurry, Cap'n. I'll show you where to find the general."

Brent clapped the young man on the back. "Lead on, Corporal." Who needed contrary women? Just wait until he was gone, then she'd see what all he'd done around the place. She'd be sorry . . . No, she wouldn't. She'd be glad he was out of her hair, out of her way and, especially, out of her bed. Probably wouldn't even miss him.

Lost in daydreams of Lar . . . Meadowlark running to him after he'd spent a long day on patrol, running to welcome him home—to *their* home . . . He was startled when Corporal Bent touched his shoulder.

"We're here, sir. The general's inside with Major Taylor."

Brent nodded. "Thanks, Corporal." Alone in front of the oaken door, Brent dusted off the arms of his jacket, then hesitated momentarily before knocking and announcing his presence.

Although he had been anxious to go to Mexico, he was suddenly experiencing reservations. He had responsibilities here. There were important things he needed to accomplish. If this summons was about leaving San Carlos now, he'd be torn between duty and desire.

Before he could get maudlin on the subject, Brent hurriedly rapped on the door and walked inside.

Major Taylor greeted him. "Come in, McQuade, and take a seat. The general received a telegram this morning that will be of interest to you, too."

General Crook looked up from where he was writing on the major's desk. "What we feared most has happened."

Brent eased into the only empty chair. "A raid?"

"Came right through my patrols near the Mule Mountains."

Brent could imagine the uproar this would create from the civilians in that area. Now they would be calling for Crook to hurry his expedition and wipe out the Apaches once and for all. "Do they know how many and who's leading the renegades?"

Major Taylor rubbed his hands together. "Chato, Bonito and Chihuahua, and twenty-three warriors."

Brent whistled. "When did they come across?"

"Yesterday, if the information we've received is accurate." The major leaned back in his chair, interlocking his fingers over his chest.

Crook stood up and paced between the desk and the bookcase lining the north wall. "I've deployed ten companies of cavalry to search the southern half of New Mexico Territory. We've alerted the area by telegraph. But catching them will be like trying to trap fleas. Our only hope is to go into Mexico. Take the battle to them."

While the general continued to pace, the major told Brent, "General Crook still has received no word from the Mexican Government granting him permission to cross the border. Until he does, I'm afraid the mission will be stalled, or even stopped entirely."

Suddenly, Crook sat down and furiously began writing. He handed Brent one of the pages and stopped long enough to ask him to wire the message.

"Sure. I'll send it right away." Brent took leave of his superior officers and headed toward the post telegraph office. It was a small desk and rickety chair, tucked into a lopsided tent. The operator was just leaving when Brent approached.

"Sorry, captain. You'll have to come back after lunch." The private stretched his arms over his head and groaned.

Standing directly in front of the soldier, so he would have to move to the right or left to get around him, Brent explained, "General Crook needs a message sent. *Right away.*"

The operator rubbed his chin and looked longingly toward the mess hall. He sighed and resignedly bent and reentered the tent. However, as soon as Brent followed him inside, he quickly pulled the flap shut. Once the wire was telegraphed, he glanced hopefully at Brent. "Do we have to wait for a reply?"

"No, no telling when it will reach the right people."

Nodding enthusiastically, the operator ushered Brent outside and tied the tent flap in place. When he turned back around, he gave Brent a smug smile. "So ole Chato is at it again. Reckon the gener'l take care o' the 'Paches good 'n proper now. Huh?"

Brent wasn't sure just how to answer the operator. It seemed everyone he talked to assumed Crook's only purpose for going to Mexico was to destroy the Indians once and for all. He looked over the top of the shorter man's head and came eye to eye with Meadowlark.

His heart literally stopped beating. She looked at him as if he had no more substance than a snake slithering in the sand. Her huge eyes were accusing and filled with hurt. When she spun and ran off, his insides sloshed cold as ice water. She must've overheard the operator's thoughtless speech. He grimaced. As far as she was concerned, her suspicions concerning Crook's mission in Mexico had just been confirmed.

Brent admitted things didn't look good for the Apaches. Public opinion was stacking against them.

The next day General Crook came to Brent. As he entered the small agency office, he took off his hat and nodded to Meadowlark. "Good morning, Miss Russell."

Her eyes lowered as she nodded, once.

Brent released the breath he'd been holding, afraid of what her reaction might be. She'd certainly frozen *him* in his tracks with a dozen cold looks since yesterday afternoon.

To distract the general, Brent placed himself between Crook and Meadowlark. "Good of you to drop by, General. Is there something I . . . we . . . can do for you?"

General Crook took off his gloves, folded them over lengthwise and then pulled them over and over between his right thumb and forefinger. "Yes, captain, there is. I'm leaving for Willcox in an hour and I have a request to make."

Brent glanced over his shoulder. Meadowlark was diligently scribbling on a piece of paper, to all intent and purpose, paying the conversation no mind. But Brent stifled a grin. He could've sworn her ears twitched. At least twice. She was a sly minx.

Brent stepped toward the general. "Maybe we should go outside."

Crook shook his head. "No need. Since you'll be staying on at San Carlos for a while, at least, I'd like for you to round up some Apache scouts."

Brent cleared his throat. "So, you think we'll go to Mexico after all."

"I'm on my way to find out. The Mexican authorities won't respond to letters or wires, so I'll go talk to them personally. The next time you hear from me, we'll all know one way or the other."

"How many scouts will you need?"

"As many as you can get."

This time when Brent darted a glance at Meadowlark, her head was down, but she'd given up the pretense of writing. Not only were her ears still twitching, but her facial expression had changed.

Her cheeks had relaxed to their normal soft hollows. The wrinkle between her eyes was gone.

The woman was up to something. He knew it. Otherwise the conversation she was overhearing would've had her up and ranting at both the general and himself.

Thank God he would be around San Carlos a bit longer. At least he could keep an eye on her and see she didn't cause any trouble. At least he could try.

Meadowlark could not believe her good fortune at being allowed to listen in on the general's orders to Captain McQuade.

She ground her teeth as she thought of the blond-haired captain. Oh, he had been cool and calm, had lied beautifully as he attempted to convince her that Crook had never mentioned his intentions were anything other than to bring the Apaches back to San Carlos.

A smile snaked across her lips. The general had the foolish notion that if the Apaches gave themselves up and returned peacefully to the reservation, there would be no need for bloodshed. Ah, and the hungry coyote would capture a rabbit and then set it free.

Her chest had swelled with pride yesterday when a friend from the Warm Springs band had informed her of Chato's raid. It had taken the army over a day to hear the news. Besides the pride, though, welled a terrible sadness. The leaders could not have chosen a worse time to cross the border.

The renegades had terrorized Mexico, and were now doing the same in Arizona and New Mexico territories. From every ranch or camp attacked, they had stolen fresh horses and traveled seventy-five to a hundred miles a day. No company of cavalry had come close enough to challenge them.

But they had killed people. At three different ranches. And stolen guns and horses and cattle. No one seemed to understand or care that it was the Apache way of life to raid and the warriors would not surrender their goods without a fight. Though they needed the cattle for food and the guns to defend themselves, the whites would demand retribution—demand the Apaches be robbed of freedom or, better yet, of life itself.

She had been furious yesterday when she heard the telegraph operator's words. And Brent McQuade had not denied their truth.

Her anger and apprehension began to diminish as Brent and the general continued to talk. They had mentioned forming a company of scouts from the Apaches living at San Carlos. Hmmm. It would be an easy thing, finding scouts, for there were many bored warriors who craved the chance to be free, no matter what the reason. And since no one Apache band felt loyalty toward another, especially if they had warred and battled over the years, of course they would help to hunt down their brother Indians. She felt no animosity for those men who decided to be scouts. It was just the way it was.

As she thought of the scouts, an idea began to take shape. It would provide the perfect answer for what she needed to do.

Meadowlark used rolled papers to shoo a horde of flies through the doorway, but knew it was a futile gesture. The pests found every tiny crack and chink in the walls and roof. She was just grateful it had been a dry spring because the gnats and mosquitoes had not been their usual problem. And only a few Apaches, or soldiers, had come down with malaria.

One particularly huge fly buzzed around her head. For the first time in over a month, she remembered another room, more flies . . . everywhere . . . Suddenly she began swinging frantically at the insect, finally beating it to the floor. She stepped on the miniature monster and ground it into the earth.

She stood perfectly still, her eyes closed, gasping for breath. Soon, her eyes flitted open and she saw another fly crawling up the sleeve of her blouse. She managed to look away and ignore it. Her outburst had accomplished nothing, but she felt better. The pressure caving upon her chest had lessened. The burning sensation behind her eyes had . . . was still there.

Standing next to the window, she was aware of the movement of a tall man in a blue uniform riding out of the compound. Curiosity turned her head and her gaze latched firmly onto Captain McQuade's straight back and the sway of his body as he sat the saddle with unassumed grace. His was a natural correlation with the horse and she drank in the sight of his taut, sinewy thighs as they constricted and gripped the leather.

Just as he reached the furthermost boundary of the post, he stiffened. Her heart skipped a beat. His head cocked to one side and she held her breath, waiting for him to turn. But he shook his head and spurred the horse into a swinging lope.

Meadowlark sighed and walked slowly to the desk, disturbed by the anticipation burning in her body at the thought that he might just *look* at her. They were adding more and more adobes to the wall between them each day.

It hurt, almost as badly as his betrayal. Yet, if she continued to increase the distance, how would she hear news of Crook's plans? There were things to which the Apache were not privy, such as the general's private thoughts and telegraphed messages.

Somehow, she had to repair some of the damage

to her odd relationship with the captain without ripping her heart to shreds. Time, perseverance and patience, and a hardening of her soul would be required, but she *had* to do it. Otherwise her plans would be worth no more than dried grass in a burning wind.

Sitting down at the desk, she scanned the compound through the space of the window. As in life, there were things she could see and things she could not. And the one most important item darkening her horizon was the fact that she still had found no clues leading to the identity of her father's killer.

She had given up thinking that the Tucson Ring were personally behind his death. Oh, they had played a part, somehow, but she suspected the actual murderer was someone right here at San Carlos. But who? And, most of all, why?

She rose and walked outside to stand in the sun. She had tried to handle it all on her own, but there were too many things over which she had no control or understanding. Looking into the heavens, she begged the spirits for guidance. "Help me . . . Please."

Brent was away from the post four days. During that time, he had no trouble enlisting over two hundred Apaches to serve as scouts for Crook's expedition. The Indians had all promised to come to San Carlos within a week's time for instructions and training, though in reality, there was little the soldiers could teach them about warfare. However, some of the Apaches had never used a rifle, and they would be shown a semblance of the army routine.

Through the entire four days he fought the sensation he'd felt as he left the agency. The sensation of eyes—her eyes—burning into his back. He remembered stopping his horse and knowing that Meadowlark was watching. At night, he lay in his sleeping bag, wondering what he would have seen if he *had* turned. Would her eyes have reflected hatred, anxiety, love—or nothing at all?

It was the thought of that studiously blank expression that had kept him moving forward. Hatred he could almost accept. But not that guarded who-cares visage. Never that. Not anymore.

He guided his horse onto a well-traveled trail. He was only a few hours from San Carlos. He guessed he'd discover her frame of mind soon. Damn it! The she-cat had the power to cause him anguish by mere thought.

Brent rode into the San Carlos headquarters late that afternoon. He looked around at the weathered adobes and the pristine rows of tents, amazed that nothing had changed in his absence. With such turmoil ravaging his life, it seemed impossible the rest of the world could remain so constant.

But that was good. At least there was something he could count on—his work and the military routine. And he looked forward to the days ahead, working with the Apache scouts and finding several white scouts to help shape his new recruits.

All in all, the next few weeks could be rewarding—if he just didn't have to contend with Miss Meadowlark Russell. Hell, she'd squirmed her way into his very soul and she was all he could think about. If he wasn't careful, she could be a life-threatening distraction. It was something he could've lived with, though, if she'd returned his feelings.

He had to ride past the office on the way to the stable. Funny, he'd made a habit of coming in the back way just to avoid this very situation. Why had he forgotten today? Was he a glutton for pain?

Of course he couldn't keep from glancing at the

door. He tried, but his eyes seemed to have a will of their own. His hand pulled back on the reins to pause, while his knees squeezed to hurry the gelding. The horse pranced uncertainly at this confused set of signals.

Meadowlark was there. In the doorway. He gulped. She was looking directly at him. Was that a smile on her face? God but she was beautiful when she chanced a rare expression of happiness.

Happy? Why? Was she glad to see him? Had she missed him?

But why? When he'd left, she'd accused him of being a traitor to her people, nothing better than a hired assassin. What had brought about the change?

Had something transpired at San Carlos that he should know about? Maybe things weren't as constant as he'd thought.

The pressure of his knees relaxed. The horse stood still in the center of the compound. Brent's gaze was anchored to Lark's. She looked so tiny and fragile. He experienced that now familiar tightening in his lower belly, that desire to cherish and protect her, to keep the world from causing *her* any more pain, too.

He cleared his throat and tipped his hat. "Evenin', Miss Russell."

Meadowlark nodded. How wonderful the captain looked, so elegant and graceful astride the big gelding. The sun was setting behind him, outlining his broad frame with golden rays of light, yet hiding his expression in shadow.

What was he thinking? Could he see through her ruse of friendship? Would he just ride on?

But was her interest in him just a ruse? Hadn't she been on edge for days, watching for him? And when she'd finally seen him, she could hardly wait for him to come close enough to see her. Her whole body was one giant nerve.

His deep, husky voice had rolled over her. Her heart still thudded against her breast. No matter what he had done before, or might do in the future, she could not deny she loved him. Right or wrong, futile as it was, she would always love Captain Brent McQuade. Apache curses tripped over her tongue to finally find escape when she softly sighed.

Her cheeks burned when he grinned. Just what was so funny about her standing in the dust on a late March evening, slapping at mosquitoes?

When he continued to sit his horse, with an air of expectancy, as if he was waiting for her to return his greeting, she asked in a strangled voice, "Did you find your scouts?"

He started to dismount. As his long, muscled body swung out of the saddle, her heart dove to her toes. She looked on in panic. She was not ready yet. She needed more time to *pretend* she cared. Or pretend she did not care. Or just to hide her true feelings—from herself as well as Brent McQuade.

As he tied his horse to the hitching rail, her mind raced. Would he expect to come inside? How could she keep him out? He would be too close. Already her flesh tingled and he was not even looking at her.

Brent loosened the saddle girth and walked over to Meadowlark. "Over two hundred warriors will be here next week."

Now she could see his face. His eyes appeared dark and inscrutable. An involuntary shiver shook her, but she managed to turn it into a shrug.

Brent frowned. What had happened to the woman? "How've things been here while I was gone?"

He lifted his hat and rifled his fingers through what she knew to be thick, soft waves. "Quiet," was all she managed to choke from her too-tight throat. She had to tear her eyes away from that one particular lock of hair falling onto his forehead.

Her eyes widened at the rush of emotion. She had not realized just how very much she had missed him, maybe even anticipated seeing him.

"That's good." Brent could hardly concentrate on the conversation, such as it was. He wanted to pull her into his arms and kiss her until she went all soft and yielding and responsive.

Meadowlark nodded. She stepped forward to remove a piece of grass from the lapel of his jacket but, instead, her fingers spread over his firm jawline and inched upward until his cheek fit in the palm of her hand. His flesh was warm and supple, just as she remembered.

Their eyes locked. More quickly than a heartbeat, their hurt and pain were temporarily forgotten. Their bodies yearned toward each other, touching, molding, healing.

Brent dipped his head, kissing her forehead, her cheek, the lobe of her delicate ear. Finally, his mouth swooped to capture her lips, igniting a blaze that neither soul cared to dowse at that moment. It was as if their coming together was fated, inevitable. That no matter what their minds dictated, their hearts demanded this moment.

But when Meadowlark made a tiny mewling whimper deep in her throat, Brent hesitated. His chest ached until he could hardly take a breath. Was it a sign that she wanted him to stop? Was she rejecting him—again? His body trembled with the force of his emotion, his love.

Meadowlark moaned with the pure pleasure of feeling his body pressed to hers. She had thought to never feel the wondrous sensation again. When he lifted his head, pulling away, she moaned once more and wrapped her arms around his shoulders, nuzzling her breasts to his chest. Even through the layers of clothing, she felt the heat, the rapid thrum of his heart; smelled that arousing scent that belonged only to him. She pressed her lips to his neck. His skin tasted slightly salty and she continued her conquest to the apex of his chin and along his jaw.

Brent shuddered. Then elation flooded his body with liquid lava as he realized that he, too, was moaning with the absolute joy of being with the woman he loved—would always love.

Quickly, he lifted her in his arms and carried her inside the office. As he kicked the door shut, he glanced through the window, checking the compound. As far as he could tell, no one had watched their passionate display.

He let her down slowly, let her body slide the length of his. He held her like that, in the circle of his arms. The faint brush of Lark's knuckles as she unfastened his jacket and then his shirt set his body atremble. The things her touch did to him . . . Things only she could do.

Sensing that she was as apprehensive as he, as uncertain of what would take place when this brief time together came to an end, he wanted to do nothing more than hold her in his arms forever. He wanted her to share his feelings, to know that he would never do anything to hurt her.

Then her hands were on his gun belt . . . his trousers and . . . him. His steps were wobbly, but determined, as he made his way to the pallet and put her down as if she were a fragile piece of porcelain.

Her velvet-soft fingers found him again. Muscles rippled across his flat belly. As if by magic, they were naked and lying side by side, reveling in the feel of their bodies. It had been a long time and they kissed and explored as if it were the first time.

Her skin was silk beneath his lips. Her body opened to him like a budding desert rose. She clung to him and his heart nearly burst with delight. If only it could be like this forever . . .

Meadowlark writhed as his fingers probed her most delicate flesh. She held his face in her palms, staring into those blue, blue eyes until she was consumed, no longer one person, but a part of a whole.

She knew now what her body had been saying all along. Whatever happened, she and Brent McQuade were destined to be joined. Their souls, their spirits, were one. She was at once filled with great joy and great distress. If only she knew what would become of them after Mexico . . . If only . . .

Her body convulsed. Brent's mouth had taken the place of his fingers. She felt as if her insides were coiled like ropes of steel. An intense sensation tautened her muscles as aching pleasure spiraled throughout her limbs.

Her hands dug into his wavy blond hair. Her back arched. Tiny explosions rocketed behind her eyelids. As her hips undulated, Brent moved up and fastened his mouth over hers to absorb the moans erupting from her throat.

He entered her with one sure thrust and they soared together. Her mouth burned a trail across his chest and it was his turn to arch his back and delve so deeply into her womanhood that he was suddenly afraid of becoming lost, devoured in depths as he sought heights never before explored.

Meadowlark held the man she loved to her breast, brushing feather-light kisses to his sweat-slicked flesh. His arms tightened around her. She felt so safe she never wanted to move. His breath, rapid, coming in large huffs against her breasts was reassuring. Sighing contentedly, she fended off thoughts of tomorrow.

Chapter Twenty-two

The next morning, Brent rolled from his side to his back. He lay still, enjoying the peaceful feeling of having had a good night's sleep. That is, he'd been able to sleep a *few* hours, which was more than usual. The remaining hours had been a blissful intermission all their own.

As if suddenly remembering he hadn't spent the night alone, he looked to one side, then the other, then sat up, startled to find he was, indeed, alone on the pallet. Then he spied Lark. Yes, she would always be "Lark" to him. She was sitting in his chair with a cup of steaming coffee, watching him over the brim as she blew on the hot liquid before taking a tentative sip.

He grinned sheepishly. "How long've you been up?"

She shrugged without spilling a drop of the savory-smelling brew. "Not long."

Brent pulled a blanket over his lap and scooted around until he found his trousers. Although their night together had been heaven itself, there was something about Lark this morning that set him on his guard.

She seemed friendly enough, he guessed, but the intimate closeness they'd shared was gone. Fine lines at the corners of her eyes seemed more prominent. When she lowered the cup to the desk, he saw the tightness of her lips. "Is something wrong?"

"No. Nothing," she lied. Meadowlark let go of the cup to hide her trembling hands. She was sorry he had awakened. The past few minutes had been enjoyable, watching him sleep, noting how much younger and serene he appeared when he was not worried about San Carlos or the Apaches or, maybe, her.

He curved his lips into a tentative smile. "May I have a cup of that coffee? Sure smells good."

Meadowlark poured the coffee and smiled a real smile, startling Brent. Pleased, he allowed the corners of his mouth to lift. Then she reached behind the desk, retrieving a plate of sticky buns. His grin widened until he couldn't help but chuckle. "I love those rolls."

She set the plate on the pallet and knelt on the far corner, keeping a safe distance between them. But when he said he loved the rolls, he looked directly into her eyes and her heart took a plunge before bobbing up to lodge in her throat.

Last night she had discovered just how easy it was going to be. All she had to do was be herself. Not only did she care, she loved, and was afraid she would have difficulty hiding her feelings from him much longer.

However, what would he say when he discovered she was using him to gather information to help Geronimo? Would he understand that it was something she *had* to do? She felt it was the only way to really prove her loyalty to her Apache heritage. She would do anything, sacrifice anything, to be of value to *her people*.

She watched Brent eat a particularly gooey piece of roll and delightedly lick the sugar from his fingers. She thought her heart would burst with the love she felt at that moment.

Would the sacrifice be too great?

Brent was suspicious. Lark was up to something. He just didn't know what.

It was nothing blatant, nothing that he could come

right out and put a name to, but he felt it in his gut. It was in the false smiles. The way her eyes glinted at certain times. The way she shied away from his touch one minute, yet cozied up to him the next.

He finished the last of the gooey rolls he now often found waiting for him on the desk, then rested his chin atop his steepled fingers. He stared at her braids. During the time since he had come to San Carlos, her hair had grown to shoulder length. He liked the braids well enough, but even better, he liked the way her hair curled in little wisps about her face and ruffled in the wind without them.

She wore a lightweight white cotton peasant blouse and a long calico skirt today. The weather was getting warmer and he caught her in the leather breeches less often. Maybe she should try a pair of those cotton pants the warriors . . . He shook his head. What was he thinking? She was a lady. It was just that he liked the way trousers clung to all of her curves and . . .

"Why are you staring?"

He started at the anger in her voice. Why was she so defensive lately? He'd stared at her before, a lot, and she'd never seemed *angry.* Embarrassed, maybe, but not angry. "I'm just lookin'."

"Why?"

" 'Cause I like what I see."

Meadowlark silently cursed. She liked what she saw, too. She could not help it. He was beautiful and she loved him. Sometimes she forgot his treachery and would allow herself to relax and enjoy his company, only to be reminded of her duty when someone mentioned Crook or Mexico. It was extremely irritating, these ambivalent feelings.

Seeing that she was uncomfortable, Brent decided not to press the issue. She would come around, one day. "Have you done any more about finding a good place to start irrigating and planting? Sorry, I've been gone so much. I know I promised to help."

She shrugged. "I found a place."

Brent frowned. "Well . . ."

"I have talked to a few men from my band."

Brent hid his hands in his lap so she wouldn't see the fists she caused him to make. Sometimes she really frustrated him over her damned inability to tell a person what he wanted to know without having to drag it out with a mule team. "What did they think?"

"They will begin the ditch tomorrow."

"That's good."

"Maybe."

He closed his eyes and counted to five. "What does that mean?"

Her eyes shot bullets. Then she scowled when she found he was not even looking at her. "It will probably only be half finished when you take the scouts to Mexico."

Brent heard the inflection in her voice. She was definitely still angry over his going with Crook. So, why hadn't she said anything more about it? "Not all of the warriors want to go. There should be enough staying behind to get a few crops planted."

He wrapped the blanket around his hips, got up and walked to the window. The wind was blowing. It was hot. Gnats covered the glass. "Have you gotten seeds yet?"

She waited until he turned toward her before she nodded.

Brent also nodded. He curled his fingers in the folds of wool and rocked back on his heels. "Have you seen Scorpion lately?" He still had the crucifix. Was still torn over whether to mention it to her.

Meadowlark's head snapped up. She had not thought of Scorpion in weeks. Had not *wanted* to. The warrior was no longer her trusted ally and there was an emptiness inside her heart. "No." She cocked her head to one side and eyed Brent warily. "Why?"

He retraced his steps and sat down again. "Don't know. Thought I might've seen him the other day, but could've been mistaken. Figured you'd know."

"He went to Mexico."

She said the words with such finality that Brent knew she believed them. But he really thought he'd seen the warrior. Just yesterday.

Brent cocked an eyebrow in her direction. "By the way, I received a wire from General Crook."

Meadowlark perked up. She wiped her palms on her skirt. This was it—the reason she had wanted to remain close to the captain—to find out about his messages from Crook. Still, she waited. But that was all he said. It was not like Brent. She cleared her throat. "What . . . Did he arrive . . . wherever he was going . . . safely?"

Brent nodded.

Her eyes narrowed. "Good."

Silence ticked between them like a timer on a stick of dynamite.

"He mentioned Chato."

Meadowlark gritted her teeth. What was the matter with the man? Was his memory failing? Could he not finish a story without all of these maddening delays? "Did they catch him?"

Brent held up his fingers and cleaned a bit of cinnamon and sugar from beneath a rough-edged nail. "No."

She shifted her bottom on the unusually hard chair. Strange, she had never noticed it being so uncomfortable before. "What did happen?" she asked, noting at the same time that her mouth suddenly felt full of sand.

"Oh, most of it's hearsay. The general can hardly believe it's true." He buffed his nails against the blanket, but winced when a jagged end pulled a thread.

Meadowlark leapt to her feet and swung around the end of the desk to confront Brent. She snapped, "Tell me, white man! What happened?"

Brent stifled a grin as he darted a glance at her outraged features. By damn, now she knew how he felt when he tried to get information out of her. At least *he* had been able to keep his frustration under control.

He cheerily recounted the general's message. "Crook said Chato made it back across the border without any of the cavalry companies ever catching sight of him. He lost two of his band; one killed, the other taken captive."

Meadowlark's eyes widened. "Truly?"

"That's what they say. All total, Chato's renegades passed through forty-five hundred Mexican troops and five hundred Americans and still made it back to their stronghold."

She walked to the window and stared out. A small smile quirked her lips as a deep pride filled her chest. It was probably one of the Apache's last great triumphs. "The general will *have* to go after them now."

Brent lay back and fluffed the blanket. "Yes."

That night, Meadowlark lay alone in her bed. Brent had stayed in the office a long time, slanting her smoky-blue, confident glances. But when she did not acknowledge his subtle hints, or even act cordial enough to exchange a few words of conversation, he became more unsure and finally slammed out the door as the evening turned moonless black.

Black. The color of the sky described her feelings perfectly. No light. No sunshine. No happiness. A tear slipped down her cheek. It was not that she did not want Brent McQuade; her body craved him, yearned for his touch. But her heart was too fragile. And knowing what must come, she could not continue to make love to him.

The tears rolled faster as she painfully acknowledged that Brent had taught her much. The value of love. The pain of betrayal. The importance of her white heritage. And thanks to the captain, she had also learned that she could use that white heritage to the good of the Apaches.

Would the Apaches see her as a traitor? Or would

they accept her for what she was—a part of both worlds. And, most frightening, what if she was never accepted by either?

Five days later an unhappy, frustrated Brent McQuade stood on the step leading up to the trading post. Several Apache women had entered earlier carrying woven baskets and pieces of leather stitched with fascinating beadwork designs. Now he moved out of their way as they emerged wearing cheap straw hats with bright ribbons dangling from the limp brims.

His shoulders raised and lowered in futility. How could the trader live with his conscience while cheating the Apaches at every turn? Brent sighed. At least the women had not come out carrying jugs of whiskey. From what Brent had seen, though, the women, who were used to doing the menial tasks of life, had a better ability to adapt to the reservation than the warriors. The men had the hardest time adjusting.

He thought of Lark's irrigation project. He hadn't had the time to ride out and see how it was progressing. His lips compressed into a hard line. No, that wasn't the truth. He hadn't gone because he didn't want to see her look of disgust when he rode up. She would think he was interfering in her business.

The woman had been damned contrary for the past few days. They'd made the best love two people could ever share, and then she treated him like a leper. One minute she'd cast him a shy, provocative smile, then turn right around and spurn him when he responded. Well, when he saw her again, he was going to tell her in no uncertain terms just how tired he was of being dragged around by the nose like some moon-eyed, sexless bull.

He was still feeling rejected and sorry for himself when he glanced up and saw a group of warriors coming in his direction. Brent recognized them as some of the Apaches from the Warm Springs band who'd decided to join his company of scouts. In a way, he was surprised they'd come, for the Warm Springs and Chiricahua, who were most numerously represented among the renegades, got along better than most of the other bands. Also, there were quite a few of the Warm Springs themselves in Mexico. Meadowlark's family, for instance.

Yet for those same reasons, he was glad to have them along. Like his brother, many of them had been to the Sierra Madres and would be assets in guiding Crook through the rugged mountain chain to Geronimo.

There was no doubt that it would be a dangerous and arduous campaign. But the excitement of treking into unfamiliar territory sent the blood surging through his veins.

Then he noticed the new sparkle in the warriors' eyes. Their straight backs and determined steps. He chuckled. Maybe the whites and Apaches weren't so different after all.

The days at San Carlos sped by as Brent acquainted his three white scouts with the warriors still filtering in to the agency. The Apaches made their own camp on the opposite side of the compound from the military tents and an anticipation-filled truce ensued.

Brent had wired his brother of the events taking place and wondered if Brandon would wait until he sent for him, or come down early and take the even greater risk of detection. He wouldn't put anything past the White Fox.

Brandon trusted the Apaches. So did Brent to an extent, but he couldn't put the image of Scorpion's crucifix and his own suspicions to rest. Anyway, if there was one traitorous Apache, mightn't there be more?

"Cap'n, they need you at the stables. Fast."

Brent waved to the corporal, acknowledging that he'd heard, then turned the sky even bluer with a string of choice curses. Damn it all! Besides being in charge of almost two hundred scouts and dealing with the hatred and distrust between them and the soldiers, and being worried about his brother's secret identity, he was also saddled with a herd of long-eared jackasses.

Mules! Sure, he could understand the general's reasoning. Fight the Apache like an Apache. The army couldn't follow trails over the tops of mountains with wagons. So mules had turned Crook's campaigns around. And the man could load a pack in a way that allowed an animal to carry twice the normal supplies and not rub a single sore on its back.

"First I have to wrangle rations," he grumbled to the dust as he hurried to the stable. "Now it's hardheaded mules. What next?"

Just as he was entering the barn, from the corner of his eye, he caught a glimpse of a big red horse. He stopped short and spun on his heel. Sure enough, Lark and the thoroughbred were only a few yards away.

A fleeting expression of what Brent described as guilt, marred Lark's gorgeous countenance for just a moment before her usual impassive mask was drawn into place. Another round of curses burned his throat. She'd probably been trying to sneak past him without being seen. "Afternoon, Miss Russell."

Meadowlark grimaced, but stopped the mare. She had hoped to escape without Brent's noticing her. Finally, she inclined her head, waiting until he walked up and patted Paloma's glossy neck.

"Nice afternoon for a ride."

She dipped her chin, at the same time darting glances all around. She had not noticed before, but it was an unusually nice day. Warm. Just enough breeze to keep the insects at bay.

"Where're you off to?" Brent's foul mood was not

improving. He hated it when she was so cold and stand-offish.

"We will see if the ditch holds water this afternoon." As hard as she tried to hold it back, excitement crept into her voice. This was a big day for her and the warriors who had worked so hard digging the irrigation canals.

Brent's hand moved close to Meadowlark's thigh. "I would come—"

"Cap'n, come quick. Roscoe's done been whomped in the . . ." A young private's eyes widened when he saw his captain talking to the pretty Miss Russell. "Oh, he's been kicked, uh, you know, where it . . . hurts. 'Scuse me, ma'am."

Brent frowned up at Lark as he stepped away from her horse. "Maybe another time."

"Hmmm." She could not get away fast enough. She kicked the mare into a gallop, not caring that she left Brent choking in a cloud of dust and sand.

The past days had been miserable, being close to him, yet so far away. Once in a while their bodies would brush against one another and a wild fire consumed her insides. They touched, but not as much as she would like. A fingertip here, a back of the hand there, was not enough, yet too much.

Soon. Very soon, Captain McQuade would be her enemy. She could not allow her body to rule her mind.

She urged the mare faster, as she had every day when she had fled the agency to come to the field. Although she had done her best to stay in the office and help with the work, it had been impossible. She could not stay and watch her own people training to hunt down their Apache friends and relatives.

Topping the ridge to gaze down on the field, her thoughts turned away from the sadness of what was to come, to the joy of the present. It had taken herself and ten warriors to clear that land. They had all worked hard, digging, hoeing, carrying rocks, labor that would have been beneath a warrior's dignity two months ago. But they seemed to have tackled the irrigation with a new sense of purpose, especially when she reminded them of their great leader Victorio and the wonderful crops they had grown under his guidance back in their homeland.

They had forgotten how hard Victorio had worked to keep peace between his people and the whites, and how he had tilled the soil with the rest of the people, using the techniques General Crook had introduced ten years ago.

Of course, San Carlos was not their homeland, would never be as rich and sustaining. But, maybe, if the ditch held water . . .

She found most of the men working near the creek. They angled a thick sheet of metal she had brought from the agency into the bank and used sledgehammers, also borrowed from San Carlos, to pound it in the damp ground until the top was level. Later, she dreamed, they would erect a better "gate" so the metal would be easier to lift and control, but for the moment, this would have to do.

Then the Indians moved the rocks and dirt from behind the metal, leaving a clear opening into the ditch. They were ready. All they had to do was raise the iron sheet and let the water flow through.

Blood hummed through Meadowlark's veins. She felt flushed. Her knees quaked when she slid from the mare and tied it to the limb of a big ironwood tree.

The warriors' faces were expressionless, but she saw the sparks lighting their black eyes. She was so proud of them. They had been resentful at first, but seemed to respect her now since most of the methods she had taught them had proven successful, and since she had not been afraid to get down beside them and work as hard as they.

A sense of satisfaction warmed her every night, if nothing else did. She blinked. Now what had caused that wayward thought?

At last, a warrior known as Squint Eye pointed toward the makeshift gate. "We open now?"

She glanced around the group of assembled men and then at the ditch. It was two feet deep. They had packed and dampened the bottom and sides. All that was left to do was to see if it held water. An air of expectancy hovered over them. A smile of reassurance curved her lips, even as she crossed her fingers behind her back, a trick she had seen her father use many times before. "Now."

Two of the men went to either side of the gate and lifted the metal until water from the creek began to run into the ditch. Once a slow, steady flow was started, two more men stacked flat rocks beneath the bottom edge to hold the sheet in place.

They all walked along the ditch, following the water. They had to stop and shore up a place where a rivulet broke through one side, but the rest seemed to hold perfectly. This time her smile was big and genuine. The warriors smiled back.

Across the canal, Meadowlark watched three more men finishing the long, neat rows where they would plant the corn. Another section was ready for melons, and yet another for squash. The ground was rocky, but the soil seemed fertile enough. And with the water . . .

Using mud to block the flow of water, they diverted it down one row and then another. The constriction in Meadowlark's throat loosened as the liquid eased down the rows and the thirsty soil soaked it up. It seemed to take forever before the water nosed down the first row and finally reached the end. Then it ran into another ditch paralleling the upper one. From that point, the water soaked into the ground, replenishing the water table. If enough standing water collected, it could be let out another "gate" into the stream.

Watching the system work, a warm glow of elation settled over her. If this field produced and the warriors were able to grow their own crops, they would be more amenable to finding other plots to clear and irrigate. The men needed to find out for themselves that some parts of this arid, worthless-looking land could be *made* to produce.

While the warriors slapped themselves on the back and waded in the lower ditch, Meadowlark went back to the mare. She felt like celebrating, too, but none of the men had seemed particularly anxious to have her join in the fun. They might respect her, but she was not one of them.

The next week passed quickly for Meadowlark. She continued to ride out each day to check the field. Brent still supervised the scouts and helped the soldiers work the ornery mules. One day he had followed her and seen for himself what they had accomplished with the irrigation, and she still basked under his lavish praise. Few people had ever taken the time to compliment her on anything she had done. Sadly, it endeared him to her all the more.

Today she had decided to go down to the stables and see what *he* was doing. They had established a kind of common ground and at least acted civil toward each other.

A small smile tugged at her lips. From the hungry look she caught in his eyes now and then, she knew his "civil" behavior could quickly change if she would give him the opportunity, as her body wished she would. Even now her nipples contracted when they brushed the soft cotton material of her blouse. Her skin tingled. There was a nagging ache in the apex of her thighs. A low, burning heat seared her lower belly.

And the sensations intensified the moment she saw Brent leading a huge jack into a nearby corral. His ruddy features had darkened with prolonged exposure to the sun. His sweat-stained shirt clung to his damp body like a second skin. The sleeves rolled up to his elbows exposed the long, elegant muscles of his forearms.

But it was the lower half of his body that kept attracting her gaze. The tight-fitting trousers left little to the imagination regarding his well-developed thighs and small, trim buttocks. Every time he bent over, she watched his pants stretch and pull across hard-muscled planes and valleys. And they were hard—steel encased by soft, pliable flesh. Flesh she had run her hands over . . .

Suddenly, Brent straightened. His head cocked to one side. Then he turned and looked directly into her eyes. Her chest caved inward. Her breath clogged her throat. She felt seared by the heat from his gaze as he seemed to reach out and . . .

"Cap'n. Cap'n McQuade."

She thought he was going to ignore the corporal's call and climb over the corral posts to come to her. But he stared at her another second, then shook himself like a great coyote emerging from a roaring river, and answered in a resigned voice, "Yes, Corporal. What is it?"

Corporal Bent hurried up to Captain McQuade and handed him a telegram. "This just come for ya, Cap'n. I think it's important."

Brent read and reread the missive. Finally he glanced up. His eyes met hers briefly and then flickered away. A sinking sensation emptied the pit of Meadowlark's stomach. "Pass the word to the men, Corporal." His words slammed against her and the pole she sat on swayed slightly. "We leave for Willcox in two days."

Chapter Twenty-three

By the time Captain McQuade was ready to leave San Carlos two days later, his good humor had been sorely tried and tested. Problems with supplies and the blacksmith's shortage of horseshoe nails had threatened to delay their departure by weeks rather than days. But Brent had managed to send a few telegrams and they were back on schedule.

A loud bray drew his gaze to a string of mules, one of which was voicing its objection to being saddled with a large pack. But the mules were not his concern today. They had been divided into five pack trains, each consisting of forty animals, a chief packer and ten assistants. Those men were to handle any difficulties with the animals that arose from now on.

It was the one hundred Apache scouts who had just left the agency that presented a problem.

Brent massaged his temples, wincing as he hit a tender spot. Yesterday an Apache woman, who'd gone to Tucson to trade her baskets, had overheard a group of men calling themselves the "Tombstone Rangers" threatening to ride out to San Carlos and "wipe out" every Apache residing on the reservation. Whether the threat was real or not, half of the scouts had elected to remain behind to protect their families and homes.

Brent couldn't say he blamed them. He was torn between leaving and staying himself. There was a certain little half-Apache who would no doubt get herself in a world of trouble if someone dared to attack "her people." At least the soldiers had been alerted and would watch for the arrival of a large group of vigilantes.

But what would the general say when Brent reached Willcox with only a hundred scouts? Crook had said he needed more—many more. Had counted on Brent and Brent had failed. Besides, this could cause a serious delay once they reached southeastern Arizona.

Standing in the agency office, Brent folded the last order he would receive and put it in his breast pocket. He glanced through the window at a column of dust that appeared to be getting closer. His hand dropped to his revolver.

Had the squaw been correct? Were the vigilantes even now approaching the reservation? In a way, he almost hoped so. They would be in for the surprise of their lives with all of the soldiers and warriors ready and waiting.

Soon he noticed the white canvas covers belonging to several wagons. He raised his hand to rub the back of his neck. Damn, but he'd be glad to get this circus on the road before he had to face any more problems. One more little thing, that's all it would take to have him perched on the highest branch of one of those cottonwoods, wide-eyed and flapping his arms like a loony bird.

As his eyes scanned the compound, he saw Lark riding out with several members of the Warm Springs band. His chest ached. He should've known she wouldn't see fit to tell him good-bye. But it hurt that she hadn't. It really hurt.

She still believed his sole purpose for going to Mexico was to annihilate the Apaches, in much the same fashion as the "Tombstone Rangers," no doubt. And he guessed he'd have to fight the renegades, if it came to that. But he hoped bloodshed could be avoided.

And Crook was of the same mind. The outcome would be up to the Apaches themselves.

Why couldn't she understand? She refused to even listen to his explanation. After everything he'd done for the Indians at San Carlos, what would he have to gain by needlessly killing others?

As she disappeared from sight, he rubbed at his eyes. At least he was leaving knowing she was here on the reservation in *relative* safety. He could concentrate on what was ahead and not worry about her—much.

He turned on his heel and strode determinedly from the room. To the soldiers and packers and scouts within hearing distance, he shouted, "One hour. We pull out in one hour."

Meadowlark and her friends were two miles from the San Carlos headquarters when she reined her mare to a halt. She explained to the others that she would not be going all the way to the Warm Springs camp and they continued on without her.

She looked back, certain that no one had followed. The captain and the soldiers had seen her leave and would be too busy to notice her return. She would stay on the outskirts of the compound, blending into the surroundings like a jackrabbit hiding in the brush.

She leaned forward to adjust the mare's headstall, then she then settled back and nudged the horse's sides to turn it around. Two riders materialized atop the nearest ridge. Meadowlark froze. The riders stopped. They all stared warily across the distance before the pair finally started down the slope toward her.

Meadowlark exhaled sharply. The man wore a turkey feather cap and a war club dangled from his wrist. He was Apache. Probably White Mountain.

Her hands relaxed their hold on the mare's reins and the dependable animal turned back toward the agency. The two riders were in more of a hurry and soon caught up to Meadowlark. She glanced curiously at the pair as they passed.

The woman, a beautiful, sienna-haired white woman, smiled and waved. The warrior, very tall and straight-backed deigned her a glance and a nod.

But she hardly noticed. She was trying to keep from gaping at shoulder-length hair the color of winter grass. The warrior was white. And he was a warrior, in every nuance of his regal bearing.

As they passed and urged their mounts into a slow lope, her eyes widened in disbelief. The White Fox. She would have recognized him anywhere. Several years ago, her mother had taken her to visit an uncle who had married a White Mountain woman. The White Fox had been the band's leader. She had thought then that he had to be one of the most handsome men she had ever seen.

And her opinion had not changed. Only Captain McQuade was better looking. And she liked Brent's darker hair color. In fact . . . She frowned. In fact, the similarities between the two men were striking. They could almost be . . . twins.

Meadowlark laughed. The captain had not even left yet, and already she was seeing his face everywhere.

Nudging her horse to a faster pace, she followed the pair. What a beautiful couple they made. The woman's dark red hair and pale skin, and White Fox's light hair and bronzed skin. They complimented each other perfectly.

In her mind's eye, she suddenly visualized images of herself and Captain McQuade as a couple. They would be as handsome together as White Fox and his lady.

What was White Fox doing at San Carlos? A curse died on her lips as she followed the couple up the last knoll overlooking the agency. Meadowlark reined her mare to the right and rode through the scouts' deserted camp. All the while she kept her eyes on the White Fox.

Among the many mules, horses, wagons and people, she soon lost sight of the white warrior and his woman. She stopped to tie her horse in a clump of mesquite and sage before continuing on foot. Ignoring the commotion, she came up behind one of the larger buildings and peeked around a corner of the officers' barracks. The first person she saw was Brent McQuade. Her heart jumped. If only Brent did not have to go with Crook . . .

Suddenly, the White Fox and the red-haired woman rode into Meadowlark's line of vision. She was stunned when the warrior slid off his stallion, smiled broadly, and clasped Brent's hands. The captain was an inch or two shorter than the Apache chief, and more heavily muscled, but other than those obvious differences, the two men were eerily similar in other respects.

She felt her eyebrows pinch together as she watched them still shaking hands. Each man lifted his free arm to grasp the other's shoulder. They laughed at their identical gestures. And though she could not hear them, she noted their similar profiles.

Her frown deepened at the affection one man might hold for another between the Apache warrior who was white and the white who warred with Apaches.

The red-haired woman waited patiently until the men remembered her, and then it was Brent who rushed around to help her down. Meadowlark's toes curled inside her moccasins. He was certainly a gallant gentleman, but did he not see she already had a man? And his hands rested on the white witch's waist far longer than was necessary. Did she not have two feet of her own?

The woman had the nerve to throw her arms around the captain. Meadowlark's scalp pricked. Then the ugly hag actually kissed him on the cheek.

Meadowlark glared at the White Fox. How could he allow his woman to manhandle Brent McQuade in such a manner?

Finally the pawing came to an end. Meadowlark sighed and leaned back against the rough adobe. These new arrivals seemed to know Brent awfully well. Surely the cunning White Fox knew of Brent's misguided mission. Surely the warrior would not condone such action against his people.

After several minutes, she peeked around the building again to find the three of them in serious conversation. She was really astonished when White Fox took the woman lovingly in his arms, kissed her soundly, then mounted the stallion and rode off with the scouts. Questions and doubts raced through her mind.

She would follow them to Willcox, then warn Geronimo. Maybe during the trip she would have a chance to find out what the great leader was doing with Crook's assassin army.

Dust rose thick in the air as the large assembly under Captain McQuade's command rode out of San Carlos. Meadowlark remained hidden, coughing and choking as they passed only a few feet from her location. She did not worry about being discovered. The clanking of bits and sabers and plodding hooves would have drowned out a herd of stampeding cattle.

She wiped her suspiciously moist eyes and her fingers came away gritty as she watched Brent's back until he was only a speck on the horizon. Her only regret was that she had not seen fit to say good-bye like the White Fox and his woman. An empty feeling in the pit of her stomach almost turned her nauseous. What if she had made a mistake? What if she never had the chance to kiss him again? What if he were killed . . .

Meadowlark gnawed at her lower lip and stepped out from behind the building as soon as the last pack train left the compound. Brushing dirt from her blouse, she ran directly into someone stepping off the barrack's porch.

"Oh, I beg your pardon. I didn't see . . . Wait. We passed you earlier on the road, didn't we? You were riding the most beautiful horse. My husband has always had an eye . . ."

Meadowlark stared dumbfounded as the woman continued to talk. The red-haired white had so many words to say so little.

". . . McQuade. Did you say good-bye to someone, too?"

Meadowlark tilted her head when she heard "McQuade." What was this woman to Brent? She had hugged him and kissed him, but had ended up in the arms of the White Fox. Meadowlark was becoming more confused the more she tried to figure it out.

Then she noticed the woman was staring. What was the question? Oh, yes, had she come expressly to say good-bye? Well, she *had* felt the need to be here to watch Brent leave. Her answer was a truthful, "Yes."

The other woman gave her a little pout. Meadowlark wondered if white women were actually taught to display their feelings with such expressions.

"So did I."

Meadowlark's stomach turned over. She swallowed convulsively. Brent had had a lot of women. Was this one of them? Did the White Fox suspect?

"My husband is . . ."

Husband! Meadowlark held a shaky hand to her forehead. She had learned of Brent's treachery a long time ago. Poor White Fox. He could not have known.

"Is something wrong, dear? You look so pale all of a sudden. Perhaps you should sit down."

Meadowlark shook her head. "I am fine," she lied.

"I hope so. By the way, I'm Hillary McQuade."

McQuade. Now she knew for sure. The name ricocheted through Meadowlark's brain. "McQuade?" She did not realize she had spoken aloud until she saw the wariness creep into the woman's eyes. Hillary? She knew that name. Brent had called for "Hillary" when he was injured and feverish. Meadowlark's own eyes narrowed.

Hillary McQuade backed up a step. "Who are you?" There was something strange about the little Apache. Perhaps she shouldn't have mentioned her husband. She was still fearful of what might happen if the wrong people learned of his double identity.

"I am called Meadowlark. Meadowlark Russell." Her spine stiffened under the other woman's scrutiny. Then bluntly, she asked, "You are married to Brent McQuade?"

Hillary's shoulders sagged with relief. She easily read the hurt and jealousy lurking in the smaller woman's gorgeous amber eyes. She could also understand Brent's preoccupation during his last visit if he had left such a beautiful woman waiting.

Hillary knew better than to make light of the situation. Meadowlark Russell seemed a very serious soul indeed. "No, I'm not married to Brent."

Meadowlark was able to take a breath, finally, yet was doubly confused. "But, you are a McQuade, are you not?"

"Yes, dear, I'm a McQuade, married to *one* of the McQuades." Hillary gave the girl time to think that over before adding, "And one's all any woman can handle."

Funny, Meadowlark mused, she had often had the same thought. Questions and answers ran rampant in her head. Did she understand correctly? There were two McQuades? One was Brent. The other had to be . . . the White Fox. Certainly. He was white . . . Suddenly she looked into Hillary's smiling eyes.

"Yes, Miss Russell, my husband is Brandon McQuade."

"The White Fox," Meadowlark whispered.

Hillary nodded.

A huge grin creased Meadowlark's taut features. But then she remembered the pain in Brent's voice when he had called for her. "Once, Brent was dreaming. He called your name."

Blushing, Hillary took Meadowlark's arm and walked her to where she and Brand had left the horse standing in the middle of the compound. As quietly and quickly as possible, she explained her engagement to Brent, her subsequent meeting of the White Fox and how the brothers met again after twenty some years apart. Rather than hide anything, she mentioned how she fell in love with Brand and how Brent met another woman.

Meadowlark snapped, "Lizabeth."

Hillary stopped and stared at Meadowlark's frowning countenance. "How did you know?"

"He called *her* name, too."

"Well, you have nothing to fear from Elizabeth, dear."

Meadowlark drew back. "I am not afraid of a white woman."

Hillary stifled a giggle. "No, I'm sure you're not. But Elizabeth hurt Brent badly. He's well rid of her."

Meadowlark considered the lost, little boy she had first sensed in Brent months ago. Just like an Apache, he had attempted to suppress his feelings. Like a man, he knew they were attracted to each other, and fought it all the way.

It was his pain and her instinct to ease his suffering that had first drawn her to him. And now she knew why.

"You're going with them to Mexico, aren't you?" Hillary looked at Meadowlark, then in the direction the command had ridden.

Meadowlark's head snapped around.

As if she could read the smaller woman's mind, Hillary said, "I saw it in your eyes, the way you kept looking after them, too. I would go, if I could."

Meadowlark believed every word. There was a quiet strength and purpose to this white woman, and she found herself liking Hillary McQuade. A lot. "Why do you stay?"

Hillary smiled a smile that brought to mind the angels Meadowlark had read about. "I'm going to have a baby, or I would have beaten you to the horse."

Meadowlark grinned. Another little McQuade. If it were anything like its father and uncle, the reservation would not be big enough to hold it.

Hillary took Meadowlark's hand. "You go on. We'll have all the time in the world to gossip when you get back."

Meadowlark nodded. Although the other woman was trying to be brave, she sensed Hillary's well-disguised fear. Giving Hillary's fingers a squeeze, Meadowlark promised, "I will look after them."

After leaving her new friend, Meadowlark went to the stables, then the trading post and finally found Corporal Bent leaving Major Taylor's headquarters. She hurried and caught up with him just in front of the vacant building. As always, she cast a few glances in that direction and wiped the sweat from her palms. "Corporal Bent, may I speak with you?"

The corporal turned, saw Meadowlark and came to an abrupt halt. A big grin lit his boyish face. "Any time a'tall."

She shifted from foot to foot. Imitating white women, she tried batting her lashes, but could not see the corporal. Finally, she sighed and asked straight out, "Corporal, I need a favor."

Bent scratched his forehead. "Yeah-h."

"I have been left in charge of the rations now that Captain McQuade is gone."

"Yeah-h-h."

She swallowed and glanced toward the empty, hovering building. "Well, I . . . just found out I have to go . . . to the White Mountain reservation because . . . a family member . . . They need me."

"Yeah-h-h."

Trying to boost her courage, she gave him what she hoped was a pitiful smile. "You have been so good to help us every week, and know as much as I do about the rations."

"Yeah-h-h-h. Maybe."

She tried the lashes again.

"You have somethin' in yore eye, ma'am?"

Meadowlark silently swore. How did white women manage to seem innocent and helpless? "No, Corporal. Will you take over while I am gone?"

"Well-l-l, I don't know."

"Please."

He looked around the compound, then scuffed his toe in the sand. "Well, I reckon I could do it."

She smiled with joy. "Thank you." Then before she realized it, she did something very un-Apache. She gave the corporal a tiny kiss on the cheek and hurried on her way.

She had one last important stop to make.

Meadowlark stopped just inside the door of the office. Brent had been in earlier, she could smell his special scent. Closing her eyes, she leaned back against the wall, picturing the way he slouched in his chair, the wicked way he smiled and that devastating dimple that dented his cheek.

Then she exhaled, took another breath to steady herself and walked over to the corner. Kneeling, she reached down and pried a loose adobe brick from the wall behind the stove. A piece of soft leather unfolded to reveal the pouch her mother had made encasing her father's watch. The pouch was beginning to crack in places where stitching and time had dried the leather. The watch lay cold in her palm.

Cold. The way she felt inside.

Meadowlark tenderly refolded the items and placed them back in the wall. Then she stood and went over to retrieve a small bundle from her pallet. With one last look around the room that had been both home and office for several months, she swiped at a stray tear. She softly closed the door behind her as she left.

For five days Meadowlark followed the captain and the scouts, staying far enough behind the pack trains to keep from being seen, but close enough for safety in case wandering troops of soldiers should happen near. She had no illusions that she had made the journey undetected. The scouts would have known she was there from the first day. But that was all right. It was Brent and the soldiers she was evading.

Sneaking. That was what she was doing. It hurt her pride to think she had been reduced to such a degrading situation. She should be riding with her people, her friends, unafraid of what she planned to do. But once they reached Willcox and joined the rest of the soldiers, Brent and the others would be too busy to pay much attention to the Apaches. Then she could blend in and set her plan into motion.

So, it was a welcome sight to see the cavalcade of soldiers, scouts and mules cross the railroad tracks and ride into the little town of Willcox. Meadowlark held back and kept the mare to the taller scrub brush. Tonight she would get ready. Tomorrow she would join the scouts' camp. When the time came, she would be prepared for the trip to Mexico.

She gathered a few twigs and made a small fire behind a yucca. Later, lying on a warm blanket with her feet toward the remnants of heat, she chuckled to herself at how the whites usually built a fire so large that it drove the people too far back for them to enjoy any warmth later, after the blaze died and only coals remained.

Thinking of whites, as usual, brought Brent McQuade foremost in her mind. She also thought of the startling discovery she had made during the conversation with Hillary McQuade.

It was still hard to believe that Brent and White Fox were brothers, but it explained the captain's unusual willingness to help the Apaches. Maybe he did understand their ways, even more than she knew. More than likely, he had also understood every word when she craftily cursed him in Apache.

Her cheeks suddenly felt as warm as her toes. One day, like the fox, she would carefully plan her revenge. An Apache never forgot, and never forgave. But she was half white and might be able to forgive Brent a lot of things someday.

Smooth ivory skin and wavy red hair cunningly robbed her of sleep that night. No wonder Brent had loved Hillary. She was beautiful and smart and totally likable, much to Meadowlark's chagrin. And the look in her eyes when she spoke of bearing White Fox's child . . .

Meadowlark looked into the starlit sky and smiled. The woman had spoken with tenderness and love shining from her soul. The baby would receive much love.

Blinking, she buried her head beneath her blanket. Love. Baby. For five days, with nothing better to do than ride and think, she had wondered what would have happened if she *had* gotten with child—Brent's child. Would he have been so gentle and caring a husband as White Fox?

Of course he would. He had already proven his concern and compassion by insisting they would marry when he was healing from his wound. He had said he loved her. And she believed him.

A baby. Brent McQuade's baby. She fell asleep with her hands resting protectively over her belly.

Captain Brent McQuade stood with his shoulders hunched, looking over the encampment. For all intents and purposes, it was a small tent city, bustling with activity. A wagon rolled past loaded with supplies and ammunition that had come in on the last train. Soldiers and scouts lounged in any shade available, cleaning their carbines and rifles.

Brent stretched and turned to look back into the tent he'd just vacated. It was the big tent the general used to receive guests and meet with officers. Besides himself, there were seven other officers accompanying the command into Mexico. They all seemed to be good, knowledgeable men who harbored no hatred or animosity toward the Apaches. They were soldiers here to do a job.

Glancing southward, he wondered how Crook was faring in his meetings with the Mexican Governors. Lieutenant Johnson had told him that the general had grown impatient waiting for word and had left four days ago to meet with officials personally. Weeks ago Crook had intimated he might do just that, so Brent wasn't surprised. He just hoped that the campaign would stop here.

A strange sensation suddenly prickled the back of his neck. He had felt it other times during the long ride to Willcox, but couldn't describe what was bothering him. He'd double-checked his orders, gone over the lists of supplies, had even gone around the scouts' camps and visited the packers and mules. Everything seemed to be in order. No unexpected problems had cropped up. So what was this . . . premonition? . . . hovering over his head?

As it had so many times since leaving San Carlos, Lark's image floated before his eyes—lustrous black hair, golden eyes, satin skin stretched over high cheekbones. Beautiful Lark. He'd actually expected to miss her more than he had, but for some reason, he could almost feel her presence.

It was a comforting thought, and he prayed that once this expedition was over, he could straighten things out with her, prove that he truly loved her and that they were destined to be together.

He had dreams of his future, and Meadowlark Russell played an important part in those dreams.

Across a large, open expanse from where Captain McQuade stood daydreaming, a small fire burned in the Apache scouts' encampment. A tiny warrior dressed in a loose-fitting gray calico shirt and baggy cotton drawers sat cross-legged, staring at the distant, solitary figure. The warrior reached up to secure the red headband about thick black hair, hoping to flatten the embarrassing, unruly curls. But trembling hands were ineffective and the small warrior had to quit.

Two other Apache scouts from the Warm Springs band had approached the fire, and now sat staring impassively. If they questioned the young warrior's sudden appearance, they did not voice it.

When the tall figure of the cavalry captain disappeared back inside the huge canvas tent, the warrior's attention wandered to the two new companions. The Apaches soon had the young warrior grinning and joining their jovial conversation. However, every once in a while, amber eyes gazed off toward the soldier's encampment, wistful, longing.

The next morning, a building sense of excitement energized the San Carlos soldiers and scouts. A telegram had arrived from General Crook, stating only that he would be in Willcox later that evening. In just a few hours they would know whether to leave for Mexico, or begin the long trip north.

Meadowlark was once again sitting near the camp fire, brewing a pot of coffee. She had hardly left her small camping area, limiting her contact to the warriors she had grown up with. They would be the only warriors who might help her if her identity was discovered.

In the camaraderie of the camp fire, she had gained a sense of belonging she had sorely missed. Would she ever have it again? She feared that even her friends would report her to the soldiers if they found out she planned to warn Geronimo and give him a chance to escape.

The warriors shared a small bottle of whiskey and offered it to her. She declined and watched wistfully as they left her fire to join a larger group of scouts boasting of long-ago raids and deeds of great bravery and skill.

Pouring her coffee into a tin cup, she blew on the rim until it was cool enough to sip the dark liquid. "Black water" the Apaches called it. It was strong and she savored the aroma as she drank one of her favorite luxuries of the white world.

About to take another drink, she glanced up to see a tall, lean warrior with white-blond hair walking toward her fire. The coffee in her throat coagulated. White Fox. Brandon McQuade. He was coming directly to her camp.

Her heart skipped several beats. Her eyes shot nervously around to see if there was someone else sitting nearby that he might be looking for. She was alone. Surely he could not be coming to see *her!* And if he was? Why? Had he seen through her disguise? Would he take her to Capt. Brent McQuade?

Chapter Twenty-four

Meadowlark tried to control her panic as White Fox drew nearer and nearer. No! He did not know her, could not have recognized her. To make doubly sure, she turned away from the fire, busying herself plucking dried grass stems from the legs of her trousers.

A pair of high-topped moccasins encasing long, trim legs walked into her line of vision and stopped. Meadowlark set her cup down rather than risk spilling the contents down the front of her shirt. She took several deep breaths and raised her eyes, forcing herself to look at the White Fox as a man would look at a man.

But when she gazed into his face, she could hardly control the sudden leap and acceleration of her heart. It could have been Brent's face staring back at her, except the soul-probing eyes were gray-green instead of cool blue. She stiffened her spine and inquired politely, "You would have coffee?"

Brandon McQuade knit his brow in a puzzled frown. For a moment, he thought he had seen recognition in those strange-colored eyes. Recognition—and something else. But then he gave the frail warrior a quick appraising glance. No, it had to have been his imagination. He had been away from Hillary longer than at any time since they were married. He just missed her, was all.

He squatted next to the fire, accepting the proffered

cup of coffee. It was mid-April, and though the days were warming considerably, the fire felt good. Then he looked up. Why would not the boy meet his eyes? "You are from San Carlos?"

Meadowlark nodded.

Brandon grinned and placed the hot tin cup in the sand. "The soldiers received an interesting telegram today."

She cocked her head, lulled by the beautiful inflection of his speech. He sounded every bit as educated and cultured as any white man. She bit her lip. Of course he should. He *was* white. She did not think of him as such because he wore the Apache breechclout and moccasins so casually, as if he were not aware of the difference in their races.

Finally, she realized he was staring, as if awaiting her response, and swallowed the lump in her throat. "We are always glad for news of our . . ." She could not say *home*. ". . . families."

Brandon shook himself. There was something about this Warm Springs warrior. Something strange—different. He could not easily describe what it was, just an instinct. The boy would bear watching. "The 'Tombstone Rangers' did not make it to San Carlos."

She almost clapped her hands together, then subdued her reaction. No Apache warrior would display his feelings in such a womanly fashion. She cleared her throat in an effort to lower the tone of her voice. "What happened?"

He grinned and took up the cup again. "After ten days on the trail, the illustrious 'Rangers' ran out of whiskey. Their bravery vanished about the same time. Close to dying of thirst, they crawled back home."

Meadowlark smiled, then laughed at the mental image White Fox's words evoked. And his eyes crinkled when he grinned, just like Brent's. "That is good news. Our people have been worried."

"They had a right to be." He finished his coffee and

sat the cup back by the fire before he rose to leave. His eyes bored into the boy until he darted his gaze toward the soldier camp. "Be sure to tell the others from San Carlos."

She nodded and managed to breathe normally until he turned his back, then almost collapsed from the sudden release of tension in her nerves.

Brandon strode briskly away, then stopped. He glanced back briefly and gave an imperceptible shake of his head. What had his brother been thinking to bring along such a puny warrior? The fellow looked greener around the gills than a tree frog.

He would talk with Brent if they were allowed to go into Mexico. Only the strongest braves would survive the long, arduous trip. And *that* one stood no chance at all.

Brent McQuade and Lieutenant Johnson and Casey waited at the Willcox depot for General Crook's train. A line of smoke billowed for miles before the engine and the one passenger car appeared.

The officers each saluted and fell in beside the general as he stepped off the platform and headed toward the mule Brent had thought to have saddled and led over for the commanding officer.

"Gentlemen, we have been given permission to proceed." With that said, the general handed his one bag to Lieutenant Johnson. Pulling on his gloves, he deftly mounted the mule, leaving his greeting committee staring after him as he rode away from Willcox and the military post.

Lieutenant Casey looked at Brent. "Where's he going?"

Captain McQuade smiled. "He's going to hold a private 'council of war.' I've seen him do it before, and heard others say it's a habit he practices whenever he anticipates a battle. He rides a ways from camp, settles back on a rock, or against a tree, and goes over every detail of the plan in his mind."

Lieutenant Johnson handed Crook's bag over to Brent until he mounted his horse, then took it back. "Well, whatever he does, he does it right. Can't say how pleased I am to be able to go along and see the general in action."

Brent and Lieutenant Casey both nodded in silent agreement.

"C'mon, men, let's go tell the others. We can give them the particulars later, after we've spoken with the general again." The energy Crook's pronouncement had sparked in Brent needed release. And so did the tension that had taken days to build in the rest of the command. Everyone had been anxious with nothing to do but wait and wonder. Now they could all focus on preparing for the journey to Mexico.

General Crook summoned his officers an hour after sundown. He had just finished a glass of milk when Brent McQuade entered the tent. "Evening, Captain. Have a seat."

Brent offered a brief salute and smiled to himself when the general dabbed a white drop of liquid from his beard. He had come purposefully early, hoping for a chance to speak with Crook alone.

The general thumbed through a stack of papers and messages, then looked down his Roman nose and smiled. "What can I do for you, Captain?"

"Not a thing, General. I just wanted to let you know that the rest of our scouts from San Carlos are on the way. The vigilante trouble was resolved and they feel it's safe to leave their families." Brent sat on the edge of the chair, twisting the brim of his hat through his fingers.

Crook was pleased. "That's good news. I was wondering what we would do without them."

By that time, the remaining seven officers began to trickle in. Included in the invitation was Brandon McQuade, dressed in civilian shirt and pants, much to his older brother's relief.

When everyone had taken their seats, General Crook cleared his throat. "Gentlemen, I'm sure you've all heard by now that we're moving into Mexico." He stopped to allow a short round of applause to finish. "We've been ordered to wait until May first to reach the border. That will give the Mexican troops a chance to get into position and allow Chato and his band to settle down and relax their vigilance.

During a pause, while Crook sifted through a few notes, the officers commented among themselves. Brent looked back at his brother, who was crouched just inside the closed tent flap. He didn't like the troubled expression on Brand's face.

"Gentlemen, on April twenty-third, five days from now, we will start for the border. Each of you will be responsible for checking equipment and supplies. Everything we take must be in good condition or it will be discarded. Check cinches and headstalls. Repairs must be made before we leave. Any questions?"

Brandon McQuade rose to his feet. "What was the Mexican reaction when you visited them? Were they willing for you to cross the border? Or did you have to persuade them?"

Crook's beard twitched. His blue-gray eyes darkened. "They are most pleased to have our help in destroying the Apaches."

Brent ran after his brother. The general's meeting had broken up only moments after Brand's stormy departure. Brent knew that the general must be wondering about Brand's dramatic exit, and then his own hasty leave-taking. But at that moment Brent wasn't concerned with General Crook.

"Brand! Wait up." Brent had to run to catch up and fall into step with Brandon.

Neither man noticed where they were walking, they just walked. Large glowing fires and tents that billowed at the foundations in the cool breeze were quickly left behind. The small fires and crudely constructed huts of the scouts grew in dimension as the brothers neared.

For some reason, that Brand wondered over later, he stopped at the same camp of the small Warm Springs warrior. He squatted and held his hands up to the fire. Glancing up, he noticed that the boy had squirmed into the flickering shadows.

"Any of that coffee left, son?" He could barely see the slight nod, and then the boy scooted the pot up next to the flames and immediately ducked back out of the light. Brand hoped the boy had not injured his neck. He held it at such a strange angle, and it was difficult to see his face. But at least he was hospitable. "Thanks."

Brent flopped down next to Brand and cast the small scout the briefest of nods before exclaiming, "What did you expect?"

Brand shrugged. Brent grimaced as he thought of shoulders about the same size as those of the timid scout's, lifting and lowering in that same noncommittal gesture.

"Damn it, Crook said that was what the *Mexicans* wanted, not what *he* planned to do."

A soft rustling of sand to his right appraised Brent of the other warrior's nervous shifting. Who was the boy, anyway? He didn't remember training anyone that small from San Carlos.

"The reason I am accompanying this campaign is to try to get Geronimo to surrender—not to *destroy* him. *If* they give me the chance."

Brent turned his full attention back to Brand. "I

know that. And the general has the same objective in mind. He told me that himself."

"And you believe him? It did not seem that was how he felt this evening."

Both men simultaneously reached for the cups being held toward them at arm's length. "Thanks." Brent's fingers brushed the scout's hand. His eyes widened. But when he glanced across the fire, the boy had scooted into the shadows again.

Brent studied the back of his hand. There was that . . . feeling again. For someone who didn't believe in ghosts, he was damned well beginning to believe he was haunted. He shook his head and looked back to his brother. Brand was the one he needed to concentrate on, not some . . . "What're you goin' to do?"

Brand took a drink of the strong liquid. "I will go with you. Somehow, I might be able to prevent a disaster."

Both men looked toward the scout when it appeared as if the poor scrawny thing might choke to death. But when one of them would have risen to help, the coughing eased to a gurgled strangle.

Finally, Brand set his cup by the fire, as he had done earlier in the day. He gazed at the slight figure and said sincerely, "Thank you for sharing your fire."

Brent followed suit, not wanting to let Brandon out of his sight for a while. However, he paused long enough to peer into the shadows, highlighted now and then when a spark popped from the fire. "Thanks again. That's good coffee. Just like I drink at home."

He waited, but when all he received was a brief nod, he quirked his lips and trailed after Brand. Damn those closemouthed Apaches. They were all alike. He got more interesting conversation from a wood-burning stove.

Meadowlark gasped for air as soon as the two men

moved far enough away from her fire. She sprawled back onto the sand, arms and legs flung wide as her lungs expanded and the trembling in her limbs ran its course.

At first, she had not believed her eyes when a white man, dressed in a cotton shirt and denims, walked toward her camp with a wildly gesturing soldier close on his heels. It had been too dark to see anything of their faces and she had logically assumed they were with the white packers. All of a sudden, the first man had the nerve to stop and hunker down right in front of her.

Then she saw the play of firelight on the pale blond hair. She immediately guessed who the soldier might be and her breath froze in her throat. Brent McQuade dropped down beside his brother. What breath she was able to suck into her lungs came in rapid, difficult to control gasps. Her heart literally jumped up and down from the contortions her chest was going through.

Several minutes later, she looked into the heavens and thanked the spirits that the men seemed so preoccupied as to hardly notice they had company at the little camp. She lifted her right hand, looking at the stars through her spread fingers. The same fingers that had touched his when she handed him the coffee. The skin still felt seared, but it was not a hurtful sensation. She pressed them to her mouth. It was just a *feeling* that coursed through her as surely as blood thrummed through her veins.

Suddenly she sat up. The McQuade brothers had been talking about Crook and what would happen in Mexico. Like herself, White Fox thought the Apaches would be shot down like wingless birds. Her jaws ached. White Fox wanted Geronimo to surrender. *She* wanted the great leader and her family to escape the Sierra Madres and live free.

If it were only possible for them to find a place to

hide, to live and live free, without raiding and causing more anger among the Mexicans and the whites.

She flopped back again. Asking an Apache living free, needing food and clothing, not to raid would be the same as placing him in prison. Maybe the reservation *was* the only answer. She would decide between now and when she saw Geronimo.

Coffee began to boil in the pot. She reluctantly rolled to her feet and moved it away from the fire after pouring herself a generous cup. Her mind pictured Brent leaning over to replace his next to White Fox's. He tried so hard to see her and she had shrunk back even further without seeming to do so purposely.

His remark about the coffee and *home*. Had he been teasing her? Letting her know that he knew who she was? No, if he had recognized her, he would have sent her back . . . home. Did he really feel that San Carlos was his home? Or was he just being polite and making friendly conversation? She hoped he would not think on his comments later and begin to wonder .

She took a drink, sputtered and rubbed her burned lower lip. A terrible thought struck her. He had *not* recognized her. Rather than feeling smug about her deception, maybe she should feel hurt that after all the time they had spent together, he did not see through her disguise.

Meadowlark looked down at her baggy clothes. It had been necessary to hide her figure, but . . . The man was as ignorant and dangerous as a blind skunk.

Tonight had been a learning experience. She had best make herself scarce if she did not want what happened tonight to occur in broad daylight. White Fox may not have known her, but she was deluding herself to think that Brent would not recognize her in the light.

She was more than happy with her decision, when

two days later, from her camp on the side of a brushy hill, she saw White Fox and Brent searching through the Apache camp.

Meadowlark sat just below the knoll of a low ridge in the shadow of an ironwood tree. One of her Warm Springs friends had told her that the pale-haired man had been asking questions about her-him. And the officers had gone through everything, ridding the packs of anything that would slow them down or that was broken or unusable.

The only thing the McQuades could have been looking for today was her. They went directly to her old camp fire and talked with the two warriors who had befriended her. When the Apaches shook their heads, the coils twining in her stomach began to unwind.

Brent and White Fox stood looking around as if they did not know where to look next. Meadowlark grinned. Maybe they wondered if the poor little warrior had been real. Maybe they thought she had been a spirit, or even a ghost. She shuddered, but thought it a perfect joke. It served them right if they thought that she was so worthless as to be left behind. She hugged her arms around her waist. Let them wonder.

But doubt began to creep up her spine. Now she would not be able to ride with the scouts. White Fox would be watching. She would have to follow—again. Yet she did not like to think of making the long trip through unfamiliar country—Mexican country—alone. She would make it. She knew she would. It was just . . . A shiver rippled her flesh.

Sinking back against the slender trunk, the only part of the tree stout enough to support even her light weight, her eyes were about to drift shut when she suddenly sat up and stared toward the railroad track. She thought she had seen something, someone familiar.

She squinted, trying to make out the rider more

clearly, but the space where she had been looking was empty. Imagination. That was all. What would Scorpion be doing here? Her hands curled into fists. Scorpion. Why would she think of him? Now? He was in Mexico.

No one had been more determined to reach the Sierra Madres than Scorpion. He would not come back with things being so dangerous, with Crook so intent in finding all of the Apaches. Would he?

She snorted with disgust. Scorpion had been dangerous when faced with an unarmed man, but she doubted he could find the courage to face General Crook and his command. Telling herself she only wanted to watch the train coming into the station, she kept slinking glances back to that spot. Nothing. Nothing but a dust devil twisting and spiraling a funnel of sand into the air.

One more sleepless night, of lying alone away from the encampment, thankfully passed. Meadowlark stretched, patted the mare, then crept to the edge of the large camp to pick up the full canteen of water left by one of her friends. Hearing approaching footsteps, she quickly slung the strap over her shoulder and copied the swaggering walk of the nearing Coyotero Apaches in an effort to move away without creating unwanted attention.

The warriors passed her by with hardly a glance, except for the one on the end not much taller than she. He slapped her on the back and grinned when she tripped from the force of the blow. He good-naturedly gestured that she join their group and prepare for the war dance that night. The next day, they would be starting the next leg of their journey, going as far as the Mexican border.

Meadowlark started to stick out her chest in imitation of the nice-looking young Coyotero, but thought better of it. Grinning, she slapped the warrior's shoulder. In as deep a voice as she could muster, she told him she was waiting for others from her own band.

With much shouting and shoving and joking, the young braves pointed in the direction they were heading. Meadowlark smiled a sickish smile and nodded, then rubbed her aching back once they were far enough away to have forgotten her completely.

Walking back up the hill, she came to the decision to attend the dance. No matter that it was dangerous, she had enjoyed the encounter with the cheerful Coyoteros. Too many nights she had sat in the dark alone. And it had been ages since she had been to a good war dance. At least since moving onto San Carlos reservation. Excitement lifted her steps.

When she reached her camp, she removed the headband and shook out her hair, feeling feminine for the first time in days. And she admitted to one other reason for going into the main encampment. Who else could cause her to take such a risk? Brent McQuade. She had not seen him since the morning he and White Fox had scoured the scout camp. She missed him. Needed to see for herself that he was all right.

Anticipating the dance and seeing Captain McQuade, caused the day to drag into a week for Meadowlark. She used a few handsful of water from her canteen and a swipe of her lavender soap that she had tempestuously added to her pack to wash the dirt from her face and upper body. One of her friends had slipped her a navy blue woolen shirt the army had issued to the scouts and she donned that over her gray cotton pantaloons.

The shirt was much too large, but she rolled up the sleeves and found a length of rope to use as a belt. Although it grieved her to plaster down her hair again, she rewrapped the headband. She sighed. The vain Apache warriors had to take almost as much time to make themselves presentable as the women.

Ready at last, she started down the hill at the same time the drums began to beat. Her footsteps coincided with the rhythm and her excitement built in pitch with the music. The sun had set and the only illumination came from the huge bonfire set between the scout camp and that of the soldiers.

Memories of other celebrations settled a somber expression over Meadowlark's features. It had been a long time since the warriors had had anything to dance about, and she was sorry the dance tonight was in celebration of tracking down their own people.

Apaches and soldiers alike stood in small groups watching the fire and some of the warriors who were already dancing, circling the blaze. Meadowlark moved inconspicuously among the scouts until she spied the Coyoteros. The shorter brave was there and she moved up close, just to blend in.

A soldier near Meadowlark whooped and she almost jumped out of her skin. Soon the rest of the onlookers began to cheer on the dancing warriors. Meadowlark was too busy searching the crowd for a double-breasted captain's uniform to pay much attention to what was going on by the fire. After she spotted Brent, *then* she could enjoy the celebration.

A kind of hush fell over the assembly. Meadowlark sensed a subtle change and stopped scanning the soldiers to glance into the circle, now crowded with figures clad only in breechclouts and moccasins. Then she saw what the others must have seen.

A figure taller and leaner than the rest, his bronzed skin a lighter and smoother color than that of his comrades had begun to dance. Sparks from the fire illuminated the pale iridescence of his hair. A blue bandanna held that light hair out of his face and Meadowlark could see the intense concentration contorting his features.

The muscles on his body and legs strained with the force of his movements. Sweat glistened on his skin. Suddenly, the White Fox leaped high in the air with a bloodcurdling yell. Meadowlark gasped and took a step backward, only to be brought up short by another body.

She started to glance around and apologize, but another shriek rent the air. Her eyes remained riveted on the scene in the circle, although her body swayed backward. She seemed to gravitate toward the warmth emanating from whomever stood behind her. It was tempting to lean against the warmth, but remembered who and where she was and stood proud and erect, alone.

Other warriors began to follow White Fox's movements as he shifted his weight gracefully from one foot to the other, faster and faster, in rhythm to the thudding beat of the drums. He leapt again, pirouetted and charged left, then right, then all directions. One knee dropped to the ground, then he sprang into the air.

More Apaches joined the dance, firing their guns, chanting their prowess in battle. Soon the White Fox blended with the rest of the warriors, whooping and yelling, their athletic bodies contorting, unleashing power and strength usually kept well hidden by life on the reservation.

A muffled curse sounded from behind Meadowlark. She cast a glance over her shoulder and her heart stopped beating. All traces of energy drained from her body. Standing dead still, she waited for the words that would foil her plans and dreams.

"Damn the bastard. Does he want to ruin everythin'?"

Then she heard a scuffling of feet and the effect of the warm presence turned to ice. Brent! She had backed into him and even stood in front of him for several minutes and had not known it—except for that warm, comfortable feeling she *always* felt when he was near.

But his eyes had been only for the dance, for White Fox. And from the sound of his voice, Brent was more upset than she had ever known him to be. Why? She backed swiftly out of the crowd and searched to see which direction the captain had gone.

There! He was walking toward a group of dancers who had just left the circle. He stopped and waited and . . . There was White Fox emerging from between the grinning warriors. As she stealthily edged closer, she saw that neither Brent nor White Fox was grinning. Instead, both of their features were set in strained, almost angry expressions.

They had moved away from the crowd and Meadowlark crouched among the creosote bushes growing nearby. Her eyes rounded with wonder when she heard their conversation. This was a side of Brent McQuade she had never encountered.

"Damn you, Brandon McQuade! Half the damned army will know who the hell you are now!"

White Fox's chest was still heaving from the exertion of the dance. "I do not think so."

Brent threw his hands in the air. "What *do* you think? That we're stupid, or blind? My God, what if General Crook recognized you? You'll be sent to prison or hanged, sure enough."

Meadowlark hissed in her breath. She had never thought of the consequences of the whites finding out about the White Fox. If the soldiers recognized the civilized Brandon McQuade as the renegade Apache leader, Brent's brother could be in terrible danger. No wonder his wife had looked so pale and wished so badly to come.

Brand tried to be the calming influence. He put his hands on his brother's shoulders, only to have them knocked aside as Brent began to pace, glancing nervously toward the soldiers ringing the fire. "You're lucky tonight, that's all. Everyone was just enjoying the spectacle. But we have yet to hear from the general."

"If it happens, it happens. I am tired of looking over my shoulder." Brand stood still. Back straight. Features proud and determined. Meadowlark thought the two brothers were never more alike than at that moment.

Brent stormed, "Damn you and your Apache philosophy! What of Hillary? What of your baby? And, hell, what about me? I won't see you carted off in chains, Brand. I couldn't bear it. We were apart too long."

Tears welled in Meadowlark's eyes. She felt Brent's pain like a knife to her own heart. More and more she was finding what lay buried in the emotions of the man, Brent McQuade. How she yearned to race over and throw her arms around his hunched shoulders and comfort him, to assure him she would always be there for him. Yet, until this campaign was over, could she make such a promise and know she would be able to keep it?

Brent looked around the barren countryside to his right, and to the war dance on his left. Warriors shouted and fired their rifles. Soldiers cheered. No one paid the two McQuades the slightest attention. He sighed. "All right, Brandon, you've made your statement tonight. But I want your promise you won't do something as stupid as this again."

From where she knelt, Meadowlark was close enough to see White Fox's eyes flash. And then his mouth quirked to the left, just like Brent's. She lost her balance slightly and caught herself by grabbing the base of the greasewood bush. The branches rustled. She froze, eyes wide, breath crushing her chest as both men spun in her direction.

There was no sound, not even a breeze. Then suddenly, a pack rat darted almost from between her feet.

The surprise of the movement caused her to bite down on her lower lip to keep from calling out.

The little animal scurried to the next bush, its hind feet kicking up a small spray of sand. The brothers grinned, the tenseness dissolved in one unguarded moment. Meadowlark allowed herself a small gulp of air.

Brandon McQuade looked at his brother. "I would like to please you, brother, but I cannot make such a promise."

Brent nodded. "Then at least say you'll be careful."

"That, I can do."

The brothers shook hands and Meadowlark crouched as low as she could when they started moving away. However, when she peeked through the branches to see if it was safe to leave, only one of the men was walking away. Brent McQuade stood a few feet from her, with his face tilted toward the heavens.

She clamped a hand over her eyes, stupidly, as if she could not see him, he would not see her. Willing her heart and breath to stop their frantic leaping and diving, she prayed he would not find her. Not now.

Brent lowered his eyes from the midnight-black sky. Clouds had rolled in that afternoon and now a star twinkled here and there as one dark layer drifted past another. Dark. Just like his mood.

Damn his brother for taking twenty years off his life tonight. If someone recognized him and told the general . . . He let the air out of his lungs in a long, long sigh. There wasn't anything he could do but wait. And like Brand said, if it happened, it happened. *Then* he could figure out what was to be done.

His lungs empty, he inhaled deeply. Suddenly, he cocked his head. Lavender? Did he smell lavender? Now that he thought about it, he could have sworn he caught a whiff right under his nose back at the war dance—about the same time he noticed his brother trying to get himself killed.

Stuffing his hands in his pockets, he started walking slowly back to the fire and the scouts, wishing he had something to celebrate. The explanation of the scent was simple enough. Meadowlark Russell. Other than during Brandon's imbecilic episode, she hadn't left his thoughts for over five minutes at a time.

It was funny, the places he thought he'd seen her lately.

Brent stopped and turned in a circle. He felt her presence everywhere. "Ah, Lark."

Chapter Twenty-five

"Ah, Lark." Brent's words stuck like knives in Meadowlark's heart. Although softly said, they were not spoken during a moment of passion or tenderness. Surely he knew why she was here. The deception was over. Geronimo and what was left of her family would be little better than bait for the wolves.

Quaking worse than an aspen leaf during a summer storm, she slowly unfolded from behind the creosote bush. Her head downcast, she waited for the eruption. Besides being disappointed in her, Brent would be furious. Only the spirits knew what he would do.

She watched the toe of her moccasin dig a hole in the sand. Why was she cowering like a whipped dog? She was the one who should be angry—incensed. Why was Brent letting the general get away with this outrage? Maybe if he talked with Crook and explained . . .

Suddenly her head shot up. She straightened her shoulders. Just because she had been caught did not mean she had lost her courage. Meadowlark glared at the spot where Brent had stood. Her mouth opened, then closed. The only proof of his presence was his footprints in the sand.

Her eyes searched the darkness and finally discovered his tall silhouette by the blazing fire. He was already mingling with some of the soldiers near the crowd still watching the war dance.

She collapsed back to her knees and looked up to the starless heavens. "Thank you," she whispered to all who could hear.

Brent McQuade was up before daylight the next morning, as was the rest of the encampment. The sky was overcast, but did nothing to dampen the enthusiasm of the soldiers and scouts. Last night's celebration had been just that—a celebration of the end of the long days of waiting and wondering.

Walking about the camp, listening to clanking gear and braying mules, he sighed and smiled. He'd gotten his first good night's sleep in weeks. Only three or four hours, but at least he'd slept. And he owed the rest to a vision of Lark. She'd seemed so near last night. And the feeling was still with him this morning.

He passed one of the other officers and asked, "Have you checked everyone's gear?"

"Some. But the general just told me to take a telegram into Willcox. Can you finish for me?" The lieutenant held up a folded paper as if to prove he really had to leave.

"Sure." Brent waved him on.

Going down the line of tents, he made certain each soldier packed one blanket and forty rounds of ammunition. All they would take to wear were the clothes on their backs. Enough extra ammo, hard bread, coffee and bacon for sixty days would be packed on the mules.

He heard a curse and looked over to see a mule sit back on its lead, nearly dragging a packer off his feet. The obstinate animal sat down on its haunches and brayed pitifully. *Maybe,* Brent thought, the extra rations would be packed.

Then he saw the general walking through the groups of mules and their handlers, inspecting the special harnesses. Every now and then he stopped to show one of the packer assistants the most efficient methods of loading the supplies.

Brent chuckled. Crook was meticulous with the mules and his men, and the soldiers liked him. They even tolerated the general's puritanical streak, admiring a commanding officer who didn't smoke, drink or swear.

The captain rubbed his eyes and sauntered toward the scouts' camp. It seemed the general inspired a good deal of loyalty, especially since nearly two hundred Indians had assembled to make the dangerous trek.

Scanning the waiting Apaches, Brent noted with amusement the differences in dress. Some were starting out in calico shirts and cotton drawers. Some wore only breechclouts. All wore moccasins and a headband of scarlet cloth.

Most of the scouts carried a Springfield breechloading rifle, a canteen, a butcher knife and a little leather case containing an awl, in case of the need to repair their most important article of clothing—their moccasins. Brent couldn't help but think the Indians were much better adapted for the long hours of travel than the soldiers.

He pulled out his pocket watch just as the call came for the officers to report to General Crook's tent. It was seven o'clock. So far, they were on schedule.

Brent walked slowly toward the tent. He had yet to talk to the general. Had he learned of the White Fox? Could that be what the meeting was about?

Come to think of it, he hadn't seen Brandon yet, either. Tension lined his face as he was shown inside for the meeting and nodded to the officers who had preceded him. Lieutenant Casey followed him in, and they all sat expectantly, waiting to hear what the general had to say.

Crook pushed his chair back from the desk, crossed one knee over the other and clasped his hands about his shins. "You men have done a good job getting everything organized for departure. I know you're all anxious to get under way, so I'll keep the meeting brief. As far as what lies ahead, I expect to reach the Mexican border at San Bernardino in about five days. On May first, we enter Mexico."

The general stood up and paced behind his desk. "Gentlemen, from then on, we'll think the going so far has been a cakewalk." He stopped and gazed long and hard at each of the officers. "Everyone in my command has been handpicked, and I want you to know I have the utmost faith in the success of our campaign. That is all, men, and I thank you. We leave within the half hour."

The officers stood, each shaking hands with the general. As Brent filed past, Crook asked, "Captain McQuade, would you mind waiting a few minutes? I'd like to have a word with you."

Brent's gut tightened at the same time he squeezed the general's hand. They both winced. Brent dropped the commanding officer's hand more quickly than he'd drop a hot coal.

When they were alone, Crook leaned his hip against a corner of the desk. His gray-blue eyes studied the young captain intently. "I understand the scouts put on quite a celebration last night."

Brent fought off a telltale frown. "Yes, sir. It seemed to boost everyone's morale considerably."

"Good. And I hear there was one warrior in particular who rallied the action."

Swallowing cotton, Brent's eyes never left the general's, whose gaze was no easier to read than either Brandon's or Lark's. "Well, yes, I guess."

"Do you know who the blond-haired Apache was?"

Hell! He took a deep breath. He'd known it was coming sooner or later. "Yes." His eyes broke contact with Crook's as he glanced toward the tent flap. Could he reach Brandon in time to warn him, or was it already too late? Was that why he hadn't seen his brother yet that morning?

Brent hunched his shoulders when the general seemed to have nothing more to say for the time being. "So, you know who he is, too?"

Crook nodded.

"You have to understand, Gen—"

The general cut him off. "But I do."

"What?"

"I've known who your brother was since he came to see me in Washington."

"You have? But—"

"He came expressly asking for me to come out here and ease the situation, which I wasn't sure at the time I could do." His beard wriggled slightly. "You know politics . . . and higher authorities."

Brent only nodded. He didn't think he dared open his mouth until he heard all the general had to say.

Crook inclined his head at the captain's deference and continued, "I decided the Apaches needed men like your brother working on their behalf. As long as he continues to work with me, we'll have no problems."

"But last night—"

"Demonstrated his care and concern."

And where his true loyalties lie, I'm afraid, Brent thought to himself. He released his breath, grateful for the general's understanding. But . . . "I've been worried. I haven't found . . . I mean—"

"I asked him to take a few scouts and check the road ahead. I don't want to chance running into more hotheads like the 'Tombstone Rangers.' "

A hesitant grin creased Brent's lips. "No, sir."

Crook did not return the smile. "Your brother could be the one person to keep this mission from turning into another war."

Hope beat in Brent's heart. Hope for the Apaches and for Lark. He'd had faith in the general all along.

Hopefully, he'd be able to go back to San Carlos and show her how wrong she'd been.

Maybe, just maybe, Brandon could make a difference.

Meadowlark watched from her camp on the small rise as the command left Willcox. She smiled when several mules bucked and kicked and crow-hopped into motion. Only one took a notion to turn the departure into a race. It took off at an ungainly, short-legged run, braying its delight at being free.

Covering her mouth with one hand, Meadowlark giggled when the jostling and bouncing scattered pots and pans and a sack of flour before a packer ran the animal down.

Once the march began, however, men and animals settled into a tedious routine, much to Meadowlark's satisfaction. But by the second day on the trail, the country flattened into excellent grassland that offered Meadowlark little means of concealment.

She had noticed that White Fox usually rode ahead and was seldom around the groups of scouts, some of which went off to hunt for the evening meal or walked off to one side out of the dust. When evening came, she decided the risk of discovery was just as great out on the trail, so she turned her mare into the cavalry remuda. The rest of the way to the border, she would be a scout.

Her two Warm Springs friends and several other warriors were gathered around a small fire, intent on a game of monte, played with horsehide cards. When she walked up to the camp, the men who'd befriended her earlier smiled and continued the game. The others watched her warily, but soon turned their attention back to the gambling.

Meadowlark sighed. It felt wonderful to hold her hands out to a fire and enjoy a little companionship, rather than the solitary isolation to which she'd become accustomed. There was nothing to fear here. Although Brent had surprised her that one time, commissioned officers rarely socialized with their lower-ranked troops, let alone a group of Indians. She was perfectly safe . . .

"Hola!"

Recognizing that deep voice, she stiffened. When Brent McQuade spoke the greeting, it definitely sounded different from when said by a Mexican or an Apache. If she had not been afraid of his seeing her, she could almost have laughed.

Almost, she grumbled, as she scooted her bottom over rocks and grass and . . . she groaned . . . cactus. The man was uncanny. Would she never be able to predict his actions?

Her worry was for nothing. He did not stop for long at their camp fire, but continued on to the white packers camp after sharing a joke with one of the warriors who spoke some English.

She did not move back to the fire, feeling safer in the background as long as Brent was in the area. She rubbed a hand over her eyes and wondered how long she would have to be on her guard.

The captain was unlike any soldier she had ever known. No other officer would spend so much time with the men under his command. And as she watched him smile and laugh with the others, she felt a deep sense of satisfaction. If she had to have the misfortune of losing her affection to a white man, she could not have chosen better. He was a fine soldier, although she did not always mean that as a compliment, and a fine man.

On the afternoon of the fifth day, the command rode into San Bernardino Springs. Meadowlark could not have told anyone the number of hours she had been walking, because she had lost count yesterday when the sun and the heat and her screaming muscles demanded that she think of anything but the discomfort of her exhausted body.

What had ever made her decide to hide among the scouts? Even after months of drinking whiskey and the inactivity of the reservation, they were in much better condition than she. And to torture herself more, now and then she would steal a longing glance at the shiny red coat of her mare, being driven with the few spare horses.

Luckily, the remuda had been turned over to three scouts who did not mind her tagging along to help see after the horse. One of the scouts was Warm Springs, another Coyotero and the third, a Chiricahau. They all appreciated fine horseflesh, although the Apaches seldom had need of a horse for long.

Her nose wrinkled at the thought of the fate of most horseflesh around an Apache camp, especially when the Indians were being constantly pursued.

But now her eyes were only for the Springs that broke out from the ground right on the Mexican-American border and flowed south into the Yaqui River. Water. Deep water. *Bath* water. Her mouth literally drooled. Later, after the camp was asleep, she would cleanse the week's worth of filth from her head and body. And maybe even wash her clothes.

Just the thought of the cool refreshing liquid lapping against her flesh was enough to make her dreamy-eyed and unaware of a person standing only a few yards away.

She sighed and turned to her right to find a good spot to make herself scarce until evening. The man turned to his left, on his way to the remuda to steal a horse to deliver an important message. Without warning, the two people stood face to face.

"Scorpion."

"Little pigeon."

They both spoke at once, surprised expressions on their faces. Scorpion looked Meadowlark over from head to toe, taking in every aspect of her disguise. Meadowlark withstood his inspection while remembering that time she *thought* she had seen him in Willcox. Yet she knew he had not been with the scouts during the past few days.

Of course, he could have been with a hunting party, or scouting ahead or behind the command. But she did not believe so. He had to be up to something. And it was probably no good.

Scorpion frowned. "What you do, dressed as warrior?"

She could not understand the man. He was acting as if nothing between them had changed. As if he had never betrayed her trust. "Why are *you* . . . here?" How could he show his face, knowing Captain McQuade was with the command? Or, since he had to have seen that Brent was alive, had he come to finish the job? Her foot tapped furiously on the packed earth around the water.

Scorpion glanced around them, then spoke in a low voice. "I go Mexico—"

She cut him off, stating warily, "You already went."

His eyes narrowed, but he shook his head and grinned. "Went back for you."

Her own eyes widened. "Me? Why?"

As if he hadn't heard her questions, he said, "You not at reservation. Know you come. Soon."

"What do you want from me?" It seemed very strange to be talking to Scorpion. He was not afraid of the soldiers passing them, busily setting up camp. He had never shown remorse for stealing her horse, or nearly killing the captain, or then running off, leaving her in his dust when the soldiers chased them. He acted as if none of that had ever taken place.

She stepped back, suddenly very apprehensive.

Scorpion shrugged. "You and me, we find Geronimo. Yes?"

Meadowlark was astounded. Why had Scorpion not gone ahead and already warned Geronimo that Crook was on his way? Something was not right. She told him, "Yes, I will find Geronimo. But I will stay with the soldiers. They may receive information that will be useful later."

Scorpion looked at her for long time. She shifted her feet. When he started toward her, she backed up. "No!"

An obscene oath colored the air. In rapid Spanish, he scorned her and angrily stalked away.

She unclamped her teeth from the inside of her jaw and gingerly laved the torn flesh with the tip of her tongue. When he stopped and looked back, a shiver ran the length of her spine. Her skin crawled. She had a terrible feeling her onetime friend could be a fearsome enemy.

Meadowlark had made a soft bed by pulling handfuls of grass and then covering them with a blanket. As she lay looking at the moon, she could tell that it was almost midnight. Most of the camp was quiet. Guards had been posted, but she had done some scouting herself and would only encounter one on her way to the farthest spring.

Sighing contentedly, dreaming of her bath, she climbed to her feet, picked up the piece of lavender soap and quietly circled the camp. If anyone had seen her at that moment, they would have thought her smile angelic. Soon, she would be clean.

As she neared the guard's location, she kept to the shadows of the few trees growing close to the water. Using the faint moonlight, she carefully placed each foot, avoiding twigs and dry grass.

She concentrated so hard on being quiet and stealthy, that when she happened to glance to her left and suddenly saw red glow from the tip of a smoke, she jumped and almost dropped her soap. She stopped and made out the shape of a man sitting back against the trunk of a bare tree, one leg bent, his wrist resting atop his knee.

He made a peaceful picture, relaxed, looking south into Mexico.

Then she noted the fit of his trousers. Moonlight reflected off polished leather. A soldier. Her vigilance slackened. She had thought all of the guards were scouts. Now she could really enjoy her bath.

With a bright smile, she still took care to move quietly, but hurried a little faster. White soldiers were not deaf, after all.

The spring glimmered cool and inviting, the surface broken only by the barest ripples as a slight breeze ruffled the water. She stood a moment, looking, knowing it might be the last opportunity she would have to completely immerse herself in water for a long, long time.

Though it was a terribly hard choice to make, she decided to wash her shirt and pantaloons first and let them dry on a nearby rock. Then she stepped into the shallow water. It was almost a reverent moment as she waded into the pool.

The liquid and cool sand massaged the soles of her feet. Tingling sensations crawled up her ankles and calves. Then her kneecaps disappeared. Goosebumps erupted over her body from sheer pleasure. The bottom leveled out when the water reached midthigh. With a gleeful smile and a deep breath, she wasted no time in sinking down until her entire body was submerged.

She resurfaced slowly, pushing short stands of dripping hair from her eyes with the palms of her hands. Rivulets of water trickled from her scalp down the back of her neck. She shivered with delight. She had not felt so wonderful since . . .

After dipping again, she lay her head back and allowed her body to float on the surface. Water lapped and caressed her flesh like tender hands kneading and . . . She had not felt so good since Brent McQuade made love to her. There! She had admitted it.

And with that defiant thought, she stood on the sandy bottom and started her bath. As much as she wanted to think of the spring as her own private domain, there were others nearby and she did not have the luxury of time.

She ran her hand down her arm and noticed something missing. The soap. It was on the bank beside her clothes. Wiping water from her eyes, she started out of the spring, reveling in the gentle pull of the water, how it tickled running down her knees.

Being careful of sharp stones cutting into her bare feet, she glanced quickly to where she had left the soap. Her heart thundered. Boots! Black, shiny boots. Blue trousers. Yellow stripe. Black holster. White shirt. Suspenders. Yellow bandana. Square chin. Dimple. Midnight-blue eyes.

Uh-oh. The spirits had deserted her.

Brent McQuade sat alone, his head leaning back against the smooth trunk of a long-dead tree. For some reason, its lonesome silhouette had called to him tonight, for he, too, was lonely.

He lit a cheroot and stared out across the border. Four days. That was all. Then the campaign began.

Suddenly restless, he shrugged to his feet and walked a little ways down a gradual incline, at the base of which was a small, tree-lined pool. Brent had discovered it earlier in the day and thought it the perfect place to have a few minutes alone to unwind.

And it had been. He'd even bathed and shaved and shook the trail dust from his uniform. And the entire time he'd thought of Lark. Images of her natural, uninhibited beauty surrounded him in this picturesque oasis.

He took a puff from the cheroot and watched waves undulate across the surface of the spring. His eyes narrowed. Waves? There was hardly a breeze. Then he saw the barest hint of a movement from between two branches. Something had dipped below the surface. He watched carefully, expecting to see a turtle or some other animal rise up for air.

The water parted. He choked on an inhaled breath of tobacco. He closed his eyes. Thinking too hard. That was all. He'd been thinking of Lark so much he'd conjured her image. He reopened his eyes. The surface was smooth.

Then his mouth went lax. The thin cigar dangled precariously from nerveless lips. A form arose and stretched flat on the water. Firm little breasts pointed toward the heavens. Water sluiced off a slightly rounded belly. Moonlight glinted off black curls at the juncture of a pair of tapered thighs.

His heart pounded against his rib cage. His loins quickened. Ever so slowly, his feet began to move. He had to go slow. Any noise or sudden movement might cause the vision to evaporate before his eyes.

Draped over a rock, he found a gray shirt and white cotton trousers. Part of a bar of soap lay at his feet and he picked it up. A figment of his imagination wouldn't leave clothing and soap lying around.

He took a quick sniff. Lavender. His gaze shot across the water. The vision, and she truly was a sight for sore eyes, was walking toward him.

Droplets of water cascaded over her shoulders and down her arms, trickled from the slender column of her neck to pearl the fullness of her breasts. His eyes feasted on her nakedness as a starving wolf would devour a trapped hare.

"Lark." God, she was real, standing directly in front

of him, staring as if he were the devil come to take her to hell.

And then the devil did begin to speak—in his ear. What in the hell was she doing down here on the Mexican border? He'd left her where he'd thought she'd be safe and waiting for him when he returned to San Carlos.

"What in the hell are you doin' here, woman?" He had no choice but to repeat his thoughts. He wasn't thinking clearly enough to say anything original at the moment.

Meadowlark opened her mouth and closed it again. For a minute, she had been under the same illusion as Brent, thinking that he was not real, just a portion of her imagination gone wild. "I-I . . . Brent . . ." She waded the rest of the way out of the pool and ran her fingers over his smooth chin.

She could not remember being happy often in her life, but just the appearance of this white soldier set her heart bubbling into her throat. Suddenly their differences did not seem so important. She blinked and felt tears joining the droplets of water dotting her cheeks.

"Damn it, quit that. I asked—" Brent saw the moisture glistening in her eyes, the sweet smile on her lips, and forgot what he was going to say. All the loneliness, all the hours he'd spent missing her, dreaming of her, flooded his heart. She was here, standing only inches from his arms.

He lifted his hands and felt her melt into his embrace. Water plastered his shirt to his chest and it felt almost as if they were flesh to flesh. His palms ran up and down her silken back, ensuring him that she was truly real and warm and his.

Meadowlark raised her head from his chest and looked into his eyes. She hoped he could read her invitation, for if he did not make love to her soon, she would surely expire from wanting and desire and . . .

love.

Brent read her invitation all right. His body responded as if a red hot iron had been applied to his person. Every nerve, every inch of his flesh cried out his hunger. In less than a heartbeat, his clothes lay discarded on the ground, and with the lavender soap still clutched in his hand, he scooped her into his arms and walked back into the water.

Where the depth of the spring had reached to Meadowlark's thighs, it lapped around Brent's knees. A deep chuckle rumbled through his chest as he kept a tight hold on her and just fell back. All the way down, she watched the bank and hissed, "Sh-h-h."

They hit the water and Meadowlark bounced in arms to land hard in his lap. If it had not been for the water's buoyancy, she feared she might have unmanned him before . . .

Her fears were unfounded. His palms covered her breasts and he nibbled her earlobe. "I'd forgotten just how good you feel." He turned her to where her legs straddled his hips, her bottom cushioned on his thighs. He looked at her, from the wet strands of hair plastered to her cheeks to every delectable feature, reacquainting himself with her long, graceful neck, and twin globes of soft, golden woman-flesh with dusky tips that puckered as he watched. The remaining parts of her body were a vague blur beneath the water.

A vague blur. But an oh-so-warm reality as he wrapped his arms around her back and pulled her close. Close. The curly nest between her thighs teased his throbbing manhood. He arched his hips at the same time he tasted a tender nipple. Gently nipping the swollen bud between his teeth, he flicked the sensitive tip with his tongue. Once. Twice. Faster.

Meadowlark arched her back, offering more of herself. The quickening sensation in her breast tingled clear to her lower belly. Warm liquid heat at the core of her womanhood contrasted sensuously with the cool water outside. She moaned when he suddenly left the one breast, which was immediately cooled by the evening breeze, to pay the same greedy homage to the other.

Her lower body pulsed to the rhythm of his tongue. Her hips moved forward until she could feel his staff nudging her femininity. She raised herself until the seeking tip of him pushed gently inside.

Brent's muscles leaped almost violently as he slipped from cool water into a heat so intense it nearly consumed him. Blood rushed through his veins, flushing his skin, increasing his heartbeat until it felt as if someone used a trip-hammer against his ribs.

"So-o-o good," he whispered.

"I have missed you." She pressed her lips to the pulsing hollow at the base of his throat.

Brent stopped breathing. It was the first time she'd ever expressed that she might have feelings for him. Real feelings. Not just a lustful attraction.

She wriggled her hips, and with her feet braced in the sand, rocked up and down before adding a few circling motions.

Brent gritted his teeth until he captured her lips in a kiss that stole both their breaths. The movements of their tongues matched the motion of their hips. Gentle ripples on the surface of the spring became rolling waves.

During the moment of release, Brent's heels dug into the sand. The unsteady floor moved with the pressure and he lost his support. On his final thrust, his body slid under the water. His arms instinctively wrapped around Lark, bracing her as she threw her head back and let her body take control. They both dunked into the spring.

Water bubbled and churned. Two heads bobbed and sputtered to the surface. Brent worriedly sought Lark. "Are you all right?"

She nodded and pushed her hair away from her face. She hiccuped and giggled. Then she looked at Brent and smiled. Before she realized it, a soft laugh escaped her lips.

Brent grinned, thought of the hilarious scene they'd have presented if anyone had been watching, and laughed, too.

Meadowlark put a finger to his lips. "Sh-h-h."

He sucked the offending digit into his mouth, wishing she would laugh again. It was a sweet, musical sound that he wanted to hear the rest of his life.

Sighing, he cupped her face in his hands, tracing his thumbs over her cheekbones. His eyes probed hers. "No matter what happens, Lark, remember that I love you."

Her lashes lowered. She ducked her head and nodded. Her tongue twitched, but she could not say the words. Not yet. Not until Crook's campaign had ended, and then maybe never. "We must go. Someone might come."

He understood her reluctance, though his heart was heavy. She wouldn't return his vow of love. He took a deep breath and reached for her hand, tugging her playfully from the water. Using his discarded shirt, he patted her body dry and then his.

They dressed slowly, hardly able to take their eyes from each other, still half afraid the other might disappear if they so much as blinked.

Brent cleared his throat. "Honey, we need to talk." He was plagued by her presence. As much as he loved her and was pleased to see her, she had to go back to San Carlos. It was dangerous here. And even more dangerous, was that look in her eyes.

"Evening, folks, nice night for a moonlight swim, is it not?" As if he had materialized from out of the sandy soil, Brandon McQuade stood less than two feet away.

Chapter Twenty-six

Brandon McQuade smothered a self-satisfied grin. "Do not worry. No one else saw the white captain and the Apache *warrior* together." He strangled on a chuckle. He had never seen two people blush so furiously that he could see their skin darken, even at night.

Brent clenched his hands. His eyes blazed at his brother. What had Brand been doing out here snooping around in the first place? Had he seen *everything?* Or had he just walked up and happened to guess correctly? "Just how long have you been here, little brother?"

With his hands splayed across his hips, Brandon stared at his infuriated sibling. He was well aware that Brent's anger was caused more from embarrassment at being caught in such a compromising situation as anything. "Long enough to direct others with the idea of . . . bathing . . . to another location."

"Oh-h." Meadowlark felt as if she could melt right into the ground. She hid her flaming cheeks beneath her suddenly cold hands.

Brent sighed, then straightened his back in perfect military form. "Well, thanks."

Brand nodded. "My pleasure." And he had the grace to look away when the woman turned an even deeper shade of scarlet than his brother. For her sake alone, because he enjoyed seeing his usually perfect brother as a human after all, he changed the direction of the conversation and said to her, "I have seen you before."

Though stated directly, Meadowlark sensed the question behind the words. "Yes. Several times." It pleased her to see the smug White Fox and the captain clearly puzzled.

Brent looked at Brand and then Lark. "I didn't know you two had met." Recalling he'd already lost one woman to his handsome brother, Brent kept a wary eye on Lark.

She preened under the jealousy Brent was trying so hard to hide. "We have not exactly met." Meeting White Fox's narrow-eyed gaze, she decided to explain quickly. "You passed me the morning you and your wife rode into the agency."

Brand studied her intently. There was something familiar . . . "Wait. The thoroughbred. You rode the big red mare." She nodded.

Brent crossed his arms over his chest. "You said *several* times."

The smooth, shimmering surface of the pool beckoned her gaze. "And at Willcox. Twice."

Both men frowned. Brent couldn't remember seeing her there. If he had, she'd been sent back to San Carlos faster than a roadrunner sped away from a fox.

Brand's eyes flared like a newly lit candle as he studied her clothing. "Ah, the little warrior that made such good coffee and listened so politely." His lips twitched when he turned pointedly to Brent. "The one I was afraid would not have the endurance to survive this arduous journey."

"That was *you?* You've been along the whole trip?" He bent over to peer into her face. "You little fool! You could've been . . . Don't you know how dangerous . . ." Her eyes were liquid amber pools. He gulped, then raised his arms in a helpless shrug. "Of course you know. How stupid can I be?"

He paced for several minutes before calming enough to come back and face her again. He shook his finger under her nose. "You're gonna turn your little tail around right now and skedaddle right back to San Carlos. You hear?"

Meadowlark drew herself up until she looked him square in the vee of his shirt. Hands fisted on her hips, legs braced apart, she stuck out her chin and declared, "Oh, I heard. But I will not go back."

"Yes, you will!"

They glowered into each other's strained features. Meadowlark racked her brain for some reasonable argument. "It will be even more dangerous if I go back alone." She allowed her voice a small quaver.

Brent snapped his jaws shut. "I'll take you." From the corner of his eye, he saw Brand shake his head. "Then I'll get someone else to do it."

With reason on his side, Brand bravely entered the foray. "The general needs every man. He will allow no one to return now."

Meadowlark realized she might have an ally, even unwittingly. "I will be quiet and stay out of your way. You will not know I am here."

Brent sniffed and inhaled the scent of lavender. "Ha! Fat chance." He began to pace again.

Finally, after a tense silence, Brand interjected, "I will help. Between us, we will keep her safe."

Brent's shoulders sagged. He directed a relieved nod to his brother. Brandon understood; knew his only concern was for her welfare. He hated like hell to take her on such a dangerous mission, but felt she'd be safer with them than on her own.

Meadowlark took exception to the high-handed statement. "I am not a child to be babied. I will look after myself."

The two brothers looked at each other and then at Meadowlark. In unison, they said, "Fat chance."

* * *

The last four days before the command crossed the border were filled with so much preparation and activity that, to Meadowlark, the days seemed to fly by. Attired once again in her scout uniform, she still bristled over the callous way she was being treated. Neither Brent nor the White Fox allowed her one moment of privacy or peace.

If that was the way it was going to be for the next few weeks . . . She darted a glance toward Brent, saw that familiar glint in his eyes as he stared back, and felt a tingling rush of heat through her body. Well, maybe she could stand his attention, for a while.

She had no choice, really. It was either be under Brent's protection or be left behind. She *had* to stay with the command. Had to beat them to Geronimo.

Brent winked. Her heart thundered. And as he turned to help one of the troopers, she swallowed down her regret that these might be their last days together.

On May 1, 1883, the expedition crossed the border into Mexico. Much to Meadowlark's delight, she had been ordered to ride her mare and stick to Captain McQuade like butter on a biscuit.

Although her disguise was effective, she could not help but notice the jealous glare in his eyes as he kept a wary lookout over his soldiers and scouts. Her heart warmed to the thought that he would protect her, no matter what, no matter who.

But that knowledge also served as a bitter dose of guilt. What if something happened to *him* because of *her?* When a situation arose that he would have to look after his own life, would he be too busy seeing after her? It all came down to the fact that she should not have been so careless as to be discovered.

The next few days were hot and dusty as they traveled down a sandy valley and into desert country. Now that she was able to ride with the command, Meadowlark searched every face that came and went, looking for Scorpion, wondering if he was traveling with them, too. But she never found him. Where had he gone? What was he up to?

The scouts were good to scour the area and bring back deer and wild turkeys. Food was plentiful, if not terribly savory. That evening, Brent happened to glance into the pot of watery stew boiling over their camp fire and gave Meadowlark an almost imperceptible nod to follow him. When they were out of earshot of the young giant of a cook, he said, "Let's go over and see what kind a cook my little brother is."

Luckily, the White Mountain scouts were handy with meat and tortillas, though Meadowlark laughed when Brent suspiciously held up a piece of the meat and asked, "What is this?" She refused to tell him and he ate it anyway.

With the sunrise, they continued down the San Bernardino Valley. Meadowlark viewed with detachment the ruins and abandoned villages destroyed by the Apaches. What she watched with caution were the mountains, rising rugged and forbidding on either side of them, slashed by hundreds of ravines they would have to cross.

The sun glared hot, draining men, women, and animals alike. But she felt sorriest for the mules, loaded down with packs, scrambling over steep hills and rocks that rolled out from beneath their small hooves. And then the mesquite and creosote grew so thick that the horses and mules had to break their way through.

Meadowlark held her legs up, wishing she had worn her leather leggings. Thorns tore at her mare's sides and its hide quivered beneath her thighs. But as she glanced around, thinking of imploring someone to help, she held her tongue. The other animals were suffering the same fate and their riders' and packers' faces were all strained with concern.

By the time they camped for the evening, Meadowlark was certain that if her mission were not so important, she would not move another foot farther. Sweat coated her body. Her hair felt thick and matted with grime beneath the bandanna. Her hands and cheeks were nicked with tiny scratches. Every bush between here and the last camp sported a piece of her clothing.

And it did not improve her disposition when Brent walked by and whispered, "Just remember, you *wanted* to come along." Ooohh, her spirit returned just thinking of wringing his neck.

The soldiers moved more slowly, and there was less conversation around the fires at night. Yet, the scouts, after trudging all day on foot, always had cheery smiles on their faces. Meadowlark found herself becoming quite short-tempered with their lighthearted behavior.

After the meal, Meadowlark, Brent and Brandon stretched out, listening to one of the White Mountain scouts play a four-holed flute he had made from a section of Spanish bayonet cane. Soon, though, Brent rolled to his feet. "I'll be back in a while. Crook's called a meeting with some of the officers tonight." Looking at Brand, he tilted his head toward Lark. "Keep an eye on our friend."

Meadowlark bristled. Brandon grinned. "I think he cares for you. A great deal."

She shrugged, refusing to look the shrewd Apache/white man in the eyes.

Her feigned disinterest did not fool Brand. "As I think you care for my brother."

Her head snapped up. "I do no . . ." Once her eyes encountered his, she found she could not lie. "Maybe. But it is not wise."

Brand lay back, resting the back of his head in the palms of his hands. "When is it ever wise to give your heart, not knowing if it will be treated lovingly or broken and scattered to the wind. But to go through life alone is like traveling through the country surrounding us now. It can have its beautiful moments, but for the most part it is bleak, barren and lonely."

Meadowlark worried her lower lip between her teeth. This man was not much older than she, yet had a lifetime more experience. And was *very* smart. "But we . . . your brother . . . and I, come from different worlds."

"The worlds are not so far apart as you think. To exist in either, one lives and hurts and laughs and loves and dies. We are all the same."

She cocked her head, staring at his profile. "I have met your Hillary."

Brandon turned his head. "And?"

"She is nice. I like her."

He looked back at the stars. "So do I."

"Has it been hard? For the two of you?" How difficult would it be, if things did work out, for she and Brent to make a life together? Was that what she really wanted to know?

"At first, it was very hard. Especially for Hillary. Our ways, Apache ways, are difficult even for Apaches at times." He glanced at Meadowlark and she returned his smile. "We had to decide that our love for each other was what mattered most. We have both given up things we loved in our past lives to build a new life together."

She nodded. Love. It was the foundation from which to build.

Brand closed his eyes. For her ears alone, he said, "Now, Miss Russell, we must try to sleep. Did anyone ever tell you, you talk too much?"

General Crook's meeting consisted mostly of discussing the condition of the men and animals after the grueling day. Brent and the other officers all reported scrapes and scratches as the worst injuries.

As they were about to be dismissed, Brent asked, "General, when we reach the Sierra Madres, and we have prisoners to return, will they be sent to San Carlos or will the government let some of them go back to their homelands?"

Crook rubbed the tip of his nose. "They have not seen fit to inform me of any decisions on that matter. I will not be able to make any promises."

Brent frowned. "I understand, but it might help when we talk to some of the chiefs, to tell them *something.*" Lieutenant Johnson cleared his throat and added, "It's all part of the army mentality, you know. If the Indians want to go back to their homeland and live in peace, then by damn, send them to a reservation *anywhere* but there."

Several of the officers chuckled, but looked guiltily at the general.

Brent nodded in agreement. "It's as if letting them live where they want is displaying a weakness on the government's part."

Crook finally stood up. "Gentlemen, I must say you are all very observant, but I warn you not to let your superiors know you've divined their politics. Now, I shall bid you good night. We have a long day ahead."

When Brent walked past, the general said, "Remember, we must not make any promises we cannot deliver later. The Apaches have to come back whether we've made things easier, or not."

"Yes, sir. I just wish we didn't have to depend on the 'or not' so heavily."

If Meadowlark had thought the last day of travel was rough, she came to a different conclusion in the days ahead as each one was more difficult than the day before.

She found a rattlesnake under her blanket one

morning and surprised the packers and soldiers by calmly telling it, "Good morning, Mr. Snake," and letting it go on its way. Of course, one of the soldiers was not so polite and quickly dispatched the reptile. Some of the more friendly wildlife included bright colored parrots, and several scouts sported new feathers in their hair. Meadowlark made out the sapphire streaks darting from flower to flower to be hummingbirds.

And as each day became more difficult and perilous, Brent grew more concerned for Lark. Sure she was as Apache as any of them, but she was a woman—small and fragile and unused to the hardships the warriors'd had to endure.

Worst of all, after climbing and descending half a dozen ridges and gorges and picking cactus out of every tender body part imaginable, by the time they camped at night, they were too tired to do anything but fall into bed and . . . sleep.

And who slept next to her? Brand. Because the soldiers might think it strange if the captain suddenly started sleeping next to the little scout.

At the same time, Meadowlark lay in her blanket every night wondering when one of the scouts would find sign of the renegades. Soon, she would have to find her way to Geronimo. But how?

Seven days after crossing the border, Brent pointed out the Sierra Madres and they finally marched straight for the mountains. The foothills were soon replaced by steeper ridges. Scrub oak gave way to cedar. Meadowlark's hands tangled in the horse's mane and her knees gripped the sleek sides so tightly that her muscles quivered like jelly.

Suddenly, a commotion ahead stopped their forward progress. Everyone strained to hear what the advance scouts were telling Crook. Word was passed down the line. A recent trail had been cut. Meadowlark's heart raced with the news. Soon.

Anticipation and excitement carried the command onward. She watched in sorrow as the scouts and soldiers checked their weapons and ammunition. Her eyes scanned the mountainsides, looking for anything that would give her an indication of where to look for her family.

Brent came to ride beside her. "The renegades must've just come from a raid. The scouts found a trail where a number of cattle were driven into the mountains."

She stared straight ahead. "Will we catch up to them today?"

"I doubt it. The scouts say the trail gets pretty treacherous ahead."

Inwardly, she breathed a sigh of relief. At least they had a good head start.

A few minutes later, the horses in front of them stopped and they pulled up their own animals. Brent stood in his stirrups and tried to see ahead. A soldier behind them called out, "Hey, what's happenin'? Why'd we stop?"

To Meadowlark's right, an avalanche of rocks skittering down a steep slope announced White Fox's arrival. The big stallion slid to a stop beside her mare.

Brent leaned over and asked, "Howdy, little brother. What's goin' on?"

Brand looked up the trail. A group of scouts had gathered around General Crook. "Someone down the line had captured an owl. You know how superstitious the Apaches are about owls. Anyway, they are telling Crook that it is a bad omen and unless the bird is freed, we can never hope to defeat the renegades."

Brent caught the look exchanged between Brand and Lark. He shook his head. "You both believe it's true, that it's bad luck, don't you?"

Brand raised his eyebrows.

Meadowlark shrugged.

Brent spurred his horse off the trail and amid a

shower of dirt and rocks, half rode, half slid back down the line. He had only been gone a few minutes when Apache yells echoed between the steep cliffs on either side of them. The column started moving again and Brandon pulled in beside Meadowlark.

She looked over her shoulder. "Where do you think he went?"

Brand's mouth quirked up on the left side, causing her to suck in her breath. "The owl is free."

She thought of the look on Brent's face when he left them and decided she would not have argued with the captain, either.

Brand took two pieces of jerky from his pouch and handed one to Meadowlark. "Keep up your strength, little bird. It will be a long time before we camp tonight."

As the march continued, she could not believe the trail they followed. It hugged the edge of a mountainside so steep that every step sent a rock bouncing down and out of sight. She had been in mountains before, but never had she seen or traveled through such immense canyons and over ridges that seemed to break right into the sky. But now she knew why Geronimo had chosen this place as his refuge. Even the spirits seemed closer.

White Fox had been right. It was almost midnight before camp was made. They were in a deep, thickly wooded canyon, with the nearest water a thousand feet below. Meadowlark slid off her mare's back and stood with her head resting on the horse's damp neck. She was tired. So-o tired.

Summoning the strength from deep down somewhere, she took extra time to rub down the mare and check its legs and hooves for sores and bruises. After what they had been through so far, no telling what was ahead.

Rather than search out Brent or White Fox, she walked through the woods to the edge of a cliff that looked like it went down and down without end. The moon was bright enough that she could see all the way across the gorge, where it was wild and dark and mysterious. Was her family there somewhere?

She started when a pair of strong, masculine arms wrapped around her.

"Sorry if I scared you. Just wanted to be sure I got a good hold on you before I said anything." Brent nuzzled his chin onto the top of her shoulder. "Some kinda country, isn't it?"

She sighed and leaned back against his solid frame. "It is beautiful."

Brent looked around and spotted a large boulder jutting out over a wide ledge. Wind and rain had hollowed out the underside, creating a shelter of sorts. He led her through a tangle of limbs and small bushes, then crawled in first to check for other, less appealing inhabitants, before holding out his hand for her to join him.

Meadowlark readily accepted his offer. He positioned her between his outstretched legs and she rested her back against the warm wall of his chest. Beneath her head she felt the steady, reassuring thud of his heart. With his arms wrapped around her and his hands clasped across her stomach, she was surrounded by peace and contentment. Her bodily aches and pains seemed to melt away with each breath she drew.

It felt good just to be held, to be in the arms of the man she loved.

Brent, too, was feeling rejuvenated. The feel of Lark's small body nestled against his thrilled him to the very core. He'd been aching to hold her like this for days. He bent his head and rubbed his cheek against hers.

Meadowlark did not flinch from the rough stubble of his beard. She lifted her hand and caressed his other cheek.

"It's hell, isn't it? Together—alone—for the first

time in ages, and we're too tired to do anythin' about it." His voice was thick and husky and sent chills down Meadowlark's spine. "I like what we are doing."

He squeezed his arms more tightly around her and scooted down into a more comfortable position. His eyelids drooped. "So do I, honey. So do I."

When his breathing became deep and regular, Meadowlark smiled. For the next few hours she would not think about tomorrow. At that moment, she was exactly where she wanted to be.

Brand roused them just before dawn. "Wake up, sleepy heads. The camp is stirring. And the general is searching for his favorite captain."

Brent muttered something under his breath that Meadowlark thought sounded like, ". . . worse'n a hound dog. Damned . . . ungrateful . . . turn'im over my knee . . ." Then, in a flash, he leaned over her shoulder and whispered in her ear, "God, I want you, Lark, almost as much as I love you."

Her eyelids fluttered. She felt a definite heat suffuse her whole body. With White Fox standing nearby, she was embarrassed to say anything, so yawned and stretched, only to stop immediately when Brent groaned. Then, against her bottom, she felt the proof of his words.

Oh, he *did* want her. With a mischievous smile on her face, she wriggled against him and quickly crawled out to stand beside White Fox.

When Brent just sat there glowering, she took White Fox's arm and began to lead him away. "Maybe we should go on and give your brother a few minutes of . . . privacy."

"Why?" Brand turned to look back but she tugged him forward.

"Because he has had a . . . hard . . . night."

Brand cocked his head and eyed the little woman/warrior warily. Then a grin spread across his lips. "Oh. By all means, let us allow him to . . . compose himself. Better hurry, big brother. I see the general coming now."

The command had traveled about five miles since dawn. Meadowlark looked up the rocky and extremely steep slope they would be ascending next and felt a queasiness in the pit of her stomach. Before she had time to really think about it, though, she felt a spray of water on the back of her neck.

She whirled just as Brent threw another handful and it splattered in her face. Sputtering, she took a threatening step toward him.

"Serves you right, after what you did this morning." He grinned and went back to the task of filling their canteens.

Meadowlark looked out over the hollowed rocks filled with pools of water. Everyone, men and animals, were slacking the thirst of a waterless camp the night before. And besides being waterless, the camp had gone without fires, as they would from now on until they made contact with the renegades.

Her eyes glowed as she thought of how snug *she* had slept last night, and she glanced back to the captain. He was so handsome in his uniform. His broad, muscular chest made a perfect pillow. And his . . . The hair on the back of her neck prickled. She turned her head. General Crook stood only a few feet away, looking directly at her.

As if he sensed her unease, Brent capped the last canteen and also turned. His muscles tensed, but he rose and strode quickly forward, placing himself between Lark and the general before saluting. "Mornin', General."

Crook pulled at one of the braids in his beard and slanted his head for one last look at the small scout. He opened his mouth, changed his mind, and indicated Brent should walk along with him a ways. "Captain, when we reach the top of the next rise, I'll be sending out several scouting parties. I would like for you to take charge of one of them."

"Me, sir?" Brent was surprised. They had white scouts that usually accompanied the general's specific patrols.

"I know this is an unusual request, but the Indians trust you and have asked for you several times. My scouts are otherwise engaged, or I would not have bothered you."

"It's no bother, General. I'm flattered. Of course, I'd be glad to help out."

"Thank you, McQuade. I'll send for you when we reach the crest and give you your orders."

"Yes, sir."

Crook started to leave, looked once more at the motionless figure behind Brent, then shook his head and went on.

Meadowlark released the giant sigh of relief—for two reasons. One, the general had not recognized her. And two, she now knew how she would get away from the command to find Geronimo.

Brent came to stand beside her. "Whew! That was too close." He looked up the face of the mountain they had yet to climb. "Well, are you ready?"

As she followed his gaze, her trepidation miraculously disappeared. "Oh, yes. I am ready."

Chapter Twenty-seven

Flies! Buzzing, nasty flies everywhere. Meadowlark swatted them away from her face as the command rode past five butchered cows. This time she did not let the insects upset her. They meant her people had food.

The trail they followed was freshly beaten down by hundreds of cattle and horses being pushed ahead of them. Now and then they passed another carcass, or two or three loose ponies roaming in the ravines.

Meadowlark's stomach churned when she happened to look down into the canyon and saw the mangled body of a cow that had fallen from the trail. She gritted her teeth and wrapped her hands more tightly in the mare's mane, shifting her weight to help the horse climb and keep its footing. And that was all it seemed they did. Climb. Her fingers were cut and blistered from the death grip she held.

Again she had to compliment Geronimo on his choice of hideouts. The country was all but inaccessible, yet there was plenty of grass and water and game.

The mare was tiring and had dropped back along the line of climbers. They were following one of the pack trains when, suddenly, just in front of her, a section of ground gave way and a whole group of mules tumbled from the trail.

"Look out! The mules!" she shouted and slid from the horse. She ran to the edge of the trail, but there was nothing she could do. The mules kept rolling—over and over. She turned her back, unable to watch what happened when they hit the bottom.

And when she turned, she was swept up into steel hard arms, only to be abruptly set down on firm footing. Brent stood rocking on his toes acting as if it were the hardest thing in the world for him to keep from crushing her in his fisted hands. But others had joined them. He had to keep control. Yet, his eyes burned into her. His jaw worked. Finally, he growled, "Are you all right?"

She nodded. "Th-the mules . . . Th-they—"

Brent winced and forced himself to look down the mountainside. An incredulous expression broadened his features. He glanced back at her and pointed. "Look."

One of the packers took off his hat and scratched his head. "I'll be damned. Wouldja looky at that."

Meadowlark tentatively took a step closer to Brent. She peered over his shoulder. Instead of finding a jumble of broken, mangled animals, all six of the mules were on their feet, looking a little dazed, but did not appear badly hurt.

She looked at Brent and smiled. He grinned back and started toward her, only to remember where they were and shutter his eyes.

A scout standing nearby said, "They go off good place. Not so steep."

And it was true. As Meadowlark looked up and down the trail, it became clear that had they gone over at any other location they would have hit massive boulders or even impaled themselves on tree branches. She closed her eyes. A powerful spirit looked after them.

Two ridges later, they topped out onto fairly flat ground. General Crook signaled Brent forward.

Meadowlark's hands gripped the mare's reins until her knuckles turned white. This was it. This would be her only chance to slip away undetected by either

Brent or his brother, who was luckily already out picketing the scouts to stand guard. She took his absence as a good omen.

The scouts had been more and more vigilant, suspecting the renegades to be somewhere close. She must find her family or Geronimo first.

When Brent rode back to tell her good-bye, she fought back the moisture burning the backs of her eyes. With so many people around, he did not try to touch her, but she felt as if she had been caressed by the tenderness in his eyes. Their blue depths were softer than she had ever seen them before.

She blinked and lowered her lashes, afraid he would recognize the emotions she was finding it harder and harder to suppress. But thinking this might be the last time she would see him like this, with the love blazing forth, she met his gaze squarely.

His lips moved. He had whispered, "I love you."

She nodded, unable to say the words, but if he interpreted the motion to mean she returned his feelings, so be it.

Brent didn't know what to think. His gut contracted as if he'd been dealt a swift kick. Had she acknowledged what he said, or was she saying she felt the same? He could hardly wait to come back and hear her say the words.

But the general had given him an assignment and he should've already left. Brand would be back soon to see she was protected. He flicked the brim of his hat and spun his mount around. If he didn't leave now, he might just ride over and haul her off her horse and take off—forgetting all about Crook and Geronimo and the damned campaign.

But he wouldn't, couldn't. He'd been a soldier too long. Without a backward glance, he gathered his scouts and rode away.

Meadowlark urged her mare in behind the last of

the scouts accompanying Captain McQuade. At first, she did not know whether to feel hurt or relieved that Brent had not deigned to look back when he had left her. Right now, she was very grateful, because he had made it possible for her to appear as if she were part of the scouting party.

Unlike Brent, however, she looked back and wished she had not. General Crook was there, staring again. She ducked her head and drummed the mare's sides with her heels, urging the animal to a swifter pace. Once they were out of sight of the camp and the too-observant general, then she could slow the horse.

She stayed within sight of the scouts, riding through a dense pine forest. Ahead of her the woods opened into a small clearing and she saw Brent waiting, gathering his scouts. She turned off. It was time to start out on her own.

Looking over her shoulder as she traveled, she was soon convinced that the captain had been too intent talking with the scouts to have seen her. The stiffness gradually went out of her shoulders as she wound through the trees and brush. The silence was deafening. She was alone. Alone and on her way to find her family.

Meadowlark angled back to the original trail, keeping to the shadows, hoping to catch sight of one of the renegade Apaches coming back for a pony or something that may have been accidentally discarded. All along the trail were items of clothing and jewelry that had obviously been taken during raids on Mexican villages.

But she rode carefully, watching for scouts as well. If one of them caught her now, sneaking around, trying to get a message to someone they now considered the enemy . . .

All of a sudden she reined the mare to one side. There was something about the ground . . . She could have sworn there was part of a track . . . Pine needles were shifting with the wind and she brushed a layer aside. There they were, a fresh set of tracks heading east. The prints belonged to an unshod horse and were traveling in a straight line rather than aimlessly foraging like the loose animals she had seen until now.

It was the first sign of hope she had found.

Brandon McQuade returned after making sure the camp was thoroughly guarded. The scouts all seemed to think it was necessary, and Brand agreed it would be embarrassing for the renegades to find them first.

Even before reporting to the general, he went to look for Brent's woman. His brother had said he would be taking out a scouting party and was worried about his little Lark. Brand smiled to himself. The little bird had done a good job so far of taking care of herself *and* Brent, from what his brother had told him.

But he could not blame Brent for being concerned. She was a beautiful woman, and it would be bad if the men found out she had duped them by pretending to be a scout.

So, he checked all of the scouts' camps. There was no trace of her. He searched the soldier camp. Nothing. Maybe she was seeing after her mare, or answering a call of nature. As the minutes wore on, and there was still no sign of her, he hurried faster.

He had just started through a line of mules when someone called to him. He turned and saw the general. Warily, he approached the commanding officer.

"Mr. McQuade, you look as if you've lost something."

Brand hesitated. "Well, yes . . . maybe."

Crook ran his hand down one of the mule's back. "Perhaps I can help."

"No, sir. I was trying to find . . . one of the . . . scouts." Brand curled and uncurled his fingers, shifting his weight from one foot to the other. His eyes strayed to the next group of packers.

"Oh, I thought you might have been looking for Miss Russell."

Brand's head whipped around. His eyes bored into the general. "Then you have . . . Who?"

George Crook rubbed the tip of his nose. "Come now, Mr. McQuade, I don't know what she would be doing *here,* but I've seen the young lady around San Carlos enough to recognize her, even disguised as she is. That beautiful face is hard to conceal."

Brand sighed and hooked his thumbs in his belt loops. "Have you seen her lately?"

"As a matter of fact, I saw her following your brother. He and a scouting party were headed east. You don't think she'd be foolish enough to do something to get herself hurt, do you?" There was genuine concern in his voice.

Shaking his head, Brand answered honestly, "I really do not know. That woman is up to something." He was already headed toward his stallion before he finished speaking.

It was well over two hours later when Brand caught up with his brother. And from the strained expression on his face, Brent guessed immediately that something was wrong.

"It's Lark, isn't it? What's happened to her?" His fingers reflexively tightened on the reins as he started to turn his horse back toward the camp.

Brand grabbed the army gelding's bit and stopped him. "She is not there. Crook saw her follow you from camp. I was checking to make sure she is with you."

"She followed me?" Helplessly, he looked around at his scouts, though he knew she wasn't there. "Why? Where did she think she could go?"

Shrugging, Brand asked, "Why did she follow the command in the first place? Was she just wanting to be with you?"

Brent rolled his eyes. "I wish it were true. But, no, if she'd been doing that, she wouldn't have worked so hard to remain hidden. And she was definitely relieved when I didn't send her back to San Carlos."

Purely puzzled, Brent rubbed the back of his neck. "Well, I've got to find her."

"I will go with you."

"I'd like nothing better than to have you along, but the general will have my hide if he finds out about this."

Brand remained silent. No sense in giving his brother any more to worry about now. The general could say something later if he wanted to. "So what do you want me to do?"

Brent hated to ask, but knew his brother could get a lot more accomplished with the scouts than he could. "Please take the scouts and see if you can cut another trail. I'll try to be back before you report at camp."

"All right, but promise me one thing."

Brent hollered over his shoulder, "What?"

"Be careful."

The captain waved and spurred his horse, jumping it over a pile of fallen logs. Yet the farther away he got, the more slowly he rode. If Lark had, indeed, followed him into the forest, she could've turned off anywhere, gone any direction. And he kept repeating the same question. Why?

His mind was nothing more than a jumble of confused thoughts when he finally bent low in the saddle, studying the ground. He stopped the horse. He'd seen two sets of tracks. One looked older than the other, and the fresher tracks had to belong to Lark's mare. The thoroughbred had such dainty feet that only a pony could make smaller tracks.

Along with his other questions, he now added, "How could his scouts have missed this sign?"

Brent followed the tracks for over an hour. He'd lose them in a rocky area, then find them again. Sometimes he followed Lark's trail when *she* lost the first set of prints. Eventually they all came together and he would try to travel faster in hopes of catching up to Lark before nightfall.

He was so engrossed in thinking of himself as the big, virile protector after his maiden, that he was taken completely by surprise when he rode through a dense growth of trees and something dropped from a limb and tumbled him from his horse onto the ground.

Rolling to his feet, he fumbled to get his gun out of the holster. Something hit him in the backs of his knees and he went down again. Before he could get up, two stout warriors pinned him to the ground. He struggled, and raised his head. A third warrior stood near his feet, his painted face grotesque in the afternoon sun.

That third man, evidently the leader, spoke in rapid Apache and Brent was dragged to his feet. One warrior yanked his arms behind his back. A leather thong cut into his wrists. Another, longer thong was looped around his neck, the thicker ends digging into his flesh. The other end was tossed to the leader, who had mounted the gelding and wrapped the leather around the saddle horn.

With a wicked grin, the Indian kicked the horse. Unused to the savage handling, it jumped sideways. Brent was jerked to the ground. Before he could get his knees under him, the Apache kicked the horse again and it took off at a run, dragging Brent by the neck. His body was pulled over jagged rocks. Thorny branches tore at his clothes and scratched his flesh. Dust clogged his mouth and nose and eyes. His shoulders felt as if they'd been wrenched from their sockets.

He rolled onto his back to protect his face, but then his hands and arms were scraped raw. The noose cut into his neck. He couldn't breathe. The pain . . .

Brent was hardly aware of the Apache slowing the horse, or of the warriors standing him up. Instinct alone kept him on his feet.

Brand McQuade and his fifty Apache scouts had

not ridden far from where Brent had left them when they encountered the white scout, Ruebush, and another hundred scouts.

"McQuade! C'mon 'n go with us. My boys spotted three Chiricahuas in the next canyon. Damned scouts got so excited, though, they fired at 'em an' skeerd 'em off. Renegades'll be on the move now."

Brand joined with Ruebush. Scouts ranged ahead and to both sides, cautiously watching for traps. Over an hour later, they ran onto two rancherias. The renegades fired before allowing Brand or any of the scouts to get close enough to talk. Too frightened and surprised that their stronghold had been discovered to put up much of a battle, only a brief skirmish occurred before the renegades, mostly women and children and older men, fled into the rugged ravines.

Riding his stallion at a dead run through the middle of the second rancheria, Brand swerved around a cluster of boulders and cut off two women. One, the oldest, was on the ground. A younger girl stood over her, brandishing a knife.

Brand held up his hand and spoke in rapid, guttural Apache. "I will not harm you. Surrender and we will see to the old woman's injury."

The girl nodded, sheathed her knife, and also said in Apache, "I know you. You are the White Fox. My mother and I come with you."

"You are Warm Springs. How do you know me?" Brand was sure he had never seen the girl before.

"Many summers ago, my mother, my mother's sister, my cousin and me, Angelita, visit relatives belonging to your White Mountain band. We did not stay long."

Brand looked down over the rancherias. "Where were your warriors? Why were they not here to defend you?"

Angelita shrugged and coyly lowered her eyes. "They are away on a raid."

Brand got off his horse and helped the older woman

to her feet. Between himself and Angelita they managed to get her out of the rocks where Brand could look at her foot. "It is only a sprain. Come. We will find a horse for your mother and go to Crook's camp. You may be able to help us."

And he hurried as he went about gathering the scouts that Ruebush had not taken in pursuit of the fleeing renegades. He did not like the suggestive way the young maiden eyed him. This one would need a randy warrior to tame her.

Meadowlark looked down on the Chiricahua Apache stronghold. Though there seemed to be plenty of wood in the area, the wickiups were poorly constructed, as if they had been put up hastily and were not expected to stay up for long.

The women were busy scraping cowhides. Children rolled a hoop through the middle of the camp. What warriors she saw reclined in the shade, some visiting with a neighbor, some cleaning their weapons or napping.

It was a typical village and she was literally astounded. They acted as if they did not have a care or worry in the world. Did they not know General Crook was camped within only a half day's ride? No, she answered her own question, they must not.

She reined the mare around a pile of loose stones. If she went down and talked to them, maybe they could tell her where Geronimo was camped. Halfway down the steep, treacherous slope, she pulled the mare to an awkward stop. A warrior on a saddled horse rode out of the trees and into the stronghold, almost directly below her position on the mountainside. Soon two more warriors walked into her view, supporting another man. A filthy, bloody man who, when he stumbled and went down to one knee, was dragged roughly to his feet again by a length of leather tied about his neck.

She covered her heart with her hand. Her eyes

burned as she concentrated on the man. There, low on his legs, she could see the color of his pants. Blue. And there, a bit of yellow. A soldier. His carriage was proud, though he could barely remain on his feet. His chest was broad and tapered to a narrow waist and hips and long, long legs.

Her eyes sought his face, but she could not see his features for the dirt. Even his hair was a dirty gray. All but one shock of light hair falling across his forehead and into his eyes. Blond hair. And now she understood why it had felt as if her heart had dropped to her toes when she first saw him.

"Brent!" She did not know she had screamed his name aloud until all heads below turned in her direction. As the mare descended the slope at breakneck speed, her eyes were fastened on the captain. She saw Brent's split lips move and nearly cried out, feeling his pain.

When she reached flat ground, she was immediately surrounded by the Chiricahuas. She sat her horse regally, proudly, and asked to see the band's leader.

A distinguished, middle-aged warrior stepped forward. "I am Chihuahua. Who are you? How did you find us?"

Meadowlark darted a glance to Brent and found that he had fallen to his knees but was struggling to rise on his own. Her throat went dry and her voice cracked as she spoke. "I am Meadowlark Russell of the Warm Springs Apache at San Carlos. That man and I"—she pointed to Brent—"have been looking for the Apaches in the Sierra Madres. We wish to tell them the great General Crook is here. He wants to speak with the leaders of the fierce Apache nation."

The chief immediately sent out two of his warriors to see if her words were spoken in truth. She nodded. Good. That would buy her time to free Brent McQuade. Again she pointed to the captain, who appeared to be glaring at her through his swollen lids.

She was grateful the Apaches were paying her little attention.

Her finger shook. "That man has come in peace and you dare to torture him." She glared knives at the smug Apache atop the gelding. "The general will hear of this. His punishment will be great and swift."

Murmurs rippled through the Apaches crowded around the mare. Some of them moved back. The chief looked into her eyes. She did not blink or take her eyes from his. He said, "You say Crook wishes to speak. Tell us what he wants from us."

"He wants you to return to the reservation. He wishes peace for all Apaches."

Her lips thinned when she saw glimmers of hope flair briefly in many of the drawn, tired faces. Even Chihuahua's.

The chief looked toward the warriors on either side of the captured soldier and commanded, "Release him. Take him to my sister's wickiup." To Meadowlark, he said, "My sister is visiting her husband's family with Loco's band. You may care for the white soldier there." Then his brown eyes turned hard. "By the next sunset we will know if your words are false."

She did not flinch from his stare. One of the warriors bent and put his shoulder into Brent's stomach, hefting the big soldier as if he were a sack of potatoes. Sliding off her mare, Meadowlark followed behind, stumbling and nearly falling when she kept her eyes on Brent rather than on the rough ground. His head lolled limply against the warrior's back and she was weak with fear.

Not so long ago he had been badly injured, and now this. Though he was incredibly strong, a man could only endure so much before . . .

She glanced back over her shoulder. The brave who had led Brent into camp was gesturing and shouting at the chief. Her hands clenched as she memorized his broad-cheeked, flat-nosed features. If Brent McQuade died . . .

Brent was carefully deposited on a pallet of cowhides and blankets. The warrior hesitated before leaving. "Crook is here? He wants peace?"

Meadowlark nodded. She had come to the Sierra Madres to help her family and Geronimo to escape Crook. Now she was telling these people the "Gray Fox" wanted them to come in peacefully. She glanced down at the unconscious captain. Brent believed that was the general's intention. He had better be right.

When the warrior was gone, she sucked in her breath and dusted her hands together, building courage for what must be done. She knelt and began to peel the remnants of Brent's clothing from his bruised and battered body. Tears rolled down her cheeks and onto the dirt caking his skin.

His hands and face and neck were scraped and cut the worst, although he was covered with knots and bumps and scratches. She untied her pouch from around her waist and turned to see if there was a kettle she could use to boil water. Stopping in midstride, she stood staring at the women standing in the doorway.

The first woman ducked her head and said shyly, "We have brought water to cleanse and agave and cypress to heal." When Meadowlark appeared disbelieving, she added, "The Great Spirit heard our words and sent the soldier to help us. We must show that we are worthy."

They considered Brent a gift from the Gods. Meadowlark blinked. Well, after all he had done for the Apache, for her, it could be true. At last she nodded and stepped aside so the women could enter. Then before she could stop them or utter a protest, they pushed past her and began clucking and fussing over Brent as if he were as precious as a newborn babe.

As worried as she was for him, she had to smile when she thought what his reaction would be if he knew three strange women were handling his naked body. His eyes would widen round as an owl's. His cheeks would redden. With much dignity, he would search for something with which to cover himself.

She knelt down close to his head and looked tenderly at his poor face. One eye was swollen. A large bump knotted his forehead. His cheeks were scratched. There was a deep cut along his jawbone. A sob caught in her throat. He must not be badly injured. He could not die. Not now. When she had come to love him so.

When Brent had been washed and his wounds treated, all but one of the Chiricahua women left to tend to the evening meal. The one who stayed was several years older than Meadowlark, and very pretty. Meadowlark was not sure she wanted the woman there when Brent awoke. She asked, "What are you called?"

"Melosa."

The woman's voice was rich and soft. Honey-voiced. That was what she was, all right, Meadowlark complained to herself. "How long have you been in these mountains?"

Melosa's eyes darkened. "Long time. Forced to come."

Meadowlark's heart went out to the woman. "As was my mother. She did not survive the journey." But she would have loved the wild canyons and tall mountains, Meadowlark thought. Her mother had always loved the mountains.

"The soldier . . . He will take us to Crook? He will take us home?"

"You *want* to go?" Meadowlark was stunned. She had thought they would run swift as deer to *avoid* Crook and being returned to Arizona Territory—to San Carlos.

Melosa felt Brent's forehead. "We have run and moved and run and hidden until we can run no more. We are tired. Our families worry. We want peace, but Geronimo make us stay and run. We are afraid."

Meadowlark sat back on her heels. These people really wanted to go back. They stayed because they were afraid to leave. All this time, she had thought that once Geronimo led them here they were happy. And free. But they were neither.

Brent groaned and opened his one good eye. "Lark?" He frowned, then winced from the strain it caused the lump on his forehead. The woman next to him was not his Lark. He licked his lips and smeared his tongue with something slick and gooey. "Lark."

She had moved closer with his first call, then moved around to his other side when the woman, Melosa, did not seem willing to relinquish her place.

"I am here." She gently took his hand, being careful to avoid the scrapes and cuts on his knuckles.

He turned his head and winced again. His throat burned when he swallowed. His voice was a thick rasp. "I was . . . afraid. What did . . . you tell . . . them?"

"That Crook was here and had sent you to talk peace."

"You," he coughed, "told them . . . that?"

She nodded.

He closed his eye. "You don't believe it."

She put a finger over his lips. "I will wait and see what happens."

Surprising Meadowlark, Melosa also spoke in English. "How does white soldier feel?"

Meadowlark cringed at the sound of that sweet voice.

Brent barely moved his head. He seemed to hurt even when he moved his eyeballs. He smiled at the Apache woman. Slowly, carefully, he croaked, "Feel like . . . been spurred . . . with five-inch . . . rowels. Thank you . . . ma'am."

Then with his fingers holding tightly to Meadowlark's, he promptly fell asleep.

The sun shone directly overhead the next day when

the Chiricahua leader entered his sister's wickiup. He nodded approvingly when he saw that the soldier was sitting up and the woman was helping him eat.

"Good, you heal quickly. Your woman speak truth. Crook has warned we must surrender in three sunrises or he will come here after us."

The Indian had such an incredulous tone to his voice that Brent choked on the small sip of broth. His throat was so sore that he could hardly swallow. He was afraid his wrists were broken, but had been assured they were not. What did they know? And he was reduced to Lark's feeding him—again. His condition did little to bolster his manly confidence.

Meadowlark eyed the Apache leader. There was something more.

"My warriors and I go to Crook. Talk. Make peace."

Immediately Brent offered, "I will take you."

The chief frowned. "No. You and woman must stay. If I do not return . . ."

The Apache did not have to finish. Brent and Meadowlark both knew they were prisoners, dependent on the general's good intentions for their lives. She stared down at Brent. "Now we will see what the general really has in mind."

A little after dawn the next morning, a young soldier, followed by two scouts, raced toward General Crook's tent.

"Apaches! We're surrounded! Apaches!"

Chapter Twenty-eight

Soldiers and packers ran to the front of the camp near the general's tent. Rifles cocked, aimed and ready, they stared at the line of Apaches riding along a narrow ridge. Scouts hovered around, intently watching the excitement.

One private yelled to Lieutenant Johnson, "Whaddo we do, sir?"

The lieutenant turned to the general. "What shall we do, sir?"

"We'll see what they want."

"But, sir, if there's a whole bunch of 'em, they could—"

"Private! That's enough." The lieutenant sidled nervously nearer the general. "Actually, he's right, General. If all of the renegades are out there, we're in a very vulnerable position."

"Which is exactly why we'll wait and see what they have to say, Lieutenant. And pass the word that the first man who pulls a trigger before I give the order . . . I'll personally hand him over to the Apaches."

Lieutenant Johnson backed up quickly. "Yes, sir. I'll do that."

General Crook asked one of the white scouts and two of the Apache scouts to accompany him to the outskirts of the camp. They waited while the Chiricahuas approached slowly, cautiously, casting clear-eyed glances around the wooded hill for signs of a trap.

Ruebush, the white scout, held up his hand, palm out. "Hola!"

The chief and five warriors rode forward. "Hola!" Chihuahua kept his rifle in his right hand, the barrel resting over his left forearm. Ruebush exchanged the customary words of greeting, while the Apache chief and the general appeared more interested in sizing up the other.

Ruebush looked at the general. "Someone's done told 'em that you're here lookin' for peace. That if 'n they come in, you'll take 'em all back to Arizona."

"Tell him that what he heard is true. Ask if he wants to surrender his band."

The scout repeated Crook's words. "Says it will take him a couple days to gather his people."

Crook stared into Chihuahua's eyes and never blinked. "Tell him he has the time. But I expect him to keep his word."

"What about them guns, sir. Should we make'em hand'em over?"

The general shook his head. "No, Mr. Ruebush, let them keep their rifles."

"Even Geronimo, if'n *he* comes in?"

"Even Geronimo. It is not advisable to let an Indian think you are afraid of him, even when fully armed."

"Whatever you say, General."

"Tell Chihuahua I'll be expecting him."

Brent opened his good eye that same morning to find Lark slumped beside him, asleep, his hand cradled to her breast. His chest suddenly ached. A deeper and more intense ache than all of the rest of his hurts put together. He blinked and felt the burning sensation of tears. God, he loved this woman.

And she loved him. He knew it as well as he knew his own name. Whether she could verbally admit to it or not, it was there in her eyes and the tender way she touched him, and protected him. And their chances of ever being together wavered in the hands of two men. General Crook and Geronimo. It was a fearsome situation.

Suddenly his fingers were squeezed tightly together. A wince crinkled his face and even *that* hurt. When he glanced up, Lark was awake and smiling at him. His heart somersaulted and landed in his throat. Finally able to summon control of his leaping muscles, he grinned back. "I-I . . ." Eyes wide, he grasped her hand tighter.

Meadowlark leaned over and picked up the bowl of agave sap Melosa had left. Bending close to his face, she whispered, "Sh-h-h. Your neck is badly bruised. This will help." She gently smoothed the thick, sticky substance on his throat.

Panic welled inside Brent. He still could hardly swallow. Death by strangulation was slow and agonizing, wasn't it?

When she finished with the agave, he watched Meadowlark calmly pour a cup of some kind of liquid. He closed his eyes and clenched his fingers. Oh, God help him! She was going to dose him with more of her foul concoctions.

He caught her wrist when she held the rim of the cup to his lips. He refused to open his mouth.

Meadowlark scowled. "Drink this!"

He stubbornly shook his head.

She heard a rustle of movement at the entrance and looked up. Melosa stood there with an amused glitter in her doe eyes. Meadowlark watched enviously as the woman glided over to sink down next to her. Then she frowned when Melosa gave her a conspiratorial wink and reached over to pinch the captain's nose closed.

Brent's eyes flew open. Even his swollen eye slitted a tad. He tried to raise himself up, but Meadowlark's hand on his shoulder was enough to hold him down. He gasped for air and she quickly poured the liquid into his mouth. With Melosa holding up his chin, he had no choice but to swallow, or truly strangle. His throat worked convulsively. Pain from the exertion drained what color there was from his face.

Surprisingly, though, once the brew trickled down his throat, it was soothing, and didn't taste *too* bad. And as he quit struggling and gasping, he found he could swallow much easier.

Melosa folded several blankets and propped them behind his back. To Meadowlark she said, "You treat the soldier like an infant. He was getting better yesterday."

Meadowlark was greatly offended. "His muscles have stiffened and are painful. It is natural that he have some trouble so soon after his injury."

Brent rolled his head back and forth between the two women. They were speaking too rapidly for him to understand much of what they said, but he knew enough to know they were talking about *him*.

"Get him up. Make him move. Melosa will help."

"No! I can manage." Meadowlark tried her best to keep from blushing when the Apache woman looked down her nose at the cup dangling from Meadowlark's fingers. She failed. Heat rose from her breasts, up her neck, and spread across her cheeks.

Melosa sniffed.

"Hey, what'd she say? What're you two arguing about?" Brent saw the hostility building between the women and noticed uneasily that somehow he'd ended up in between them.

Meadowlark harrumphed. "He is my man. I know what is best for him."

"Then you will have no man at all if you treat him so."

Oh! That some stranger could say such a thing about the strong, brave, wonderful captain. Meadowlark snarled.

Melosa taunted, "My small son is more a man than your white—"

Brent saw it coming. He saw Lark stiffen, saw her

hands curl and literally felt the explosion ready to burst from her small, taut form. He gritted his teeth and willed himself to move. Just as she leapt at the other woman, he pulled himself up farther and caught both of her wrists in his hands.

His muscles bulged and strained. Sweat beaded from every pore. Gradually he urged her arms to bend and he brought their hands in against his chest. Her body came to rest at his side. The fire burning in the amber depths of her eyes flickered to glowing embers. When she leaned forward and pressed a tender kiss to his lips, he fell back onto the pile of blankets, completely bemused.

Meadowlark also looked over to the grinning Melosa and smiled.

Between the two women, they helped Brent to his feet. Although he wasn't quite able to keep the pain racking his body from showing on his face, he never uttered a sound. Meadowlark went warm all over when Melosa looked at her and said, "He is a big man."

Suddenly Brent reared back and put a stop to his hobbling gait. Those words he'd understood. He was half afraid to look down at himself, but when he did, he croaked, "What the hell is this? Where're my pants?"

Meadowlark's lips twitched. Did he think she would allow these other women to eye his beautiful body whenever they wished? She happily informed him, *"That* is a breechclout."

"Damn it, I know what it is. What's it doin' on *me?"* His raspy voice was getting stronger.

"Your pants were torn. But . . . if you want, I will take it off—"

"No! No. This will . . . have to . . . do. I guess." God, he still felt naked.

All of a sudden, he realized he was walking without the women's support. He grinned and looked over to find them standing to one side, with identical blank expressions, as if it was no surprise at all. And really, once he started moving, the initial distress of stretching his abused muscles began to wear off.

The rest of the day he alternated between resting and walking, resting and bending. The cut along his jaw bothered him some, especially when he puckered up and tried to give Lark a kiss.

Small fires were lit and the evening meal of beef stew with wild onions simmered in large kettles, when a teenaged boy came running into the stronghold. "Chihuahua's back. They're coming."

The returning warriors rode into the camp amid clouds of dust, snorting horses and happy greetings from the people crowding around. Chihuahua held up his hand for silence. "First we will eat and rest. Then you will hear Crook's words."

A large fire was built in the center of the village. It was well after dark when the Apaches began to gather, singly, in pairs, or by families. Meadowlark and Brent joined those seated close to the flames. The night was cold and she snuggled next to his large, warm body.

Brent wished he understood the change in Lark's attitude. She had never acted so affectionate—and he loved every minute of it. He put his arm around her shoulders and pulled her closer. The imprint of her soft, petite body cuddled so sweetly beside him would be branded on his flesh and in his mind forever.

He felt ten feet tall when she was with him like this. There was nothing he couldn't do. His shoulders sagged slightly. Except, perhaps, marry the woman he loved.

At last, the chief stood in the center of the circle of people around the fire. "Hear me. This day I have spoken with the great chief Crook. I told him my people wanted to live in peace and that we would come to his camp willingly. I told him I would need time to gather those who wish to return to Arizona. He granted us that time. In two sunrises, I will leave here for the general's camp. Come, or stay. I will force no one to accept my decision."

Brent held on to Lark. This was a start. But what would Geronimo decide to do?

Brent and Meadowlark accompanied the main force of Chihuahua's band to Crook's camp while the chief and several of his warriors looked for more of his people who had scattered into the mountains.

Brandon and a small group of scouts rode in at about the same time and Brand immediately went in search of his brother. "You look like you fought wolves and came out on the wrong end, big brother."

Shaking, hands with Brand, the captain retorted, "Thanks, you look good, too. Any word on Geronimo?"

Brand nodded. "He and several other chiefs, and most of their warriors, have been away on a raid. We should hear from them soon."

Meadowlark looked between the two men. From their forced expressions of nonchalance, she figured they probably wondered the same things as she. Which would Geronimo do first? Fight, or come in and talk to the general?"

Groups of women and children swelled the Apache population all day. Meadowlark anxiously scanned the arrivals, hoping for sight of her aunt. The person she encountered first, and was most surprised to see in Mexico, was Angelita.

She rushed to give her cousin a hug and then laughed at Angelita's wariness over being approached so rudely by a "scout." "It is Meadowlark, Angelita."

"Meadowlark? What are *you* doing here? Dressed like that?"

Meadowlark shrugged. "I might ask the same of you. I thought you were still at San Carlos."

The Warm Springs woman replied, "I had to come. There had been no word from my mother or brothers and sisters. And when Crook arrived, I became more fearful for their safety."

"Did you find them?"

"Yes. But first we were captured by the scouts and the White Fox. Oohhh! He is so-o-o handsome. Then he and Crook asked me to take messages to the renegades to surrender. Yesterday I found Geronimo's camp and . . . my mother was there."

"She is all right?"

Angelita smiled. "All except for one swollen ankle. And she is very anxious to return to Arizona Territory."

"Did you see Geronimo?"

"No. But the others in the village will tell him. He may come today."

Meadowlark looked toward the tent where Brent was resting. That meant that Geronimo might come as early as tomorrow. As early as tomorrow . . . She would know whether she could share her love with Brent.

Able at last to get around without hobbling, Brent rolled out of bed early the next morning. The first thing he did was look toward the camp where Brandon and Meadowlark were sleeping. He saw her, sitting cross-legged, sipping from a cup. He smiled. The sheen of her whiskey eyes reflected across the distance. Or was it just he could imagine them sparkling in his mind's eye? He frowned. Had she just raised her cup slightly? In greeting?

It was almost over. His fingers twitched as if they could already feel her silken skin naked beneath him. He pictured Lark and his mother together. Two ladies of fiery spirit. His mother would just love Meadowlark, would enjoy showing her the sights of the big city.

He was interrupted from his daydreaming by a commotion in the cliffs overlooking the camp. Soldiers stood with guns drawn, pointing to fully armed Indians running and jumping from crag to crag.

"Don't shoot," Brent shouted to the troopers. If the Apaches were going to fire on the camp, they could've done so earlier and taken them all by surprise.

Brand ran up to General Crook, who was standing beside Brent. "I will talk with them. They are afraid they will be hurt if they come in."

Crook listened to the Apaches on the mountainside shouting down to their comrades. "Tell them they won't be harmed. Until Chihuahua has had his chance to bring in his band, the hostilities are suspended." He walked out to get a better look at the Indians. "Do you think they are a part of Geronimo's band?"

"I will find out." Brand took along another scout and walked out to meet with several warriors. Most of the others, still afraid of a trap, remained high above the camp. Eventually, when they saw that the Apaches who had surrendered were being fed and treated kindly, they began to wind their way down.

There were thirty-six warriors, and were led by Geronimo.

Meadowlark saw the famed Apache leader and ran straight to Brent. Geronimo. The chief was really here.

Brent looked down into her eyes and she swallowed her heart back to its rightful place. He knew. What happened here today could influence the rest of their lives.

Brent was tempted to pull her into his arms, in front of God and everyone but, instead, gave her a brief smile of encouragement and turned back to watch the famous renegade leader. He was not disappointed. The warrior *looked* like a man who had fought and survived many battles. Old bullet wounds dotted his muscular body. Eyes as black as coal glowed fierce and intelligent.

One of the scouts interpreted for the general when Geronimo spoke. "I am Geronimo, Apache chief come to talk with white chief Crook. Hear me. I am a peaceful man who always wanted to live in peace. Any man prefers peace to war, but a man can only be pushed so far. My people were mistreated and driven away from San Carlos. The Mexicans offer bounties on Apache scalps. They lure us into their towns to trade and slaughter us as if we are no better than animals. They will smile and lie. They cannot be trusted.

"Like the great lobo wolf, the Apaches are fading from the earth beneath the guns of the white man. The chiefs in Washington give us land, then five times take back pieces of that land. They take the gold, the silver, the good farmland, until there is nothing left the Apache but weekly rations that feed us for three days. Once we were 'Tin-ne-ah.' The People. Now we call ourselves 'In-deh.' The Dead. We can fight the white man. We can fight the Mexican. But we cannot fight you both together. And we cannot fight so many of our own people."

The chief looked around at the Apache scouts, then looked Crook in the eye. "I ask for fair treatment. A trial. If I cannot make peace, my warriors and I will die in these mountains, fighting to the last."

Meadowlark swiped at the tears on her cheeks. She had moved closer to Brent and could tell from his grim countenance that he had been moved, too. Turning her gaze to the general, awaiting his answer to Geronimo, she happened to catch sight of someone familiar among the surrendered Apaches. A young man resembled . . . She squinted her eyes, looking closely.

The general chose that moment to speak. "I offer renegades in the Sierra Madres the chance to surrender. I will not make peace. I am tired of your disobedience and outbreaks. You wage war on whites and Mexicans and I cannot talk terms with a man wanted by two governments. If you are willing to lay down your arms and go to work farming, I might allow you to go back. But perhaps it would be best if you choose to fight."

The general stood straight as an arrow, staring at the Apache leader. Behind Crook, someone cocked a rifle.

Geronimo appeared disconcerted.

Meadowlark held her breath. Betrayed. That was the only word to describe what Crook had done to Geronimo. Her head spun from side to side, waiting for the gunfire that would massacre the Apaches.

Her eyes collided with Brent's. Betrayed by the general, as Brent had betrayed her. Because of her, Chihuahua and his band had surrendered. Because she had finally come to believe Brent's words—to believe in Brent.

All of her fury turned on the captain. Tears of rage and frustration blurred her vision. She lunged at him, her fingers curled into claws to tear at him, to punish him savagely for the pain that he caused her and her people.

Brent had been so intent on Geronimo's reaction that only sheer instinct caused him to turn in time to see Meadowlark's attack. Deftly, he ducked her hands and lowered his shoulder, catching her in the stomach. As the air whooshed from her lungs, he slung her over his shoulder and strode from the campground and into the forest. He walked until he felt her movements begin to increase and heard her choking and gasping for breath. He stopped and eased her to the ground.

Meadowlark was even more incensed. Arrogant white man! He had taken her from her people. Whatever fate they were to suffer, she would suffer. Air filled her lungs. She struggled harder, beating him with her fists, kicking with all her might, hoping to hurt him as he had destroyed her.

Brent captured her fists and wedged his body between her legs. She continued to fight. He had no other choice but to weight her down with his heavier body.

Rendered helpless, with his long form pressing her

into the earth, his legs imprisoning hers and his hands trapping her arms above her head, she spat, "I hate you." And then she cursed herself for being unable to think of anything better to say than those feminine white words.

"Damn it, Meadowlark," he growled. "What's the matter with you?" He could hardly swallow because of a blow she'd delivered to his throat.

She sputtered and spit and finally choked, "You heard. Crook betrayed Geronimo. *You* betrayed me!" She was so angry that she hardly noticed his hips nudging her. Barely felt his chest nuzzling her breasts. Tried to ignore the tingle permeating her body—that always coursed through her when he touched her.

Brent was momentarily speechless. Betrayed? He found his voice, though it grated like gravel in his throat. "What the hell are you talkin' about?"

Exhausted, Meadowlark quit struggling. It was over. For the Apache. For her. But as she lay there, afraid to move, to create even more contact with Brent's body, she noticed something. Silence. There was no sound of gunfire, or screams.

But she glared wickedly at Brent. "What does your General plan on doing next to humiliate my people?"

Brent shifted, trying to ease some of the sore muscles that were screaming their discomfort.

Meadowlark gritted her teeth. She would not think of the intimate way he was touching her.

His bewilderment was fast evaporating. "*My* general is only trying to ensure that *your people* have a lasting peace."

She scoffed, "By insulting Geronimo."

He lifted his weight onto his elbows and Meadowlark nearly cried out loud when the light brushing of his chest caused her nipples to harden. Now her body was betraying her. She jerked her arms free and pushed his shoulders. "Get off me. I cannot stand for you to touch me."

Brent cursed. He was tempted to stay right where

he was, to keep her pinned down until he could talk some sense into the hardheaded she-cat. But for once, her face was very expressive and the mutinous scowl assured him that nothing he could say would change her mind or temper her feelings.

He rolled off of her and scooted over to lean his back against the trunk of a tall pine. His temples throbbed, threatening to explode the top of his head. His thick skull was finally receiving the message. Everything had gone wrong. She hated him. Couldn't stand to be around him, much less have him touch her.

Meadowlark's resolve almost crumbled as she scrambled to her feet and saw the dejected slump of his shoulders. How could he appear so hurt and innocent? He had to have known what Crook was going to do.

She stood with her hands braced on her hips, eyes blazing. Just to make sure he understood, she gave in to a display of emotion and shouted, "Crook made Geronimo crawl to him to talk of peace, then refused his gesture in front of his people. That is the worst betrayal of all."

Looking toward the camp, she shook her head, bewildered. "I expected the soldiers would shoot Geronimo down. Yet they did not. Why?"

Brent's voice was listless. God, he had lost her, and for no reason. "Crook knows what he's doin'."

"What?" Meadowlark was so agitated that she literally danced around his outstretched feet.

He looked up and leaned his head back against the rough pine bark. "How many times has Geronimo spoken of peace before and then broken his word? Crook has to make the chief understand that it can't happen again. You've seen what's happening in Tucson, and with vigilante groups like the 'Tombstone Rangers.' Time is running out for the Apaches. Geronimo *has* to come to terms with a lasting peace."

"But Crook—"

"Give his plan time, Meadowlark. You'll see." He pushed to his feet and stood staring at her. He felt as if his heart was on his sleeve, out in the open, for her to take or to break.

Meadowlark turned away and wrapped her arms about her waist. She had to, or she would have lost the last defensive thread of her anger. Why did he not do something about the cut on his chin? It had reopened. *She* had reopened it.

A deep sigh shook her small form. She swallowed her pride and spun around to go to him. But her heart withered. He was gone.

Geronimo talked with General Crook two more times during the next few days. After the second meeting, Meadowlark was walking past the general's tent when she happened to hear Brent speaking. Her legs went weak. Her feet dragged to a stop. She did not intend to eavesdrop, just wanted to listen to the deep, soothing rumble of his voice.

"What do you think, General? Is he going to come in?" Brent tried to show an interest in what was going on with Geronimo, but found it too difficult to concentrate on anything for long.

"I think he will. But he's going to have to hurry and make up his mind. Our rations are running low with so many people to feed. We'll have no choice but to leave day after tomorrow."

Brandon McQuade sat forward. "I think what you said about removing the squatters and miners who do not possess a legal title to their land will help. And I told him that you had been resisting *more* efforts to cut the size of the reservation."

Brent added, "I think what's worrying a lot of the renegades is the rumor that they will be sent to Indian Territory. San Carlos is bad, but at least its close to their homelands."

"They will not be sent to Indian Territory. I have

enough pull in Washington to see to that, if nothing else," Crook huffed.

Meadowlark flinched when she heard the scrape of wood against gravel. Someone was getting ready to leave and she did not want to be caught here in the soldiers' camp. Someone might get the wrong idea and think she had come to see . . . someone.

As she scurried toward her own camp, she nibbled at her lower lip. Had she been so wrong? Had the general really had a plan in mind all along?

She had seen her aunt yesterday. The woman had been thrilled to be going home, to be free of Geronimo's domination. The chief had been the cause of a lot of their hardships. He should not have *forced* people to leave the reservation who did not want to go.

But more than the accusations against Crook, the hurtful words she had hurled at Brent gnawed at her conscience. She had aimed to hurt him, and had. And now it appeared she would have to choke back those words, or truly lose him.

Always prideful, she had seldom been the one to back down from an argument, or admit she was in error. Now she had a choice to make—pride or love. Weighing the two together, it would cost her much more if she let a man like Capt. Brent McQuade get away.

That night, Meadowlark rolled up in her blankets under the watchful eyes of the White Fox, or Brand, as she was trying to remember to call him. She sensed him staring at her, even with her back turned, and shuddered. She could probably talk to him, confront him with her stupidity. But what could he say that she had not already told herself?

Besides, he had never indicated one way or another what he thought of Brent's relationship with a half-breed Apache. She sighed as guilt again ate at her insides. Now she was mentally taking her frustrations out on *him*.

At least he looked at her; something Brent had not done for two days.

Sunlight streamed through a hole in the blanket and into her eyes. Meadowlark sat up abruptly, embarrassed to discover she had overslept. She swallowed and folded the blanket neatly, avoiding having to face the person sitting by the fire.

When Brand handed her a cup of hot coffee, she had no choice but to accept it or make an even bigger fool of herself.

"Sleep well?"

She nodded, then bristled when she thought she saw his lips twitch. Well, she had. For about an hour.

"Geronimo is coming back today."

She glared at him. "Oh?" What was he saying? Did he already know why she was so unsettled lately?

"His people have had enough warfare."

Nodding, she knew he was telling her that *somehow* there was going to be peace. The soldiers would not have to fight the Apaches. There was nothing to keep her from loving the captain as he deserved to be loved. A tear slid down her cheek and she turned her face so he would not see.

More and more often nowadays, she seemed to be succumbing to her weak white heritage. More and more . . . Suddenly, she tilted her head and studied Brandon McQuade. The White Fox. She could think of no one she had admired more. He was white. And the woman who had endured such hardship as the White Fox's captive, and then married him to live on an Apache reservation. Hillary McQuade was white. Of course, there had been her father. One other came to mind. Brent McQuade. A truly honorable and courageous man, who was not afraid to right a wrong. Maybe being *half* white was not so terrible.

A hushed murmur drifted through the scout camp. Geronimo was coming.

Meadowlark and Brand walked together to Crook's

tent. They stood among the surrendered Apaches who were smiling and happy to put an end to their lives of being hunted like animals. They were all looking expectantly toward the great chief.

From where she was standing, Meadowlark could only see Geronimo's back. The leader was facing General Crook and . . . Brent. It was difficult to hear what was being said, but she, and most of those around her, caught "want peace." Excited chattering drowned the rest of the conversation.

She looked over to Brand to see what he thought of Geronimo's words, but he was staring at the two leaders. Then, suddenly, over Brand's shoulder, she saw him. Scorpion. Only a few feet away. And he held a rifle pointed at . . . Geronimo? Or Brent McQuade?

Chapter Twenty-nine

Meadowlark fought down the panic threatening to immobilize her. With hardly a second thought, she pulled her knife from her moccasin.

Brandon grunted when she pushed past him and then yelled at her to stop. There was no time to stop and try to explain. Brent could be killed within those few seconds. She had to get to Scorpion.

Once, she had vowed the man would never harm Brent again and it was one promise she intended to keep. Her feet seemed to float on air as she ran. Her eyes were glued to the finger Scorpion was slowly squeezing on the trigger. Legs straining, lungs bursting, she launched herself into the air. Was she too late? Too late.

Then her body barreled into the slight warrior. The rifle pointed skyward just as he pulled the trigger and stumbled to the ground.

Scorpion was back on his feet in the blink of an eye, grinning wickedly at the tiny little woman who had the nerve to threaten him—with a knife, no less.

As she advanced toward him, wielding the knife as if she knew how to use it and would gladly do so, he stopped grinning. But then an evil leer tilted his lips as he drew a pistol from his waistband. "Little pigeon grow big talons. But you no stop Scorpion."

He raised the pistol. Meadowlark shifted the knife and started to lunge. An arm wrapped around her middle and lifted her off her feet as gunfire reverberated the air.

Her eyes never left Scorpion as the gun tumbled from his fingers and he crumpled to the ground, clutching his bleeding shoulder. She snapped her head around to see Brandon replacing the barrel of his rifle into the crook of his arm. And then she looked at the man holding her. The man whose touch set her nerve endings aflutter even in the midst of battle.

All of a sudden she was plopped back on her feet. The knife was wrenched from her fingers. Brent leaned down, glowering at her. "You damned little fool. You could've gotten yourself killed. Don't you know any better than to take a knife against a man with a gun? I oughtta turn you over my knee. You . . ."

Meadowlark rolled her eyes and they came to rest on Brand. He had a funny little quirk on his lips, and Meadowlark recalled hearing Brent scold the younger McQuade in much the same manner as he was chastising her now.

For him to treat her so could mean only one thing. He still loved her. Really loved her to treat her like one of the family. Encouraged, she stepped boldly up to him and effectively silenced his rambling tirade with a kiss.

His arms quit gesturing long enough to wrap around her. His lips molded to hers. When she broke the kiss and lifted her head, he looked at her questioningly.

Grasping his arm for support, she turned to her onetime best friend, Scorpion. Guarded by two soldiers, he returned her gaze with hate-filled eyes. Her mouth felt as if it were suddenly stuffed with cotton, but she asked, "Why?"

Calmly, as if she were stupid not to know, he replied, "Revenge."

"Revenge? On who?" It was unimaginable that the kind, friendly warrior she had known could be this hateful, bloodthirsty monster. "Who were you aiming for? Geronimo, or the captain?"